Deborah Carr lives on the island of Jersey in the Channel Islands with her husband, two children, and three rescue dogs. She became interested in books set in WW1 when researching her grandfather's time as a cavalryman in the 17th 21st Lancers.

She is part of 'The Blonde Plotters' writing group and was Deputy Editor on the online review site, Novelicious.com. Her debut historical romance, *Broken Faces*, is set in WW1 and was runner-up in the 2012 Good Housekeeping Novel Writing Competition and given a 'special commendation' in the Harry Bowling Prize that year. *The Poppy Field* is her second historical novel and a *USA Today* bestseller.

🐦 @DebsCarr
🅕 @DeborahCarrAuthor
📷 @ofbooksandbeaches
deborahcarr.org

Also by Deborah Carr

Mrs Boots of Pelham Street

Deborah Carr

OneMoreChapter

One More Chapter
a division of HarperCollins*Publishers*
The News Building
1 London Bridge Street
London SE1 9GF

www.harpercollins.co.uk

This paperback edition 2020

First published in Great Britain in ebook format by
HarperCollins*Publishers* 2020

A catalogue record for this book
is available from the British Library

Ebook ISBN: 978-0-00-837711-3
B Format Paperback ISBN: 978-0-00-837712-0

Set in Birka by Palimpsest Book Production Ltd, Falkirk
Stirlingshire
Printed and bound in Great Britain by CPI Group (UK) Ltd,
Croydon CR0 4YY

To my daughter Saskia, with love and admiration for all that you've achieved

Prologue

March 1891

Florence Boot gave one last look out of her living room window. As she took hold of the heavy velvet curtains, she smiled at the purple and orange crocuses that her husband Jesse had planted for her several months before. She sensed someone watching her and looked up to see one of her neighbours smiling from the amber glow of the gas lamp across Wellesley Road. Florence waved. It had been another tiring day working alongside Jesse at the Boots store on Snig Hill. She enjoyed living in Sheffield, although Jesse had been ruminating more often lately about returning to his native Nottingham at some point soon.

At that moment all Florence looked forward to was spending a quiet evening at home relaxing with Jesse, their nine-month-old daughter Dorothy, and their two-year-old son John in their cosy living room.

Florence tugged at the heavy curtains, drawing them together against the cool evening air. She turned to watch her husband slowly rotating the handle on the zoetrope that was keeping their children amused on the colourful rug in front of the fire. This was her favourite time of day, when their two live-in domestic servants had gone up to their rooms, and Eliza, who preferred to live out, had left for home.

Dorothy burbled happily, more interested in sucking her thumb than what was happening in front of her. John, on the other hand, chuckled loudly each time Jesse stopped moving the handle to suddenly rotate it again.

'He's besotted with that toy you bought him for his birthday, Jesse,' Florence said as she sat on her high-backed chair. 'Let me know when your arm is tired, and I'll take over.'

John gave another deep belly laugh as the pictures flickered in front of his face. Florence wondered if maybe he should be moved back from the toy – seeing those pictures flickering speedily in front of his young eyes must be tiring – but she didn't like to interrupt their fun.

'I'm hoping he'll grow tired of the moving slides soon enough,' Jesse said, grinning as he glanced up at her, his blue eyes twinkling with amusement. 'But he doesn't seem to be losing any interest just yet.'

Florence laughed and watched the three most important people in her life. She couldn't help thinking how lucky she was to have been blessed with so much happiness. She wondered how her younger sister Amy's life would have been if she had found someone like Jesse to settle down with. Florence smiled at the thought of her independent sister and what she would say if she was to hear her ever voice this opinion aloud.

'What are you thinking about, my love?' Jesse asked, as John giggled at the pictures moving animatedly in front of him.

'Only that for a woman who never wished to be married, or indeed ever expected to have children, I'm entirely content with my lot.' She smiled at the irony of how different her life had turned out compared to what she had always imagined she wanted.

Jesse laughed. 'You are still an independent woman in many ways, my dear. Never fear on that score.'

She was, and she knew it. Florence stifled a yawn, not wanting Jesse to notice how tired she was, especially as she had only recently persuaded him that continuing to work long hours now that she was a mother with two small children was not taking its toll on her in any way. Despite being thirteen years older than her, Jesse had proved to be a very forward-thinking husband and hadn't minded too much when she had insisted on working after John's birth. She was careful not to give him any reason to think that it might be time for her to spend her days at home bringing up their children, now they had two of them to care for.

She also did her best to ensure Jesse relaxed as much as possible when he was at home. The last thing she intended letting him do was worry, or spend time planning his next venture with the Boots Pure Drug Company. He needed at least a few hours each day enjoying time with his family when he could forget about business and simply be himself.

Florence took a calming breath and sat forward slightly in her seat.

'I'm not as independent as I used to be,' she said, 'and I'm happy for it.'

He looked up at her from his place on the rug and sat back

on his haunches. 'Tell me,' he said quietly. 'I know there's something bothering you that you've been wishing to discuss with me. What is it?'

She wasn't sure why she was surprised that he had noticed her nervousness. Florence loved that Jesse cared enough not to let any anguish she might feel continue unduly. She would have to voice her fears, because now that Jesse had become aware of them he wouldn't let things lie until she had shared them with him. She also knew they wouldn't go away until she had told him. She reached out to take his hand and gave it a gentle squeeze.

'I want us to try for another child.'

She waited anxiously for his response. Florence didn't elaborate, allowing Jesse a moment to absorb her thoughts. She watched him frown thoughtfully. He forgot to turn the handle on the zoetrope.

'Papa, Papa,' John whined, pushing Jesse's arm to get his attention.

Jesse ruffled John's hair. 'You try now, my boy,' he said, taking John's pudgy little hand and placing it on the handle of the zoetrope. 'Turn it, slowly, like this.' He kept his hand over John's smaller one and turned the handle several times until the toddler became used to the motion. Then, as he rose with a little difficulty to his feet, Dorothy began to grizzle and he picked her up. He stood by Florence's chair, still not catching her eye.

Jesse kissed the top of Dorothy's dark hair and then passed her down into Florence's arms, before bending and kissing Florence.

'I'm happy to try for another child, if that's what you want.'

Florence was relieved. Now that she had two children, the need for another was intense. She felt her cheeks flush. 'You won't mind?'

'Not about having more children. Only that I worry for you taking on too much,' he said. 'I know you insist that you are fine coping with all that you fit into your days, but I wouldn't be a caring husband if I didn't notice that on occasion, like this evening, you're weary.' He sat on his chair next to hers and took hold of Dorothy's little hand, smiling silently down at John.

'What is it?' Florence asked, seeing his eyes well up.

He turned his attention back to her. 'I want you to be the happiest you can be, Florence.'

'I know that.' She didn't understand the direction their conversation was going.

Jesse stared at her in silence for a moment. 'You're going to tell me that you want to keep working when this next baby is born too, aren't you?'

He knew her too well. 'Yes,' she admitted, glad to get this point of contention out of the way. 'I am. I know most women would be happy not to work.'

'But you're not most women, Florence,' he interrupted fondly. 'You are truly unique, and I love you for it.'

Florence sighed. 'I know you do, and I'm grateful to you for caring about me enough to let me make my own choices about working.' She hesitated. 'I sometimes can't help wondering though if I'm being selfish giving in to my need to continue working alongside you at Boots. There's so much more that I want to achieve for the female employees working for the company, and I can't help them if I'm not there. And, unlike other women, I have the freedom to take my children with me to work and look after them there.'

He stared at her for a moment. 'And you think you'll be able to cope with three children to care for? You're already tired looking after two on occasion. Especially now John is wanting to spend more time moving about, rather than sitting in the office playing with his toys?'

Florence knew Jesse made sense. She wished she didn't feel such a need to continue working, and could act more like other women lucky enough to enjoy her social status, but it simply wasn't in her to do so. She had no idea how she would make it work, that was the truth of it, but she was determined to at least give it a try.

'Yes, I'm sure,' she said, sounding more confident than she felt. Florence knew from experience growing up that it was better to ask for more than you expected to receive.

'Then I won't challenge you over your decision,' he said, leaning down to help John with the zoetrope once more. 'However, if I do feel you're struggling, then I will have to say something to you. Agreed?'

'Yes,' she said, grateful not to have to quarrel with him about her decision.

John grizzled and tired of the zoetrope, pushing the cylinder over.

'Come to Papa,' Jesse said, scooping John up into his arms. He sat back in his armchair and, placing John on his knees, bounced him up and down to distract him from the toy.

'I can't believe that at the age of forty I'm discussing becoming a father for the third time,' he laughed.

Florence breathed in the familiar scent of her baby girl's head and watched Jesse with his beloved son. Her heart felt as if it was filling almost to bursting point. She had so much to be grateful for – was she right to wish to continue working? Was it fair on John and Dorothy, and the next baby, if they were lucky enough to have another one, for them to spend so much time in an office with her? Or was she simply being greedy and selfish?

Florence thought back to when she was younger and living above her parents' stationery shop in St Helier. She used to go downstairs from her parents' flat to the shop where her mother worked long hours alongside her father. The only difference between her childhood and her children's was that financially her parents had both needed to work. Florence believed she had gained her work ethic from watching how her parents lived their life and hoped that by continuing to work, if nothing else she would be teaching her children, especially her daughter, by example.

Florence wanted Dorothy to grow up knowing that women should have the right to make their own choices. Why should women not continue working if they chose to do so? She also wanted her son to be raised believing that it was normal for a mother to elect how she conducted her life. As far as she was concerned, she couldn't do those things if she did as society commanded and stayed at home.

What about Jesse though? she wondered. Was she asking too much for him to continue accepting that his children be brought to the office on a daily basis, while he was trying to work in his office next door? He had such a heavy responsibility on his shoulders already, trying to keep control of expanding their stores and factory departments. Did she have the right to be so stubborn? Or was she simply being greedy?

She contemplated her concerns as she hugged Dorothy to her, her hand resting on the tiny round belly, as her daughter kicked her legs back and forth. If Jesse was happy for her to carry on as she had been doing, then who was she to argue? She really was the luckiest woman she knew and would be forever grateful that Jesse's sister Jane had suggested he travel to Jersey to recuperate from his breakdown six years before. Her life would have been very different if they had never met. Florence knew she would have been happy, because she had loved living in Jersey and working with her father and sister at W H Rowe's Stationers, but nothing gave her as much joy as the life she led now.

She was married to a man who not only adored her, but who most of the time accommodated her wishes. He gave her the freedom to be herself and the lifestyle to allow her to continue working even though other mothers were forced to remain at home.

'You have given me an inordinate amount of joy since our marriage, dearest Florence,' Jesse said, distracting her from dwelling further.

'And,' she said, taking his hand in hers, 'you've done the same for me, my love. We are very lucky to have found each other.'

PART ONE

Chapter 1

January 1892

'Mrs Boot?' Agnes Tweed, Florence's secretary, knocked quietly on her office door.

'Come in,' Florence called, wincing as her baby gave a couple of kicks inside her stomach. It was hard to believe that John was now three, having celebrated his third birthday the previous week. Dorothy was already nineteen months old now, and in three months Florence would be giving birth to her third child.

She and Jesse had fitted so much into their lives since their marriage and Florence could barely believe all the things they had achieved together and how far they had come since then. Business had been continually increasing and now Jesse was in the stages of completing the paperwork to take over the rest of the factory building on Island Street.

She wondered how much bigger their empire would need to be to satisfy his ambitions. They had over eighty staff working at that factory already, most of them women whom she had recruited to work there. Florence enjoyed being able

11

to give the women placements in the various departments. There was no reason they wouldn't be as capable as men at packing, bottling, and working in the printing department. In fact, Florence mused, the female employees had proved themselves very worthy when it came to advertising, laboratory work, and also looking after the business accounts.

Florence had been proud when, on the way to the office that morning, Jesse had told her that they would soon be able to open their thirtieth store. She was amazed but knew that their success was bolstered by them both working up to fourteen hours each day, despite the slow decline in Jesse's health.

The door opened slowly and her secretary peered around it. The smile on her face disappeared as her eyes rested on John's empty cot next to Florence's desk.

Florence glanced at the pulled-back crochet blanket her mother had sent over specifically for her daughter Dorothy's birth last year. She had to admit, if only to herself, that working in late pregnancy while caring for a three-year-old and a toddler was rather more tiring than she had anticipated. Not that she had any compulsion to share her thoughts on this with Jesse. If he realised how exhausted she felt at the end of each day he would soon put a stop to her going to work, at least until this baby had been born and she had taken time off to recover from the birth.

'Master John and Dorothy are awake?' Miss Tweed asked, trying not to peer too obviously over Florence's desk at the little camp beds behind it.

'They were getting restless.' Florence could see the disappointment on the woman's pale face and suspected that Miss

Tweed had come in before the store opened to see the children before anyone else had the chance to. Florence wished her secretary would find the young man she had confided that she longed to meet so that she could settle down and have a family of her own. Florence thought of her own intention as a young woman not to marry and give up her independence, and how those plans had dissipated when she had met and spent time with Jesse. It hadn't taken long for her to discover how enjoyable it could be to spend time with him over anyone else.

She heard Miss Tweed mumble something. Florence had noticed that Miss Tweed never failed to find an excuse to take John to her tiny office next door to play with him. She liked Dorothy too, but there was something about John that charmed her. It was such a shame that she wasn't a mother herself. Not that Florence would relish losing the meticulous woman to motherhood. Miss Tweed made her and Jesse's days far easier with her excellent shorthand, typing, and organisational skills, but the thought of someone missing out on the joys of having their own children now that she had experienced it for herself saddened her.

Florence was aware that her intention to continue working like she had before John was born had been naïve. She hadn't considered the debilitating tiredness she'd feel after disturbed nights nursing him, and then Dorothy, through recent head colds. Nor had she envisaged her need to be the one to nurse her children, rather than allowing one of the domestic servants to take over from her and give her a little respite during those disturbed nights.

'Miss Pilbeam kindly took them for a while,' Florence explained, realising that Miss Tweed was waiting for her to answer. 'John was a little grizzly. I asked her to keep him and Dorothy busy while I finished writing this letter to the widowed mother of one of our shop assistants.'

Florence did not elaborate about the unmarried girl finding herself in the unfortunate predicament of expecting a child. She had needed to speak at length to Nellie Blythe the previous evening. Florence didn't want anyone else to know she had spoken privately to the young girl, so had arranged for her to stay behind after the shop had closed for business.

Miss Tweed left the room and Florence swallowed away tears that were threatening to overwhelm her. She put her emotional state down to lack of sleep and still being shaken by Nellie's terror at facing her mother. Florence had come to understand the shame girls faced when one of them fell pregnant with an illegitimate baby; she had seen it happen enough times now, unfortunately. She wished there was something she could do to help Nellie and counteract the dreadful stigma that the poor girl was about to come up against.

Florence didn't want Mrs Blythe disowning her daughter, like so many other mothers felt compelled to do. She understood that they mostly did it to show their contempt for their daughter's actions to the rest of their community, hoping that some of the shame the girl had brought on her family might be dissipated.

Florence could never imagine being able to turn her back on her daughter, regardless of what she had done. Was this, she wondered, because she had enough money to travel away somewhere with her daughter if such an event were to present itself? No, she decided. Her children were worth far more to her than either her standing in society or her reputation.

Florence gazed sadly at the empty chair on the opposite side of her desk where Nellie had sat trembling as she sobbed into a damp handkerchief.

Miss Tweed's light knock on her door brought her back to the present. Florence looked at her and was about to smile but seeing the concerned expression on her secretary's face frowned instead. 'Is something the matter?'

Miss Tweed closed the door quietly behind her and, lowering her voice, walked up to Florence's desk. 'I'm afraid there's been an incident, Mrs Boot.'

Something she wasn't going to like, Florence suspected. 'Go on, what is it?'

Her secretary cleared her throat. 'I'm afraid several of the women have been discussing Miss Blythe.'

Florence frowned. She took a deep breath, hoping that what she was about to hear wasn't anything to do with her meeting with Nellie the evening before. 'Yes, please go on.'

'Apparently . . .'

Miss Tweed didn't have time to finish her sentence before Jesse barged into the room. He opened the door with such ferocity that it flew back, slamming against the office wall, making her and Miss Tweed jump in shock.

'Thank you, Miss Tweed,' he snapped, interrupting her. 'Kindly leave me to discuss the matter alone with my wife.'

Florence glared at Jesse, stunned by his rudeness. She went to stand. 'Whatever's happened?'

'Don't get up,' Jesse said, taking a seat where the previous evening Nellie had sat sobbing. Miss Tweed closed the door gently behind her.

Jesse closed his eyes briefly. It seemed to Florence that he was either trying to calm his temper or building up to telling her something he didn't expect her to like. She didn't fancy either option but waited for him to elaborate.

'I gather you asked young Nellie Blythe to come and speak to you last evening,' he said, scowling, his usually gentle eyes appearing like glints of blue granite.

Florence winced. She hated it when Jesse was angry with her, but it also irritated her when he pulled rank. 'That's right,' she said defensively. 'She has a personal issue and I wanted to help her with it.'

Jesse slammed his hands on the desk between them. He took a deep breath. 'From what I hear, it seems that you trying to help this young woman has now aggravated matters.'

'How?'

'One of the other assistants noticed Nellie hanging back before coming up to your office. Honestly, Florence, what were you thinking, asking the girl to come here?'

Florence had no idea what she had done wrong. She had called many of the women to her office when she needed to speak to them about something private. 'I don't see why that's an issue,' she argued. 'Anyway, it's none of the women's business what I discuss with their colleagues.'

Jesse stared at her silently for a moment before replying. 'Florence, the woman followed Nellie up here and listened outside your office door.'

She gasped, dumbfounded that anyone could have the gall to do such a thing. 'Are you certain?' Jesse nodded. 'Well, who was it?'

'Myra Ellis.' His eyes narrowed.

Florence could see Jesse was irritated with her for what she'd done and annoyance with him rose.

'I've always been slightly suspicious of that woman,' Jesse said half to himself.

Florence pictured the bird-like member of staff. She had also been unsure whether to take the woman on, but her references had been good enough. Apart from her personal dislike of Myra, she had no reason to refuse to give the woman a job.

'We should fire Myra,' Florence insisted instinctively. If the woman was capable of spying on one of her colleagues and then repeating what she had heard to the other assistants, she wasn't the sort of woman that Florence wanted to have connected with their Boots stores.

'That was my first thought, too,' Jesse said, his anger seeming to subside slightly. 'But if she's capable of this sort of behaviour, then what else is she capable of?'

'I'm not frightened of what she might do!' Florence snapped, furious with what Myra's actions could mean for Nellie. 'Think of the repercussions for Miss Blythe.'

Jesse sighed. 'I understand what you're saying, Florence,' he said, his voice controlled and sounding almost patronising. 'However, does it occur to you that although the women might not like what Myra has done, her actions will make them fear her and also what she might do to them, should they cross her?'

'Don't act all superior with me, Jesse,' Florence said, glaring at him. She might have put herself in this position, but it angered her when he talked down to her as if she was one of their children. 'I'll speak to Myra.'

Florence knew she would have to take a little time to calm herself down before attempting to do so, otherwise she might lose her temper with Myra Ellis completely and fire her on the spot.

Jesse shook his head. 'No. We should speak to the women in Nellie and Myra's department and tell them that a private conversation between yourself and a member of staff was listened to. Let them know that the culprit is known to us, and that should anyone ever do such a thing again, then it will mean instant dismissal.' Florence opened her mouth to argue, but Jesse raised his hand and continued dictating to her the action they would take. 'I'll then call Myra up to my office and give her a stern talking to. I'm going to warn her that I don't want her spreading rumours about other members of staff. I also want her to know that I'll be watching her. Hopefully she'll be more concerned about losing her job than spreading more nastiness around the store.'

Florence understood what he wanted to do but thought she should be the one to do it. 'Have you quite finished?'

He frowned. 'Yes.'

'Fine. Now I'll tell you what I think, if you'll give me the chance to speak.' She narrowed her eyes at him. 'I took on Myra, so I should be the one to speak to her.'

'She will be far more bothered by a scolding from me than from you. Don't you agree?'

Florence was not in the mood to concede to Jesse's instructions. Not today. 'No. I'm happy for you to speak to the staff, but I believe I should face Myra, alone.'

Jesse frowned. 'Florence, I have more experience with the staff than you. I think you'll be making a mistake.'

'I disagree, Jesse. I employ the female staff, therefore it makes sense that I reprimand them. If I let you do this, then I'll lose any credibility I have with them.' When he didn't reply, she added, 'I insist, Jesse.'

Jesse stared at her thoughtfully. 'I can see that there's no compromising with you on this. You must do what you think best. But you will need to be very careful when choosing your words with that woman.'

Florence nodded, happy to have taken charge of the situation once again.

'Fine,' Jesse said, wearily. 'You are a stubborn woman at times, Florence. I just hope you know what you're doing, that's all.' He sighed. 'Let's go and speak to the women now, before the store opens.'

They went downstairs and Florence stood next to Jesse as he addressed the staff. She glanced from one woman to the next to try and gauge their feelings as he spoke. Jesse didn't mention Nellie by name, but Florence sensed that most of the woman knew who it was that she had met with the previous evening. Her heart ached for Nellie as the poor girl stood near the back, shamefaced from being the centre of so much attention, albeit not direct.

'I want to hear no further reports of such behaviour,' Jesse scolded, concluding his talk. 'Any further actions of the type

I've mentioned will result in instant dismissal. Does every one of you understand?'

A chorus of 'Yes, Mr Boot' rang out.

'You may all return to your stations.'

The women turned to go, some whispering to each other as they moved. 'Apart from Myra Ellis,' Florence announced. 'Please come to my office in two minutes.'

Florence caught the look of annoyance on Jesse's face and realised that once again she had done the wrong thing. Maybe she shouldn't have singled out Myra in front of the others, she thought as she walked with him to the lift.

'Why did you do that?' Jesse asked as the lift doors closed behind them.

'Everyone out there who knew about what had happened, also would have known that it was Myra who listened at the door.' Florence's instincts told her that Jesse was right to be concerned, but it was too late now to rectify it. 'I saw the look on poor Nellie's face as you were speaking. She was mortified to be the subject of the women's gossip. And all of it was instigated by that dreadful woman. I don't care if she's embarrassed. Maybe it might teach her a lesson not to do it again.'

'Somehow I doubt it, Florence.' He took her hand in his. 'Please, think carefully before speaking to her. You don't want your words to be the catalyst of another drama for Nellie, or any other poor girl who finds herself in the same predicament.'

Florence didn't. 'I will,' she assured him, wishing she felt as confident as she sounded.

'My love, I know you enjoy your work and I love having

you working next to me, but I think that sometimes you try to fit too much into your days.'

'Because I've made a mess of this, you mean?' She glared at him, waiting for him to disagree.

'Yes, if I'm honest. You're not making the right choices on occasion and it concerns me. I wish you'd listen to me, when I try to help you.'

She knew he was making sense, but she worried that if she agreed with Jesse, he might then insist she reduce her working hours, and she wasn't ready to relinquish any control of her work.

Florence confronted Myra a few moments later. She had expected the woman to glare at her stony-faced and indignant, but instead Myra begged for forgiveness and cried the entire time Florence was talking to her, but she couldn't help wondering if they were crocodile tears. Myra didn't seem like the sort of person to suddenly become tearful and apologetic, but she would have to give her the benefit of the doubt in this instance.

Later that day, when some of the staff were taking their lunch break, Florence popped down to the shop floor and when no one else was nearby discreetly asked Nellie to come and see her again.

'I'm so sorry for what happened after our chat last night,' Florence said. 'As you know, Mr Boot has spoken to the women and I've met with Myra Ellis and given her a talking-to. I hope the matter calms down a little now.'

'Thanks for trying, Mrs Boot,' Nellie sniffed. 'But now they all know the state I'm in.' She burst into fresh tears, pulling a creased handkerchief from her uniform pocket. 'Me mam's going to kick me out, Mrs Boot, I just know she is.'

'You don't know that for certain.' Florence tried to reassure her, aware that she had never met Mrs Blythe so had no idea how the woman would react. 'Would you like me to write to your mother?'

Nellie looked up, her blue eyes puffy from crying. 'What would you say?'

Florence had no idea, so took a moment to try and come up with something. 'I presume that your mother is concerned about what the neighbours might say about the, um, situation. Is that correct?'

Nellie blew her nose and sniffed. 'Yes, Mrs Boot. Me mam will say that 'er next door will 'ave been waiting for somethin' like this to 'appen, so she can say she always knew we was not as good as 'er.'

Florence hated the thought of someone relishing another person's misery. 'I can write to your mother and let her know that I'm happy to give you a reference, so that once the baby has been born, you'll be able to find work.'

Nellie looked stunned. 'You'd do that for me, Mrs Boot?'

Florence felt a pang of sadness that the girl sitting in front of her was so grateful for any help, especially when she had been instrumental in Nellie's situation becoming common knowledge among her peers. How desperate she must feel, Florence thought miserably. 'Yes. I'll happily help you find something at one of our other stores, where there's less chance of the staff there knowing your business. Would that make you feel better?' she asked.

'Yes, very much.'

'Then I'll write saying the same to your mother. Hopefully it will pacify her and she won't be as angry with you as you fear.'

'That's very kind of you, Mrs Boot. Thanks ever so much.'

'It'll be my pleasure, Nellie. Now, dry your eyes and go and eat some lunch.'

She watched Nellie leave. Her head ached and more than anything she would have loved to take half an hour to lie down and close her eyes, but she needed to write to Nellie's mother without delay. She had suspected a few weeks previously that Nellie was putting on a little weight around her waist, but the girl had been so thin before that Florence had thought the extra weight had suited her. She hadn't thought for a moment that Nellie could be carrying a child.

Florence recalled the girl's interview with her almost a year before. She had been barely sixteen, but desperate to prove herself capable of carrying out her role as a junior shop assistant. She had been one of the staff Florence had taken on at the Goose Gate shop, but within months she knew that she was one of her best employees.

She thought how Nellie had mentioned living with her disabled younger brother and widowed mother, who, if Florence remembered correctly, also suffered from poor health. Florence believed the mother's troubles were due to arthritis. How, she wondered miserably, was Nellie expected to survive without a weekly wage, let alone adding the responsibility of bringing up a baby without a husband? She had no choice but to let her go, but it didn't make doing it any easier. Nellie's situation had struck a chord with Florence and she was determined to find a way to help her, if she possibly could.

Chapter 2

'Drink your milk and then Mama has a treat for you,' Florence said, holding out the small cup for John to take. She had a batch of his favourite gingerbread biscuits that she had baked for him the evening before hidden in a tin in her desk drawer. Enticed by the temptation of a treat, John took the cup and drank.

'I have today's mail for you, Mrs Boot,' Miss Tweed announced, entering Florence's office and smiling down at the children.

'Thank you,' Florence said, having not heard her secretary's knock. 'My mind is everywhere today.'

Miss Tweed handed several envelopes to her. Florence thanked her and after her secretary left the room noticed the top letter had her mother's neat handwriting on it. Sighing, Florence picked up her letter opener and sliced open the top, wondering if this would be another one of her mother's caring but critical letters. She took out the single sheet of paper, suspecting this wasn't a chatty tome, but something more serious playing on her mother's mind. She unfolded the page and read.

27 Queen Street
St Helier
Jersey
28th January 1892

14 Wellesley Road,
Sheffield

Dear Florence,

I am writing this against your father's wishes, but felt the need to stress my thoughts to you as I believe any caring mother should.

I was aware of your insistence to continue working after John and then Dorothy were born, despite my advice to the contrary. I overheard your sisters speaking earlier today after one of them had received a letter from you and have to admit my shock that your husband is still allowing you to continue your work after your third baby is born.

I am aware that you enjoy being part of your husband's stores, Florence, however, you are a mother now and your babies need to come first in your priorities, as does your health.

I understand also your need for independence, but in this case I feel that you are making a mistake. Haven't I always worried about you being too independent for your own good? I am surprised to still be berating you on this now that you are a married woman. I had expected your husband to take you in hand and instil some sense into you.

I am compelled to stress that now is the time for you to leave your husband to run his businesses. Mr Boot is a successful man, of that I am fully aware, but I believe that his ambitions may be encouraging you to act in a way that could be detrimental to the wellbeing not only of yourself, but also of your children.

I am aware that you will be unhappy to read these words, but women of means, such as you enjoy, should not be out at work, Florence. It is simply not acceptable. They should remain at home to run their household, and be satisfied to do so. I would be comforted if you could reassure me that you will at least consider my thoughts on this matter.

On a different note, I happened upon Mrs Wolstenholm today when I ventured downstairs to the shop with a letter for your father. She asked how you were finding married life. I refrained from mentioning to her about your working situation, because I couldn't bear for her to spread gossip about the family, as I feel sure she might be compelled to do.

There, I have said my piece. I must finish this letter now if I am to catch the next post. Please do not be angry with me for my sentiments, I mean only to help you find the most appropriate way forward. Your father sends his best wishes, as do I. I hope you know that I am only writing this to you because as your mother I feel it my duty to do so, and also because I care that you make the right choices.

Your caring Mother.

Irritation flowed through Florence, making her want to tear up the letter and give her mother a piece of her mind. Why was it that women were expected to stop doing something that fulfilled them because they had a family? It was unfair and, in her opinion, unjust. No, she would not do as her mother asked, she thought defiantly. She had the opportunity to continue working and be a mother, and that was what she intended doing.

Florence might have given up her younger ideals of being an independent woman when she agreed to marry Jesse, but she refused to believe that being married meant she should lose all sense of herself. Why were people so judgemental of others? Nellie Blythe was condemned for becoming a mother without a husband, and Florence was criticised for continuing to work when she had one. Surely women deserved the right to decide how they lived their own lives without others accusing them of doing wrong, Florence mused. Her mother might have had to conform to her husband's wishes, and to an extent Florence didn't mind compromising with Jesse, on occasion, but she did not believe that compromise should always be on the side of the woman, despite what society seemed to think.

Now she had a daughter, Florence intended to ensure that Dorothy grew up to be an independently thinking woman. No daughter of hers would ever be subservient to a husband, not if she had her way. She believed that Jesse would feel the same way too. Wasn't he always telling her that it was her zest for life and independent nature that had attracted him to her in the first place?

Florence took a deep breath and tried to calm down. She didn't want to say anything to her mother that she would later regret and decided that she would not send back a hasty reply. She would wait a while and think through what she was going to say when she did. Her mother meant well, of that Florence was certain, and she had always been open with Florence about not understanding her need for independence.

Florence was also painfully aware that most women would agree with her mother. She had overheard women at the stores, especially since John and then Dorothy's birth, whispering behind their hands that her place was at the hearth with her children. She rubbed her eyes. She loved her work but there were times, like these – when John had kept her up half the night, unable to sleep after a nightmare – that Florence wondered if she was right to insist that she could be a working mother. Why couldn't she be satisfied to stay at home with her babies, like other women? What was so wrong with simply running the family home? She sighed. It just wasn't the life for her, whether other people agreed with what she did or not.

The last time another woman had given her a disapproving look was only the week before when she had carried Dorothy on her hip and led John by the hand to go and speak to several members of staff.

None of this mattered to her, not for the most part anyway. She never presumed to question their choices as parents, and didn't think they had the right to criticise hers. She couldn't help wondering, now and then, if some of the women giving her dirty looks had been concealing their envy at her independence.

She might be a married woman and one of some standing, but nothing would erase the shop girl from Jersey that she had originally been. She loved being a working mother but sometimes missed the peace and tranquillity of Jersey, especially at times like this when she was over-tired and emotional. Her mother had worked, although not the long hours that she insisted on doing. Florence tried to think if she had ever felt neglected in any way by her parents. No, she hadn't. Her childhood might not have been luxurious, but it had always been filled with love and warmth, unlike that of many other women she had met through Boots.

Florence hoped that her children would see her hard work as something to be proud of and to emulate, not something to resent. She couldn't help feeling that she was walking a fine line between being ambitious and trying to do too much.

She enjoyed working hard to help Jesse achieve his plans for his growing empire, and working closely with him helped her to keep a close eye on his health. It was harder for him to hide things from her if she was in the next office.

She wondered if his being thirteen years older than her might be what kept him working at the level he did. Maybe, she thought, it was her fear of Jesse's health deteriorating that increased her determination to continue working so hard and by taking the children with her into work, they were able to spend more time with Jesse than they otherwise would.

Florence valued their hours spent together as a family. It soothed her to think that she was being supportive of Jesse despite his tendency to overwork. She was relieved he still remained fairly strong and she believed that her watching over him and his diet helped keep it that way. She had every intention of continuing in the same way and hoped that with her love and support her husband would carry on as he was for many more years to come.

Florence knew that she and Jesse had much to look forward to and she was going to see to it that they enjoyed every second they had together.

Chapter 3

Two days later, Miss Tweed walked into Florence's office and quietly informed her that someone was waiting to speak to her.

'She doesn't have an appointment to see you, Mrs Boot, but she insists that she isn't leaving until you listen to what she has to say.'

Florence frowned, anxiously. 'Do you know her, or what it's about?'

'She doesn't work here, but she said she's come about her daughter Nellie Blythe. Would you like me to try and get her to leave?'

Florence's heart plummeted. She hadn't expected this to happen. Surely, she couldn't have made the matter even worse? She looked at her two children playing peacefully in the corner next to her. She wasn't sure what to expect from Mrs Blythe and didn't want the children to witness any unpleasantness. 'No, that won't be necessary', she said. 'I would like you to take the children while she's here though, please.'

Miss Tweed nodded enthusiastically. 'I'd be delighted to.'

Florence turned to her children. 'John, Dorothy? Would you like to go for a walk with Miss Tweed now?'

Both children immediately forgot their toys and beamed at her. 'Yes please, Mama,' John said, answering for both of them. 'Come on, Dothy.' He reached out and took his sister's small hand in his and pulled her to her feet. Then, without a backward glance, they went to her secretary's side.

'Thank you,' Florence said. 'Please show Mrs Blythe in.'

Florence stood and waited for Nellie's mother to enter her office. 'Mrs Blythe,' she said, walking around her desk to shake the woman's hand.

Mrs Blythe reluctantly did as expected of her and then took a seat when Florence gestured towards a chair, where a couple of days before her daughter had sat.

'I presume you're here to discuss my letter about your daughter, Nellie?'

Mrs Blythe nodded slowly, the tightness of her mouth clearly showing her displeasure. Florence couldn't understand what she must have done wrong and waited for the woman to speak.

'Mrs Boot,' she said, her narrow lips pursed. 'I got your letter 'bout my Nellie. I wasn't happy that she told you her news before me. It's private and not to be shared with her betters. I'm ashamed of her, I don't mind admitting that much. What makes it worse though is that you and, she tells me, Mr Boot knows about this.'

'Mr Boot doesn't know, Mrs Blythe,' Florence assured her, aware that it wasn't true, but knowing that there was no way Mrs Blythe could know that he did. She hoped her reassurance might help calm the woman a little. Florence could see why Nellie had been frightened to face her mother. She was a stern lady and looked most formidable. A young girl reliant on her for a home might well be worried to upset her. 'And I made sure to speak to Nellie after everyone had left.'

'That's something, I suppose.' She studied her gnarled but immaculate hands.

Florence suspected that Nellie hadn't mentioned about Myra Ellis listening to their conversation and sharing it with others. She didn't know whether to speak or wait for Nellie's mother to continue. She watched as the woman decided what to say next and wondered how old she must be. Surely Mrs Blythe couldn't be more than forty, or forty-five? She looked seventy though, with her wizened face and stooped shoulders. How much had this woman suffered, Florence mused. Yet she was like so many other women who had to find ways to feed and care for their children with little or no assistance from others.

'I didn't mean to offend you by speaking to Nellie or by writing to you, Mrs Blythe,' Florence said, hoping to alleviate the woman's annoyance at anything she had done.

Mrs Blythe looked up. 'I know you didn't, Mrs Boot. I'm sure you thought by putting my daughter's shame on paper that only I would see it.'

Florence was shocked. 'I'm sorry, did I do wrong?'

Mrs Blythe straightened her shoulders. 'Yes, although I'm sure you had the best intentions.' Florence didn't understand what could have happened. 'It's not your fault that I have a nasty, nosy neighbour, a Mrs Ellis.' Florence gasped. Surely

Myra wasn't the neighbour to whom Mrs Blythe referred? Florence's heart pounded as she waited to hear more.

'Well, this time it wasn't her what done it, but that spinster daughter of 'ers. Myra.'

Florence hardly dared ask, but needed to know what had happened. 'Myra Ellis is one of the staff members here, at Boots. What has she done?'

'Mrs Boot, we don't often get no mail,' Mrs Blythe continued. 'So when that busybody next door saw the postman coming our way, she pretended she was Nellie and took the letter intended for me.'

Florence winced, unsure whether it was from the baby's sudden kick or her horror at what had happened. 'Please, go on.'

'That little—' Her face reddened, and she shook her head. 'No, I can't use such names in front of a lady like you, Mrs Boot, but, well, she opened your letter. Now that harridan has made it her business to make sure everyone in our street knows that our Nellie is in the family way.'

Florence bit her lower lip, horrified to have made Nellie's situation so much worse. Jesse had been right. She should have listened to him and taken his counsel instead of believing she knew better.

'I'm so sorry, Mrs Blythe, I really am. I was only trying to make things better for Nellie when I wrote to you.'

Mrs Blythe shook her head.

Florence's heart pounded. 'Is there anything at all that I can do?'

'No.' Mrs Blythe stood and, holding her shawl tightly at

the front, walked to the door. Then, turning to Florence, she added, 'I know you meant well, Mrs Boot, truly I do. But with all due respect, you can't know 'ow it is for the likes of us. Our lives aren't like yours. Now everyone will know, and there's no way my Nellie can be taken on at any of your other shops. That Myra Ellis will see to it that word spreads and she's bound to make it her business to tell others working here about Nellie, too.'

Florence walked over to join her. 'I truly am very sorry for my part in this, Mrs Blythe,' she said, aware that repeating her apology didn't help Nellie, or her mother, at all.

'I believe you are, Mrs Boot, and I know there was no 'arm meant. I just wanted you to know what's 'appened, so you'll know not to try finding work for Nellie at one of the other Boots branches.'

The woman departed and Florence stared at the closed office door. How could she have been so stupid? With her clumsy attempt to play the good fairy, she had managed to make not only Nellie's situation much worse, but also her entire family's. Florence closed her eyes and sighed heavily.

'I am such a fool,' she said returning to sit at her desk and putting hands over her face. 'Why couldn't I leave well alone?'

'Why, what have you done?' Jesse asked closing the office door quietly. She gasped to see him there, unaware that he had walked in. 'I was going to my office when I saw that woman leaving. Miss Tweed told me it was Nellie's mother.'

He walked to stand behind her and gave her shoulder a gentle squeeze and kissed her lightly on the head, before taking a seat opposite her.

Florence shook her head, barely able to control her tears. 'I've been such a fool, Jesse.'

He crossed his arms. 'You're not a fool, Florence. You're a kind woman, who has probably taken on too much. You're exhausted and that's what's affected your judgement. Why don't you tell me exactly what's happened and maybe together we can find a way to make things right?'

Florence cringed. 'I'm not so certain that's possible.'

'You let me be the judge of that.'

She explained everything that had happened, aware that there was no reason not to confide in Jesse about Nellie's situation now that she had in effect found a way to announce it to the Blythes' entire neighbourhood.

He listened intently, not speaking until she had finished. 'Ahh, I see.'

'I thought I was helping the poor girl,' she said, wishing she had never taken it upon herself to do something without first speaking to Jesse and making sure she was doing the right thing. Why had she been so foolish? 'I'm so angry with myself. It's frustrating seeing these girls suffer so much, when all they need is someone to care and help them in some way.'

'Yes, but that's not how it turned out this time, is it?'

Florence shook her head. 'No.' She gave him a pleading look. 'What can I do to make things right? There must be something, isn't there?'

Jesse stared at her thoughtfully before shaking his head. 'Not on this occasion, no. I think the best option is for you to do as Mrs Blythe requested and leave well alone.'

Florence couldn't stand to think that she had made such

a mess of things. She stood up, panic-stricken, and paced back and forth behind her desk.

Jesse got up and went to her. He took her by the shoulders to stop her. 'Calm yourself, my dear. Upsetting yourself over this will help no one, least of all Nellie.'

'But I must do something, Jesse. I can't leave things as they are.'

'You have no choice in this instance. All you can do, my darling, is to learn from this and maybe next time you wish to help someone, think things through from their perspective. Speak to me about it. I've lived here all my life; I've been that poor child who had to save their shoes so I had a decent pair to wear to chapel on Sundays. I'll understand better than you how the communities around here work.'

His words made sense. 'I'll do that,' she agreed, hating to think of Jesse's younger life being so much harder than hers had been.

He pulled her into his arms and hugged her. 'You're trembling. Try not to worry too much. You are kind, that's all. Maybe a little naïve. All you wanted to do was help. I'm sure Mrs Blythe knew that your actions came from a place of caring.'

Florence thought so too. She also knew that whatever Jesse said, she would have to find a way to help Nellie somehow. The next time though, she would take much more care about how she did it.

'First though, I'm going to have another word with Myra,' Florence said, watching Jesse for his reaction. 'I don't know about you, but I think she's gone too far, and I want to dismiss her. I don't want someone as malicious as her working for Boots.'

She waited for him to argue, but instead Jesse nodded. 'I was going to suggest doing the very same thing.'

Chapter 4

February 1892

Florence was busily checking through references for prospective new female employees when Jesse walked in carrying a large envelope and sporting a wide smile on his face.

'I have a surprise for you,' he announced proudly as he unwound the scarf from around his neck and dropped it on the edge of her desk. She sensed an underlying nervousness about him. 'Here, read this.' He withdrew a letter and held it out for her to take.

His enthusiasm was infectious, and Florence couldn't help grinning. She enjoyed it when Jesse was excited about a new project and suspected that he had probably already signed for whatever it was he was about to show her. She just hoped she was as happy with it as he seemed to be.

Florence read the letter. Twice. Then, trying to remember to keep smiling, she looked up at him. 'You've bought us a house? At The Park?'

She had been to several dinners held by friends who were

residents of the smart estate but had never considered that they might move to live there too.

'Yes. I've named the house St Heliers in honour of your hometown.' When she didn't reply immediately, his smile slipped slightly. 'Did you see the illustration of our new home attached to the back of the letter?'

Florence took the letter back. All she could think of was how busy they both were and that the last thing she wanted to do right now, especially as she was heavily pregnant, was to move to a new house. She flipped over the front sheet to study the huge brick house that Jesse had apparently bought for them. It was enormous. How had she come to this only six years after living most of her life in a small flat above a shop?

'What do you think? Do you like it?'

Florence liked the house well enough, but would have preferred a little time to let the idea that they would be relocating sink in. Their days were already filled with work, looking after John and Dorothy, and in two months' time they would be welcoming another baby into their family. How was she supposed to fit in a house move and finding extra servants as well?

By the look of the houses she had seen when visiting the estate, the three women employed at their Wellesley Road home would not be able to cope with the extra work needed to run a house so much larger than the one they currently lived in.

Florence loved living in her double-fronted home on Wellesley Road. She would have enjoyed living there for longer, although now Jesse had taken on the lease for a new store at Pelham Street, she had suspected they would be moving closer to that location and back to Nottingham, just not this soon.

Jesse was ever practical, and it was too far for them to travel to work in Nottingham's town centre. He had spent time working there, staying in the small flat they had lived in as newlyweds above the Goose Gate shop. She also knew how much he missed her and the children when he stayed away overnight. It made sense and, if she was honest with herself, Florence had suspected on a couple of occasions that Jesse had ambitions to move to a larger home. Florence still wasn't certain that she was ready to do so yet though.

'It has a library and a conservatory,' he added. 'Florence?'

She looked up at him and, hating to see the concern expressed in his deep eyes, pushed her doubts away. How could she refuse this wonderful husband of hers anything at all? Hadn't he done all that she had asked of him, allowing her to keep working and being proud of all that she had achieved for Boots?

'It's a bit of a shock, that's all.'

Jesse sighed. 'I'm sorry to drop this on you, especially now,' he said resting his hand on her rounded stomach. I know the timing is dreadful, but I knew this was the house for us. You're happy though? To move to The Park?'

She forced a smile. 'How can I not be? Most people would give all they had to live in such an impressive home. Anyway,' she said resting her hand on his, 'when do we need to move there?'

Jesse's eyes narrowed. 'Soon, I'm afraid.' He bent to kiss the top of her head. 'I know it's not the most convenient timing but I feel it's the right thing for us to do.'

By now, Florence knew when Jesse was open for discussion

about something and also the occasions when he had no intention of changing his mind. This was one of those times.

'I'd better start making arrangements then, hadn't I?' she said, unable to help feeling a tingle of excitement at the thought of living in such a majestic house.

* * *

The next two weeks were a blur. The only time she wasn't dictating letters to Miss Tweed about their relocation to the new house, Florence was making endless lists. She loved a challenge and this was certainly one of those. The excitement drove her on despite her tiredness. She had never imagined living anywhere like St Heliers and couldn't help feeling a sense of pride that Jesse had achieved this for them in so short a time.

Florence began to think of all the connections she could make being one of the residents of this well-respected estate. There were bound to be new acquaintances that she could ask to support her charities and help with local projects that they might not yet know about. Her children would have a large garden to play in. She smiled and reasoned that the benefits of this relocation were bountiful and endless.

Florence rested the palms of her hands on the base of her back. She ached all over, but she was doing a little too much for someone who was seven months pregnant, so it was hardly surprising. It would be worth it. Jesse was beginning to give her concerned looks, but the only concession she made to this big change in their life was to finish work earlier each day and come home for an hour's rest between working at her office and overseeing the packing up of their belongings.

Harriet, their older general domestic servant, led the packing and was as organised as Florence had hoped she would be. Eliza watched over the children, sorting and packing their clothes, linen, and toys, while Beth kept on top of the cleaning in the house.

Soon the boxes filled their dining room ready to be taken from their Wellesley Road home to St Heliers House. Florence had asked Miss Tweed to write to two agencies for the extra servants they were going to need. She was sorry that Eliza had decided not to continue working for them after their move to The Park, but it was too far for her to travel each day from her own family home. Harriet and Beth, the scullery maid, were coming with them. Neither wished to find alternative work and Florence believed that they were rather excited about the prospect of living in a larger home.

Florence called Harriet to the drawing room the night before their move.

'As you're probably aware, I've been interviewing a few new servants. The new house is much bigger than this one and it will be too much for you and Beth to look after. There's a new under housemaid called Violet, as well as a footman. His name is Joseph Meadows.'

'Yes, madam,' Harriet replied, enthralled by this news.

'Mr Boot will need a valet, so we're looking to engage someone to fit that role. The reason I've asked you here is not only to let you know about the new servants, but also to tell you that I'll need a lady's maid.' Harriet's eyebrows lowered slightly. Florence could see she was probably wondering what that had to do with her, so added, 'I was hoping you might like that role, Harriet?'

'Madam?'

Florence smiled, hoping to reassure the shocked woman. 'You know more about my daily routine than anyone other than my husband,' she said. 'I trust you and feel that you are the obvious candidate, should you wish to be. What do you say?' When Harriet didn't answer, Florence was concerned and added, 'You don't have to, naturally, but maybe you might need some time to consider the offer. Obviously, you'll have more responsibility and an increase in your salary, but if you're happy to remain looking after the domestic duties downstairs then I'm happy for you to take charge of the more junior staff.'

Harriet clasped her hands together and beamed at Florence. 'No, madam. I don't need to think about it at all. I'm a little shocked to be asked, that's all. I'd be honoured to be your lady's maid, very much so.'

Relief flooded through Florence. She had been hoping that Harriet would agree to the promotion. She had never had a lady's maid before and wanted to have someone she knew and liked, since whoever it was would be working very closely with her; Harriet was the perfect person to carry out the role.

Florence stood. 'I'm delighted. I'll inform Mr Boot and you can start your new position from the day of our move.'

'Thank you, Mrs Boot. I'm very happy you asked me.'

'And I'm delighted you've accepted,' Florence replied honestly.

* * *

Florence stood at her bedroom window and stared out at the trees and garden to the rear of their splendid new home. The move two weeks earlier had gone well. The new valet she had sourced for Jesse, Henry Trimble, was discovered drinking after only two days and his employment terminated. Florence always made sure she explained to every member of staff during their interviews that she and Jesse believed in temperance. She wanted prospective staff to be aware that they didn't allow alcohol in their home either for themselves or for their servants. They were aware that to some this would not be acceptable and wanted servants to be able to make the choice before confirming that they would like to work for them at St Heliers.

'Mr Meadows is very conscientious at his work,' Jesse said when she broke the news to him that his valet had left rather suddenly. 'Maybe he will be happy to act as my valet if we offer to increase his wage accordingly?'

Florence liked the idea. She also liked Joseph Meadows and had been hoping that Jesse would make exactly this suggestion.

'Very well, I'll ask him,' she said.

Thankfully Meadows was happy to do as she and Jesse asked, and explained that the increase in his wage meant that he would be able to send more money home to his elderly parents in Devon each month.

Everyone was settling in nicely to the new house and both Florence and Jesse were particularly delighted with Mrs Rudge's baking abilities. She ran her kitchen with a kindly but firm hand and never failed to produce delicious meals, which Florence was especially happy with as there always seemed to be something to tempt Jesse's appetite when he was feeling unwell.

The new under housemaid, Violet, and a kitchen maid, Annie, were due to start working for them in the next two days and Florence felt like a weight had been lifted from her shoulders and that it was beginning to feel like the new servants had worked for her and Jesse for months. They had still to settle on a footman to replace Meadows, but Florence was wondering if they really needed to find one, or if it was an unnecessary addition to the household.

She decided to speak to Meadows and ask if, when he wasn't looking after Jesse, he might agree to act as footman.

'I'd be happy to, Mrs Boot,' Joseph Meadows had said. 'To be honest, Mr Boot is out so much of the day that I'd feel better if I had other work to attend to during that time.'

Florence turned and walked out of her beautifully decorated bedroom, with its smart patterned wallpaper in pale blues and subtle yellows and large rug that matched the tones exactly. Jesse had surprised her, yet again, by arranging for new wardrobes and chests of drawers to be made to match their existing bedroom suite. He had known Florence would not want to replace it with a new one, but also that the larger bedroom would need more furniture.

She arrived at the spacious landing with its sweeping staircase flowing gracefully down to the open hallway and stopped to take in the vibrant colours of the large flower arrangement that one of their neighbours had sent to them as a welcome to the area.

The children had rooms on the upper floor and the servants had their accommodation in the attic with a back staircase taking them down to the kitchen so that they could come and go without any visitors seeing them. Jesse had been right. This house had been meticulously planned and was a delight to live in.

Florence walked through to her new library. She still had more books to find to fill the shelves completely, but that was a treat she was going to take her time to enjoy. She stood by the fire and rubbed her hands together slowly. The baby moved and she caught her breath for a second. Jesse, as usual, had been right about buying this house and moving their family to this place. The red brick house wasn't beautiful, but it had character and the grounds were stunningly beautiful. It gave them all the space they needed to grow, especially with this new baby about to arrive.

Florence's heart swelled with happiness and optimism for their future. 'We're going to be very happy here,' she said to herself. 'I just know it.'

Chapter 5

March 1892

'You must eat your lunch, John,' Florence said, attempting to spoon steamed apple into her son's mouth. He usually fed himself but wasn't very keen on today's pudding. 'A little more and then you can carry on playing with your toy horses.'

He narrowed his deep blue eyes briefly before opening his mouth like a little bird. Florence giggled gleefully and quickly deposited the spoonful into his mouth.

'There, that wasn't so bad, now was it?'

She wiped his face with a muslin square and handed his two toys back to him. How she loved this little boy of hers. He was already showing signs of stubbornness, just like his parents, she thought with amusement. She bent down and kissed the top of his head and couldn't help trying to imagine what sort of man he would grow up to be. A kind one, she hoped.

Her thoughts were distracted by a knock at her office door. 'Mr Boot has asked that you join him in his office,' Miss Tweed said, smiling at John.

'Mr Boot?' She hoped nothing had happened to him. He had been a little quiet of late and Florence suspected that he might be suffering from more pain than usual.

'Is everything all right, Mrs Boot?'

Florence closed her eyes to gather herself. 'Yes, perfectly fine, thank you. You took me by surprise, that's all. There's nothing amiss, is there?'

'I'm sorry, I hadn't meant to. And no, I'm not aware that there's anything wrong.'

'It's not your fault, Miss Tweed. Will you watch over John while I go to see my husband?'

'I'd be delighted to,' she replied, stepping further into the room and immediately making her way to crouch next to John's play area.

'Thank you.' Florence left the room feeling a little silly for sounding panicked, but sometimes her worry for Jesse's health made her nervous. Thankfully, his infirmity seemed to have slowed down in the past year. She was certain this was helped by her insistence that he rest more than he had been used to doing, and because she kept an eye on his diet, ensuring it was as healthy as possible at all times. Florence never admitted to anyone how she was always on guard for any deterioration in her husband. However, much to her embarrassment, this time she had been careless enough to let her fears show to an employee.

She walked the few steps to his room and knocked lightly. 'Come in.'

She opened the door and walked in to find him standing behind his desk. Her heart swelled with love for the man who had given her so much more than she had ever imagined wanting. His hands rested on the lower half of the plans which were unfurled on the mahogany and tooled-leather surface with paperweights holding the curled paper on either side.

'What is this?' she asked, intrigued as she joined him and tried to make sense of what the plans might be for.

Jesse looked up, the smile on his face showing how happy he was to see her. 'These are the plans for the Pelham Street store. I wanted to show you, so that we could begin working on designs and layouts throughout.'

She thought of all the ideas she had come up with for the store and hoped that Jesse would allow her to utilise most of them. It would be the first place where she would be able to visibly make her mark, with her ideas for decor and new departments with stock that appealed to more customers than the items they currently sold. It would be somewhere that was almost as much hers as Jesse's. Florence was determined to use whatever opportunity he gave her to show just how much foresight and intuition she had, and how it would bring in the vast numbers of new customers they would need to make the business pay.

'There's a huge amount of floor space and on several floors too. We're going to have to think of what we can use to fill the entire area.' She studied it further, aware that she needed to slowly introduce all the ideas she had for this store. 'I particularly like the idea of having a gallery supported by a colonnade of cast-iron pillars,' she said, picturing how it would look once finished.

He looked at her thoughtfully then smiled proudly. 'I

thought that design feature would play to your creative instincts,' he said.

'And we're going to need to employ quite a few more people here than at most other Boots stores, if we are to cover all the new departments we're going to need to use the building to its maximum potential.' Florence felt Jesse's eyes on her as he considered this notion.

'I agree,' he said. 'I was also thinking that you should be charged with the taking on of the female employees for this store and also the interior decoration. What do you think?' His eyes glinted as he waited for her reaction to what she suspected he had known she would want to hear.

Florence opened her mouth to speak but when the words didn't form, she closed it again. She was grateful for this proof of his confidence in her abilities, especially when she had managed to get things so wrong when dealing with the Nellie Blythe situation. Florence beamed at him.

'I'd like that, very much.' She leant forward and kissed him.

'There's no one I trust more than you, Florence.' He rested his hand lightly on her rounded stomach. 'I trust you to bear my children; there's nothing more important in my life than that. I also know that there's no one better to work beside me. Haven't you proved your business worth to this company already in these past six years?'

'I like to think so,' she said, not reminding him of the times she had got things wrong. 'I love working with you, Jesse, I hope you know that?'

Their lives had been such a whirlwind, building up their home and family life together. As Florence had gradually become more involved in Jesse's daily working life, she barely had time to draw breath. Now they were planning what was to be their most impressive store to date and, despite feeling a little weighed down by this third pregnancy, Florence's enthusiasm for the project grew.

He kissed the tip of her nose. 'I most certainly do. Look,' he said, pointing at the area on the plan depicting the shop fronts. 'I took note of your suggestion to bring in an art nouveau style for the doors, window design, and decoration on the stonework. What do you think?'

'I'm honoured,' she said, running her fingertips lightly over the area on the plans. 'It's going to look very impressive, don't you agree?'

'Yes, I do.'

Her mind raced. Florence could just picture the new Pelham Street premises, and a mixture of fear about how they would pay for this, and excitement that it would be Jesse's biggest venture yet, fought for supremacy. She took a deep breath to calm her mind. She didn't want to show him any sense of panic now that he had given her such a huge compliment.

'We're going to have to think carefully about how we want the store to work.' She focused her thoughts for a moment, wanting to make the most of this opportunity.

'Go on, tell me what's on your mind,' he said laughing. 'I can almost see your brain whirring with ideas.'

Florence wasn't going to let the opportunity to share her thoughts with him pass. 'The experience we wish the customers to have when they visit Pelham Street . . . it has to be very much a Boots store, naturally, but I think we need to ensure that we make a bigger statement than usual with this store. It's an opportunity to appeal to a new type of customer and widen our appeal. Don't you think?' she asked, her enthusiasm growing as she spoke. 'We need to show that although we are still chemists,' she said to reassure Jesse, 'we are now much more than that, and Boots offers so much more to customers than ever before.'

He didn't answer for a moment but studied the plans in front of them thoughtfully. After a while, Florence began to think she might have offended him. It wasn't something she ever wished to do. She opened her mouth to speak, as Jesse looked at her and shook his head.

'You are right. What you say makes perfect sense. It is time to expand not just our business but the way we do business.' He put his arm lightly around her waist. 'I love your enthusiasm and your talent for innovative ideas.'

Florence sighed, relieved to see he wasn't upset with what she had said. 'That's a relief. For a moment I was concerned I'd said something wrong . . . again.'

'Not at all, my love.' He turned his back to the desk and leant against it, pulling her gently towards him. 'We might disagree with each other's ideas at times, but do you know that since we've been working together everything about this business has been much more enjoyable?'

Florence leant forward and kissed him. 'I'm happy you think so.'

'I do. I enjoy sharing our working life as well as our private times. Most couples only get to share a few hours each morning and evening.'

She sighed. 'I'm forever grateful that you let me take part in the running of the businesses. It means the world to me that I can immerse myself in your work next to you.'

Jesse's smile slipped and he cleared his throat. 'I thought that working next to my mother was special, but I had no idea how much more satisfying it could be to work with my wife. I'm the lucky one, Florence,' he said gazing at her, his eyes shining. 'To have found a wife with the business acumen and love for Boots that you do is a gift that I'm certain I don't deserve.'

'Nonsense.' She stroked his right arm. 'We were meant to be together. It's fate that has ensured we are here now.'

They gazed at each other and Florence didn't think she could ever love anyone more than she loved Jesse.

Jesse's arms dropped from her sides and he turned back to focus his attention on the plans once more. He pointed at a space above the stairs. 'This is the upstairs gallery. I thought we could display pictures there.'

'Yes,' she said, her mind racing as her enthusiasm rose. 'Maybe also have glass and fancy goods, too?' Florence was going to enjoy spending time planning how to make this the most fascinating shop in Nottingham.

'We must get this right.' Jesse leant forward and pointed at one of the areas near the front of the shop. 'I thought the pharmaceutical department should go there. Right at the front. After all, it's what most people visit Boots shops for.'

Florence didn't agree. She took her time to look at the detail of the new store and knew that whatever they did at this place could set a precedent for what customers expected from the future of their stores.

'You're not sure?' Jesse asked looking at her.

Florence didn't think that now was the right time to delve into this matter. She decided in that moment to wait until the shop was ready for stock to be displayed to show Jesse what she had in mind for some of the departments.

'Florence? Tell me what you're thinking.'

But perhaps saying something now would at least would help her gauge how far Jesse was happy to go when it came to changes for the Pelham Street store.

'If the customers mainly come to Boots for their medication and herbal remedies, which they do, then why don't we place the pharmacy at the back of the store? That way everyone coming to the shop would need to first pass our other departments. What do you think?'

He turned his attention back to the plans and stared at them, his eyebrows lowered in a thoughtful frown. 'Tempt them on their way to buy their medicine, you mean?'

'It's merely a thought for you to consider.' It was something she felt strongly about, but knowing Jesse as well as she did now, she had learnt that arguing with him usually led to a stand-off where no one was the winner. It didn't come very naturally to her, but she had discovered that using subtlety worked far better than blunt honesty where her husband was concerned.

She waited for him to speak again, not wishing to push her idea onto him, letting him take onboard her suggestion calmly.

'Hmm.' He tapped his moustache with his forefinger for a few seconds without speaking. 'What goods were you thinking of selling at the front then?'

She knew she had to be very persuasive and gave the matter some thought.

'Items to attract people who might be looking for a gift for someone, or even a treat for themselves. Handbags, purses, perfume, or picture frames.' Her excitement grew the more she imagined all the different items of stock she could source for them. 'The list is endless. And, as we build up the business further, we will no doubt have more ideas of things that should sell well and bring in more customers to the store.'

He stared at the plans and nodded thoughtfully. 'I do see what you're saying.'

She sensed he was about to add a *but* to his comment.

'But Boots is a chemist, first and foremost. It's what we do and why people come to our stores. The pharmaceutical items need to be at the front of the store. They always have been and should continue to be.'

She held back from arguing with him. She was a relative newcomer to the business, which was Jesse's after all. She would have to come up with a way to make him see that her idea would be the best way forward for Pelham Street store.

He studied the plans, once more. After a moment's silence, Jesse asked, 'Did I mention that work on the printing department is almost complete?'

'Already?' She knew he was trying to distract her, but went along with it. 'I hadn't realised.'

'I felt it was needed urgently,' he explained. 'This way we can print our own stationery without outsourcing at extra cost. You know, labels and anything else necessary that the company needs.'

Florence had thought it a brilliant, if initially expensive, idea when Jesse had first told her of it. She trusted his business acumen and knew that if there was a way to save money, then Jesse would find it. She just hadn't expected him to be working on this idea so soon. But Florence had known Jesse long enough to know that he didn't care for boundaries. He was fond of saying that every problem had a solution, and he never wasted any time in working out the best way to make it happen.

'I didn't want to trouble you,' he explained. 'You already have enough going on, what with work and this pregnancy.'

Florence thought back to how nauseous she had been for the first few months with this baby, but had believed that she had hidden it from him. Not well enough, it seemed. 'I understand your wish to protect me, but I'd rather know what's happening. I hate being left out of your new projects,' she said, not wishing him to see how hurt she felt at his omission, but unable to help herself.

'I'm sorry, I only thought . . .'

She didn't want him to feel badly, so gave him a smile. 'It's fine. Now, about Pelham Street. I'm looking forward to it being opened. Have you decided when that might be?'

'We need to check that we're happy with everything first,' he said, leaning, she thought, a little heavily on his silver-topped cane.

Florence studied her husband carefully. She had been so wrapped up in all her responsibilities that it occurred to her she might not have kept such a careful eye on Jesse. 'Then we have a lot to do.'

'We do,' he said. 'Hopefully the printing department will be finished in the next few days and I'll be able to show you around.' Jesse frowned and rested his hand on Florence's back. 'I think you've had enough for today,' he said. 'Shall we go home now?'

She closed her eyes briefly before nodding. 'With pleasure.'

Chapter 6

April 1892

Florence couldn't believe it was already April. They walked around the factory and she made sure not to walk with her usual lengthy stride. She linked her arm through Jesse's, wanting to take her time and not overexert her husband.

'There's no need to rush, is there?' she asked, smiling to soften her words. She made a point of resting her gloved hand on her stomach, knowing that he would assume she wanted them to slow down because of her heavily pregnant state.

Florence had made a point of keeping an eye on Jesse's health since their marriage. She was grateful for her husband's determination to keep as active as possible by doing his rounds to various Boots stores on horseback. But she couldn't miss the sadness in his voice when he reminisced about how he used to take daily dips in the River Trent and always enjoyed lengthy treks across the countryside, many times walking the thirty-seven miles from Sheffield to Nottingham before his health had broken down just before they had met.

She decided soon after their marriage that as a concerned

61

wife she should care for her husband, as she would expect him to do for her. She knew that Jesse was too proud to admit when he was in any pain, but thankfully his health had held up better than either of them had expected.

'This is going to save the firm a lot of money in the long run.' Jesse took hold of her hand with his free one. 'And we won't have to wait for printed materials to be delivered to us. We can print whatever we need immediately.'

'And it will give more people work,' she said, happy at the thought that by this expansion to the business they were also helping others. She knew that Jesse relished this part of their lives as much as she did. Having the means to assist others to get along in the world was certainly the best feeling, she thought. Well, after having her children and husband in her life. She felt truly blessed to have so much joy in her life, and it made her feel better to think that she was spreading her luck among others.

She had seen first-hand the deprivation some unfortunate families experienced when she had met Lily Buttons years before in Jersey, but nothing had prepared Florence for the enormous scale of the poverty she had witnessed here in the lace district in Nottingham. Florence usually felt positive that she could find ways to help make improvements in people's lives, and for the most part she was satisfied that she had managed to help a lot of the people she had come into contact with. Sometimes, though, it concerned her that no matter what she or Jesse did to try and help others, there would always be too many people suffering in silence whose names they would never know.

Florence spent many sleepless nights worrying about how best to help people faced with seemingly insurmountable problems that could be lessened if only they had the money or her assistance to help them fight back. She was determined to make it her life's work to focus her attention on improving the lives of as many women and children as possible. First, though, she needed to deal with today's issues.

He gave her hand a gentle squeeze. 'It will certainly do that.'

They strolled into the printing department and Florence stared at the large machinery in awe. This was all theirs and should save them a lot of money. She was impatient to see it all working.

'The staff you interviewed for this department,' she asked thoughtfully. 'When do they start working?'

'Monday. I thought they should begin as soon as possible.'

Florence was pleased. She always enjoyed adding new names to the employee register. It gave her a sense of comfort to know that she was sharing her blessings with others and giving more women a way to earn a living and thereby feed their family.

He withdrew his gold half-hunter pocket watch from his waistcoat pocket and clicked it open. 'It's getting a little late. I think we should return to the office so you can have some time sitting down and maybe take tea. I don't want you to overdo it and tire yourself. You still need to visit the factory today, and we're going to stay with friends at Snig Hill this evening, don't forget.'

Florence was struggling more than usual for some reason

today. Her back ached and she had a slight headache coming on. She wasn't certain how she was going to deal with the manager and her worker who had recently been repeatedly late to work. The manager had wanted to dismiss the woman, who she believed was causing a disruption in the team where she was positioned, but Florence had decided that she would speak to the younger woman first to ensure they weren't missing a good reason for her change in behaviour.

'Good idea,' she said, happy to agree to Jesse's suggestion. She wished she could forget about the situation at the factory and go home to relax. Florence was aware that the manager was used to dealing with issues such as this one, but the employee in question had sent a note to Florence's office appealing for her to step in and treat her leniently over the matter. Florence felt obliged to at least go and see for herself what was going on. 'Let's go.'

They took their time walking back to the office. She relished these quiet moments alone with him. It reminded her a little of the strolls they used to take in Jersey before they were married. Those days seemed so long ago now and Florence wondered at how much her life had changed since then. She was amused to think how busy she had supposed herself to be before her marriage. Now, though, she was a mother and responsible for a household consisting of both her growing family and several members of staff.

Florence could not help wondering what she must have done with her time before she had married her husband and moved away from Jersey. She linked her arm with his. They had so much to look forward to – a new baby and a huge store in Pelham Street. It was sometimes difficult to imagine that she had once thought herself fulfilled.

It broke her heart to think that women were scorned for having a baby out of wedlock. How, she wondered, could the thought of bringing a new life into the world be so joyful to some and so shocking and vile to others, simply because a woman either did or did not possess a marriage licence? It seemed so cruel and unfair.

They arrived home just over an hour later. Meadows took their coats.

Jesse thanked him and turned to Florence. 'We have an hour to ready ourselves before the carriage takes us to the Bradshaws' at Snig Hill. I wish it was longer and you had time to rest first.'

Florence shook her head and smiled. 'It's fine. I can rest in the carriage on the way there. Don't worry, I'll soon be ready.'

Florence hurried up the stairs. She checked on the children, giving them both a cuddle and then explained to Harriet that she and Jesse would be away from home overnight. She hated the thought of leaving the children, but thankfully she rarely needed to. This time, however, it would be too far from to return home at the end of the evening.

'Please don't worry, Madam,' Harriet said. 'I'll take good care of the little ones.'

The carriage ride was tedious, probably more so because Florence's back ached for the entire journey. It didn't matter how she placed herself on the padded seat, she could not find a position that gave her any comfort.

'You're here,' Helena Bradshaw exclaimed, welcoming their

carriage as it drew to a halt outside the pretty but modest home that was so like Florence and Jesse's former home on Wellesley Road.

Florence waited for Jesse to step out of the carriage and take her hand. It was good to be back among old friends. She hugged Helena, glad to see her once again. They had been good neighbours when she and Jesse had lived in the area.

She accompanied Helena into their comfortable home, listening as her friend chatted to her excitedly and shared the local gossip that she had been saving up.

Half an hour later, the four of them were in the warm living room exchanging their news and having a reviving cordial when pain shot through Florence's stomach. Groaning in shock at the intensity of it, she instantly realised that it was a contraction. No wonder she had been experiencing backache all the way to Snig Hill, she thought. She was in labour.

'You are unwell?' Jesse rushed to her side from where he had been standing in front of the fireplace.

Florence shook her head. 'I think this baby has decided to make an untimely appearance.' Mortified, she gave Helena an apologetic look. 'I'm so sorry, this is dreadful timing.'

'You must not concern yourself,' Helena said. 'I am excited to welcome a new baby into this house.' She waved her hands to get her husband's attention. 'Gerald, instead of staring at Florence, why don't you go and tell one of the servants to make the second spare room ready for Florence.'

His eyes widened and after slamming his glass down so hard on the occasional table next to him that it cracked the stem, he carried both the top and bottom of the glass and left the room. 'Mabel,' he bellowed, the panic in his voice obvious to them all.

'What do you need me to do?' Jesse asked quietly.

'Try to remain calm,' Florence soothed, trying her best to keep her voice steady. The last thing she needed was for him to panic as much as Gerald seemed to be doing.

Florence heard footsteps running through the hall. The door opened and a frightened young girl stood in front of them. 'You took your time,' Gerald snapped.

'Mabel,' Helena said, her voice gentle. 'Please put on your coat and run to Doctor Jacobs's home and tell him that we have a guest who is about to have her baby. You know where it is, don't you?'

'Yes, madam. I'll go there immediately.' She looked relieved to be escaping from the house.

'Gerald, you need to calm down. Go and ask Betty to boil some water and bring towels. I'll need her to help me get the spare room ready, too. We need to settle poor Florence as soon as possible.'

'Thank you,' Florence said, wishing she had taken the time to consider that she might be in labour when she first felt the twinges earlier in the day. She winced as another contraction took hold.

Jesse paled. 'Is there anything I can do, my love?'

'I'm sure the doctor will be here shortly.' Florence was aware that if the servant was going to fetch him on foot it couldn't be too far away. She hoped he was at home and didn't waste any time coming to her. 'Why don't you stay here with Gerald when he returns to the living room? He can keep you company.'

Jesse seemed unable to move for a moment. For a man who was always in control, the only occasions Florence recalled him being almost stupefied with fear were when she was giving birth to their children. 'I'm fine, Jesse. I know what I'm doing, don't forget.'

'If you're certain there's nothing I can do to help?'

'Your wife is in safe hands.' Helena rested a hand on Florence's right shoulder. 'She'll be well cared for, Jesse, and I'll let you know how things are progressing.'

Helena took Florence's empty cordial glass from her shaking hands and placed it on a table. 'Now, my dear, let's go and help you settle down to wait for Doctor Jacobs. He should be here shortly.'

Florence hoped Helena was right.

Florence accompanied her hostess into the hallway. Her foot was on the first step when another contraction took her breath away. She gripped hold of the bannister, panting as the pain took over. As soon as it passed, she and Helena slowly made their way upstairs.

'Here you are, madam,' Betty, a red-faced woman of about forty, said, placing fresh towels on the chest of drawers near the window. Helena left the room while Betty helped Florence to change into her nightdress.

Florence wished for a moment that Harriet was with her, then reasoned that she much preferred her to be looking after the children. She waited while Betty hurriedly made up the bed.

'There you go, madam.'

Florence thanked the maid and got onto the bed.

Moments later Helena returned with a small tray holding a glass and carafe of water. 'I thought you might need these.' She helped Florence sit forward and plumped up the pillows behind her. 'There, that's a bit better. We want to make you as comfortable as we possibly can.'

Florence heard the front gate slam shut. She willed it to be the doctor. As friendly as Helena was, she couldn't help feeling a little vulnerable being away from home. It wasn't what she had planned for the birth and she missed having familiar people nearby.

Seconds later, there was the sound of footsteps clambering up the stairs before a rapid series of knocks on the bedroom door.

'Come in, Mabel,' Helena said, giving Florence an apologetic look.

The maid ran into the room, struggling to catch her breath.

'Will you keep the noise down and try to calm yourself,' Helena hissed between clenched teeth. 'Mrs Boot does not need to be disturbed like this.'

'Sorry, Mrs Bradshaw,' Mabel said, looking, Florence thought, on the verge of tears.

'Did you find the doctor, Mabel?'

'Yes, madam.' Mabel swallowed and took a deep breath. She glanced at Betty, as if surprised to see her still in the room.

Florence could see the older woman was trying not to lose her temper with the young maid. She didn't want the poor girl to be given a hard time on her account. 'Everything is perfectly fine,' Florence said, hoping to defuse the situation between the two maids. 'Now, can you tell us what Doctor Jacobs said?'

'He said I'm to tell you that he'll be along momentarily,' Mabel said. 'He just wanted to let his wife know where he was going.'

Before Florence could reply, they heard the sound of the front gate closing. There was a collective sigh of relief. Seconds later the doorbell rang.

'That'll be him now,' Helena said. 'Go and let him in, Mabel. Betty, I think you probably need to make a cup of tea for Mr Boot and Mr Bradshaw. They've both had rather a shock this evening. Make one for yourselves, too, you are both going to need to keep your strength up tonight . . .'

* * *

Three days later, Florence kissed Jesse and watched as he gave their new baby a peck on her tiny head.

'She suits the name Margery, don't you think?' Jesse asked.

Florence could tell he was delaying the moment he would have to go.

'Jesse, we've had this conversation several times over the past few days. Now, you really need to leave, if you're to get home before the children are put to bed.'

'I know, but I hate to leave you behind,' he said miserably. 'It doesn't seem right, somehow.'

She smiled at him and reached up to rest her hand on his cheek. 'We've been through this. The doctor has insisted I stay here for a while. It won't be for long.'

He bent to kiss her. 'I promise I'll return to check on you as soon as possible.'

'Don't fret about me,' Florence reassured him. 'I need to go home and cuddle our other children. They'll be missing us terribly and I can't bear to think of that. Tell them I'll be home again in a few days and I'll be bringing their new baby sister with me.' She smiled at him, hating to see him go, but glad that in a few hours he would be back with John and Dorothy. 'You've also got work to do, don't forget. It'll keep you busy and the time will fly by. Just you wait and see.'

He didn't look convinced.

Florence was relieved when Helena knocked on the bedroom door. 'How's the mother and baby?' she asked popping her head around the door before joining them. 'I'm sorry to interrupt you both,' she said. 'But I was passing the room and overheard your concerns, Jesse. This can't be easy for either of you, but Florence is right. Your other children need you and you'll no doubt have a lot of work to be getting on with. Gerald and I are happy to look after Florence while she's recuperating from the birth. We promise to make sure she and baby Margery have the best care possible.'

'You see?' Florence gave Helena a grateful smile. 'Doctor Jacobs insisted I couldn't travel for at least another ten days. Come back then and the three of us can return home together.'

Jesse nodded slowly. 'I don't seem to have much choice.' He kissed her once more and rested his hand briefly on baby Margery's tiny head, before doing as she asked and leaving the room.

'I'll show Jesse out,' Helena whispered, as she left to accompany Jesse downstairs.

Florence hadn't expected to cry. She was overwhelmed, hearing Jesse shout his goodbyes to Helena and Gerald before the sounds of horses' hooves trotting away, pulling Jesse's carriage on its way to Nottingham. She gave in to her tears, unable to stem their flow, and reached for a handkerchief. She blew her nose with her free hand and then bent her head to breathe in the scent of her beautiful baby's hair. She wasn't feeling nearly as happy to be left behind as she wanted Jesse to believe.

After a few moments of self-indulgent sobbing, Florence took a deep breath. She needed to buck up and make the most of this time alone with her baby girl. She didn't doubt that life would take over again as soon as she returned to Nottingham. Even if she stayed away from work for a few weeks, Florence knew it would take a little time to settle the baby in at home. She also intended making up for her extended absence to John and Dorothy once she was back at St Heliers. She determined to enjoy every last moment of whatever peace she could glean. The next few months were going to be busier than ever and she wanted to build up her strength while she could before returning to work and focusing her attention on the move into the new store in Pelham Street.

Chapter 7

October 1892

Pelham Street

The following six months passed by in a blur of baby feeds, bedtime stories, and trips back and forth to Pelham Street. Finally, baby Margery was in a routine that suited Florence and they had employed a nanny to look after John and Dorothy on the days that they preferred to remain at home and play in the nursery.

Florence's figure was almost back to how it had been before her pregnancy and now, as she sat in her new bigger office, she was ready to work on the finishing touches before the big opening.

She loved this office. It gave her enough space to accommodate the three children in a corner of the room where they played when they were with her, while she worked at her desk.

There was a familiar knock on Florence's office door and she could tell by its gentleness that it was her secretary. Florence sat back in the button-backed leather chair Jesse had bought her to mark the opening of their new Pelham Street store and screwed the top back onto her fountain pen. 'Come in, Miss Tweed,' she said keeping her voice low.

'Thank you, Mrs Boot.' Her secretary's eyes scanned Florence's desk briefly before she continued. 'Mr Boot asks that you join him in No. 2 Department. There's something he wishes to speak with you about. I'll keep an eye on the children for you, if you wish.'

'Yes, please. I shouldn't be too long.' She looked down at the two small cribs in the corner of the room, one holding Dorothy and the other baby Margery. Florence's heart swelled with love for her daughters. 'The girls have only recently fallen asleep, so you shouldn't be disturbed.' Florence loved having her precious children in her office, but also enjoyed a quiet moment alone with Jesse when he requested her company. 'I'll go to find my husband immediately.'

She turned the piece of paper she had been writing on face down onto her blotter. She was a little stuck over what to write anyway. Despite having dealt with many troubling issues amongst the staff, Florence always liked to try her hardest to find the best resolution for everyone involved. Now she was having to deal with an employee who had found herself in a difficult predicament, although Florence wasn't supposed to know any details about why the girl was leaving. Having been pregnant three times now she recognised the signs only too well. She had promised to draft a reference for the girl, aware that she wasn't moving on to other employment but to motherhood. Florence wanted to help her have the necessary reference should the girl ever be in a position to be able to return to work. Her thoughts shot to Nellie Blythe and the mess she had made of things when trying to help her. She had learnt a lot since then – at least she hoped she had.

Florence stood up slowly and strode out of her office to find her husband, but was unable to shake off thoughts of Nellie Blythe.

Her own life was so different to the lives of the women she employed, and regrettably had to occasionally dismiss. Yet, she reflected, her life could have been quite different had she not met Jesse. She doubted she would have had any children or married. As she walked across the plush store carpets, she recalled her joy at becoming his wife at the St Helier town church that sunny August day, her head filled with excitement for their anticipated life ahead. She hadn't been disappointed. Jesse had made her happier than she had dared ever imagine.

She also suspected that he was as surprised as she was at how naturally they both took to having their small brood. Florence smiled to herself; thinking about her babies always gave her a warm, fuzzy feeling. One of the store assistants caught her eye and assumed Florence's smile was meant for her and reciprocated the greeting. Florence stopped briefly to speak to the girl and one other who was working nearby.

'Everything as it should be?' She glanced around the department where the handbags and gloves she had sourced were now displayed with precision.

'Yes, Mrs Boot,' the younger one answered, her cheeks reddening slightly. 'We've almost finished unpacking the stock. This department will be ready in lots of time for the opening next week.'

'Thank you. You've both done a sterling job.' She took in their young, bright faces. They both seemed so proud of their work, which was exactly what she aimed for.

'Thank you, Mrs Boot,' they answered in unison, smiles on their faces.

'I'd better dash – Mr Boot wants to speak with me and I mustn't keep him waiting.'

She hurried away, wondering what Jesse wanted to show her that couldn't wait until after the store closed.

Florence found him speaking to two of their shopfitters, a tape measure hanging around his neck, as he seemed to have most days now. Both men were listening intently to what he was saying. Jesse was waving his arms about animatedly as he spoke. Her mood dipped. Jesse was angry about something, that much was obvious to her. Knowing how he hated to be interrupted when he was sorting out an issue, she decided instead to check how the final touches were coming along in the next department.

Florence quietly greeted several members of staff as they busily unpacked silver-plated mirrors, combs, and brush sets from chests lined up along the half-filled counters. She was grateful to have Jesse's confidence in her taste for items, so much so that she was now in charge of sourcing all the stock for anything not connected to the chemist side of the business. She smiled to discover there had already been a delivery of the crystal powder jars she had ordered from Paris a few weeks before. The ones already on display were sparkling brightly under the electric lighting she had suggested Jesse install in the store.

The new lighting was her favourite installation. It showed off their stock far better than the old gas lamps did in the other stores. Jesse's confidence in her instincts and taste had boosted her own confidence. He often complimented her on her flair for interior design, proving his sincerity by incorporating most of her suggestions at this new store.

Florence recalled with amusement that although Jesse might believe in some of her ideas, he still took a lot of persuasion before agreeing that handbags and some smaller women's items, such as prettily packaged manicure sets, would sell well. Thankfully, she thought as she studied a nearby display, on this occasion she had been proved right.

No, despite her mother's reservations, she had been deliriously happy with her husband. She smiled to herself, picturing the photograph she had commissioned of her with John and Dorothy in her arms and Jesse looking down at them with utter adoration. It was her favourite picture and had pride of place on the marble mantelpiece in their drawing room at home. She made a mental note to arrange for a new photo to be taken showing all three of her children with her and Jesse.

She had been so deep in thought that she hadn't realised Jesse had finished his discussion and was standing next to her, hands on his hips.

'Is everything all right?' Florence asked, unsure whether she was going to like the answer when she noticed he was glaring in the direction of the beautiful items she had just been watching the girls unpack.

Jesse turned his attention to her and with his right arm outstretched, asked, 'What is that?'

Florence wasn't certain exactly what Jesse was referring to. She looked in the direction of the display cabinets and counters but couldn't see anything amiss. 'What? It looks fine to me.'

'The layout of this department is all wrong,' he bellowed, his face turning puce with rage.

Florence wondered for a moment if he was going a little mad. 'In what way do you think it's wrong? We agreed the layout months ago.'

'Yes, that's what I thought, too. Why then are the toilet and fancy goods you've introduced being displayed at the front of the shop? You know full well that the pharmaceutical counter is always stationed near the door. It takes the primary position in the shops. We are a cash chemist before anything else, not a department store.'

The shop assistants immediately stopped unpacking and swapped stunned glances with each other.

Florence had hoped she was being subtle enough with the way she was slowly incorporating new stock into the stores. She had obviously misread Jesse's answer when they discussed this latest rearrangement and tried to recall exactly what had been agreed. She noticed the two shopfitters slink backwards out of the line of fire and didn't blame them. She would like to do the same herself.

'You agreed with me when I said these should be at the front,' she said, remembering as soon as she had spoken that Jesse had said the idea was worth thinking about.

Horrified that she had taken his comment as an invitation to make these monumental changes to their new store,

Florence decided to try and turn the misunderstanding around to her advantage.

'If you think back, you'll recall that I said your idea to move the layout around was worth considering. However,' Jesse said, his voice lowered, which Florence knew meant he was trying hard to control his temper and was therefore extremely angry with her, 'I did not, at any time, agree to it. I want everything put back to how it should be. Now!'

The shopfitters ran forwards and the female assistants immediately began repacking the chests with the stock.

'Stop, everyone,' Florence shouted. She was not going to be dictated to or dismissed like a naughty schoolgirl. She was Jesse's wife and he needed to take her opinion on board. 'Please wait. Just for a moment.'

She turned her attention back to Jesse. 'The pharmaceuticals are essential items,' she said, willing him to listen to her. 'Look at the counters.' Florence indicated the polished mahogany with a sweep of her hand. 'They are pleasing to the eye. I know, without any doubt, that they would be far more enticing for passers-by looking into the windows if they had pretty, shiny items displayed on them, rather than simply medicines.' She became more determined to win the argument as she spoke. 'People don't come into the store to browse for pills. They come in specially to buy them.' She saw Jesse's expression change and hoped he was rethinking his decision. 'They are essential items and people either need them or they don't. As far as I can see they barely need any selling.'

'So now you're telling me that my advertising campaigns are a waste of money. Is that what you're saying?'

Florence gritted her teeth. 'For pity's sake, Jesse,' she snapped. Why was he being so infuriating? He seemed determined not to understand the point she was trying to make. 'No, that's not what I'm saying at all,' she said, her voice becoming clipped as she tried to refrain from showing how angry she was with him. 'I do, however, believe that if we have these items displayed as customers enter the store on their way to buy their medicines then they will be tempted to buy them as they pass. For example, imagine a lady coming in to purchase a tonic; she notices one of these beautiful silver-backed dressing-table sets and decides to treat herself. She's still going to continue on to the cash chemist, because she still needs that tonic. If the chemist stock is at the front of the shop she won't even see the beautiful items we now have to offer her and we will have lost that sale, and the many sales that could have followed. Don't you agree?'

Jesse glared at her. 'No, I do not.' He turned to the shopfitters. 'Do as I've already told you and rearrange this floor.'

Florence watched as he marched off to the lift. Her head ached, no doubt due to the temper she was trying to suppress. She loved Jesse, but he could be impossible sometimes. He was too used to doing things his way, she thought. She understood why he found it difficult to have someone questioning his decisions, but if he wanted her input into the business, then that's what she would give him.

Florence returned to her office, determined to find a way to make Jesse see sense. She couldn't simply stand and continue arguing with someone who had decided the matter had been concluded. No, she needed to be more subtle than that. For the rest of the day and at times during the night when sleep eluded her, Florence tried to find a way to solve the issue. She knew she was right about the layout of the floor. She didn't mind deferring to his decisions most of the time, especially when he felt so strongly that he was right about something. After all, he was the one who had built this business to where it now was, not her. But she had worked beside him, and she knew much more than he obviously thought. This time, she knew she must make him see sense.

The following morning, when Jesse was away visiting one of his other stores, Florence left the children at home and took a hansom cab to Pelham Street. She summoned the two shopfitters to meet her where their argument had taken place the day before.

'I'd like the biggest mirror you can find put up on that wall over there,' she said, pointing towards the toiletry goods on the wall halfway along the main counter.

The men looked at each other, a worried expression on both their faces. 'Ooh, Mrs Boot, I don't know if that's the right thing to do,' the older of the two men said, nervously.

She understood why they weren't in a hurry to encounter Jesse's anger if they did the wrong thing.

'I will take full responsibility for everything,' she reassured them. 'Please do as I ask.'

Later that morning, after Florence had been trying to keep busy and not worry too much about Jesse's reaction to what she'd done, Miss Tweed entered her office.

'Mr Boot has requested that you join him down—'

Florence had been waiting for such a summons and immediately stood up. She smoothed down her skirt and took a deep breath, ready for whatever battle awaited her.

'Thank you. I can imagine exactly where he wants to meet me. Wish me luck.'

Miss Tweed frowned, looking confused as she held open the office door for Florence to leave the room.

Florence took the lift down to the ground floor and was reminded as she always was, whenever she saw him near the modern apparatus, how proud he had been to have installed the first passenger lift in Nottingham. She spotted Jesse straight away, standing in his knee breeches and staring at the mirror.

'What is this?' he asked as she walked over to join him.

'The mirror?' Florence asked, playing for a little time, to think how she was going to reply.

Jesse gave her a sideways glance. 'Yes, that.'

'It occurred to me that if the pills and potions need to have the prime position in the store, then the toiletry department should have a mirror to throw a little light on it. Don't you agree?'

She waited while Jesse took his time thoughtfully studying the changes that had been made behind his back. Eventually he rubbed his chin. 'I suppose it does improve the area somewhat.'

Encouraged, Florence agreed. 'I think it makes the floor space seem twice the size, don't you?'

Jesse nodded slowly. 'It does.' He sighed. 'All right, Florence. I think in this instance we can come to a compromise and maybe we should keep both the pharmaceutical and the toiletry stock at the front of the store.'

'What a wonderful idea, Jesse,' Florence said, happy to give him the credit for finding a way to keep them both happy. She knew that this small victory would mean that she could now encourage him to introduce the same layout into the rest of their stores.

Florence glanced around her to check they weren't visible to any of their employees. Seeing they were very much alone, probably because no one wanted to become involved in their quarrel, she leant forward and gave Jesse a quick peck on his smiling mouth.

'What's that in aid of?' he asked, his eyes widening in surprise.

'Because I love you, that's why,' she whispered as a storeman walked past them.

He took hold of her right hand in his and gently pulled her closer to him. 'We make a great pair, don't you think?'

Florence pretended to give his question some thought, then nodded. 'Yes, most of the time.' Her head still ached. She rubbed her temples lightly with the tips of her fingers. 'You are unwell?' Jesse whispered. 'I worry that you do too much.'

'Nonsense,' she argued, forcing a smile. 'I'm simply weary from not turning in for bed early enough last night. My own fault. I'll make up for it by ensuring I have enough sleep tonight.'

Recalling that she had left Miss Tweed looking after the children, and happy to leave Jesse before he thought to continue with this conversation, she added, 'Right now, though, I need to go back to my office. Miss Tweed might enjoy spending time with the little ones, but she has a lot of work to be getting on with and I don't want her insisting on staying late today to finish everything.'

She daren't tell him that on occasion she might agree with him. Florence was concerned that if she gave in to Jesse's request and took more time away from work, he might decide that being at home with her children was the correct thing for her to do after all. She was not about to take that chance and had no intention of giving it up any time soon.

Chapter 8

May 1893

The months passed quickly and Florence presumed it must be due to her days being so busy. She was walking a fine line trying to balance motherhood with her working life, but Jesse never let up in his ambitions to build their empire and she did not want to be left behind. Sometimes it was a struggle to ensure that she gave herself time to relax. The children needed her attention, as did her workload. Mostly, she covered up the crises in her confidence when she wondered if she might have bitten off more than she could chew by trying to be all things to everyone. Florence knew she had one chance to make her double life work.

She took a bite of her toast and honey and smiled across the dining-room table at Jesse.

'Did I hear you speaking to one of the servants about John staying at home to play in the nursery today?' Jesse asked, folding his newspaper and placing it next to his side plate.

Florence finished her mouthful. 'Yes. He sometimes becomes a little restless having to sit for long hours in my office when

I'm very busy. I thought he'd prefer to stay at home and play. Annie offered to sit with him while we're out and the new nanny is away collecting all her belongings from her previous position.'

She thought of the previous woman who had come to look after the children. She had only lasted a few months, unable to hide her disapproval that Florence insisted on taking the children with her to work most days.

'But what am I supposed to do all day if the babes aren't here?' the woman had complained. 'I've never been in this situation where the mother looks after the children all day. It doesn't make sense for me to be here if I don't have any children to care for.'

Jesse took a drink from his teacup before placing it down gently in its fine porcelain saucer. 'Won't that mean that Violet will have to take on Annie's chores in the house? Is that fair?' His smile faded.

Florence felt a pang of concern. Jesse was right. 'Violet didn't seem to mind when I mentioned it to them. I think it'll be fine. I'll check though before arranging to do this another time.'

'As long as we take care not to let Violet feel as if she's taking on the majority of Annie's work,' he said, wiping his moustache with his napkin. He gazed at her thoughtfully before placing his napkin down on the table next to his place.

'What is it, my love?' she asked trying to remain positive.

'You know I treasure your instinct about the stores and have utmost confidence in all that you do.'

She nodded, concentrating on not letting her growing concern show.

Jesse continued. 'You seem to have grown in stature over the past few years. You've taught me more than I could imagine about what to sell and how to manage the staff. Your assistance has helped the business attain heights I hadn't expected to reach for many more years, if at all. Did you know that?'

She had suspected as much, but was grateful to him for acknowledging her work. 'Tell me what's bothering you.' She wondered if maybe he was struggling to tell her that he didn't truly approve of Dorothy and Margery still being brought to work with her. 'Jesse, if you wish me to stop taking the girls with me to the store then simply say so.'

'And you would listen?' he teased.

Florence was glad he was aware how far he could push her when it came to the children.

'It's not that I don't wish for them to be there, you know I do.' He moved the teaspoon on his saucer to one side before looking back at her.

'Then what is it?'

He hesitated and stared at her thoughtfully.

Florence relished the openness in their relationship, even more so than his confidence in her business abilities. 'Jesse?'

He cleared his throat. 'I'm frightened that you've taken on too much.'

'Carry on,' she said, trying not to sound defensive.

He must have noticed the tone in her voice. 'I'm not criticising you in any way, please don't ever think that. You do a marvellous job, as I've said, and I can't ever imagine being at the store without you there next to me.'

'Well then,' she said, soothed slightly by his assurances.

'However, now we have three children . . .'

Florence had no intention of going down this route with him. 'I can cope,' she interrupted angrily. Even if she found it a struggle, she wasn't ever going to admit it.

'You really should take things a little easier now,' he argued. 'Even if it's only while the children are so small. I spoke to the doctor and he intimated that you should slow down, just a little.'

Irritated that the physician had spoken to Jesse about her without her knowledge, she scowled at him. 'He had no right to discuss me behind my back. I'm not a fool, Jesse.'

'I know that perfectly well, but—'

She could see Jesse was getting upset. She hated to think she was the cause, so raised her hand to interrupt him. 'I promise you that if I feel like it's all getting too much, or that I need to rest, I'll return home straightaway.'

He thought about what she had said for a few seconds. 'You will?'

She stared at her husband's sweet face, his brow lined with a frown and his beautiful mouth tight with worry, and knew that she couldn't upset him further.

'I know you always want the best for me and I love you for that. I'll admit that I'm slightly more tired than usual at present, but this is an unusual time. We're between nannies, Margery is only six months old, and we've been working on the new store. Things should ease off soon.' When he didn't seem convinced, she added, 'I have taken on board what you've said, though, and will look for a way to take things slightly easier for the time being.'

'Good.' His face relaxed into a smile. 'I'm not expecting you to stop working entirely. I know well enough that's not something you'd ever wish to do.'

She wanted to make him happy, so she determined to make a few changes to her daily routine. Florence thought quickly. She had no intention of giving up work, or of leaving her daughters at home. She also worried that if she did take time out it might set a precedent and she'd then battle with Jesse to return to work. Then it came to her.

'I'll finish earlier in the afternoons,' she announced. 'Just for the time being. You and I can still take the girls to the store together each morning, but I'll bring them home with me for the afternoons.' She was happy with her compromise and hoped he would be too.

He mulled over her suggestion. 'I enjoy our mornings, too. Perhaps there should be days when the girls remain at home with Nanny though?'

Florence wasn't completely happy with the idea. She had taken some persuasion to leave John at home since he had reached the toddler stage and wasn't as content to spend so much time in her office, preferring to be taken for a run around in the park near their house. But she couldn't deny that what Jesse was saying made sense.

'I'll take them to the office in the mornings, then. On days when I'm extra busy at meetings, we can arrange for the carriage to bring Nanny to collect them at lunchtime. Only on busier days, mind.'

Jesse's smile widened. 'I agree. I like it when we can come to a compromise,' he said, a twinkle in his blue eyes. 'We

both know that there are times when it is a little more difficult to do so. I imagined this might be one of them.'

It dawned on Florence why he had been so concerned to
broach this subject. Jesse hated it when they quarrelled, but
as much as she wanted to please him, Florence also knew
that, to be happy, she needed to stand up for what she wanted
too. She reached out and took his hand, giving it a gentle
squeeze.

Jesse grinned at her. 'I will still want you to return home
earlier in the afternoons, too. On that I do insist.'

He was right, she knew that, and was happy to agree. 'For
the time being only,' she acquiesced.

'If you insist. I worry that if you push yourself too hard,
you might become ill, and I couldn't bear that.'

Florence's heart ached. The very last thing she wanted to
do was cause Jesse to fret about her. She placed her napkin
on the table and walked over to stand behind his chair. She
hugged him from behind, kissing the top of his head.

'My dearest darling, I never want you to worry unnecessarily about me. I am very well and intend to remain that
way.' She stepped beside him and bent down to kiss him.

'Good,' he said taking her in his arms and kissing her back.

Chapter 9

June 1893

The days were getting warmer and Florence was looking forward to the summer. She didn't particularly like having to wear a corset under her dress in the hotter months and wished there was a more comfortable mode of dressing, but as the carriage stopped in Pelham Street, she smiled to think that they might be able to eat their dinner with the children outside this evening for the first time this year.

Florence held three-year-old Dorothy in her arms as she stepped down from the carriage.

'Wait until I help you down,' she instructed John, who did as she asked and leant back against his father's legs until she was ready. 'Right, take my hand now, please.' She clung on to John's tiny hand as he climbed down and then waited for Jesse to bring Margery, and the coachman to hand Jesse his briefcase.

Florence gazed up at the Boots logo she had grown to love. It was the same one Jesse had designed ten years before, a simple yet appealing sign that she felt certain would stand the test of time.

'Ready?' Jesse smiled as the doorman opened the door for them.

Florence beamed at him. She loved moments like these, when they were all together. Their own perfect little family. Miss Tweed was waiting for them inside the main door, her hands resting on the handle of Margery's pram. The same pram had been kept here for John and also Dorothy and it warmed Florence's heart to see the familiar navy object that had kept each of her babies secure while they slept as tiny babies next to her desk.

Jesse lowered the sleeping child carefully, so as not to wake her, and then covered her with a blanket. Each of them was well versed in this daily routine now. Slowly she was finding her way to make most of her days more easy-going. As long as none of the children were battling an ailment, then they were usually very easy to look after at the store.

John giggled and ran the few steps to Miss Tweed. He hugged her legs tightly. Miss Tweed wobbled briefly and then bent down to ruffle his hair.

'Good morning, Master John. You seem very chipper today?'

'Bithkit?'

Miss Tweed knew she wasn't supposed to give the children any treats, so that Florence knew what they had eaten while they were at Pelham Street. She didn't want their meals ruined by sweeties, but she was unable to hide her amusement that John had shared something she suspected Miss Tweed was hoping to keep between the two of them.

'I, er, have a small tin of digestives in my desk drawer,' she admitted, her cheeks flushing with embarrassment. 'I gave John half of one the other day. Sorry, I know I shouldn't have done.'

Florence didn't want to upset her secretary and knew that Miss Tweed's unexpected awareness that John didn't know to keep these exchanges to himself would probably be enough to stop her doing it again.

'It's fine, really,' Florence reassured her and led the way through the store. 'The occasional half a biscuit is fine. I only worry if it becomes a daily occurrence.'

Dorothy wriggled, wanting to be free of her mother's arms, so Florence put her down onto the shop floor so she could walk.

'No running off now, Dorothy,' Florence said firmly. 'You must come with us upstairs.'

Dorothy took Miss Tweed's free hand and Florence took the pram from her.

Jesse thanked the doorman, Alfred, an elderly man who had begged Jesse for work after losing his previous job. Jesse had given him a chance and the man seemed to idolise him.

Florence followed Jesse through the art nouveau building, taking in the perfection around her as staff made their way to their stations, ready to greet their customers. Each employee looked immaculate. She was delighted to think how each one of them had worked hard to settle into their roles at the store. Their dedication to their work was evident every day. Pride coursed through Florence. She couldn't help feeling grateful to these women for their repayment of her trust that they would work hard for her, and loved being the one Jesse had assigned to take on the female staff and oversee their welfare.

Jesse stopped to chat to a member of staff on their way through the store. Florence greeted the women in the dispensary, thinking how professional they looked in their immaculate uniforms and also, she was relieved to note, how happy.

Moving on to the women preparing to begin another day on the perfumery counters, Florence's thoughts drifted to her old friend Lily Buttons. They exchanged letters occasionally and she always made sure to take her out for tea whenever she travelled home to Jersey, but she couldn't help thinking that at some point Lily would want more than to stay on the island. She hoped that Lily's father's regular terms in prison wouldn't hold her back. Florence still believed that Lily could make something of herself in this world given half a chance.

While Jesse stopped to speak to one of the storemen, Florence walked over to the stationery department. It was her favourite area in the store and, although it was so much bigger than the floor space in her father's store in Queen Street back in Jersey, it always reminded her of being a young girl working with her sister and Lily before her marriage. She had possessed so many dreams back then, Florence recalled. One of them had been to run her own business one day. This might be Jesse's business, but she truly felt a part of it. Here she was in this impressive new shop showcasing products, many of which she had been the one to source, and it was a dream come true.

Florence spotted one of the displays wasn't quite as well put together as she would like. Unable to help herself, she parked the perambulator against the nearest wall out of anyone's way.

'Is anything amiss?' Jesse asked, concerned.

'Not at all, but you know what a perfectionist I am. I've just seen something that needs my attention. You carry on to your office with Miss Tweed and the two older children, and I'll follow shortly.'

Satisfied that Margery was still sleeping and could be left for the moment, she went to rearrange diaries that had recently been received from the supplier.

'Mrs Boot, I'm so sorry,' the supervisor said, seeing her and hurrying over to join her. 'Is something the matter?'

Florence looked at the pale, pinched face of the woman, who was wringing her hands.

'No, I was just passing and thought this display could be better placed, nothing more,' she said trying to reassure the woman that she was not in any trouble. Florence took hold of the sides of the wooden frame showcasing the display and moved it several inches to the right. 'Now, if you could help me move these crystal ink pots and the paperweights slightly further apart,' she suggested thoughtfully, 'I believe that will improve the setting. We want to show everything off to its best advantage under these electric lights, don't you think?'

'We do.' The supervisor smiled, relaxing as she helped.

'There, that's a little better. I'll stand back a bit and see if I'm right.'

Florence walked back to where she had left Margery and studied the display. She smiled, satisfied. 'Yes, we were right,' she said wanting to include the supervisor in her achievement. 'That looks perfect now.'

'Thank you, Mrs Boot,' the woman said looking, Florence

noticed, much more confident as she glanced at one of the other assistants approaching the department.

Did she make the women nervous? Florence wondered. She hoped not. She liked to think of herself as having earned their respect as a fair and thoughtful employer. She never wanted any of her girls to be scared of her; it would be devastating.

Florence took hold of the perambulator handle just as Jesse returned, presumably to see what had made her stay back in the stationery department. She gave him a knowing look. 'We both know you can't bear not to be in control and wanted to see what I was doing,' she teased.

Jesse opened his mouth to argue. 'You're quite wrong,' he said, looking indignant at her accusation. 'I thought I'd accompany you to the lift. The perambulator can be a trifle awkward to manoeuvre.' He took the handle from her and pushed it as they walked to the lift.

Florence hid her amusement, but secretly enjoyed it when Jesse was unable to hide his inquisitiveness around her.

Once in her office, Florence went to lift Margery from the pram. 'Let me,' Jesse insisted, kissing the tip of his baby daughter's button nose.

Florence watched him, happy to give him as much time as he needed around the children. There were too many times when Jesse's work kept him in his office, either here at the store or at home. And when he wasn't working, he spent hours out on his horse accompanying one of his managers to visit other stores and their factories on his rounds.

Jesse cuddled baby Margery and ruffled the heads of his two older children as they played happily in the small playpen at the back of her office. It was an idyllic scene until John reached out and snatched Dorothy's favourite teddy, making her wail in indignant fury.

'Naughty boy,' Florence said softly, as she took the toy from his hands and passed it back to Dorothy. 'You mustn't tease your little sister.'

'Do you need me to help with anything, Mrs Boot?' Miss Tweed asked quietly.

'No, thank you. I'm sure you have more than enough to be dealing with. If you come back to take some dictation at eleven o'clock that should tie in nicely with their morning sleep.'

Jesse cleared his throat. He beamed at his three children and sighed contentedly. 'Well, I suppose I'll go to my office and press on.' He turned to Florence and gave her a kiss.

'You have a busy day today?' Florence asked, pulling the hatpin away from her hat and taking it off.

'No more than usual.'

John tried to take Dorothy's teddy again, causing her to scream. Margery began to whimper, and then cry. Florence placed her hat on her desk and shook her head. 'You go and I'll try to placate these three.' She stared at him, willing him to leave the room before he began fretting again about her coping with the children while at work. 'Go on, I'll have these three settled all the quicker if there's no one else in here but us.'

He hesitated, before doing as she asked.

'You'll bring them in to my office for some lunch later?'

Florence placed her hand on his cheek. 'Yes, I'll order food to be brought in from one of the restaurants we like.'

He looked over at her neat desk, the only items on it being a silver-framed family photo of her and Jesse with their two older children, a blotter, pen stand, and her leather-bound diary..

'What do you have scheduled for today?' he asked.

She walked to her chair and sat. Then she opened her diary and ran her finger down the page. Before she could reply, Miss Tweed knocked gently twice and entered. She produced Florence's daily list of tasks and placed it on her leather-topped desk. 'You asked me to remind you to be sure that Mr Baxter has the carriage here to take you to the factory this afternoon.'

Florence could not think for a moment what the meeting was about.

Miss Tweed seemed to read her confused expression and added, 'It's for the dispute you were having a meeting about.'

'Dispute?' Jesse scowled. He looked from Miss Tweed to Florence. Florence gave him a reassuring smile.

'Thank you, Miss Tweed,' Florence said. 'Please check that the carriage will be waiting for me with enough time for me to reach the factory and have ten minutes to speak to the manageress.'

'Yes, Mrs Boot.' Miss Tweed looked from Florence to Jesse and chewed her lower lip nervously.

Florence appreciated all her secretary did for her but wished that she had not timed her reminder of the appointment quite so badly. 'I'll call for you in a little while when I'm settled in.'

Her secretary looked relieved to be given leave to go from the room.

Florence watched Miss Tweed rush off to do as she had

asked. She could not help thinking that as much as she found some of the disputes between management and the female employees upsetting, it gave her a lot of satisfaction when she was able to resolve matters to everyone's satisfaction.

She realised she hadn't answered Jesse's question. 'Yes, it seems that this time it's over a man and there's been an altercation between the two women.' She didn't miss Jesse's expression darkening but decided not to comment on his reaction. Florence was aware that after her agreeing to return home earlier every day, he wasn't going to be impressed that she intended going to the factory this afternoon. 'It probably sounds more dramatic than it is.'

He scowled and walked over to the playpen and ran his right palm lightly over Dorothy's head, smoothing down her hair.

'Do you think, on this occasion at least, that I might be the better person to see to this matter?' Jesse frowned, unable – or possibly, Florence mused, unwilling – to hide his concern.

Florence closed her eyes for a few seconds in an attempt to stop her temper rising. She did not need to be made to feel guilty about choosing to work as much as she did. She already had that to battle with on a daily basis. When would he stop fretting about her being unable to work hours as long as his? Or perhaps he was concerned that she would handle this situation badly again, like she had with Nellie Blythe? She was determined to prove that she had learnt from that situation, that she could manage the girls under her employ.

'How would it look to our employees if I did as you suggest? For all I know, one or both of these women could be mothers themselves. They would not be allowed to leave work early to rest. Neither of them is lucky enough to be in the privileged position that I am in.'

'That is no fault of yours, Florence,' he said keeping his voice low.

'I know it's not, but it makes me feel that I need to work harder as their employer to prove that I support them.' She could see Jesse's opinion wasn't affected by what she said. 'I'm sorry, my dear, but I have no intention of handing over my responsibilities. The power my position in life bestows on me enables me to help these women and it's an opportunity I'm determined to use to everyone's advantage.'

She didn't add that it was what she hoped someone would do for her, if the circumstances were reversed. That, she decided, was what she would do, otherwise what was the point of her continuing to work at all?

He shook his head. 'You are a stubborn woman.' She went to argue, despite her awareness that he was right, but he held up his hand to stop her as she took a deep breath. 'However, your strength of character and determination to help others are part of your personality and part of why I love you so much.' He smiled. 'Are you certain you'd rather deal with this?'

Florence loved her husband and trusted his judgement but was not about to let him take on jobs that she felt were her responsibility. She was relieved he didn't argue any further. She didn't want to be late to her meeting. How would that look to the women waiting to see her?

'I think we both know the answer to that question.' She raised an eyebrow and smiled. 'Now, I think you need to go to your office and let me look at what else is in my diary today.'

He hugged her. 'I'll leave you to carry on.'

Jesse tapped the bottom of his cane a couple of times on the floor as he stared at it thoughtfully. 'I'm aware it must be frustrating for you when I act this way.' He didn't meet her eyes. 'But I'm only trying to protect you.'

'My love, I know you only have my best interests at heart. Your reminder that I take good care of myself is welcomed, not resented.' It occurred to her to use the moment to her advantage. 'However, it works both ways and I expect you to do the same.'

Jesse's face softened and he laughed. 'Fair enough. I know when I've been dismissed.'

Florence stood and stepped around her desk to kiss him. 'You have. Now, let's have no more of this talk. You'd better go and press on with your work and I'll do the same.'

Chapter 10

Florence arrived home tired but happy. It had been a good day. The sun had shone and takings were up. She had also managed to catch up with a pile of outstanding letters, and Jesse had taken a rare afternoon off to spend some time at home with the children.

The smell of beeswax polish greeted her as she entered the hallway, and the pinks, purples, and white in the arrangement she had created from flowers cut from her garden the previous day brightened the already light room.

'Good evening, madam,' Beth said, greeting her. 'May I take your coat and hat for you?'

'Yes, thank you.' Florence unpinned her hat, as she stifled a yawn, then unbuttoned her coat and, slipping it off, handed it to Beth. 'Is my husband upstairs with the children?'

'He's upstairs, madam.' She took the coat from Florence's hand and stepped back when Florence hurried past her up the stairs. She suspected he might be changing for dinner, so headed immediately to his dressing room.

Hearing voices, Florence watched from the hallway as Harriet carried an empty tray from their bedroom. Her dark eyes widened to find Florence standing there. Florence placed a finger to her lips and shook her head, mouthing for Harriet to leave the door ajar. Nodding, she did as instructed and went downstairs.

Florence stepped forward, willing her skirt not to rustle and alert Jesse to her presence. Peering in through the gap her heart swelled as she watched the man she loved so deeply humming to himself as he took several pills, swallowing each with water from a glass and carafe that Harriet had just left behind. He then finished brushing his hair at the wall mirror.

Florence knew she shouldn't be watching him, but it was such an unexpected opportunity to gaze at Jesse without him being aware of her doing so that she couldn't help herself.

She heard Harriet telling off their scullery maid, Beth, for some mischief that she had done and smiled to herself. Hearing the familiar voices of her home soothed her soul after the long afternoon she had spent at the factory while the two women, Iris and Agnes, had found a way to compromise over their differences. Florence had been determined not to leave until their issue had been resolved.

The last thing she had intended to do was leave the factory having to fire one or both of the women involved. To do so would mean that she had their lack of an income on her conscience. Florence couldn't bear to think of children going hungry and suffering because their mothers found themselves without an income due to a decision she had made. There was always a solution to be found, Florence believed, although she was aware that some were more difficult to find than others. This one had taken a little time, but thankfully, for now at least, the problem had been resolved. She hoped that both women found a way to move on from the man they had become involved with.

John's voice, deep for such a little boy, echoed from the nursery on the floor above as he bossed Dorothy about. Florence rested her left hand on her heart when she heard Dorothy standing up to him and then Violet insisting they both got into their beds.

'Your mother will be here to tuck you both in very soon,' Florence heard her saying. 'What will she think if you're both still up when she comes to kiss you goodnight?'

'She won't mind,' Florence heard John say. She stifled a giggle.

Her children were so strong-minded, but, as Jesse liked to tell her when she commented on their characters to him, 'What can you expect when you think who their parents are?' He was right, too. She and Jesse were both pig-headed at times, each always certain that their idea was the best. Why would her children ever be any different?

Hers was a happy household and she was grateful for it. Florence couldn't imagine a life better than hers right now.

She heard movement in Jesse's room and watched as he reached down to pick up one of the gold cufflinks she had bought him for his most recent birthday. He had been delighted with the embossed linking of their two first initials and had delighted her by wearing them every day since. Jesse always preferred the presents she chose for him that were practical as well as beautiful.

He fastened the first cufflink, singing quietly to himself.

She could see joy emanating from his reflection in the mirror. She had to cover her mouth with her hand to stop herself from making a sound. He went to pick up the second cufflink, stopping abruptly, his outstretched arm frozen. She watched his face contort into a grimace as he grabbed the top of the dressing table, his singing replaced by quiet groans.

Forgetting her hiding place, Florence gasped and ran to help him. Quickly remembering his distaste for drama, she immediately covered her horror and in a calm voice, asked. 'My darling, is anything the matter?' She dragged a chair from its place near the window, trying not to let him see how much her hands were shaking. 'Here, take a moment and sit. You seem tired. I think you've been working a bit too hard these past few months.'

'It's nothing,' he insisted, taking her hands in his and lowering them. 'A slight case of indigestion, nothing more.'

The strain in his voice belied his reassurance. She wanted to believe him, but was too aware of his delicate health to simply accept his affirmation that there was nothing to worry about.

'Do you think we should maybe call for Doctor Braddock to come and check? It won't do any harm.'

'No,' he said, as she suspected he would. 'It was nothing. Truly.' He stood and, taking her face lightly between his hands, leant forward. 'I took my painkillers a little later than I was supposed to, that's all. Now,' he said, taking a deep breath, 'how are you after today's events at the factory?'

She wasn't surprised to hear him voicing his concerns. 'I'm sorry. I know I'm much later home than I intended to be.'

She saw him relax into his seat slightly. His pain must be easing a little, she thought, relieved.

'Now, Jesse,' she gave him a pointed stare as she knelt down in front of him. 'Don't think that you can change the subject that easily. If you're not well, I don't want you to hide it from me. Promise me you won't, otherwise I'll worry unnecessarily.'

He leant forward and took her in his arms, kissing the tip of her nose. 'My beautiful wife, you worry far too much about my health. However, I will do as you ask. It's a particularly busy time with the business growing and I have probably been worried by how quickly it's been happening. I am fine though.'

'Well, everything at the factory seems to be running as smoothly as possible and now that the Pelham Street store is up and running, I think we can both take it a little easier than we have been doing. Just until we press on with our next big project. Don't you agree?'

She rested her head on his shoulder and breathed in the soapy smell from his face. He had just shaved. The familiar scent calmed her. She knew she couldn't push herself harder and expect him to take things a little easier, so they needed to at least try to take a little more time for relaxation as a family.

'You look beautiful, as ever. Why don't you freshen up and change your dress and we can go downstairs for dinner and catch up properly with what has happened in our day.'

Florence freshened up and asked Harriet to check that the fire was lit in the living room, then went upstairs to kiss her children goodnight.

A floorboard squeaked under one of Florence's feet as she approached the nursery door where John and Dorothy shared a room. Florence heard stifled giggling and Violet whispering that they should wait quietly for their mother.

She took hold of the handle and slowly pushed open the door, poking her head around it before it was fully open. 'Are my babies still awake?'

'Me not baby,' Dorothy said, lisping slightly.

'You are,' John argued. 'I'm a big boy.'

Dorothy scowled at him and then looked back at Florence, her eyes shining with unshed tears. 'Not a baby? Margy baby.'

Florence stepped inside the room. 'I'm so sorry to keep you late, Violet. Has Nanny gone for something to eat?'

Violet nodded. 'I offered to sit with them, madam. They're the sweetest children.'

'Most of the time,' Florence said smiling. 'It's time you went home to your family. Come in a little later in the morning if you like and apologise to your mother for me, will you?'

'Please don't worry, Mrs Boot. My mum is still happy from you sending me home with the cream and eggs earlier this week. She won't mind me staying on a bit with my kids and these two are so well behaved.'

Florence wasn't so sure about her children being such beacons of good behaviour, but she was grateful to Violet. 'Ask Harriet if she can spare you some of that lamb pie we had last night; maybe your husband would enjoy that and it might save you having to cook for one evening.'

Florence didn't like to presume but had learnt since the

time Violet had come to work for her that any food she could spare for them was always welcomed with delight.

'Thank you very much, Mrs Boot. I'll go and ask Harriet now.'

Florence smiled at the young woman who worked so hard for her and then turned and leaned over the raised edge of Dorothy's cot bed under one of the windows. 'You are not a baby, no,' she assured her daughter as she leaned forward and kissed her forehead. 'You are a little girl who needs her sleep. Now, turn on your side and close your eyes.' Dorothy did as she said, placated by her mother's words.

Relieved to have pacified her daughter, Florence walked over to John's bed and kissed his forehead. His little arms reached up around her neck and he gave her a tight hug.

'Love you, Mother,' he said, letting go of her and yawning.

'And I love you, too. Did you have fun today with Violet?'

He nodded sleepily.

Florence covered his arms with his bed clothes and stroked his hair gently as he fell asleep. She pulled the curtains together more tightly to cover a gap at the top. The longer they slept, the longer she and Jesse were able to do the same, and Jesse needed his rest.

She left the room and walked the few steps to the baby's room where she found Margery sleeping peacefully, sucking her thumb. Florence sighed happily. She couldn't believe her youngest child was already fourteen months old. A pang of sadness shot through Florence. Margery would be her last baby, of that she was certain. She knew she was pushing herself as it was, working each day, with the three children she already had.

Being at home with her babies was when she was at her happiest. As much as she loved her work, it was times like these that she relished the most.

Florence went downstairs to meet Jesse in the living room a short while later. He was bent down and placing an extra log on the fire. She found it incredible to think that nothing on his face gave away any pain he might feel. If she hadn't been secretly watching Jesse earlier from the doorway, she would have been none the wiser about him suffering today. How many times did he hide his pain from her? she wondered. He was obviously adept at covering his ailments, and, she suspected, diverted her attention from him by focusing on how much he worried about her work commitments.

She would have to be more vigilant, she decided. She was determined to ensure he didn't overdo things and the only way to do that was to keep a keener eye on him. As much as both of them wished he had better health, Florence knew that Jesse wasn't nearly as robust as he led everyone to believe. She was determined to have Jesse in her and the children's lives for as long as she possibly could, which meant being stricter with him over the next few months.

Chapter 11

November 1893

Florence stepped out of the way of a pink-faced delivery boy carrying a heavy box along Pelham Street. She found it hard to believe that yet another year was racing to its conclusion. Did the months seem to pass so quickly because she worked such long hours? She didn't know, but she would have welcomed a few more hours in each of her days to fit everything comfortably in and not feel like she was struggling to keep up with everything most days.

She gazed up at the logo bearing her married name and then at the large shop windows filled with displays that included all the trimmings any person could wish for at Christmas.

This would be the eighth Christmas she and Jesse had spent together. As with the previous seven, Florence intended making the event a peaceful one. It was one of the few days a year when they could be alone with their children.

They would attend chapel in the morning as they always did each year, and return home for their family lunch. She could just picture the scene, and then afterwards she and

Jesse would spend time sitting happily together as they watched the children playing with their new toys. She loved those times when neither of them had any demands on their time as a family. It was a rare occurrence and one that Florence guarded fiercely. She and Jesse had made a habit over Christmas of sitting and reflecting on all the blessings that had been bestowed upon them in the previous twelve months.

That wasn't for a few weeks yet, though, and before she could spend any more time dreaming of their Christmas together, she must ensure that her customers had everything they needed at their disposal. Florence strode into the grand department store and exchanged pleasantries with several customers. Stopping occasionally to chat to members of staff on the ground floor, Florence spotted an immaculate assistant charming an elderly, well-dressed customer on the perfume counter, before moving on through stationery. The women she had employed to work at the store were turning out to be perfect ambassadors for Boots as the customers' first connection to the business.

She knew that Jesse's ethos for his stores had always been 'health for a shilling' to help as many people struggling financially to be able to afford medicines. Now, though, Boots was opening its doors to more affluent people wanting to treat themselves, which increased their takings and, Florence was satisfied to note, enabled Jesse to finance further shops to bring cheaper medicines to even more areas.

Florence passed the manicure sets and handbags in No. 2 Department. It was her favourite department, probably because it had been entirely her idea. She had been uncertain whether she had ordered enough of the latest perfumes from France, rouge dishes from Portugal, and the delicately scented soaps and body lotions she had discovered from various places in England. She was happy to note that she had calculated her orders well.

Satisfied that everything was working smoothly, Florence slowly walked up the elegant staircase, her hand gliding up the polished bannister on her way to the upstairs gallery. She meant to check on some newly introduced fancy goods, when she spotted Jesse talking to a customer.

'Mrs Boot,' someone whispered next to her.

Florence couldn't miss the urgency in the shop assistant's voice. 'Yes, what is it?'

They both smiled politely at a passing customer and when the woman was far enough away not to hear them speak, the girl replied. 'One of the women has fainted in the dispensary downstairs.'

'Thank you for letting me know,' Florence said, motioning for the girl to go with her. She walked as fast as she could back down the stairs without actually running, not wanting to alert anyone to the drama unfolding.

'Where is she now?' she asked the woman keeping step next to her.

'They've taken her into the back room for a sit down, but thought I should come and find you to see what you wanted us to do.'

Florence nodded a greeting to a regular customer near the cosmetics counter but continued on her way down to the pharmacy department. The girl led the way down the wooden stairs into the department and was relieved to see two assistants calmly serving customers as if nothing was amiss. Florence smiled at them and bade the customers a good morning before going into the back room and closing the door behind her.

She could see by the pale face of the woman sitting on a chair near a small desk in front of her that she was unwell.

'What happened?' she asked, recalling that the woman's name was Gladys. 'Is there something we can do for you?'

Gladys looked up at her, eyes wide with embarrassment. 'I'm so sorry, Mrs Boot. I've no idea what came over me.' She went to stand, but Florence placed a hand on her shoulder and pushed her gently back down.

Florence thanked the assistant who had come to find her. 'Return to your work now; I'll see that Gladys is looked after.'

The girl did as she was asked, leaving Florence and Gladys alone with the manageress, Ruby.

'She's insisting that she's fine to return to her post,' Ruby said doubtfully, her arms folded across her chest as she stared at Gladys.

Florence had seen this before and suspected she knew what was behind Gladys's fainting episode. 'What did you have to eat for breakfast?' she asked quietly, not wishing to sound in any way accusatory.

Gladys picked at a slight dent in the oak desk. 'I, well, that is . . .' She sighed. 'I didn't have time for anything this morning, Mrs Boot.'

'You didn't have your daily cocoa?' Florence asked, aware that it was all that a lot of the women consumed before starting a long day at work.

Florence still recalled the first time she had learnt that many of their female employees went without breakfast to ensure that there was enough food for their husbands and children. Jesse once explained to her how many women on a low income not only gave the majority of their food to the rest of their family, but also believed that when they could afford to buy meat, it should be fed to their husband as the head of their household. She found the notion staggering. It wasn't as if these women didn't work a full day, too.

Florence could not help feeling affronted on the women's behalf when, after finishing a day's work, they would be expected to return home to tend to their children and prepare a meal, while most of their husbands relaxed in front of the fire, or enjoyed a pint down at the local public house. Jesse thought she worked hard, which Florence knew she did, but she wasn't expected to go without a decent meal to feed others and she was lucky enough to have servants to do all her housework and prepare their food.

She had grown up without any luxuries, but her family had never gone without food and her father had always insisted on everyone eating a hearty breakfast before starting their working day.

'I was running a bit late this morning,' Gladys explained, her voice shaky. 'One of my kids wasn't well and I had to wait for my neighbour to come and sit with 'im. I'm so sorry, Mrs Boot. It won't happen again.'

Florence could hear panic rising in Gladys's voice and, wishing to calm her, grabbed hold of a nearby chair and pulled it towards her.

Florence sat facing Gladys. 'Please don't fret. These things happen,' she said, patting the woman's trembling hands. 'Ruby, please send for a large mug of cocoa for Gladys and ask if there are a few biscuits that she might eat.'

Ruby pursed her lips at the back of the woman's head. 'Don't be expecting this special treatment every morning, Gladys,' she snapped. 'Mrs Boot has more important things to do with her time than sort out breakfast for you.'

Gladys looked up at Florence, tears welling in her eyes. 'I promise I'll make sure I'm on time in future, Mrs Boot.'

'I'm sure you will,' Florence soothed, hating to see Gladys so apologetic when what she needed was reassurance. It was one thing to arrange for cocoa to be provided for each of the women every morning, but there must be something else she could to do assist them further. She would have to give it more thought.

'Ruby, I believe we all know that on occasion things happen that are out of our control. I think Gladys has had enough of a fright without us making matters worse for her. Now, please do as I ask and send for some refreshment.'

Florence was angrier with Ruby than she let on but didn't like to undermine Ruby's authority over the women, or humiliate her by telling her off in front of Gladys.

Florence waited for Ruby to go and carry out her orders before she turned to Gladys. 'Now, I don't want you to worry about what's happened this morning. Being a mother and working is difficult, I know that much. If there's anything I can help you with, at any time, please come to my office and speak to me. Will you promise me that you'll do that?'

Gladys stared at her thoughtfully.

'Gladys?'

'Yes, Mrs Boot. I will.'

'Good. Now, drink your cocoa and if you need a second cup, you just say so. I want you to feel up to returning to work before leaving you here.' Florence wondered if Gladys would ever come to her to ask for anything. She hoped that she would.

Ruby returned and Florence took her to one side. 'I don't want you to say anything further to Gladys,' she whispered, glancing over her shoulder to check that she wasn't being overheard. 'I think Gladys has had enough of a shock this morning having fainted.' She paused and stared at Ruby, hoping she was taking on board the gravity of her words. 'We provide the cocoa as a benefit to the women and we must be aware that some of their home lives are more difficult than others. I expect you, as someone in authority at Boots, to look out for the women in your care and to come to me with any concerns you may have. Can I leave you to do that for me, Ruby?'

Ruby swallowed, her eyes wide. 'Yes, Mrs Boot.'

Florence wondered if this was the first time Ruby had truly thought about her responsibilities towards the women in more junior roles to hers. It seemed to her that Ruby had experienced some sort of awakening.

Ten minutes later, satisfied that Ruby wasn't going to give Gladys a hard time, Florence watched as Gladys sat eating a biscuit and sipping at her cocoa.

'I'll leave you to it,' Florence said. 'I'd better press on; it's always such a busy time before Christmas.'

'Thank you very much, Mrs Boot,' Gladys said.

Florence smiled at her, relieved to notice that the colour had returned to the woman's cheeks and that she seemed much better than she had earlier.

Chapter 12

Christmas 1893

Florence helped Jesse hang three Christmas stockings from the plaster mantelpiece for the children. She felt an almost childlike excitement for the next day when their children would come down and discover the gifts that Father Christmas had bestowed on them.

Jesse put his arm around Florence's waist and they stepped back to admire the scene in front of them. Their Christmas tree, which Jesse had arranged to be delivered to the house four days before, now had a prominent position in the corner of the room between the large living-room window and the fireplace. They had decorated the tree with oranges covered with cloves and thin red ribbon, as well as baubles and strings of glass beads.

Lastly, she and Jesse had helped John and Dorothy to hang little boxes that they had decorated under Florence's watchful eye with pieces of doilies and coloured card. She waited until they had both gone to bed to hang up small pieces of fudge made by their cook, Mrs Rudge. Florence enjoyed wrapping each inch-sized square in coloured tissue paper. She was delighted to note that their tree not only looked beautiful, but the pine, orange, and clove scents emanating from the decorations gave the room a perfect Christmassy atmosphere.

'Do you think they'll like their toy theatre?' Florence asked, looking at the largest present sitting under the tree, which she had wrapped the evening before. 'I know the children each have new toys for their presents, but I wanted something that we can all enjoy together as a family tomorrow.'

Jesse pulled her to him and kissed her. 'I think it's a stroke of genius, my darling.'

Florence smiled, happy to have made the right choice for a family gift. 'Mrs Rudge has prepared all the food that she's certain we'll need for the next couple of days. She's left me a list of everything and I assured her that if we need anything cooked I'm perfectly capable of managing while she's with her family.'

'I'm aware you're able to cook, Florence, but are you certain you want to spend your Christmas doing so?'

She was. She used to love helping her mother in the kitchen when she prepared their family Christmases in Jersey and wanted to be able to feel like she was contributing something to making her own small family's food extra special.

'Yes, perfectly.' Florence sighed. 'I've given the staff the next two days off, but we do still have Harriet, Ethel, and your valet downstairs. I would rather they take the time to relax and celebrate this special time of year for themselves though, but I do know that if I need them for anything they'll be happy to assist me.'

'We have loyal servants, Florence,' Jesse said thoughtfully. 'They seem to enjoy making this a very special time of year and for that I have you to thank, once again.'

'Nonsense,' she said modestly. 'I do know that we're going to have a quiet day, just the five of us together. I'm looking forward to spending time together alone as a family and can't wait to see the children's faces when they come in here tomorrow after chapel.'

He hugged her tightly to him. 'Neither can I.'

'I've had new outfits made for each of them, too,' she said, thinking of the dark blue and white sailor suit she had waiting for John, the pretty pale blue pinafore dress for Dorothy, and a smaller version for baby Margery.

Jesse smiled. 'I look forward to seeing them dressed in their new Christmas finery. And you, my darling, do you have a new dress for tomorrow?'

'I do, but you'll have to wait to see it.'

* * *

The following morning, Florence, Jesse, and the children sat in the carriage on the way home from chapel.

'You've all been very well behaved.' Jesse gave her a look that she knew meant he was wanting to share a surprise with them. She nodded, smiling.

Jesse ruffled John's hair as he sat beside him. 'Your mother and I have a present for each of you.'

'What is it?' John asked, his eyes wide as he stared up at his father.

Florence watched the two men in her life, and her heart swelled. John was such a sweet, kind little boy and she hoped that he grew up to be very like his father, although probably less stern than Jesse could be on occasion. She looked down at the baby in her arms and smiled at Margery's cherubic face. Then turned to watch Dorothy sitting with her thumb in her mouth as she listened to John chatter with his father.

'Do you like your new dress, sweetheart?'

Dorothy nodded and grabbed the material where it covered her knees. 'It's pretty.'

'It is,' Florence agreed. 'And you look very beautiful wearing it.'

Jesse caught her eye. 'I haven't mentioned how lovely you look in your new gown, my darling. It suits you very well.'

'Thank you,' she said, pleased that Jesse had noticed and liked what she was wearing. 'It's a slight change of style for me and a simpler line compared to what I've been wearing the past couple of years.'

They arrived home and, having discarded their coats and hats immediately, made their way to the living room. The first thing Florence noticed was the smell of pine filling the room. She breathed it in and smiled. For Florence, this was the second-best thing about Christmas – the festive scents from the small boxes of dates, the small crystal bowls filled with sugared plums, and visiting the kitchen to watch Mrs Rudge stir the Christmas pudding and take the spice-filled Christmas cake from the oven.

Then she spotted a tray of cordial and holly-shaped shortbread biscuits that one of the servants had thought to leave for them. The fire was lit too and the room felt cosy. It was the perfect welcome after their outing in the cold weather.

Florence placed baby Margery in a cot that she had asked to be brought into the room the previous day especially for the festivities. She picked up one of the sugar-coated biscuits and took a bite, the buttery pastry crumbling into her mouth and delighting her taste buds.

'Look, children,' she said, hoping to entice them with something light to eat before they began unwrapping their gifts. 'Don't these biscuits look pretty? They're tasty, too. Do you want one?'

Both children immediately turned and eagerly rushed over to her. They were hungry, as she had expected them to be after a busy morning out of the house. She handed a biscuit to each of them and then passed the tray to Jesse. 'Try one.'

They all did as she suggested and each stood ravenously eating their biscuit and making a crumbly mess all over the Persian rug under their feet.

Florence smiled at Jesse as their small children ate and then raised her eyebrows questioningly as she glanced at the brightly wrapped presents under the large fir tree.

Jesse nodded. He picked up a linen napkin from next to the plate of biscuits and shook it open, then, taking each of the children's small hands, wiped off the crumbs.

'Now, do you wish to open one of your presents? The others presents will have to wait until after luncheon, but Mother and I think you've both been very good and deserve to choose which one to open now.'

'Yes,' they both shrieked, jumping up and down in excitement.

'Right. I'll point out the presents that have your names on them and then you can decide.'

Florence sat down on the sofa nearest to Margery's cot and stroked the little girl's chubby cheeks. She really was a beautiful baby, Florence thought happily. She gazed over at her wonderful husband kneeling in front of the tree and indicating to the older two children the presents that they would be able to open at some point during the day and knew that however successful they might be, all she ever wanted or needed in this world was to have these four people close to her to be truly happy.

Finally, their decisions made, Jesse waited for each child to sit on the floor before handing them their present. He then joined Florence on the sofa and took her hand in his.

'Look at them, aren't they perfect?'

She swallowed away tears of happiness and smiled. 'They are and we are two very lucky people.'

He raised her hand and, turning it over, kissed her palm. 'I wonder each day how I was ever lucky enough to meet you and end up with such a delightful family. You have given me so much joy, Florence. I hope you know that.'

She did, mostly because he told her regularly how very happy she made him. 'And you have made me the happiest of women, Jesse. You know you have.'

John discarded the paper covering his present. Pulling open the box, he cried, 'Mother, Papa, it's a boat.'

'It is,' Jesse said, waving him over to join them. John handed the boat to him and stood by Jesse's knees, gazing at the present in front of him. 'We'll take it to the park in a few days and I'll show you how to sail it. Would you like that?'

'Yes, Papa. Now?'

Florence laughed. 'No, poppet. It's Christmas Day and we're going to be eating a big lunch, but maybe tomorrow.' She looked at Jesse. 'What do you say, Papa? Shall we all go out to the park tomorrow so you and John can sail his new boat?'

Jesse handed his son the boat, pulled him into a hug, then let him go and ruffled his hair. 'Tomorrow it is then, if the weather is dry.'

John beamed at them and went to sit back on the rug and play with his present.

Florence looked over at Dorothy, struggling to open a large box. 'Do you want some help?'

Dorothy shook her head. 'No, Mother. Dot do it.'

She and Jesse laughed. 'She's such a determined little girl,' Florence said to him.

'I wonder who she takes after,' he teased.

'It could be either one of us, I think.'

Dorothy eventually managed to take her new doll from the box and the two of them sat comfortably watching their children enjoying their new toys.

Florence looked at the clock on the mantelpiece and saw that it was nearly one o'clock. 'You stay here with the children and I'll go and take the presents to the servants who have stayed behind for the festivities and then prepare our luncheon. Mrs Rudge was kind enough to put the turkey into the oven and prepare the vegetables, so all I need to do is boil them, make the gravy, and then I'll call you to help bring it to the dining room.'

'Why don't I carry the presents through to the kitchen?' he suggested. 'That way I can make sure to thank them all and then I'll come back and sit with the children while you take through the rest.'

She helped Jesse sort through the gifts and when Florence was satisfied that every member of staff had been accounted for, she gave Jesse the presents and sat back to wait for him to return.

Twenty minutes later, Jesse walked back into the living room. 'They seemed very happy with the food and gifts that we've given to them.'

Florence was relieved. She was confident in buying for the stores and also when choosing gifts for those closest to her, but although she knew most of her servants very well, she worried that they received few gifts in a year and wanted to be certain that what she had chosen to buy for them from her own family was the best gift possible.

She had presented Christmas presents to each of the other servants before they had left for their family celebrations. Each had been asked to visit her in her drawing room, where she chatted to them about what they would be doing and then thanked them for their hard work serving her and her family over the previous twelve months. She knew how much she had appreciated her father, or even Jesse, noticing when she had worked extra hard and achieved something important to her and believed that to commend her staff for all that they did was something that would enrich their lives too.

'I'll go and prepare luncheon now. The children should be fine for a while.' She reached the door, opened it, and then, suspecting Jesse wouldn't be as strict as her about the treats in the living room for the children, she said, 'No more than one sugared plum for John and Dorothy.'

She knew she was right to say something when Jesse turned and grinned at her, a mischievous twinkle in his pale eyes. 'I wouldn't dream of it, my darling.'

'Good,' she giggled.

'Call me if you need help with anything at all,' he said moving over to sit next to Margery, who was now sleeping soundly in her cot.

Florence left them and walked out to the hall and down to the kitchen. Mrs Rudge was standing at the range cooking.

'I hope you're preparing the food for you and the servants, and not our Christmas lunch,' Florence said, certain that she had caught Mrs Rudge looking after their food. 'I did want you to have time to yourself today.'

Mrs Rudge wiped her hands on a cloth and smiled. 'Now, Mrs Boot, we both know that I'm happiest in my kitchen preparing tasty meals for this household. The servants are just finishing their lunch now and I thought I'd come back in here and check on your meal. You work hard all year round and this is my way of helping you today.'

'Well, that's very thoughtful. Thank you.'

'I know you wish to do some of the cooking though, so I will leave you to finish everything off.' She hesitated, her eyebrows lowering into a frown. 'Unless you would rather I finish it for you. Harriet would be happy to serve you, despite what you said about us not working today.'

Florence was horrified. 'No, thank you. You've already done

far too much and I don't want Harriet disturbed. She works very hard and Christmas is a day for everyone to take time to rest and, if it's your choice, to worship.'

Mrs Rudge handed Florence an apron and waited for her to put it on. 'I'll be leaving for my sister's house in an hour or so,' she said. 'But I've left a game pie for you and Mr Boot for your supper in the pantry. I made it yesterday, and if I do say so myself, it looks as if it's one of my special ones.'

Florence put the lid on the pan of vegetables and turned to the cook. 'That is very kind of you, Mrs Rudge. Mr Boot, as you know, is very partial to game pie. I'm sure he'll thoroughly enjoy eating it this evening. Now, if you've no reason to stay here, why don't you leave for your sister's home now. I'm sure she must be looking forward to seeing you.'

Forty-five minutes later, John and Dorothy chatted excitedly at their places at the big dining-room table where they were only allowed to eat on very special occasions. The table was decorated with the family's best silver and crockery for her and Jesse, and second-best for the children. Harriet had placed the best crystal glasses for her and Jesse's water, and tumblers for the children, but the centrepiece was a large silver epergne with one large crystal dish at the top and six smaller ones on a lower tier. The top bowl was filled with sugared almonds and the lower ones with tantalising treats and flowers. It was the only colour on the table. There were two silver candelabra, one in front of her place and one at the other end of the long mahogany table in front of Jesse, both sporting two creamy white candles.

Jesse served the meat and passed the children's smaller

plates to Florence, who gave them a few vegetables, two roast potatoes, and a little gravy. She didn't bother to serve them with redcurrant jelly; it was far too tart for her children's taste buds.

Finally, they all sat with their food in front of them. The children were impatient to eat but knew to wait until grace had been said. Florence put her hands together and gave a pointed look to each of her children. They each copied and all closed their eyes in thanks as Jesse said grace.

'Amen,' they said in unison.

Jesse smiled at each child and then at Florence. 'Time to enjoy your mother's delicious meal.'

The double dining-room doors were open to the living room so that they could hear if Margery woke, but she didn't stir and Florence was able to sit and enjoy a perfect, if a little excitable, meal.

'Mother, are there more presents after?' her son asked.

Florence nodded. 'Yes, but only if you both eat up all your vegetables.' She doubted the children would want any pudding and decided that maybe she and Jesse could enjoy their evening after they had eaten the game pie.

They hadn't needed a fire in the dining room with the doors open to the living room. Florence didn't like to be too hot, nor did Jesse, and both knew that to heat the room too much would cause the children to become fractious.

It was a perfect lunch and she was pleased to see that Jesse looked to be enjoying their small family lunch as much as she and the children were.

'Well done, children,' she said, praising them when Dorothy

finally finished her last mouthful of food and placed her small fork on her plate. 'Papa will lift you down, Dorothy, and then we can all return to the living room and open the rest of your presents.'

The afternoon was spent playing with the children on the floor in front of the fire, while Margery chewed on her new teething ring that had a silver doll hanging from it.

Later, after feeding the baby and giving the older children a light supper of soup and a bowl of delicious trifle, she and Jesse put them all to bed and returned to the living room. He added two logs to the fire and stood with his back to the hearth, warming the backs of his legs.

'Shall we swap our presents to each other now?' Jesse asked. He didn't wait for an answer and went over to the tree to pick up a beautifully wrapped gift.

'You may as well bring yours, too,' she teased, knowing how much he loved to receive surprises from her. She had taken a lot of trouble to design this gift for him and hoped very much that he liked it.

Jesse's hand went straight to the small present on one of the higher branches of the tree. Florence had made sure she had placed their presents to each other on high branches well out of the children's reach.

'Here you are, my darling,' he said passing the larger box to her and sitting next to her. 'You go first.'

Florence gave him a smile and did as he asked. She could tell he was impatient for her to see what he had bought for her. She carefully undid the pretty pink bow tied around the rose wrapping paper and wound it lightly around two of her fingers. Then, placing the bow in her lap, she removed the paper. Seeing the dark blue leather box, she pressed the tiny brass clasp and opened the lid to reveal the prettiest necklace she had ever seen.

'Do you like it?'

How could she not? she thought, mesmerised by the fine gold chain dotted with small diamonds every half an inch around the bottom half of it. Attached to each diamond was a tinier chain with oval aquamarines hanging from each one. The gem in the middle was double the size of the others. She gasped at its beauty. 'Jesse, this is far too extravagant.'

He shook his head. 'I saw this, and immediately thought it matched the colour of your eyes.'

Her eyes were darker, but if he wanted to think that they were this exquisite azure colour, then she wasn't going to argue. 'Thank you, I adore it.' She turned her back slightly to him and held the ends of the chain up at either side of her neck. 'Will you do up the clasp for me?'

He did as she asked with a little difficulty due to his misshapen fingers and stood up. He reached his hand out to her and she took it and got to her feet. They walked over to the large mirror above the mantlepiece. Florence gazed at the gems sparkling brightly from the reflection of the flames in the fireplace below.

'You spoil me, Jesse,' she whispered, enthralled by the necklace.

'Not at all.' He kissed the back of her left shoulder. 'It suits you even better than I had imagined it would.'

They returned to the sofa. 'Now,' she said. 'Your turn.

Although I must warn you that I can't compete with what you've bought for me.'

'Good,' he said kissing her cheek. 'I want to be able to give you things you love.'

'Open yours now.'

She sat silently as he unwrapped the box and opened it to reveal the gold stick pin she had had commissioned. Jesse studied the circular top with their initials in the middle and those of their children linking to them in a filigree pattern from top to bottom in order of their age. She wondered if she might need to explain her thought process behind it when he didn't speak for a few moments.

He looked up from it and kissed her. 'It's beautiful. I can keep all my precious ones connected to me when I wear this, wherever I might be.'

'You like it then?'

He looked stunned. 'I love it, as you knew I would. You know me so well, dearest Florence.'

Satisfied, she sat back with him and gazed at the pretty Christmas tree, now depleted of its presents. She cuddled up to Jesse and, content with simply sitting close to him in the warm, pine-scented room, flickering candles on the mantelpiece casting shadows up onto the patterned wallpaper, she closed her eyes.

They sat there in comfortable silence until Jesse's stomach rumbled. Florence heard him chuckle and did the same. She sat up straighter in her seat.

'Where are you going?' Jesse asked holding her gently by the arm.

'To find some food for us. I've heard how hungry you are,' she said, amused. 'And now realised that I'm a tad peckish too.'

'What shall we eat?'

'Mrs Rudge mentioned a game pie that she made especially for this evening. I'll go and fetch some for us.' She stood and smoothed down her skirts. 'You stay there and I'll be back shortly.'

She left the living room and walked through to the kitchen. Now she thought of it, she was ravenous. Florence was quiet so as not to disturb the servants. She could hear laughter coming from behind the closed door to their parlour, so she took a tray and laid two places on it. Then she went into the larder to find the game pie. The shelves were ordered with everything grouped together tidily. Florence lifted a teacloth thinking she might have discovered a smaller one than Mrs Rudge usually made, but it was an apple pie.

'How odd.' She was confused. She thought back to her conversation with Mrs Rudge and was certain the cook had mentioned placing the pie in the larder for them. Where could it be then, if it wasn't there? Now she couldn't find it, she yearned for the merest taste.

'Ooh, madam,' Harriet exclaimed, stepping back in surprise as Florence stepped out of the larder. She narrowed her eyes. 'Is anything the matter?'

Florence explained about Mrs Rudge and the pie. 'But it doesn't seem to be there now. Could she have stored it elsewhere, do you think?' Florence hated the thought of Mrs Rudge going to the trouble to cook the pie and then her and Jesse not bothering to eat it.

Harriet shook her head. 'No, madam. It would have been left for you in there, I'm certain of it.'

She frowned and thought for a while. 'I'm not sure what to say. Mrs Rudge will be back late tomorrow evening. I can ask her then, if you wish?'

Florence didn't want Harriet to feel that her annoyance had anything to do with her. 'Yes, please, Harriet. Right now though, I need to take some supper through to Mr Boot. Do you have any idea what else Mrs Rudge might have left for me to give to him?'

'Would you like me to make up a tray for each of you?' Harriet asked, her pink cheeks an even deeper shade than usual.

'That's very kind of you, Harriet,' Florence said touched by her maid's offer on her day off. 'But no, I'll have a look and put something together for us. You go back and enjoy yourself. And thank you.'

A few minutes later Florence returned to the living room with a tray of cold meats, salad, and some cheese and bread. She had included two small bowls of pickles from some jars she had found in the larder. She set the tray down for them to eat on a table in front of the sofa.

'No game pie then?' Jesse asked, disappointment etched on his handsome face.

Florence's heart constricted. She didn't like to let him down ever and especially when there was something he was looking forward to. She explained about her conversation with Harriet.

'I'll speak to Mrs Rudge about it on her return from her sister's.' She served him a plate of the treats in front of them. 'Now, let's enjoy this food, it looks delicious.'

She sat next to Jesse on the sofa. Despite the disappointment with the pie, everything else had gone well. She had enjoyed spending time with Jesse and the children away from work. It had been wonderful not to have to worry about her staff, or any of the other constant queries or small jobs that made up her working day, wonderful to take time to focus on those closest to her and watch them having fun.

Jesse cut a portion of ham and, sticking his fork into it, dabbed on a small amount of Mrs Rudge's delicious pickle and held it in front of Florence's mouth for her to eat.

'Tasty?' he asked after she'd chewed and swallowed the morsel.

'Very.' She watched him eat some of his food.

The break away from the business had done Jesse the world of good, too. He seemed more relaxed and less strained than he had done recently, Florence noticed with relief. She loved days like these, when she and Jesse spent time with the children away from their usually busy lives. They had both been doing far too much, each working hard to make sure that the factories were producing all that was needed to supply the shops for the busy Christmas period. Now, though, they could take things easy, at least for the next few days. It was exactly what they both needed.

Chapter 13

St Heliers House, The Park, Nottingham

Florence's hansom cab pulled up outside her house a few days later. She shivered despite her warm coat as she stepped down, shocked to hear her scullery maid, Beth, shouting hysterically.

'You liar, I never took anything!'

Florence clenched her jaw as she paid the driver, trying to act as if neither of them could hear the commotion carrying on inside her home.

'You did,' Mrs Rudge shouted. 'And what's more, I'm going to tell Mrs Boot as soon as she's back home.'

Florence thanked the driver and, furious to be embarrassed by her servant, rushed inside the house. It had been a long, tiring day and the last thing she needed was for her neighbours to hear two women arguing from inside her home. She didn't bother to remove her hat or coat, but dropped her bag onto the hall table as she marched to the back of the house and into the kitchen.

'What is the meaning of this!' She noticed the back door was open, which must have been why their voices had carried so clearly to the driveway. 'Beth, close that door this instant.'

Beth and Cook gaped at her, both obviously shocked to see her unexpectedly in their domain.

'Now!'

Beth scurried to do as Florence asked.

Florence took in the messy kitchen table covered with used bowls and utensils before smelling something burning. She turned to see smoke coming from a pan behind her. 'Harriet, take that pan off the range before it burns dry.'

Harriet immediately grabbed a cloth and removed the pan, taking it over to the sink and running cold water into whatever had been inside.

'Now, I don't know what's been going on whilst I've been at work, but whatever it is, there's no excuse to make this much noise. I do not expect to come home and hear two women screaming at the top of their lungs.'

'She called me a liar,' Beth grumbled, giving Mrs Rudge a sideways glance.

Florence took a deep breath. She could see Mrs Rudge's fury by the thunderous look on her rounded face.

Mrs Rudge, her ruddy face even redder than usual, took a deep breath. 'Sorry, madam, I should have spoken to you about what I've discovered, but Beth cheeked me and I lost my temper with her.'

Florence looked at Beth. 'I can't imagine Mrs Rudge accusing anyone without reason,' she said. 'Tell me why you think she believes you lied.'

Beth scowled and stared at the floor. 'She said I've been stealin' food from the larder.'

Florence was shocked. Cook kept a tight rein on the food orders and what was stored at the house. 'Is this right, Mrs Rudge?'

'It is, madam.'

Annie, the under housemaid, interjected. 'I saw Beth once meself, takin' some of the crackers Mrs Rudge was keepin' for the children's tea.'

'That's enough from you, Annie Andrews,' Cook snapped, crossing her arms over her chest. She raised her head defiantly. 'I'll thank you to mind your own business.' She turned her attention back to Florence. 'I did accuse her, Mrs Boot. And I know for a fact that I'm right to do so.'

Annie pouted and stomped out of the room.

'You're the liar,' Beth said through gritted teeth. 'Not me.'

'That's enough, Beth,' Florence said, taking off her hat and placing it on a small table by the door. She unbuttoned her coat. It was warm inside the kitchen after the cold of her carriage journey back from the store. 'You'll be given your turn to speak.'

She really wanted to go and cuddle her children, but this situation needed to be settled between her cook and maid before Jesse's return home. He would be exhausted after overseeing another day of sales. The sales, especially when successful, were exhilarating and very exciting, but they could also be manic, which was why she had decided to leave the children at home today with Violet. She hoped they couldn't hear the cacophony from these two women from their bedrooms two floors above. This place was her sanctuary, Jesse's too, and he needed peace when he was at home, not disruption and noise.

Mrs Rudge muttered something under her breath, then added, 'She did steal from the larder, Mrs Boot. Do you recall the game pie I made for you and Mr Boot for Christmas?'

Florence recalled her disappointment when she hadn't been able to find it. 'Yes, I do, but there wasn't any game pie,' Florence replied. 'I must admit I was a little confused by—' She didn't finish her sentence as it dawned on her what Cook was intimating.

'I'm sorry, madam, but I spent a good few hours preparing that pie for you,' she said, giving Beth a furious glare. 'When Harriet told me you couldn't find it in the larder, I admit I couldn't understand what might have happened. Then it occurred to me that there could only be one other person who had the opportunity to take it.'

'What about Violet?' Beth suggested, sniffing and wiping her nose on the back of her hand.

Cook rounded on the younger girl. 'Violet had already left to be with her family when I put that pie in the larder. The only other person in the house who could have possibly taken it was you.'

Florence studied the younger girl. She didn't seem to be even trying to hide her guilt, despite crying noisily and staring at the floor. Why had Beth done such a thing? she wondered. Hadn't they given her enough food? Was her wage too low? Florence had imagined the girl to be happy working for them.

Cook addressed Florence once more. 'Because of what happened, I set a few small traps with food and the like. I did it in the evenings when Violet had gone home and timed it so Harriet and the others weren't around. I wanted to be sure that I had proof that it could only have been Beth. I'm sorry, Mrs Boot, I know this leaves you in an unsavoury position, and' – Mrs Rudge narrowed her eyes at Beth – 'I truly hate doing this, but I can't share rooms with a thief. I don't think you and Mr Boot's kindness to us deserves to be repaid by one of your servants pinching from you either.'

Florence knew that Mrs Rudge was a kindly woman who would never see anyone lose their job if she could think of a way to salvage it. She struggled frantically for some way to remedy the situation without having to dismiss Beth. Florence could barely take in the enormity of what she was forced to deal with, especially at such a miserable time of year. She hated to think that this naive girl had been silly enough to put herself in a position where she would have to be let go, but try as she might, Florence couldn't think of another way to resolve the bad feeling that now pervaded the servants' quarters.

'Beth, do you have anything to say in your defence?' Florence asked, willing the maid to come up with something she could use to help her find a way out of this mess.

Beth shook her head and gave a loud sniff. 'You had so much other food for the two days we were away. I didn't think no one would miss it.'

'That's beside the point,' Cook snapped. 'It wasn't your food to take, young miss.'

'Is there a reason you felt compelled to take the pie?' Florence asked, hoping the girl might come up with a reasonable excuse she could use to pacify Mrs Rudge. 'Is there a problem at your family's home? Did you feel the need to take food to them maybe, for the festivities?'

Beth shook her head. 'Not really, madam.'

Cook snorted and shook her head. 'See, she can't even pretend she was trying to help her family,' Cook grumbled. 'You don't even look as if you feel at all guilty for stealing, my girl. If you found it so easy to take this, then what else might you have pinched, I'd like to know?'

Beth's face reddened. Florence was surprised to realise that it wasn't in embarrassment, but in anger at being found out. She was stunned. She obviously hadn't known the girl nearly as well as she imagined she'd done.

'But it's only food and it's not as if anyone will go hungry without one stupid pie,' Beth argued.

Mrs Rudge gasped at Beth's rudeness. She stepped forward and raised a hand. Florence realised she was about to slap the girl, so immediately stepped in between them.

'Beth, if you wanted something to take home to your mother,' Florence said, wearily, 'all you had to do was ask Cook for something. Isn't that right, Mrs Rudge?'

The cook pursed her thin lips. 'Yes, Mrs Boot, it is.'

It occurred to Florence that the older woman was hurt that one of the maids who helped in her kitchen had taken it upon herself to steal from her. She also wondered if Cook's fury might have been made worse by the prospect that food she had ordered and would have to account for in her books had gone missing.

Florence wished there was some other outcome she could think of for Beth, but knew that she had no choice. She would have to dismiss her. The realisation made her heart sink. 'I'm afraid you'll have to leave this house, Beth. You do know that, don't you?'

'Yes, madam,' she whispered.

Florence hoped that the repercussions of what Beth had done might stop her from ruining any future jobs she'd have. Being light-fingered was not something any employer would take kindly to, not when they had to trust the people living at home with their families.

'Will you be able to go to your mother's this evening?' Florence asked, unable to let the girl leave without knowing that she had somewhere else to sleep, however upset Cook might be about the theft.

Beth nodded. 'She said this would happen,' she mumbled, looking contrite.

'Your mother knew what you'd done?' Florence was shocked that Beth's mother had not insisted she return the pie immediately. At least that way they'd have been none the wiser and Beth would not now be out of a job.

'She wasn't best pleased, but said that it looked tasty, so we might as well eat it and hope you didn't miss it.'

Florence opened her mouth to speak but was lost for words. She hung her head for a moment, trying to gather her thoughts before looking back at Beth. If this was how her mother had reacted, she mused, then maybe Beth had no experience of understanding the upset that stealing from someone caused. 'You do realise it's not the pie that's the issue here, but the fact that you stole it and that by doing so you've lost the trust of those in this house?'

'Yes, madam,' Beth said, looking sullen.

Harriet stepped forward. Florence hadn't seen her enter the room and wasn't sure how much she'd heard. 'We all know that you wouldn't see us go without, Mrs Boot,' she said, scowling at Beth with distaste. 'I had a silver St Christopher on a chain that went missing several weeks ago. When I asked Beth if she'd seen it, she denied it. Did you take that too, Beth?'

'What would I want with your stupid necklace?' Beth sneered.

Florence was horrified. How long had this girl been stealing from this household? 'Beth, have you taken other things? If you have, now is the time to return them.'

Beth's eyes widened. She looked stunned by the insinuation that she might have stolen more items. 'That wasn't me, madam. I promise.'

Florence almost believed her until she caught Beth giving a triumphant sideways glance at Harriet, whose face was now pinched with anger.

Florence had had enough for one day. 'I think there's nothing more we can say about the matter.' She shook her head, miserably. 'Mr Boot will be home soon. He'll be expecting a hot meal. Mrs Rudge, please make something while Beth goes to her room and packs her bag.' She stared at the young maid, sad that her time with them had ended in such a dreadful way. 'I'm sorry it's come to this, Beth, but you leave me no choice, I'm afraid.'

Beth hung her head, miserably. 'I know, Mrs Boot. I've been a fool and I know I must go. It was nice living here though, while it lasted.'

'Little minx,' Cook mumbled as she grabbed hold of a pan. 'Madam, please don't feel badly. It isn't your fault what's happened and I'm sure Beth will have learnt a valuable lesson for the future.'

'I do hope so,' Florence said. 'How will you cope without her here though? Do you know of anyone who might want her position?'

'I'm not sure, but I'll have a think.'

'Thank you.' Florence was grateful to the woman for keeping an eye on things when her back was turned. She needed honest people in her home. 'I'll leave you to it. I need to go and say hello to the children.'

Florence picked up her hat and left the kitchen, needing desperately to hug her babies and push away the sad end to her day. She couldn't help wondering if there was another way she could have resolved the matter with Beth. Her footsteps were heavy as she climbed the stairs to the children's nursery. As she walked, it dawned on her that though she had not been able to find a way to keep Beth, maybe Beth's unacceptable behaviour might help resolve someone else's situation.

Chapter 14

By nine o'clock the following morning Florence was sitting in a hansom on the way to Nellie Blythe's home. She still had Nellie's home address from when she had sent the letter to her mother that had caused so much trouble.

Florence recalled only too well how her initial attempts to help Nellie Blythe had gone awry in the worst possible way. This time, though, she knew better and would be far more careful. She would speak directly to Nellie and her mother and hopefully they would approve of what she had in her mind.

'Red Lion Street, madam?' the driver said. 'Also known as Narrow Marsh. You sure you want to go there? It's not somewhere where we usually take a lady like yourself.'

'Yes, that is the place I need to visit,' Florence said.

'Fair enough.'

Florence decided that rather than announce her arrival and give Mrs Blythe any chance to rebuff her second attempt at helping her daughter, she would turn up and hope for the best.

The houses she passed by in her hansom as she neared

Red Lion Street became more and more derelict. Florence couldn't help feeling nervous about what she was intending to do. She also found it difficult to imagine how Nellie was coping with caring for a young baby, her mother, and her brother in one of these squalid homes. The hansom drew to a halt outside a house with broken windows stuffed with damp card and old newspapers. Children stared at her as she looked out of the window.

The driver climbed down and walked round the hansom to open the door for her. 'Are you sure this is where you want to be, Mrs Boot? It's not the best neighbourhood, if you don't mind me saying.'

'Thank you for your concern, but I am exactly where I need to be.' She stepped down and checked her hat was straight. 'Wait for me here, please. I shouldn't be very long.'

Florence was more certain than ever now that she was doing the right thing coming here to find Nellie. She heard a baby screaming inside the property and a woman in the next-door house bellowing at someone. Florence didn't give herself time to think further, but raised her gloved hand and knocked several times on the front door.

Moments later it was opened by Nellie. At least she thought it was her. Maybe Nellie had a sister she hadn't known about, Florence wondered.

'Mrs Boot?' Nellie said, her hand shooting up to her hair as she tried to pat the wild curls into some semblance of order. 'What are you doing here?'

Florence noticed a group of onlookers had congregated on the other side of the road. They stared and whispered to each other, no doubt speculating why she had come to Narrow Marsh.

'You'd better come in,' Nellie said, her baby resting on her right hip. 'Please watch your beautiful clothes on the walls though, as they're rather damp.'

Florence followed Nellie into a room that despite its peeling paper, damp walls, and cracked windows had a small fire in the grate and was very tidy.

'You've, er, met my mam,' Nellie said, blushing as she gestured towards Mrs Blythe, scowling at her from a threadbare armchair near the meagre fire. 'And that's my brother Tommy.'

'Hello, Mrs Blythe. I hope you don't mind me visiting unannounced,' Florence said. 'I was hoping to speak to you and Nellie about something.'

Mrs Blythe stared at her warily. 'You're here now, so you may as well say what you've come to say.'

'Would you like to sit down, Mrs Boot?' Nellie asked.

Florence shook her head. 'Thank you, but no. I don't have much time and I have to be back at the office.' She explained about being unexpectedly down one servant in her house. 'I know you wouldn't want a live-in position, but was wondering if you might be interested in coming to work at my home as a scullery maid?'

Florence could see the surprise in Nellie's face and wasn't sure if she was offended or simply shocked at the suggestion. She looked at Mrs Blythe to try and gauge her reaction, but she was watching Nellie. She waited for her offer to be considered. 'I'm afraid it's not much. I know that my naivety made matters worse for you last time, Nellie, and for that I'm still mortified.'

'It's fine, Mrs Boot,' Nellie said, shooting a look at her mother.

Florence could see that Nellie seemed much stronger since having her baby. 'If it's all right with you, Mrs Blythe, I think a position in my household would work for Nellie. It would be a fresh start and would provide her with an income.' She clasped her hands together. 'It's entirely up to you. I thought I'd come here and ask you first, before going to the agencies to find someone.'

'The cat got your tongue,' Mrs Blythe said. 'Well, thank Mrs Boot for her kind offer, Nellie girl.'

Florence had to concentrate on not showing her relief at Mrs Blythe's reaction. Finally, she could feel as if she had made amends for her past error. It was a relief to have found a way to help Nellie and atone for her own stupidity.

'You don't have to if you'd rather not take the position,' Florence said quickly before the two became angry with each other. 'I have always felt badly that you lost your position at the factory for something that was unrelated to your work, which was very good, I might add.'

'I'm sorry,' Nellie said. 'I'm still a little shocked to see you here. I'd love to come and work for you and Mr Boot at your home, though I'm not sure where it is.'

'Here's my card,' Florence said, taking one from the bag hanging from her wrist. 'It has the address.' She handed it to Nellie, who studied it briefly.

'When would you like me to start?' Nellie asked, looking much happier than she had on Florence's arrival.

'How about next Monday?' Florence suggested. 'It will give you time to organise the baby and anything else you might need to sort out.' She wasn't sure if Nellie's mother would be able to care for the little one.

'She'll be happy to,' Mrs Blythe said, quickly. 'I might not be the best on these pins of mine, but Tommy gets things for me and can hand me the baby when I need him to. He's a good boy.'

Florence smiled and looked at Tommy, who smiled back.

'Thank you, Mrs Boot,' Nellie said. 'I'd be very happy to start work.'

'That's settled then. Now, I had better make my way to Pelham Street, or my husband will wonder where I've gone to. It was nice to meet you again, Mrs Blythe, and you, Tommy.' She placed a finger on the baby's cheek. 'And you, little one.'

'I'll show you out,' Nellie said, smiling.

They reached the door and Florence opened it and stepped outside. 'I never asked your baby's name, Nellie.'

'It's Joey, Mrs Boot.'

'Well, he's a bonny baby indeed. I look forward to seeing you next Monday.'

Nellie followed her to the door of the hansom and waited for Florence to climb in and settle herself on the padded seat.

'Thank you very much, Mrs Boot. I was horrified when me mam went to speak to you that day. I tried to stop her, but she wouldn't have it.'

'You have nothing to apologise for, Nellie. It was my mistake and your mother had every right to be upset with me.'

'Well, that's as may be,' Nellie said, looking unsure. 'I'm

ever so grateful for your offer of a job though. It'll make all the difference to my family, really it will.'

'It's my pleasure,' Florence said, honestly. The driver closed the door and she gave Nellie a quick wave, delighted that this time she had done the right thing and made Nellie's situation better. It was a huge relief.

Being able to give a job to a young girl who desperately needed employment helped make the upset of having to let Beth go the evening before slightly less painful.

Why was it, Florence thought as the hansom took her through the streets, that women were overlooked and seen as useless once they had borne children? It didn't make any sense to her and annoyed her deeply. These women should be valued, not looked down upon. Weren't they the ones who kept families together?

She sighed angrily. She was tired of the unfairness of it all. Her life might be very different to that of the women who worked for her, but, unlike them, she had the power to make changes and she was determined to use her position to do just that.

She arrived home aware that, despite Jesse's hope that she would resist taking it upon herself to try and help others without speaking to him first, she had done exactly the opposite. She joined Jesse in the living room where he was about to drink a cup of tea that Violet had just served to him. Florence watched Violet, thinking that she was another young woman who worked all day and would no doubt shortly return to her own home to begin preparing supper for her young family. These women never seemed to have time for themselves.

Jesse raised his cup halfway to his mouth, stopping when he noticed Florence's arrival. Before he had a chance to ask her where she'd been, Florence told him all about her visit to see Nellie.

'After the last time, I'm a little annoyed that you didn't discuss the matter with me first,' he said, looking hurt.

'I'm sorry,' Florence said. 'But I knew if I thought about it too long that maybe I'd talk myself out of going, and I didn't want to do that.'

'It seems that you did the right thing.' Jesse gave her a reassuring smile. 'And was Nellie happy with your offer?'

Florence stood in front of the fire to warm her hands. 'Yes, very happy. Nellie's looking forward to coming and working here.' She couldn't help thinking of the other women she had seen in the neighbourhood.

'What's the matter?' Jesse placed his cup back on the saucer on the small table next to him. 'Why don't you sit down and tell me what happened?'

Florence took a moment to try and calm herself, before doing as he had asked.

'You seem a little cross. Was Mrs Blythe rude to you?' he asked, reaching out to take her hand.

'Not at all. I have to admit, though, that I am angry,' she said, enjoying the comfort of his warm hand in hers. 'Seeing where Nellie lives, and how much of a struggle it is for her to cope, made me think not only about her but about the other women who work for us.' She shared the thoughts that she had been having on her way home.

Jesse listened silently and, when Florence had finished

speaking, said, 'And you want to find a way to help them, I assume?'

'Yes, I do.' She couldn't understand why he needed to ask. 'Wouldn't you?'

'Yes. But don't you think we already have more than enough charitable projects to focus on? When would we fit in more?'

She had no idea, but that didn't mean she was going to give up on wanting to help these women without even trying.

'Florence, I want you to promise me that you'll not do anything rash?'

'Like what?' she asked, irritated with him for not being as upset as she was about the issue.

'You have a family of your own, and –' he raised his eyebrows as if to make a point of his next few words '– work longer hours than many of these women. You cannot take on every cause that concerns you. To do so would make you ill.' He lowered his voice. 'Your first priority is to focus on the responsibilities you already have, Florence. If you then feel you have the time and energy to take on this battle, do it. To be honest, though, I don't see what there is that you can do to make a difference. Isn't it about changing society's attitudes to women? That is an issue too enormous even for you to solve, don't you think?'

'Maybe,' she said. But she was determined to find a way to make a difference. Surely there was something she could do? Even if she made small differences to some of these women's lives they would know that they weren't alone and that someone did care about them and all that they struggled to face each day.

She looked at Jesse and could see that his concern was for her. She was glad to have someone who cared so much for her welfare. She didn't like to worry him unnecessarily, so decided that until she came up with a way to help these women she would keep her thoughts on the matter to herself.

Chapter 15

January 1894

The post-Christmas sales were going exceedingly well throughout all the Boots stores, Florence was pleased to discover. Surely now Jesse would take things a little easier, if only while he struggled to shift the cold that had plagued him since the start of the new year.

Florence was at the top of the stairs on her way to her office when she heard a female voice.

'Good morning, Mrs Boot.' It was a voice she recognised, but initially failed to place, that called out to her. Florence turned to see a pink-cheeked face grinning up at her from under a rather elaborate hat.

'Lily Buttons?' she asked, shaking her head in disbelief, stunned to come face to face with someone from Jersey. 'Whatever brings you to Nottingham, and especially at such a cold time of year?'

'I've been saving up to come and stay here,' Lily replied.

Florence looked at the young woman in front of her. Gone was the underfed girl she and her sister Amy had pleaded with their father to employ and here was an immaculate, poised woman. She could not have been prouder of her young friend.

'You're looking very smart. You're no longer the young girl I first met.'

Lily laughed. 'I was thinking a similar thing about you. I almost didn't recognise you,' Lily said, her voice quieter than before. 'You're so . . .'

Florence laughed. 'Old?' she suggested, amused by the surprise on Lily's face.

Lily giggled. 'Not at all. I was going to say posh, but I suppose grand is more what I meant.'

'That sounds pretty old to me.' Florence couldn't help teasing Lily and was repaid with a wide smile. It was a joy to see someone from her hometown here in the shop. 'My father has given you time off work from Rowe's Stationers, I see.' A thought occurred to her. 'Or have you left there since your last letter?'

Florence studied the young woman in front of her. Lily had changed so much in the years since Florence and her sister Amy had rescued her from her brutal father. Even Jesse had become involved in protecting Lily that day she had come into the shop to hide from him.

'I've given in my notice,' Lily announced. 'I thought I'd come to the mainland to see if I can find work here.'

Florence could not imagine that her father and sister would be very happy at losing such a hard-working shop assistant.

Lily must have noticed the shock on Florence's face. 'It's fine,' she said reassuring her. 'They were happy for me to come over here and try my luck. In fact, Mrs Rowe, well, your mother,' she added awkwardly, 'expressed an interest in helping out at the shop on occasion. I didn't want your father to struggle to find enough work for me, to justify my wage. I'd also been thinking about travelling to Nottingham for some time. It sounds like such an exciting place in your letters and I've been wanting to see your smart shop ever since you wrote and told me some of the plans that you and Mr Boot had for it.'

Florence was delighted Lily was trying to make something of herself. 'I'm very pleased for you,' she said honestly. Florence glanced around her quickly. Everything seemed to be in perfect order and nothing appeared to require her immediate attention. 'Do you have time to come with me to my office? We can have some tea and biscuits and catch up with what's been happening in St Helier.'

Lily smiled at the mention of tea and biscuits. 'Yes, I'd love that. Do you remember how you were so kind to feed me tea and biscuits when I first began working at Rowe's? I was such a skinny little thing back then.' Lily seemed to stand up straighter, as if to add substance to her words.

Florence couldn't help thinking about Gladys from the factory and how little gestures could make all the difference to someone's life. She felt proud of her part in Lily's break from her troubled past. If she had achieved nothing else in her life, knowing that she had been instrumental in Lily finding work, learning to read, and gaining the confidence to become the elegant young woman she now was would be very satisfying. Like her, Lily had worked hard to overcome obstacles and become the independent woman she was now.

'Please, come this way. Mr Boot might even have time for a quick chat. He usually pops into my office to catch up with me around this time each day.'

Florence walked slowly next to Lily, allowing her time to take in the different objects on display. Lily stopped every so often to admire something – a picture frame, or glass paperweight.

'They're beautiful, aren't they?' Florence said. 'Those paperweights are from Scotland. I particularly like them. Jesse has a blue one on his desk in his office at home.

'How wonderful to spend your day among such beautiful items.' Lily stroked her gloved hand lightly across the crystal object. 'One day I'd like a house decorated with beautiful things like these.'

'There's no reason why you can't make that happen, Lily,' Florence reassured her. 'You're clever and have always been dedicated to your work.'

As they walked to her office, Florence thought about their backgrounds and how different they were. She had never had cause to fear her father, or dread returning home, unlike Lily. Lily's drunken father had spent much of her childhood either in a public house, brawling, or locked up in jail, leaving Lily, the eldest of several siblings, to find a way to help support her mother.

Florence liked Lily very much, but most of all she admired the girl's strength of character. She had watched Lily rise up from her difficult start in life, having had barely any education, and couldn't help feeling a touch of pride at her part in helping Lily to become the self-contained woman walking next to her. *Look at Lily now*, Florence mused. Seeing her young friend, so changed from the neglected girl she had once been, reminded Florence of the difference she had also made to Nellie's life. She had the power to change women's lives just by giving them a helping hand. The thought made her even more determined to do the same for others.

They entered Florence's neat office. She sensed Lily taking time to study the warm, homely room where Florence spent so much of her working day.

'The children aren't here yet, unfortunately. They're being brought in to see me for an hour later. It's a shame that you've missed them; I would have loved you to have met them today.'

'That's a shame,' Lily said staring at the cot at the back of the room. 'I was hoping to see them.'

'We'll have to make sure that you do then. Please, take a seat,' Florence said, waiting for Lily to do so before sitting herself. 'Would you like some tea now?'

Lily shook her head. 'No, thank you.' She smoothed down her skirt. 'I suppose you'll be wanting to know why I'm here.'

Florence had assumed Lily was visiting the store to let her know she was in Nottingham and say hello. She frowned, concerned. 'There's nothing wrong, is there? And, of course, you must tell me if there's anything I can do for you while you're here.'

'I hear all about the grand Boots stores when your father speaks about expansions and how clever Mr Boot is with his knack of placing advertisements,' Lily explained. 'And, naturally, I learn more when you write and tell me about your trips to Europe buying stock, and how each of the children are doing.' Lily's gaze fell on Florence's tidy leather-topped desk, before she looked around the room. 'This is a lovely office.' She pointed to the silver-framed photograph on Florence's desk. 'Is that John, Dorothy, and baby Margery?'

Florence turned the frame slightly towards her. 'It is,' she said unable to help smiling at their cherubic faces looking so angelic for once. She worried that Jesse favoured the girls, but kept her concerns to herself as she waited while Lily struggled to continue to answer why she was visiting the shop.

Lily took a deep breath. 'I want to make something of myself, Florence. I've saved to come here in the hope that you might have a vacancy somewhere and be able to offer me a position in this store.' Lily hesitated. 'Do you think that's at all possible?'

Florence didn't ask why she hadn't thought to write to her in the first instance, if this was what she wanted. Lily knew her address, after all, and it might have saved her a journey. Then again, Florence thought, smiling, she was delighted to see her friend.

As if Lily had heard her thoughts, she added. 'I have to admit I was worried that if I wrote you might not see my letter.'

Her words perplexed Florence. 'Why on earth would you think such a thing?'

Lily clasped her hands together and rested them on her lap. Florence could see her knees shaking slightly and it dawned on her how difficult this was for her younger friend. 'Well, I thought that if your, um, assistant, opened your mail, maybe she'd think I had a cheek approaching you for work.

She might believe I was taking advantage of our friendship and not pass it on to you. You must have many people wanting to work in a smart place like this?'

They did, but none of them were Lily, Florence thought, smiling. Wanting to put her at ease, she said, 'I'm glad you made the journey to see me, Lily. Firstly, it's a wonderful surprise to see you here so unexpectedly. As far as work, I'd be happy to look into vacancies and see what I can do for you.'

Lily visibly relaxed. 'Oh, thank you, very much. That's incredibly kind of you, Florence.'

'How long are you staying in the area?' Florence asked, picking up her fountain pen. 'If you can give me an address, I'll contact you in the next day or so and arrange for us to meet again. We can go through whatever's available that I think might suit you.'

Lily beamed and stood up. 'Thank you ever so much.' She unclasped the top of her small leather bag and reached inside. Pulling out a slip of paper she handed it to Florence. 'I've written down my address.' She blushed slightly. 'Just in case you asked for it.'

'Are you certain you don't want some tea and biscuits before you go?' Florence didn't like to think of Lily going back out into the cold without having a warm drink and something to eat.

'No, thank you. I don't wish to take up any more of your precious time. You've been very generous seeing me for this long as it is.' Lily gave Florence a wide smile. 'I was ever so nervous about coming here today.'

'Why? You know me well enough!'

Lily seemed to consider her words before speaking. 'I knew you before you were married, when you were Miss Rowe and before you were Mrs Boot. A lot has changed since then.'

'We've kept in touch though. The only thing that's changed between us, Lily,' Florence said, walking around her desk to take Lily's gloved hands in hers, 'is that you and I are eight years older. And, I must say, those years have served you well.'

'Thank you, Flo— er, Mrs Boot.'

'Please, call me Florence when we're in private. If I find you a position here, which I can assure you I will do, then you'll need to address me like the other staff, as Mrs Boot. Now, though, we are simply Lily and Florence.' She pulled Lily into a brief hug. Letting her go, Florence stood back. 'It truly has been a joy to see you again.'

'Thank you,' Lily hesitated. 'Florence.'

They laughed as Florence walked Lily to the office door. 'Are you sure you don't want to wait and see Mr Boot?'

'Not today,' she insisted, looking, Florence thought, rather terrified at the prospect of meeting Jesse again. 'I'm sure he's far too busy to be making small talk with me.'

Florence went to argue, then, aware of Lily's unease, opened the door and held it back for her friend to exit.

'I really appreciate this, Mrs Boot,' Lily said as Miss Tweed walked up to the door looking surprised to see someone coming out whom she hadn't shown into Florence's office.

'Bye, Miss Buttons,' Florence said, happy to have spent time with her old friend. She determined to do what she could to help her in whatever way she needed.

Florence waved Miss Tweed into her office. 'I'd like to know the vacancies we have in the store for senior shop assistants.' Lily had been taught by her and her sister Amy, and if Lily's work satisfied her own father enough for him to keep her on for all these years, then that was good enough for Florence. She trusted Lily implicitly and wasn't going to miss out on employing someone as personable and hard-working as her. Lily would soon find a position in any of the various outlets competing with Boots if she didn't find something for her at Pelham Street.

'I'll add it to my list of things for tomorrow morning,' Miss Tweed said, making a note on the pad in her hand.

'No, I'd like it done today, please. Put aside anything on today's list and make this a priority.'

Miss Tweed raised her eyebrows almost imperceptibly. Most people probably wouldn't have noticed, but Florence knew her well enough to see that for once Miss Tweed's professional exterior had been breached. She gave a single nod and left to do as Florence had asked.

Florence studied the piece of paper Lily had given her with her temporary address written in her neat rounded hand. She didn't know the boarding house where Lily had booked in to stay, but recognised the name of Pepper Street and didn't think it was too far for Lily to walk.

She and Jesse now had thirty-three shops to run and having someone as dependable as Lily Buttons working for them would be a great asset. She was honest and hard-working, and Florence wanted to help her find a foothold in Nottingham.

Florence was certain Lily could be happy there, too. She

might only have lived until now on a small island, but Florence knew that it was a fascinating experience to start somewhere new.

Florence stared at the photo of Jesse and her children on her desk. John, Dorothy, and Margery would never know the deprivation or cruelty that Lily had been accustomed to for most of her life, and she was grateful for that. Lily would make a perfect manageress for one of the departments and that was the role Florence hoped to offer her in a letter later that day.

She felt honoured to be in a position to help out her old friend and, she thought, it was going to be exciting to be able to share memories of Jersey with someone else who had grown up there.

PART TWO

PART TWO

Chapter 16

March 1901

Florence stared at the date on the newspaper. 'I still can't believe it's the twentieth century.'

'It has been for the past fifteen months, my sweet.' Jesse took a sip of his tea and gazed at her over the rim of his cup, the skin at the corners of his eyes crinkling in amusement.

Their lives were good and she felt certain they all had much to look forward to, but whatever Jesse said, it still felt strange to her. The old Queen Victoria had died two months before and Florence wasn't sure if she was prepared for all the changes that seemed to be happening. They had over two hundred and fifty Boots stores now, and the year before, Jesse had bought a chain of sixty chemist branches from one of his competitors. She had expected him to slow down a bit now that he was in his fifties. She should have known better.

She was grateful that her children were settled, for the most part, although Florence had begun to notice how much more sternly Jesse was now acting towards John compared to the way he was with the girls. She thought back to an incident the evening before when Jesse had arrived home and found John and Florence reading quietly in the conservatory.

'You should be out with your friends somewhere,' he had said, 'not sitting inside with your mother reading.'

Florence had noticed her son's hurt expression. 'He's doing nothing wrong, Jesse. Reading is a perfectly acceptable pastime.'

'When I was his age I was working, not lazing around doing nothing.' He waved for John to stand. 'Put that book away and go and find something to do outside. Invite one of your friends over to play tennis, get some fresh air, instead of sitting in here all day.'

Florence locked eyes with her son and smiled. 'Go on, darling. Do as your father asks.'

'Yes, Mother.' She watched her son leave the room, his shoulders stooped. He was upset at being told off and rightly so, she thought.

As soon as she was certain John was out of earshot, Florence turned on Jesse. 'That was uncalled for,' she snapped. 'He was doing nothing wrong.'

Jesse sat in the chair next to hers, a scowl on his face. What had brought this mood on? she wondered. The business was flourishing, as far as she was aware. And even if it wasn't, Florence thought, Jesse had no reason to take out his bad mood on John.

'Are you going to tell me why you were so mean to John just then?'

Jesse smoothed his moustache with his right thumb and forefinger before turning to her. 'I worry that he's not tough enough to take over from me one day.'

'He's twelve Jesse, not twenty. Anyway, you don't mind when the girls sit and read with me.'

'That's different.'

Florence felt anger building up inside her. 'And why is that, Jesse?' she asked, daring him to answer without thinking.

Jesse looked at her. 'You know what I mean.'

'No, I don't. You're always easier on the girls, and it's not fair on John. He idolises you and it hurts him deeply when you pick on him.'

'I don't. I can see you're looking for an argument,' Jesse grumbled, 'and I'm not going to give you one. If anything, you're the one who overprotects our son. Have you considered that?'

'Nonsense. I treat him the same as the girls.'

Jesse harrumphed. 'Then maybe you shouldn't. He needs to be tough if he's going to take over at Boots someday, not soft.'

Jesse's attitude towards John frustrated her. It was the main bone of contention between them and it bothered her to see that rather than resolving the issue, they seemed to be moving further apart in their feelings towards their son.

'John is a kind boy who likes to spend some of his time reading. You should be glad of that, especially as last week you were telling him off for not focusing on his studies enough.'

'Reading novels is not the same as him paying attention to his schoolbooks, and well you know it.'

'That's as may be,' Florence said, focusing on keeping her voice controlled before continuing. 'But reading novels hasn't done me any harm, or would you disagree with that?'

'No, I wouldn't.' He frowned at her. 'Do we have to row about John, again?'

'Yes, if I think it's necessary. As I've tried to explain to you before, John is only twelve. He's a child, and only one year older than Dorothy. Yet you don't pick on her. They both have plenty of time before having to decide what they want from their futures.'

Jesse opened his mouth to say something then seemed to think better of it. She suspected he had been about to argue that he was harsher with John because he was a boy. Florence stared at Jesse silently. She was glad that her husband knew better than to use that reason for any argument, especially with her.

'Maybe,' she continued, 'John won't want to work for Boots. Have you thought of that? Maybe one of the girls will be better at running the business.' Florence knew she was testing Jesse's patience now, but couldn't help herself. If he believed she was capable of working to the level she had proven herself able to do, then why not one of her daughters?

Jesse shook his head and smiled at her. 'I know what you're getting at, and I won't discuss it, Florence.'

She didn't blame him. Jesse knew her well enough to know when she would stand back and let him bellow and rant, and when, at times, she was not in the mood to allow him that freedom. John's happiness meant too much to her to keep quiet. She had said her piece now, though, and hoped Jesse had taken her words to heart.

'Please think before snapping at John, Jesse. It distresses him, and it upsets me.'

Jesse considered her words silently. Then, reaching out, he took her right hand in his left one and kissed the back of it.

'I don't like to think that I upset him, or you. I'll try to do as you ask in future.'

Florence was surprised to hear Jesse give in to her request so easily. She studied him. He had been thoughtful for the past few days. Despite him insisting that nothing was wrong when she had probed him about his mood the previous evening, Florence suspected that he did have something on his mind that he was keeping from her.

She rang for tea and picked up her book to continue reading while they waited for Violet to bring the tea tray and set everything out on the table. When Violet had left them alone, Florence closed her book.

'Jesse,' she said, softly, 'I know there's something worrying you.' He didn't react, so she tried once more. 'Please tell me what it is before I start imagining all sorts of horrible scenarios.'

'It's nothing, truly. Now, please stop fretting. You worry too much about me, and about John and the girls. We're all perfectly fine. Why don't you come for a walk with me out to the rose garden after we've finished our tea?'

Florence hated to think of herself as a fretful mother. She found it difficult enough dealing with her own mother when she took it upon herself to start trying to dictate how Florence should bring up her children, or deal with her working life.

'Good idea,' she said, giving him a smile and pouring them each a cup of tea. She decided to let the quarrel go. For now.

* * *

The following morning at breakfast, Florence gave the children permission to leave the table and waited patiently while Jesse finished the last mouthful of his buttered toast. He sat back in his chair, staring at her thoughtfully for a moment. Florence noticed that Jesse's forehead was shining.

He saw her watching him and, taking his handkerchief from his pocket, wiped his forehead. 'I'm fine, before you ask,' he said, pushing the material back into his trouser pocket. 'It's a warm morning, nothing more.'

Florence didn't agree. It was warmer than usual at this time of year and the spring morning sunshine poured into the dining room, but it wasn't hot enough to cause Jesse to perspire like this.

'Are you quite well?' she asked, going to stand and check him for herself.

He waved for her to remain seated. 'Yes, I'm fine. Don't fret, Florence.'

'Well, something is amiss and if it's not your health, then what is it? Tell me,' she insisted, trying but unable to read his expression. She knew Jesse extremely well and could usually gauge his thoughts, but this morning all she could fathom was that there was something bothering him that he knew she wouldn't like. 'Jesse.'

He sighed and after a brief pause said, 'I think John should be sent to boarding school.'

The air around her stilled. Had she heard right? Florence stared at him silently, shocked to hear her husband suggest she send her boy away. She could tell by the steely glint in his eyes that he was determined to follow this through.

Panic coursed through her and her breathing quickened.

'What? You can't be serious,' she said, aware that he was. By the way he was clenching his jaw, she could tell that he was ready to quarrel with her over this idea of his.

Jesse raised his hand to stop her saying anything further. 'I've found the perfect place.'

'No! I won't have it, Jesse. I simply won't.'

As if she hadn't spoken, Jesse added, 'The school is in Cambridge.'

'Cambridge?' Her mouth dropped open in horror. 'Cambridge is miles away. Jesse, he's only twelve. He can't possibly be sent away. He's not ready for it.'

Jesse's face relaxed. 'Ah, so you do agree that he should go at some point. Then why not go now?'

Florence covered her face with her hands. She wanted to scream. She had just played into Jesse's hands. She lowered her hands and glared at him. She might have started this conversation on the back foot but Florence had no intention of giving in to Jesse's suggestion simply because he believed that he knew better for their son.

Jesse reached out to take Florence's hand, but she snatched it back, placing both her hands on her lap.

'Dearest, let me explain,' he said quietly. 'I was working long hours with my mother when I was younger than John is now. Our son needs the best education we can find for him, and I believe that the school I've found will be perfect for him.'

Florence forced herself to calm down. Her mouth was dry and she took a sip from her teacup. She wasn't going to get anywhere with Jesse if she argued with him; she needed to be far cleverer than that. She took a deep breath. 'Tell me about this school then.'

Jesse's expression softened. 'It's called The Leys School. It's primarily for boys from Methodist families, so John will be with likeminded boys.'

'We've never visited the place, nor do we know anyone who's attended the school,' she said, hoping to find ways to change his mind. 'How could we possibly know whether it will suit John?' She lowered her voice so that no one outside the room could overhear what she was about to say. 'We both know that John isn't the most academically minded child. I would hate for him to be forced into a situation where he'll be unhappy.'

'I see your point, of course I do,' Jesse said, giving Florence a little confidence that maybe he was willing to listen to her. 'However, I can tell you that this is the most marvellous school because I've been to the place.' Florence gasped in shock that he could do such a thing behind her back, but it seemed that Jesse was too focused on his clever planning to notice. Florence listened as he continued with enthusiasm. 'I've met the headmaster and a couple of the pupils and I know that if John gives the place a chance, he'll be very happy there.'

Florence clenched her fists. Her whole body tensed as she struggled to contain her fury. 'You visited the school? When? You never told me.' How could he be so underhand? Her heart pounded as she tried to contain her rising temper.

Jesse frowned. 'It was last month, when I went out inspecting some of the southern stores.' His eyes lowered. He slowly pushed the silver butter dish back from his place setting.

'I know I should have told you, but,' he said, looking back at her again, 'I expected you to react like this.'

'Good, then you know me a little better than I was beginning to think you might,' she snapped, disliking Jesse for the first time in her life.

'Florence, I thought it made sense for me to see if it was the right place for John to attend before speaking to you about it. I didn't want to upset you if it wasn't necessary.'

'Then you don't know me nearly as well as you think, Jesse.' She hated that he had done this thing behind her back. 'How many other things have you done that I don't know about?' She knew she was being nasty, but Jesse had hurt her and at that moment she wanted to hurt him back.

Nothing meant more to her than her children and their welfare. Jesse had never made any big decisions about the children without first bringing the suggestion to her. He had always been satisfied to leave the children's upbringing to her and for him to remove that responsibility from her so suddenly and about something this important devastated her.

'I don't see why you've done this, and to do it in such a clandestine way is not like you at all. At least I thought it wasn't.' She realised she was on the point of tears, but swallowed her upset and focused on making him listen to her point of view.

'I didn't intend for you to be so upset by this,' Jesse said, his voice soft and, Florence thought, almost apologetic. 'If I didn't like the place then I would have said nothing and saved all this upset from happening.'

'But you do like the place,' she sneered.

Jesse nodded. 'I do. Florence, it's a brilliant school and the buildings and surrounding area are exceptional. I truly believe it'll be the making of John.'

She closed her eyes, unable to speak for a moment. 'Jesse, I always insisted on taking my children to work with me when they were smaller because I was determined to continue working, but I also wanted to be certain that I never became a distant mother,' she explained, her voice controlled to try and keep her passion out of it. 'I've always kept my children close. I don't see the point of having children if you farm them out to other people. To do so doesn't make any sense – not to me, at least.'

Jesse rubbed his eyes and groaned. Florence could see he was as frustrated at their impasse as she was. 'You were sent to board at a convent in Brittany,' he argued. 'You told me you were happy there, Florence.'

She had been . . . eventually. 'Not at first I wasn't. I would have much rather attended a local school on the island and returned home to my parents' flat each night to eat with them and spend time with my family. I missed my mother and father when I was away from them.'

Jesse pushed his seat back from the table. Florence could see he was trying to keep a tight rein on his temper. Jesse was used to her standing up to him, but she always chose her battles and usually managed to entice him to change his mind in some clever way.

Florence took a deep breath. If she was going to stand her ground on this matter, she would need to be able to speak, and right now the tears she was battling to hold back were restricting her ability to do so. She swallowed the lump in her throat. This time, Florence was too hurt to hold back from this face-to-face argument. John was her son and she was not going to have her feelings swept aside as if they didn't matter. She realised Jesse was speaking.

'And did it do you any harm to be sent away to school?'

It hadn't, but that wasn't the point as far as she was concerned. 'That was my parents' choice. Now I'm a parent and I will make the choices for my children that I see fit.'

Jesse stood up and threw his napkin down onto the table. He had clearly had enough of this argument. His face was puce with irritation and Florence knew it was because he hadn't got his own way. She also suspected that he realised he had overstepped the mark and was feeling a little guilty. She didn't care.

'Yes, Florence, but what you seem to be forgetting is that I am also John's parent. As his father, I believe it will do him good to be sent away to boarding school, so he will be sent.' Florence opened her mouth to object angrily but before she managed to, Jesse added, 'He needs toughening up, rather than spending so much time with his younger sisters.'

'So, as far as you're concerned the decision to send John to boarding school is a *fait accompli*?' She dared him to agree.

He stared at her for a few seconds. 'I don't have time to continue with this row.' Jesse pulled his watch from his waist-coat pocket. 'We need to leave in five minutes. I will not be late arriving at the store. I presume you are still accompanying me to work?'

As much as she would have liked to tell him that he could go in by himself, she had several meetings in her diary that she needed to attend. 'I'll be ready, but, Jesse, as far as I'm concerned nothing has been decided and this matter isn't finished with yet.'

'It is, as far as I'm concerned,' Jesse snapped, marching out of the dining room.

* * *

Later that morning, Florence stood next to Jesse as they surveyed their Boots Booklovers' Lending Library with its cosy feel and polished mahogany counters. She could barely look at him, and had managed to stay away from him since their arrival at the shop – until now. Florence had tried to keep her mind focused on her work and not dwell on their disagreement, grateful for the two meetings she had already taken part in with suppliers. She was still fuming from their quarrel earlier that day, but had no intention of letting any of the staff or customers know that they were hardly speaking to each other.

'I'm not certain how we've progressed from supplying cut-price medicine to lending books to people,' Jesse grumbled.

Florence wasn't surprised he was still angry with her. He liked his home life to be calm and hated it when they were at odds about anything. This was his doing, though, she reasoned, and she had no intention of deferring to him when it came to her son's education.

Jesse straightened a vase on the small table nearest to them. She could see he was acting awkwardly, but wasn't sure why. 'This has been a dream of yours for a while now,' Jesse said, his voice gentle. 'I trust you when you insist that having this department in our store will bring in more customers.'

Ah, so that was it, Florence realised. Jesse was trying to appease her by focusing on the lending library. She scowled at him. If he thought anything he had to say would soothe her hurt, then he was sorely mistaken.

Then it occurred to her that although he was trying to please her by saying how he believed her idea would work, he was also speaking loudly and letting those nearby know that this wasn't a department that he had initially believed in.

Another put-down. That's two in one day, she though angrily. She didn't want anyone to hear Jesse's doubts about this new feature in the store. They couldn't expect customers to tell their friends to come and borrow books if the owner had little confidence in the library.

'Keep your voice down, Jesse,' she hissed.

He seemed confused for a moment, then it must have dawned on him why she didn't want him speaking so loudly. 'I just meant that it's taking me a little longer to become used to this idea than it seems to have taken other people.' He took his handkerchief from his trouser pocket and wiped his forehead once again.

Florence watched him push the damp, crumpled material back into his pocket. No sooner had he wiped his forehead than the sheen reappeared. When he had told her he was fine over breakfast, she had put his flushed skin down to his annoyance with her, but this was something else. A niggling concern seeped into her mind. He really didn't look very well. Had she been so angry with him that she had failed to notice he was going down with some illness? she wondered guiltily.

Florence resisted the compulsion to rest her hand against his brow, reasoning that it would embarrass him and bring it to everyone's attention that he was unwell. She didn't need to feel his forehead to know that he was ill.

'Jesse, are you all right?' she whispered, putting her anger about his earlier actions aside.

'Stop fussing. I'm fine.'

She knew by his denial that he had no intention of discussing the matter further. Maybe he was simply suffering from a head cold. She hoped so. Jesse hated being ill and mostly brushed aside any concerns she ever had. Florence understood how difficult it must have been for him to become used to the subtle changes in his health, but wished he'd be more open with her when he wasn't feeling very well.

She caught him glaring at her. 'Maybe they have a need for these books that you don't have,' she explained, returning to the safer subject of their lending libraries. 'You and I are lucky enough to have access to any books we choose to read. Making this lending library available for everyone willing to come to the store only encourages people who might not be able to afford to buy new books. We want to encourage reading and literacy as a whole, surely,' she said, becoming more impassioned. 'I want to make people aware that reading is available for everyone, not just the privileged few.'

Jesse thought for a moment. 'I understand that, but it is an odd department to have at the back of a store.'

They had argued several times over this issue and Jesse had only given in to her insistence after she had promised that if this plan of hers didn't work at the Pelham Street store, then she would not challenge him further with any of the other stores.

Florence disagreed. 'I rather think it's the perfect place for it to be. Readers coming to select a book might see other items as they pass counters on their way through to here. It's a good way for them to discover things that they hadn't even realised they wanted or needed. You mark my words, it's going to be a huge success.'

Florence hoped she was right. It had taken a lot of persuasion to finally get Jesse to agree to progress from the revolving bookcase she had insisted on installing at their Goose Gate store to this splendid lending library. Florence recalled how books had always sold well at W H Rowe's Stationers when she worked for her father, so there was no reason why people wouldn't take this new project to their hearts. She had every intention of spreading the word to as many people as possible about this new service Boots was offering their customers.

Aware she needed to make a further point to Jesse, she left his side to go and speak to an assistant who had just finished serving a customer. 'How is everything going?'

'Very well, Mrs Boot,' the young woman answered, picking up three books from the counter that needed to be returned to the shelves. 'We had quite a rush on first thing, but it's a little quieter now. Probably because people have gone back to work after their lunch break.'

Florence thanked her and went back to Jesse. He didn't look at her, or speak, just turned and walked away. Confused, Florence followed him. He seemed to falter by one of the displays nearer the front of the store. She watched him anxiously. He was behaving very strangely and it troubled her. Jesse seemed to be staring silently at some ornaments. They weren't the usual kind of thing he focused on but he seemed thoughtful, so she waited in the background to see what he would do next.

Jesse turned his head to her and opened his mouth, but instead of speaking, his face paled and he reached out to clutch at the edge of the counter. Florence gasped as Jesse's eyes rolled back in his head and he crashed heavily to the floor.

'Jesse?' Florence raced to his side and fell to her knees, terrified that he might have died. She felt for a pulse in his neck, her hands trembling. Sighing with relief, she closed her eyes when the tips of her fingers found one.

Why hadn't she persisted with him earlier when she'd noticed he wasn't himself? Instead of taking care of her husband she had fought with him about John's schooling. She would never forgive herself if their last morning together had been spent at odds with each other. Florence bit her lip to keep focused. This wasn't the time for panic or tears. Jesse needed her help. She unfastened his jacket, waistcoat, and the top button of his starched collar to help him breathe more easily. Then, withdrawing her handkerchief from her skirt pocket, she dabbed it lightly on his forehead.

'It's all right, Jesse,' she soothed. 'You're going to be fine. I'm here and I'm not going to leave you.' She felt his hand twitch next to her knee and had to clear her throat so she wouldn't give in to her tears.

Florence heard footsteps running nearby. 'Quick, call for an ambulance,' she commanded the nearest shop assistant. The girl ran off and others stood waiting for Florence to give them orders. 'Bring me a blanket for Mr Boot and some cold water.' Florence struggled to remain in control of her emotions. 'Send for Doctor Mason. Albert on the door knows his address. Hurry. Tell him that Mr Boot has collapsed and is unconscious. As soon as the ambulance arrives, we'll take him to the Nottingham General Hospital, the new Jubilee Wing,' she added as the new extension that had only just opened came to her mind.

Lily ran over to join her, crouching down on the other side of Jesse. 'Florence, oh heavens. Tell me, how can I help?'

Florence realised that customers were standing around and watching. The last thing Jesse would want now was an audience. 'Remove these people as quietly and as quickly as you can, please, Lily. See that this area is cordoned off so we have some privacy until the ambulance arrives and Jesse's been taken to the hospital.'

'Right away.' Lily immediately turned and began moving customers and shop assistants away from the area. 'Please move back,' she heard Lily demand, her voice slightly shaky but brooking no argument. 'There's nothing for anyone to see here.'

Florence was grateful for her friend's thoughtfulness and turned her attention back to Jesse. Where was that ambulance? she wondered, aware that it had only just been called for.

'You're doing well, Jesse,' she assured him, unsure if he could hear her, but knowing that if he could, he might be calmed by the sound of her voice. 'The ambulance will be here shortly and you'll soon be more comfortable in bed.'

She took a deep breath to fight against the panic threatening to overwhelm her and rested the palm of her right hand against Jesse's clammy cheek. His skin was grey. Florence was terrified that if medical help didn't come soon she might lose him. She couldn't let that happen, especially not now. Not when they had been so deeply embroiled in the worst family disagreement they'd ever had. Why had he chosen that morning to tell her about his plans for John's schooling? Regret squeezed at her heart. For all these years most of their conversations with each other had been happy, love-filled words. Why had they quarrelled today of all days?

Florence had always known that there was a possibility that Jesse would go before her. It was something she had pushed from her mind since their marriage. Since Jesse's physical breakdown just before they had met, his health had held up. She couldn't bear his body to let him down now, fifteen years later. The fear that this time Jesse might not have the physical strength to fight back terrified her.

'You're going to be fine, Jesse,' she whispered. 'I just know it.'

'The ambulance is here, Mrs Boot,' Albert said quietly, arriving at her side with two men and a stretcher. Florence went light-headed with relief.

Lily rushed over to her. 'Florence,' she said forgetting their agreed formality when at work. 'If there is anything at all you need from me, please let me know.'

Florence gazed blankly at her dear friend's face, comforted to have her nearby. 'Thank you, Lily. I'll call on you if I need to.'

She clutched Jesse's hand, as the ambulance men placed him gently onto the stretcher. They covered him with a blanket and lifted him. Florence reluctantly let go and stepped back, giving them space to pass. Seeing them carrying Jesse away was too much to bear. Florence struggled to contain herself, holding the damp handkerchief over her mouth to stifle her cries.

Lily must have noticed. 'He's strong,' she reassured Florence quietly. 'Keep your faith, Florence. Jesse will fight this with all his might. I know he can do it.'

Florence wasn't sure how much strength he still possessed. At least Jesse would have a decent chance being treated in the new wing of the hospital, she thought, trying to remain positive. She and Jesse had read about all the place in the newspapers recently with its latest equipment and electric lighting. She knew that Jesse would receive the best medical care in Nottingham; she just prayed that it would be enough to save his life.

Chapter 17

April 1901

Nottingham Hospital

Lily had insisted on accompanying Florence to the hospital. It was comforting to have her friend by her side. Now, as they waited in an area assigned for family members, she breathed in the smell of disinfectant that filled the room and waited for the doctors let her know how Jesse was getting on. She wished she was somewhere private and able to give in to her tears, but knew that she would have to do her best to hold on to her emotions until she was back at St Heliers House.

Lily took Florence's shaking hands in her own. 'Would you like me to fetch you a cup of tea, or some water perhaps?'

'Th-thank you, no. I don't think I'd be able to swallow anything.' She glanced up at the clock on the wall. 'Why do you think they're taking so long? We've been here almost an hour and I still don't know how Jesse is.'

'I know,' Lily said. 'I'm certain they'll come and speak to you soon.' After a moment's silence, Lily added. 'Has anyone sent a message to St Heliers House to let the servants know you won't be back for the children for a while, or would you like me to ask someone to let them know?'

Florence had been so focused on willing Jesse to stay alive that she hadn't given any thought to anything or anyone else. 'The children,' she whispered guiltily, unsure what to do. She didn't want to worry them unnecessarily, but they would work out that something was amiss if both their parents didn't arrive home when they had been expecting them to.

'I can take a carriage to the house and let Meadows and Harriet know what's happened and they can tell your cook to go ahead and feed the children, maybe?' Lily asked quietly.

Relieved that her friend was thinking clearly when she obviously was unable to, Florence nodded. 'Yes, please. I think it'll be less frightening for everyone if you're the one to go and tell Meadows and Harriet. They're sensible and will know what's best to say to the children.'

'Fine, I'll go immediately,' Lily said, letting go of Florence's hands and standing. 'Shall I come straight back here, or would you rather I ask someone else to come and sit with you?'

Florence thought of her friends and it dawned on her that the only person other than Lily whom she would choose to be going through something this terrifying with her was her sister Amy. Unfortunately, Amy was in Jersey and she needed someone nearby.

'No, I'd rather you came back to sit with me. If you don't mind, that is?' She took in her friend's furrowed brow and tear-filled eyes and hated to think that she might be forcing Lily to spend time sitting in the hospital, a place that so many people were frightened to enter for fear they might never leave. Or was that only people who were admitted? she mused, aware that her mind was beginning to ramble in panic.

Florence took a deep breath to steady herself. 'Please don't feel that you have to return here though, Lily. I know how intimidating hospitals can be to some people.'

'Not to me, they're not,' Lily insisted. 'I'll leave right now and find a cab and be back as soon as possible. I shouldn't be too long.' She reached down and gave Florence's right hand a gentle pat. 'Try to stay calm. Jesse's tough and will do his best to fight whatever it is that's made him ill today.'

Without a further word, Lily ran off along the corridor and out through the doors. Florence watched her go, wishing her friend didn't have to leave her, but grateful to her for making sure that her senior household staff knew what had happened and could deal with the children's needs accordingly.

A man in a white coat walked in her direction and it took a moment for Florence to register that he was a doctor and was making his way to speak to her.

'Mrs Boot?' Florence nodded and went to stand. 'Please, no need to get up. I'm Doctor Jenkins and I've been looking at your husband. I'm afraid he's very poorly at the moment. We're not sure if he suffered a stroke, or if his collapse was due to something else entirely. I gather that he's previously had a physical breakdown, is that correct?'

She couldn't imagine how the doctor could know this and surmised that maybe Lily had given the information when they had first arrived and spoken to the sister who had greeted the ambulance.

'Yes, that's right. It was in '85, but although his health has slowly declined, he's been mostly well and rides each day, works long hours, that sort of thing.'

She couldn't make out whether the look the doctor was giving her was one of regret at what he was about to tell her, or sadness for Jesse's situation.

'He is going to live, isn't he?' she asked, unable to bear the thought of hearing the worst answer.

'We hope so. Everything is being done for your husband, Mrs Boot. We'll know more in the morning, hopefully, but I think the best thing you can do is go home and try to get as much rest as possible. I was told that someone was waiting with you.' He looked around as if expecting to see another person nearby.

'Yes, my friend was here with me, Miss Buttons. She's taken a cab back to my house to alert the servants, but she'll be back shortly.' Florence didn't want to leave without seeing Jesse and reassuring herself that he was still alive. 'May I see my husband before I leave?'

The doctor thought for a moment. 'Briefly. For a minute, two at the most. Come, I'll escort you myself.'

Florence went to stand, but her legs were so shaky that she immediately dropped back down in her seat. 'I'm sorry, I don't know what came over me.'

'Take your time. There's no rush.' He took her hands in his and helped her to stand. 'Do you think you can walk along the corridor to the end? He's in a room not too far after those double doors.'

Florence insisted that she could and together they walked

to the private room where Jesse lay, eyes still closed, on the hospital bed.

Florence went to his bedside and rested her hand on the right side of his face. 'Is he sleeping –' she cleared her throat '– or unconscious?'

'He's been given something to help him sleep.'

Florence stared at her darling husband, his pallor grey, and leant down to kiss his forehead. 'Don't leave me, Jesse,' she whispered before kissing him again and turning to leave the room.

'I'll take you back to wait for your friend,' the doctor said. 'If you come here at around ten in the morning, we should know more then.'

They walked through the double doors back to the public corridor and Florence was relieved to see Lily waiting for her.

'Thank you, Doctor Jenkins,' she said. 'My friend is here and will accompany me home. I'll see you in the morning, as you suggest.'

Now she just had to wait for Jesse to recover.

* * *

Florence was unable to sleep. By the time dawn appeared, she was thoroughly exhausted and relieved when Harriet thought to bring a cup of tea to her room, together with some buttered toast topped with local honey.

'Mrs Rudge insists that you drink this and eat the toast. She said you'll need something in your stomach to face the day.'

Florence had little appetite, but knew her cook was right

and forced herself to eat the breakfast. Jesse was the love of her life and she could barely cope with the notion that one day she might have to live without him next to her. He needed her to be strong. She wouldn't be able to support Jesse, or the children, if she became ill. She needed to look after herself and this was a start.

An hour later, Florence was washed and dressed and had spoken to each of her children to reassure them that as soon as she knew anything about their father's situation she would send word to them.

'Can we come and see Father?' John asked.

'No, I'm afraid not. He needs his rest. Maybe soon though. I'll have to wait for the doctor to give permission for you to visit.'

She left for the hospital, aware that if she wasn't allowed to stay then, rather than returning home, she would go on to the office and see to anything that needed her attention. There would be Jesse's rounds to be covered by one of his managers and also meetings of his that needed to be postponed.

Doctor Jenkins asked for Florence to be shown through to his office, where he told her the good news that Jesse's condition had improved slightly overnight.

'I've examined your husband this morning and spoken to him. We think he's suffered another physical breakdown.' Florence groaned; her pain at the thought of this happening to Jesse was physical. 'I suspect,' the doctor continued, 'that this might have been brought on by overwork and his system being weaker due to the slow decline in his health.'

'But you think he'll be all right?' she asked, willing the

doctor to reassure her that Jesse would be returning home with her at some point.

'I believe so. I'm afraid he'll have to spend time recuperating though, and probably for several months. It will mean a change to his usual work routine. First, though, we need to get him to that point. We have a way to go before thinking along those lines yet.'

She focused on the thought that Jesse would be home again soon. At least, he would if she had her way about it. Thankfully they could afford to hire a nurse, should he need it. It occurred to Florence that she would need to watch over Jesse when he was back with her at St Heliers. She didn't like to think how he would take to reducing his working hours. Jesse had never taken things easy. Even after his first breakdown when he had come to Jersey, he still took her out most days. She knew well enough that Jesse was hopeless at taking instruction from anyone else, even a doctor.

'My husband isn't very good at doing what he's told when it comes to slowing down,' she admitted.

The doctor rested his elbows on his desk and clasped his hands together. 'I'm afraid that if your husband doesn't follow my suggestions, his health will continue to decline but more rapidly than he's experienced so far. This collapse has been brought on by the strain he's put on his already weakened body. It can't be taken seriously enough.'

Florence promised to do her best to make sure Jesse did as he was told, but knew that it was going to be a battle. They still had to deal with their opposing thoughts on John's education. She pushed that issue aside. Now wasn't the time to focus on that particular problem. This was a matter of Jesse's life and she wasn't ready to allow him to damage his health further.

'May I visit my husband now, please?'

'Of course you can, Mrs Boot. I just wanted to let you know how things stood. You'll need to watch your husband when he's out of his doctor's sight.' He smiled. 'Don't worry, I know that there's only so much you'll be able to do to persuade him slow down, but if I or your personal physician can't be around, then you need to be the one to control his daily movements.'

The doctor walked her to Jesse's door. 'He's in here. I'll leave you to speak to him privately.'

Florence thanked him and entered Jesse's hospital room, barely able to breathe. She was nervous to see him, frightened that he might appear worse than he had the previous day at the store. Her eyes widened to find him propped up on several pillows. He looked sullen, which didn't surprise her, although he brightened when he noticed she was standing by the door.

'You're looking much better,' she said, relieved to note that his skin tone now had a pink tinge to it. She went to the side of his bed and bent over to kiss him. Then, taking a seat next to his bed, reached out and took his left hand in hers. 'You gave me a terrible fright yesterday, Jesse.'

'I know, my darling. I think I gave myself rather a shock, too.' He gave her a half smile. 'Has Doctor Jenkins spoken to you about me? I presume he has.'

'Yes. He said . . .'

Jesse closed his eyes for a moment, irritated, as she knew

196

he would be, by being told to slow down. 'I know what he'll have said. He told me the same thing, and I know you're going to be even more vigilant about me working than you were before. Aren't you?'

Florence inclined her head and smiled. 'What do you think?'

Jesse groaned. 'I thought as much. But I still have to continue working, Florence.'

She noted the determined tone in his voice. She knew that Jesse needed to work. He had never known anything else and to expect him to stop entirely was fruitless.

'I know. First, though, you must rest and get well. I'll spend time with you each day and then go to the office. I know the business well enough to see to anything that requires your attention.'

'You can bring it home to me.'

Florence didn't argue, not wishing to upset him. 'We'll take each item of work as it comes in and I can discuss what you want doing, if you like. Will that suit you?'

'Not really, but I have a feeling it's the most I can hope for.'

'You're right. Now, the first thing we need to work out is how we're going to make sure you get better.'

Chapter 18

June 1901

The two months since Doctor Jenkins had agreed to discharge Jesse to Florence's care had been easier for both of them. Jesse's mood lifted as soon as he was allowed to leave the hospital after Florence assured the doctor that she would take on a day nurse and a night nurse to oversee all Jesse's needs until such time as he was well again. The weeks had seen a mixture of moods. On occasion, Jesse had been happy recuperating at St Heliers, but he sometimes found it impossible to hide his frustration at not being allowed to work from his office over the Pelham Street store.

Now though, as Jesse started to feel better, he was becoming more irritated at still spending his days at home. Florence knew he was used to a lifetime of being busy and it wasn't natural for him to take things easy. It was becoming more strained between them as Florence tackled the tricky subject of him still having to wait until the doctor gave him permission to start back at work on a part-time basis. All she had to do was continue to persuade Jesse that taking things easy and allowing his body the time to recover were the quickest way for him to be allowed to return to work.

Despite his frustration, Florence refused to give in and insisted that he follow Doctor Jenkins's orders.

'This sitting around all day is infuriating,' Jesse shouted, his face puce from temper. 'If you don't want a madman living in this house then I'm going to have to return to work, and sooner rather than later.'

Florence hated seeing him restricted to the house; she had been working longer hours than usual to cover Jesse's work as well as her own. She longed to return to her usual working times and wished there was some way she could help speed up Jesse's recovery. But there wasn't. The doctor had given them his orders, repeatedly. 'Jesse, the doctor specifically said you were to have at least another month's rest at home.' It took all her effort to keep her voice level and not let her irritation with his constant demands show.

Jesse slammed his hand down on the table next to his chair. 'Then he's a fool.'

'We both know that's not the case.' Florence knew she was fighting a losing battle. Jesse was not a man to be held back from doing what he wanted. For now, though, she would do all she could to keep him resting at home, even if his temper was becoming intolerable. 'Look,' she said, spotting Lily walking up the driveway, a heavy bag in her hand. 'Here's Lily now bringing you some paperwork. Isn't that kind of her?'

'It is,' Jesse agreed grumpily.

'I'll bring it into you, so that you can work on it and I'll take tea with Lily in the conservatory.'

Florence had seen Lily a couple of times at the Pelham Street store and had invited her to the house to have tea with her and a catch-up.

'Miss Lily Buttons,' Meadows said moments later, announcing her arrival.

'Thank you, Meadows. Please arrange for tea to be served in the conservatory and bring some for Mr Boot in here. He has work to do.'

Florence stood and beamed at her friend. 'It's very good of you to come by today. Thank you.'

Lily walked over to Florence and gave her a hug.

Jesse waved at her and smiled. 'It's very good of you to bring this paperwork to the house for me. I appreciate you doing so.'

'It was my pleasure,' Lily said, taking the large leather bag over to where Jesse sat and placing it on the table in front of him. 'When Florence asked me to visit, I said yes immediately. I'd never turn down an invitation to tea at St Heliers,' she said with a laugh.

'Well, it's very kind of you anyway.' Jesse caught Florence's eye and grinned at her. 'I think my wife will be delighted that you've brought me something to stop me from bemoaning my situation for a few hours.'

'And you'd be right to think that, Jesse.' Florence sighed and shook her head. Now that he was happy once again, his charm shone through and she immediately forgot her annoyance with him. She linked arms with Lily. 'Come, let's go and take tea in the conservatory and leave Jesse here to lose himself in his work. It's the happiest I've seen him for the past few days.'

They left the room and walked down the hall to the conservatory. Once inside, Lily breathed in deeply.

Florence watched, amused. It was something Lily always did when she entered this room.

'I don't know if it's the sunshine pouring into this room, or the blissful scents of the . . .' Lily hesitated and then said, 'You said it's a Stephanotis Floribunda?'

'Yes, that's right,' Florence grinned, not surprised that Lily remembered the name. 'Also known as the Madagascar Jasmine. Isn't it heavenly?'

'I love the smell of this plant. It makes me feel like I'm on a tropical island.' Lily beamed. 'Not that I'd have any idea what that might smell like.'

Florence motioned for Lily to sit next to her at the rattan table. 'It was very good of you to bring all that paperwork for Jesse. It looked heavy. You should have told me and I'd have sent the car to collect you.'

'No need,' Lily said. 'I enjoyed the walk.' She unpinned her hat and, pushing the hat pin back into the straw crown, placed it on the spare chair next to her. 'I said I was happy to help you with anything you need.' She gazed at Florence thoughtfully. 'How is Jesse getting along? I thought I noticed a bit of tension between the two of you when I arrived. Is he doing as the doctor ordered and taking things easy, or is he finding it all very difficult?'

Florence rolled her eyes heavenward. 'He tries his best to do as little as possible, but you know Jesse. We've had various managers coming to the house to meet with him, or I'm delivering notes to them with instructions on what he wants doing at various stores. He always has to be in control and I'm sure it's because he's scared that everything will collapse if he doesn't keep an eye on it at all times.'

'I suppose it's only natural when you've spent so many years working hard to build up a business.'

Florence agreed, but still wished he would learn to trust people and allow them to prove they had enough experience to carry on without him, at least for short periods of time. She was about to answer Lily, but Meadows entered the room followed by Violet.

Violet placed her tray down on the side of the table and took from it the crockery, cutlery, napkins, and a cake stand with neat cucumber and egg sandwiches, several scones, slices of lemon cake, and little pots of cream and fresh strawberry jam. Then she picked up her tray and Meadows put the silver teapot, strainer, hot water pot, and milk jug in its place.

'Thank you both,' Florence said. 'Please tell Mrs Rudge that this all looks delicious.'

She waited for them to leave the room before continuing with what she had been about to say. 'You're right, Lily. I understand Jesse's concerns.' She went to pour the tea, but stopped. 'I don't know what I'd have done without you as a confidante these past few months. You're the only person who knew me before I married Jesse that I feel able to speak to openly. I couldn't speak to Amy, or my mother, because for some reason I worry that they might think Jesse and I are at odds.' She shrugged. 'Which of course we are, but not in a way that's detrimental to our marriage. You don't make judgements; I think that's what I'm trying to say.'

'I'd never do such a thing,' Lily said. 'We all need to speak to someone.' Lily hesitated before continuing. 'I think sometimes all we need is to share our worries with a trusted person. It always helps to hear ourselves voicing what's worrying us out loud. When I do that I can usually work out a solution for myself.'

Florence thought about what her friend was saying and agreed. It made sense. 'Still, I do appreciate your discretion. Thank you.' She indicated the cake stand. 'Please, help yourself.'

'Thank you, this really does look almost too good to eat.' Lily giggled. 'Not that I intend to let that hold me back.' Lily took a cucumber sandwich then an egg sandwich and placed them on her plate. 'You've always been a friend, Florence. It's the very least I can do to be a friend to you when you need me.'

'I appreciate it, Lily. I really do.'

They ate and drank in silence for a while, each lost in their own thoughts.

Lily eventually wiped her mouth with her napkin and draped it back onto her lap. 'How's the situation with John and his schooling? Any changes there as far as Jesse is concerned?'

'No,' Florence said, sipping at her tea before replacing the cup on its saucer. 'I'd hoped Jesse's illness might have made him rethink his decision and allow me to keep John at home.' She sighed miserably. 'It frustrates me to have to fight for what I believe is right for my own son.'

'His son, too, though,' Lily reminded her quietly. 'I can only imagine how hard that must be for you.'

'It's incredibly difficult for me to deal with.' Florence

couldn't believe they still hadn't found a way to come to some sort of compromise. Usually she was able to persuade Jesse, or didn't mind too much about him getting his own way, but this was different. 'We haven't spoken about it much since Jesse's return home. I'm frightened he'll have a relapse if I push him too far, so I'm careful not to antagonise him. He has mentioned that he'll soon need to enrol John at the school if he is to go. There's always a determination in his voice when he refers to it. I can tell that he's still as set on sending him there as he was before he fell ill.'

Lily rested her hands on her lap. Florence could see she was preparing to say something. She always asked Lily to be honest with her and knew that whatever Lily was preparing to say would be something she considered to be in Florence's best interests.

'Florence, I've been thinking.'

'Go on,' Florence said, giving her an encouraging smile.

'Are you one hundred per cent certain that you're right and Jesse is wrong about sending John away?'

'Yes, I am,' she said, surprised that Lily might think her wrong to insist John didn't go.

'I know you want the best for John, but so does Jesse.' She looked at Florence silently for a moment before continuing. 'I suppose I'm trying to say that Jesse has been so unwell, do you really think it's worth continuing to fight with him over this? If John doesn't like it, then at least he gave it a try. Jesse's still rather frail and needs all his strength to focus on getting well again. He shouldn't be using valuable energy fighting about this, however important it is to both of you.'

Florence couldn't deny Lily was making sense, even if she didn't want to agree to what she was saying.

Lily smiled. 'Surely you have more chance of him relenting if he sees that John doesn't take to being at boarding school. Don't you think? Nothing will be lost, apart from maybe a term away from home. Who knows, maybe John will enjoy being there?'

Florence listened to her friend's wise words. She hated rowing with Jesse, especially when he was still unwell. Lily was right. He needed to reserve all his strength.

'I hope you don't mind me being so blunt?' Lily asked, frowning. 'I mean only to try and help.'

Florence poured them both a fresh cup of tea. 'And I am grateful for your honesty. You make a valid point,' she said thoughtfully. 'I'll speak to Jesse one more time about it and if he's still adamant that he's right, which he will be, then I'll agree to defer to him over this. If he was well, though, I wouldn't be so eager to give in to him.'

Lily laughed and instantly covered her mouth. 'Sorry, but you are funny sometimes.'

Florence was confused by Lily's unexpected reaction. 'Why?'

'You, talking about being eager to give in.' She gave Florence a sweet smile. 'You've been standing your ground for over two months over this. I'd hardly call that eager.'

She was right, Florence thought, seeing the funny side. 'Lily Buttons, drink your tea, that's enough cheek from you.'

Florence spent another hour chatting and laughing with Lily. It was good to be able to speak honestly without worrying about anyone overhearing. When Lily had gone, Florence sat and thought about what she had said. She didn't want to relent and give in about John's schooling, but neither did she feel able to continue to push the matter any further with Jesse. The last thing she needed was for him to have a relapse. The thought of having such a thing on her conscience terrified her.

She went upstairs to see him.

'Jesse,' she said when he was sitting in his dressing gown at the table. 'I hate to argue with you when you're still not fully recovered, but I still don't like the idea of sending John away.'

Jesse gave her a weary glance and lay back against the chair rest. If he was trying to make her feel guilty, he was succeeding. 'I'm sorry, Florence. As I've said many, many times, I believe I'm right about this. Please, trust me on this. I know I'm right.'

'I know you think you are.'

Jesse might have been the one struck down physically, she mused, but mentally she was exhausted from weeks of over-work and concern about his health. He might have improved enough to be allowed back home, but it was obvious to both of them, and certainly to his doctors, that his collapse had taken a drastic toll on his body.

'If I wasn't certain that this was the best way forward for John, then I am now.'

'What do you mean?' She couldn't imagine what could have made him more determined than he had been before.

'I've had many weeks lying and thinking about my health,' Jesse said, almost to himself. 'I'd like to think that I'll go on for ever, but this breakdown has shown me that I must be realistic.' Florence went to argue with him, but Jesse shook his head. 'No. Please hear me out. Whether you like it or not, I'm going to need John to step up and take over from me at some point.'

'You're saying that I'm not capable?' She didn't even try to hide her hurt at his words. 'Have I not proved myself already? Is my work not valuable to you?'

Jesse closed his eyes. She wondered for a moment if he had fallen asleep, but then he opened them again and gazed at her. 'Your continued support, both as my wife and at work, is invaluable to me. You know it is.'

He had a strange way of showing it, Florence thought miserably. 'Then why insist that John be sent away, if I'm strong enough to run the business, should the need ever arise?'

Jesse's expression hardened. 'For pity's sake, Florence. Will you never simply accept a decision? Do you always have to quarrel with me?'

'That's unfair, Jesse. There are many times when I keep my thoughts to myself and let you carry on as if you have my full support. This is not one of those times. I don't wish my son to be sent away. That's the end of it,' she added with as much determination in her voice as she could muster.

Jesse shook his head. 'I'm sorry, but I refuse to give in on this issue.' He took a deep breath. 'Please, Florence. I'm asking you to defer to my judgement. Let us move on from this impasse.' He reached out his hand, now showing the effects of the rheumatoid arthritis that was manifesting itself so visibly. Florence took his hand in hers.

What choice did she truly have? She had tried her best and exhausted them both. How could she keep arguing with such a sick man? A sick, stubborn, and infuriating man, and one she loved deeply.

Florence sighed, her heart heavy with disappointment and the sense that by giving in to Jesse she had let her son down. She desperately hoped that would prove not to be the case. She had to trust that John would be as happy at this new school as Jesse felt certain he would be. If he was wrong and John was unable to find a way to settle in at The Leys, then she would never forgive herself for letting him go.

Chapter 19

July 1901

'Mrs Boot will see you now,' Florence heard the manageress, Miss Barton, say to one of the women outside the office where she was seated behind a tidy oak desk. Florence smoothed down her skirt and waited for the woman to follow Miss Barton in to join them.

'This is Iris Smith,' Miss Barton said, not taking her eyes off the sullen girl now standing in front of Florence, her hands clasped together in front of her skirt. Florence saw that her left eye was slightly swollen. 'I thought you should speak with her first because the gentleman in question –' Miss Barton hesitated briefly '– is Miss Smith's apparent intended.'

Florence wished there wasn't a need for her to become involved in such a personal situation and although she had been told the bare bones of the situation by Miss Barton earlier, she focused her attention back on Iris.

'Miss Smith.'

'Please, madam,' Iris said, her face reddening. 'Me mam is goin' ter kill me if I lose me job.'

'Hush,' Miss Barton hissed. 'You wait until Mrs Boot asks you to speak.'

'Sorry, Mrs Boot, Miss Barton.' She looked from Miss Barton to Florence. 'You can call me Iris, Mrs Boot.'

'I told you to wait until you're spoken to,' Miss Barton snapped. 'Now be quiet.'

Florence glanced at Miss Barton and hoped that her eyes conveyed her wish for the woman not to be too harsh on the girl. 'Iris, Miss Barton has explained to me some of what happened, but I'd be grateful if you could let me have your version of events.'

Iris stared at the floor for a moment. Then, looking across at Florence, she said, 'We was friends, me and Aggie Flack, since school. We've 'ad our ups an' downs, but nothin' like this.' She stopped speaking and stared blankly at Florence.

For a moment Florence wasn't sure why she just stood there, but thinking it might be because Iris didn't know how much to say, she nodded. 'Go on, please.'

Iris picked at the skin on the side of her right thumb. 'We was goin' ter get married until she set 'er sights on him,' she said, her voice breaking with emotion.

Florence's heart ached for the poor woman. She didn't like to ask about their living arrangements, or whether they had children, which she gathered was something that happened occasionally. 'Would you like to take a seat, Iris?' Iris shook her head. 'Your relationship with the gentleman concerned, is there any chance of it continuing?'

Iris shook her head. 'He was a wrong 'un, I knew that really. Aggie, she'd told me many times not to take on with 'im.'

'It seems that she was right,' Miss Barton said quietly, her eyes widening as soon as she'd spoken the words as if she hadn't meant for them to be said out loud. 'That is to say . . .'

'How are you and Miss Flack now?' Florence asked, hoping this matter was somehow resolvable. 'Do you think you can work together after this incident?'

'I dunno, Mrs Boot.'

Florence wished Iris had assured her otherwise. Not being able to find a way for the women to work together would mean she would have to move one or both of them off the factory floor to work elsewhere. She was aware that neither had the skills to work in the shop, nor were there any vacancies for them at the current time. The last thing she wanted to do was dismiss either one of them.

'Thank you, Iris. If you'll wait outside for a moment while I have a word with Miss Flack, please.'

She watched Miss Barton follow Iris out of the office and poured some water from the glass jug into the small tumbler that Miss Barton had placed on the desk for her before her arrival. The cool drink helped clear her head a little.

'Miss Flack?' she asked the younger woman as she walked over and stood in front of her where Iris had been moments before.

The girl nodded. 'That's me, miss.'

'Mrs Boot,' Miss Barton corrected, glaring at her. 'I'll thank you to respect your betters when you're in here.'

'Sorry, Mrs Boot,' Aggie said, her shoulders slumping slightly.

Of the two women, this one was the prettier, Florence decided as she placed her glass back on the desk. She also looked much tougher than Iris for some reason, her wide blue eyes staring confidently back at Florence despite her telling off.

'Do you want to tell me what happened, Miss Flack?' Florence noticed the parallel scratch marks on Aggie's neck.

'She, Iris that is, caught me kissin' Bert this morning outside my 'ouse, just like I meant her to.'

Florence shook her head. 'You wanted her to see you with him? Why?' She was intrigued. Surely if the girl was having a secret liaison with Iris's intended the last thing she would do is kiss him where she knew her friend would catch them.

'That's right. I like Iris, really I do. Well, I did until she attacked me this mornin'.' Her hand went to the marks on her neck as if recalling the pain of Iris's fingernails as they cut into her skin. 'I've told her ever since she got with 'im that 'e's bad news.' She leant forward, her eyes glistening. 'And 'e really is. She wouldn't believe me though. No matter what I said. I decided I needed to show 'er just how rotten Bert was. I flirted with him a bit, for a few days, like. Then I got my little brother to take a note to Bert tellin' 'im there was somethin' I needed to tell 'im and to meet me at a time I knew Iris would be callin' on me to walk with me to work.'

'So you planned all this?' Florence was shocked at the lengths Aggie had gone to simply to prove a point to her friend. 'What did Miss Smith do?'

'Well, I thought she'd lose it. You know, like hit me, or him, but she stuck 'er nose in the air and marched off to work. Bert ran after 'er, but she told him to bugger off.'

'Miss Flack! That's enough of that language. Apologise to

Mrs Boot immediately.' Miss Barton looked as if she didn't know whether to pass out or slap Aggie.

Aggie's cheeks flushed. 'I'm sorry, Mrs Boot. I mean, Iris told him to, er, go away.'

Florence nodded. 'Yes, I understood as much. So, it wasn't until later on that your altercation with Miss Smith occurred?'

'No, er, yes. That is, I thought she was just sulking, so I tried to explain to Iris about what I'd done, when she flew for me.'

'Ah, I see.' Florence was torn. She understood the logic behind Aggie's plan, although didn't agree with it, and she also could see why Iris had felt so betrayed by her friend. 'Wait outside, please, while Miss Barton and I have a discussion, and we'll speak to you and Miss Smith shortly with our decision.'

'Yes, Mrs Boot.' Aggie walked slowly over to the door. Florence thought Aggie looked as if she was deep in thought as she reached out and took hold of the doorknob. Instead of walking out immediately, she turned. 'I really am sorry, Mrs Boot, and to you, Miss Barton, and to Iris, if I'm honest. I never meant for this to 'appen. I was only trying to fix something that I know wasn't my business to sort. If you must blame someone, it should be me. Iris has kids and I don't want them to suffer because of what I done.'

Florence relaxed slightly, relieved to hear Aggie's apology. It would make sorting this delicate matter out much simpler now that one of the women had taken responsibility for the reasons behind their fight. She hoped Iris could hear what Aggie had said from where she was sitting in the hallway.

'Thank you, Miss Flack. I appreciate your sentiments.' She waited for Aggie to leave and close the door behind her.

Florence looked over at Miss Barton. She knew she wanted to find a reasonable solution to the situation and believed that the manager did, too. 'What are your thoughts on this, may I ask?' She motioned for the woman to take a seat opposite her at the desk. When Miss Barton hesitated, Florence said, 'Please, sit.'

Miss Barton did as she was asked and stared thoughtfully at her lap. 'We're not supposed to tolerate fighting in the factory,' she said. 'I don't know how we can resolve this without dismissing the women.'

Florence could see she needed to point out a few things to the woman, sensing she did not wish to say the wrong thing to Florence. 'Are they good workers?'

'They are.'

'You say that they were good friends up until today, so I presume this is the first time they've ever fought with each other.'

'That is correct.'

'Then I think we need to ask Aggie to apologise to Iris, face to face. If she accepts the apology and they both promise never to become embroiled in something like this again, then we can give them another chance. Do you agree?'

Miss Barton nodded several times, looking much happier. 'I think that's very fair of you, Mrs Boot.'

'Good. Please call them back in here.'

Moments later the two sullen women were standing in front of the desk once more. Florence explained what she and

216

Miss Barton had discussed and without hesitation Aggie apologised to Iris.

'I'm sorry, too,' Iris replied quietly, looking sideways at her workmate. 'You did try to tell me to say ta-ra to him, but I didn't want to. Don't do nothin' like that again, will yer?'

Aggie shook her head. Florence glanced at Miss Barton and exchanged a smile with her.

'Good,' Florence said clasping her hands together. 'Do you both think you can remain working in the same team?'

The women nodded immediately.

'Fine. Then Miss Barton and I have agreed that this sort of behaviour must never happen again, because if it does you will be dismissed instantly and without a character reference.'

'It won't, Mrs Boot,' Aggie assured her.

'No, never, Mrs Boot,' Iris added.

'Good. I'm glad to hear it. Now, if Miss Barton is happy for you to return to the factory floor . . .?'

Miss Barton nodded. 'I am.'

'You may go.'

'Thanks, Mrs Boot,' they said in unison.

'You won't tell me mam about this, will yer, Miss Barton?' Iris asked, her face taut with fear.

'No,' Miss Barton said. 'Not this time.'

Aggie nodded and went and opened the office door. Iris gave a little curtsey and followed her out of the room.

Florence waited for the women to leave and close the door behind them before asking, 'You know her mother?'

'No,' she said. 'And I wouldn't presume to contact her about anything that happened here at the factory, but if the thought of me maybe doing so at any point makes Iris Smith take a moment to think before she reacts, then I'm happy for her to believe I would. Do you mind?'

Florence shook her head and stood. 'No, I don't think there's any harm in Iris having a deterrent that helps her stay in her job.' She glanced at the clock on the wall and noticed the lateness of the hour. Jesse would be unimpressed with her tardiness, especially after all she had promised him.

'I really must hurry along,' she said. 'I'm happy we've been able to resolve the situation to everyone's satisfaction.'

'Thank you, Mrs Boot. So am I.'

As Florence sat in the carriage taking her home, she thought of the two women and how pleasant they had been in the office. It was hard to imagine them fighting and the thought shocked her. She thought of herself as an ex-shop assistant, but how similar to their lives had hers ever truly been? She hadn't worked in a factory, of course, but she had worked for a living. She might empathise with these women, but she realised she could never really know what it must be like to live the lives they had to struggle through. It made her even happier to know that despite what had happened, both women had been given a second chance to keep their jobs at the factory. No one would be going hungry on her account this evening. The thought soothed her.

Florence thought back to the chaotic mess she had made of Nellie Blythe's situation nine years before. She couldn't help feeling a sense of pride when she thought of everything she had learnt in those intervening years. She had had to make a concerted effort to listen to Jesse's advice many times.

Jesse, despite her best protestations at the time, had turned out to know better how to deal with Nellie's particular situation. Florence smiled to herself. She really had learnt a lot since then.

Chapter 20

July 1902

Florence folded her arms as she stood at the front door. She couldn't believe Jesse was about to go out on horseback to do his rounds. She had hoped that his breakdown the previous year would make him consider his actions more carefully, but yet again he was ignoring any warnings by her or the doctor to adapt his lifestyle to fit his physical situation.

She watched angrily as he stepped up onto the mounting block and, taking his horse's reins from Meadows, placed his foot into the stirrup and with some difficulty swung his leg over the rear of his horse and settled into the saddle.

She had tried her best to dissuade him from accompanying one of his managers who had taken over Jesse's rounds checking on several of the nearest stores, while he had been recovering from his breakdown. The man was waiting patiently on his own chestnut gelding for Jesse to be ready to leave and if he had any concerns about Jesse's welfare, he hid them well.

Florence wished Jesse would accept that now was probably time to consider giving up riding altogether. He had celebrated his fifty-second birthday the previous month and since his breakdown had lost much of the strength in his legs. She knew he had no intention of doing as she asked but she couldn't help worrying every time he rode his horse what might happen if he was to take a fall.

'What if the horse shies away from something, and you lose your seat?' she had argued over breakfast that morning. 'The fall could kill you, Jesse. Have you thought of that?'

She went outside to try her best yet again to make him see sense before he left. 'Jesse,' she said quietly, standing next to the muscular left shoulder of his huge grey mare. 'Are you certain you won't change your mind? It would be much quicker and I imagine more comfortable for you both to do your rounds by carriage.'

Jesse frowned, not bothering to hide his annoyance with her. 'We've already had this conversation, Florence,' he said quietly through gritted teeth. 'As I said then, I've not fallen from a horse in years. I have no intention of doing so today. This is the way I've always done things,' he said, tightening the reins. 'I'm well again now and don't see any reason not to carry on as I usually do. Now, please move out of the way, I don't wish you to be trampled on.'

Florence glared at him in frustration, but did as he asked. 'You might be much better than you have been, but neither of us can truly say that you are well enough to carry on as you did before this illness, Jesse. Why not conduct the inspections by carriage? It's a more sensible option, don't you think?

'I do not,' he snapped, then, smiling at her, he put his

gloved hand to his mouth and blew her a kiss. 'I'd better get on. I'll see you later.'

'You are an infuriating man! Do you know that?' she asked, her irritation with him melting away. His stubbornness was part of his personality, after all.

Florence was glad that she had been able to see Jesse off before starting her own day at Pelham Street. The shop was busier than ever and she needed to plan what stock would be needed for the coming Christmas. She arrived at the store and almost bumped into Lily on her way to the lift.

'Walk with me?' she asked quietly.

Lily fell into step next to Florence. 'Is everything all right?' she asked, also quietly. 'You seem a little down this morning.'

'I'm finding it rather quieter at home without John around.' She sighed. 'The girls are their usual noisy, fun selves, thankfully, but I do miss him.'

'You're bound to.'

Florence missed her son terribly since she and Jesse had travelled with him to Cambridge several weeks before to settle him in to The Leys School where he was now boarding. Florence had been trying hard not to show her emotions too much and lower the rest of the family's spirits.

'Have you spoken to Jesse about it?' Lily asked as they stepped into the lift alone.

'Yes. He tried to appease me by saying that John will have an exeat one of these weekends,' she said. 'I hope he does, then he can come home and spend some time with us and tell us properly how he's settling in.

'Jesse even admitted to me that although he feels that

sending John away was the right thing to do, a part of him is struggling now that he's gone.'

'He told you that?' Lily asked, her eyebrows disappearing into her fringe.

Florence pulled a face. 'I know. I was as surprised as you at his admission.' The lift slowly rose to the top floor and Florence continued, 'I keep telling myself that I didn't enjoy the convent I was sent to in Brittany at first. Everyone spoke French and I missed my parents, siblings, and Jersey very much.'

'I'm not surprised.'

'For a time, I resented my father for insisting on sending me away to school.' She frowned at Lily. 'I'm hoping John doesn't feel badly towards me or Jesse for sending him off. I couldn't understand why I had to go to France when there were perfectly good schools in Jersey. I soon became used to it though and learned to speak fluent French, but, more than that, I discovered how other families lived. It was a valuable experience. I keep telling myself that John's experience will be valuable for him. Despite my initial dislike of the convent I was sent to, I loved it there in the end, as I hope John will learn to love his school.'

'I'm sure you're right,' Lily said as the lift stopped and she waited for Florence to step out. 'You shouldn't worry about a decision you both took a long time to make. John is a friendly young man and I'm sure he'll be fine,' Lily insisted.

They reached Florence's office. 'Come in for a while, will you?' said Florence.

Lily walked in and sat down. 'What's worrying you then, Florence?'

'I'm probably being over-sensitive, but I can't help sensing from John's letters that he's not as settled as I would have hoped him to be by now.'

'Can you visit him there?'

Florence shook her head. 'I was thinking about writing to the headmaster and asking if John can come home to spend a weekend with us, sooner rather than later.'

Lily's face broke into a grin. 'That sounds like a splendid idea. You should do it.' She bit her lower lip. 'Have you mentioned this to Jesse yet?'

'I did.'

'What did he say?'

Florence smiled as she recalled their conversation the evening before as they sat and read by the fire. 'I'm relieved for both our sakes that he thought it was a good idea. He also said that it will be good to spend time with all of the children together again.'

'I'm so pleased, Florence.'

'I'm going to write to the school this morning. I have to admit that I'm looking forward to seeing him very much.'

'I'm not surprised.' Lily stood. 'I'd better return to the shop floor.' She grinned. 'I don't want anyone thinking I have special treatment.' She smiled at Florence. 'I'm really pleased that Jesse is happy for you to ask for John to come home again soon. I think being able to speak to him should put you at your ease.'

Florence hoped so.

After Lily left, Florence sat in her silent office and gazed at the area where the children's cots had been when they were babies. She had valued that time with them so much, despite others looking down on her for taking her children to work. As far as she was concerned, no one had the right to dictate how she brought up her children. No one apart from Jesse, of course, and even he had to fight to get his way, Florence thought, amused.

Her heart contracted painfully. It was hard to imagine that John was now twelve, Dorothy eleven and Margery nine years old. Where had the time gone? The next thing she'd know, each of them would be married and bringing up children of their own.

No, thought Florence, shaking the thought from her head. She was not going to think such things. She was determined to enjoy that time when it came to it, but for now, she was going to spend as much time as she could with her children, while they were still young enough to want her company. And, she reminded herself, when John was allowed home from boarding school for a weekend or the holidays.

She unscrewed the top of her fountain pen, took a piece of her personal embossed paper, and began to write a letter to the headmaster.

Florence welcomed being kept busy all day. Her father had written to ask if they would consider selling the lease of the small Boots shop Florence and Jesse had set up in Jersey next door to her father's stationery shop back in 1896. Florence sighed, as she read how her father thought the shop would be perfect for him to extend his business into and pressed her to encourage Jesse to consider selling the lease to him.

Florence sympathised with her father, but had no intention

of doing as he asked because, unbeknownst to her father, her mother had quietly told Florence that he was finding work rather difficult on some days and, rather than building his business in his sixties, he should be thinking about retiring sooner rather than later.

She wrote back to him gently repeating that she and Jesse had bought that shop to obtain a foothold for the Boots company on the island. It was true. She also didn't think the timing was right to sell just yet, which she thought was kinder than to say she didn't think he could cope with a larger business. She hoped her father would forget about his plans to expand his business, for a while at least. Her mother was tired of helping run the stationery shop and would be furious with Florence if she ever did sell to her father. Not that she, or Jesse, had any intention of doing so. Instead, they hoped that when her father did finally retire they would make him a generous offer to buy Rowe's Stationers and extend into that shop, rather than the other way around.

Florence knew it was what her mother hoped would happen in the future. It would be a way to help her family and also tie something from her past into her future.

* * *

John was given permission to return home the following weekend, despite it being so close to the end of the school year. The mood at St Heliers had risen considerably. Everyone, both family and servants, was looking forward to his return, as they always did. Florence wished John could be at home for longer than a couple of days, but it was better than nothing. Jesse had already left for the train station to meet him and bring him home in a hansom.

Florence had spoken to Mrs Rudge the previous evening to check that all John's favourite foods had been stocked, or prepared, and gone up to his bedroom to stand in the middle of it, comforted to see his bed made and fresh towels on the towel rail under the window. Life at St Heliers felt complete when John came back.

It was soothing to know that soon John's bedroom would be inhabited again by him. Florence was even looking forward to seeing his things left about the house, something that usually irked her. She smiled, thinking how differently mothers saw their children when they weren't with them all the time.

It had been several weeks since she had seen her son, but a lot of her time had been spent focusing on her Booklovers' Library, which had taken off rapidly since its inception. Florence visited the library each day, witnessing the neat organisation of the department, where each book had a green shield imprinted on the plain red, blue, or green cover of the book, and it made her smile.

She sometimes asked for a couple of books to take home for herself and, once a selection had been brought to her, Florence would sit at one of the small tables and look through the books, checking that they were as clean as she meant them to be. She liked to sit quietly and read, taking in the conversation about her and hearing what customers thought of the lending library. Whenever she visited, the place was always pristine, with small vases of fresh flowers on the tables. She also mentioned to the manageress when she heard of any particularly interesting novels that had been published, desperate not to miss good new books that had come onto the market. She wanted her Lending Library to be up to date at all times. If they weren't then customers might lose interest and Florence wasn't about to let that happen.

Initially, it was the regular customers that she noticed making the most of the library books. Slowly though, women she hadn't seen before in the shop began coming in specially to choose a book. Some of them initially seemed reluctant to spend time studying the shelves, but then started to gain a little confidence. Florence sensed people were beginning to feel like the library was theirs as much as anyone else's. Which, of course, it was.

'Mother, Mother,' Dorothy shrieked from downstairs. 'John's here.'

Florence opened the windows of John's room to ensure fresh air had been circulated. Hearing Dorothy's excited shouts, she went to step into the hallway but had to take a step backwards to avoid her youngest daughter, as Margery charged along the hallway from her own bedroom to the top of the stairs.

Florence loved that her children were so close. The girls' excitement had increased almost hourly over the last few days. Florence understood why. John might not be the most studious of boys, but he was fun to be around and kind. His sisters had missed his presence very much, probably even more than she and Jesse.

By the time Florence reached the open front door, Jesse was stepping out of the hansom and waiting for John to appear. Seconds later, he almost leapt out, not bothering with the small metal step, and raced to his mother to give her a hug.

Florence laughed at his enthusiasm, as he almost unbalanced her. She hugged her son tightly, relishing the warmth of his arms encircling her waist. He eventually let go and stepped back and Florence studied him for a moment. It was wonderful to have his bounding energy in the house once more and to know that for the next two nights he would be sleeping in his own bed upstairs.

'You've grown taller. Don't you think he has, Jesse?' she asked ruffling John's fair hair as he walked over to join them after greeting his sisters.

'I thought as much when he stepped off the train.'

Margery grabbed hold of John's right arm. 'Come and see what Papa has done in the house. It's for all of us. You'll love it.'

Margery pulled him inside the house and towards the back garden with Dorothy running along after them.

Jesse seemed more content than he had been in a while. She went to stand next to him and put her arm around his waist.

'She's been dying to show him the new tennis court, hasn't she?' Florence asked, aware that the girls had been chatting about what they thought John's reaction would be when he saw what Jesse had arranged at the back of the house at the end of the lawn.

'She certainly has. He'll love it and I look forward to playing a few matches with him.'

Florence laughed, picturing father and son competing against each other. 'And I'll be watching.'

'I thought it was something the children would enjoy this summer, and it's also a good way to warm up if it's cold later in the year.' Jesse laughed and gave her a kiss on the cheek. 'Come along, let's go inside and have some tea. I'm parched. It's been a long afternoon and I think we're going to have a busy evening ahead of us, don't you?'

Florence sighed happily. 'Yes, I think you could be right.'

They called for some tea and crumpets to be brought to the living room. Florence knew how much her son loved to eat toasted crumpets and asked Violet to tell the children to join them in the living room as soon as they were ready.

John arrived first and spotted the treat waiting for each of them on a plate.

'Mother, how did you know? I've been hoping that you'd ask Mrs Rudge to make these for me today.'

Florence handed him a plate. 'I wanted you to have all your favourite things waiting for you,' she admitted. 'Here. Sit down and eat it before it cools too much.' She poured him a cup of tea and placed it on the table next to his chair. Florence lifted the lid on the muffin dish where Mrs Rudge had stacked several more crumpets, aware that John's appetite for them would not be satisfied with just the one. She served Jesse and then turned her attention to Dorothy and Margery. 'Girls, take yours now too, please.'

Florence watched each of her family savouring their

afternoon snack as she ate her own. Once again, Mrs Rudge had surpassed herself.

'Tell us how has this term been,' Dorothy said. 'Mother and Father told us that you were having fun, but were you? Really?' She looked at her brother doubtfully as she took the last bite from her crumpet.

John looked from Florence to Jesse and back to his sister. He gave a slow shrug.

Jesse mumbled something under his breath and Florence tensed. The last thing she needed was for Jesse to pick a quarrel with John so soon after his arrival home. 'Buck up, John. You've been there almost a year now. I'd have been delighted if my parents had been able to afford to send me somewhere like that.'

Florence noticed the muscles in John's jaw working as he tried to suppress his irritation with his father.

'How's everything going, John?' Florence asked.

John smiled at her. 'Mostly, it's fine,' he said, not giving away very much. 'I miss being at home with all of you though. The food's all right, but not as good as it is here.'

Florence listened intently. She wasn't sure if his words made her feel any better. 'Have you made any friends yet?'

'There are enough boys at the school for you to get on with a few of them, surely,' Jesse grumbled.

'Please let John speak for himself.' Florence gave him a sideways glare. If he ruined her time with John this weekend, she wouldn't let him forget it.

John gave his answer some thought and smiled. Florence noticed that his smile reached his eyes and seemed genuine, and for the first time since his arrival home, she felt herself relax slightly.

'Yes, a few. There's one chap in particular.' John grinned. 'He's from Canada, Vancouver in fact. He said I can go and stay with his family at their apple farm in the summer. Will you mind?'

Florence hated the thought of John going away for an entire summer just when she was hoping to make the most of having him back at home for a decent length of time. 'I think you should wait until you know him better, don't you?' she said, happy at her quick thinking.

'Your mother's right,' Jesse agreed. 'The last thing we want to do is book a passage for you all the way to Canada only for you to fall out with the chap and then not wish to go.'

'I can't see that happening,' John argued quietly, but Florence could see that their comments made sense to him.

'Maybe next year,' she reasoned, relieved her son had made some friends. Everyone needed friends, especially close ones they could rely on and be able to confide in, like she did with Lily. 'What's the name of this Canadian boy?'

'I want to know why they farm apples,' Dorothy said and giggled.

'Yes,' Margery said, coming to sit on the arm of John's chair. 'I thought people had animals on farms, like cows and pigs. I've never heard of someone farming apples.'

John nudged her playfully, grabbing her arm when she almost slipped off the chair.

'Children, calm down,' Jesse said shaking his head. 'John's only just returned home and we don't want to have to deal with any scrapes while he's here.' He pointed for Margery to go and sit on a nearby chair.

Violet brought in more tea for Jesse and Florence and apple juice for the children. While they sat and drank John explained more about his daily routine at the school.

Jesse finished his tea, placed his cup on the saucer, and put it down on the table in front of where he sat next to Florence. 'It's not as bad as you thought though. And it'll soon be the summer holidays, don't forget.'

'I know. I'm looking forward to them, especially now we've got the tennis court. I'm beginning to feel more like I belong at the school. I think most of the new boys feel the same way as me when they first arrive and they do say the first year is the hardest to cope with.'

'Is it really that difficult for you there, John?' Florence asked, concerned. She hated to think of her son finding it hard to fit in.

He looked over at her and didn't speak for a moment, then smiled. 'It's not so bad. It's school, isn't it? I don't think it's supposed to be fun. We do a lot of sports though, which I enjoy, and go to church at least twice a week. It's what I expected only a bit better, I suppose.'

'That's good to hear,' Florence replied, relieved to know her son wasn't struggling as much as she feared he might. She had spent so many hours worrying about him since he had begun at the school. It was an enormous relief to know that John was coping. Florence still slightly resented Jesse for insisting that John attend a school so far from them, and couldn't completely banish her guilt at giving in to her husband despite her concerns. Her children's happiness was the most important thing in the world to her, and she would never forgive herself if her initial misgivings had proved correct and John had been miserable.

'Tell us about your Canadian friend,' Jesse said.

John shrugged. 'His name is Frank Hamilton. We mostly like the same kinds of things and we laugh a lot together. His mum is Canadian and his dad's Scottish.'

They chatted a little bit more and then when the children had all finished their tea and crumpets, Florence said, 'I'll ring for Violet to come and collect these plates and I think you should go and say hello to Mrs Rudge, John. I know she's looking forward to seeing you, as are the rest of the servants. I think they've all found it a little too quiet here without you thundering around and asking them for things.'

He wiped his mouth on his napkin and stood. 'Yes, I'm looking forward to seeing her, too. I need to thank her for making these for us today. She's always so thoughtful.' He smiled at Jesse and then Florence. 'It really is good to be home for a couple of days. Thank you for arranging it for me.'

'We're delighted to have you, my boy,' Jesse said, smiling. 'Aren't we, my dear? It's good to have our boy home again.'

'It is.' Florence sighed happily before standing and walking over to the fireplace and pulling the wide cord to summon Violet. 'Your case should be in your room by now, so after you've said hello to everyone, why don't you go and unpack and settle in for a bit. I'm sure you want to spend some time with your games and books in your bedroom.'

He smiled and gave her another hug. 'I do, Mother. I'm

mostly looking forward to being able to sleep in my own bed again. The one here is much more comfortable than the one at school.'

'May we go with John, Mother?' Dorothy asked.

'Yes, may we?' Margery asked, popping the last of hers into her mouth.

'Of course. Run along and I'll call you all a little later.'

Florence waited until the children had left the room and Violet had tidied away their tea things, before settling back down on the sofa next to Jesse.

'Is something the matter?' he asked, taking her hand. 'Nothing's amiss, is it?'

Florence didn't want to pick a fight with Jesse but was struggling to cope with his attitude towards his son. 'I wish you wouldn't be so hard on John.'

'I'm no harder on him than any caring father would be.'

Florence wondered if Jesse genuinely believed what he was saying, or maybe he was acting the way his father had when he was younger. Either way, she didn't like it and said so.

Jesse took her hand in his. 'I don't think you realise how much he has to learn if he's going to take some of the pressure off me when he's finished his education.'

Florence tensed. 'I know better than anyone, surely. I've been the one working with you these past years, haven't I?'

'Yes.' Jesse frowned. 'That isn't what I meant.'

'Then what?'

Jesse was silent for a moment. She could see he was struggling to answer her question. 'I worry that he hasn't got it in him to take over.' He hesitated. 'When the time comes.'

Florence went to speak but Jesse hadn't finished what he was saying. 'When I was ill recently, I had a lot of time to think about the future, whatever there is left of it for me.'

'Don't say that,' Florence snapped, not wanting to think such things.

Jesse patted her hand and kissed her on the cheek. 'We both know it's inevitable and I worry about what will happen then.'

She didn't like to admit that she had also worried about the future, but always resolved any concerns by telling herself that Jesse had an excellent team of managers working for Boots and that she could do whatever was needed for the business. Even train John, if it came to that.

'All I want is for you and John to get on,' she said, her voice barely above a whisper. She cleared her throat. 'I never imagined that you two would clash like you do. It's heart-breaking for me to witness.'

Jesse turned to her, a stricken look on his face. 'We will be fine, Florence. Please don't worry. I love my son, very much. I simply want the best for him and from him. Even though I say it myself, he has large shoes to fill and I'm sorry, but I can't help my concern that he won't be able to manage it.'

'He will,' Florence replied, not certain at all that she was right. 'He's young yet; let him enjoy this time before he has to focus on the business.'

'I'll try.' Jesse inclined his head as he gazed at her. 'Please don't worry so much.' He watched her as she sat thoughtfully. 'What are you thinking?'

'Just that I'm relieved to hear John has made friends and

seems to have settled in at school. Having him back here with us reminds me how different it is when he's not here, though, and I know I'm going to miss him twice as much when he leaves again.'

Jesse gazed at her thoughtfully for a moment. 'So will I.' Florence was relieved to hear Jesse say as much. 'And I'm sure his sisters will do, too. But sometimes you have to make sacrifices, my darling, and this is one of those times. I know you had your doubts,' Jesse said, kissing the back of her hand, 'and that John going away to school is difficult for you, but I truly believe it's going to be the making of him. He's told us he's fine and we have no reason to disbelieve him.'

She just wished that John and Jesse would find a way to get along more easily. There were many positives to having the money and status that she and Jesse now enjoyed, Florence mused, but having to educate their children in this way was one of those aspects of their lifestyle she would have rather done without.

Chapter 21

August 1902

Florence enjoyed marking the time around her birthday by arranging outings for her staff. She had been doing it for many years now but this year she was working hard planning the intricacies of taking five hundred of her female employees for a day out at the seaside. After a lot of thought and discussion with Jesse and then Miss Tweed and Lily, she had decided that they were to go by train for a day to Skegness. It was somewhere Florence had never visited and she liked the idea of her initial trip there being one that her employees could also enjoy.

'I believe that visiting new places and having new experiences inspires people. Don't you agree, Agnes?'

Agnes pushed her spectacles further up her narrow nose and looked up from writing on her notepad. 'I do, Mrs Boot.'

'We've been on many adventures and the response from the girls is always positive.' Florence tapped her chin with the and of her fountain pen as she tried to think of anything she might have overlooked in their detailed planning.

She had been told many times by the women how grateful they were for the days out that Florence and Jesse took them on. She knew that most of them appreciated the events because without them they might not have been able to go on an outing on their own accord, due to lack of funds or leisure time. Each time she enjoyed hearing back from them about how much they had enjoyed themselves.

These were her Dear Girls, and if Florence could find a way to ensure that these women saw something in themselves they hadn't seen before, then she would do all it took to make it happen. She thought back to how little she had known of the world when her life had only extended to the nine-by-five miles of her home island. Now, though, she had been lucky enough to travel to New York, several times, as well as various places on the continent on buying trips. She knew England much better than she had done and had even visited Scotland twice with Jesse. Florence wanted to share as much as possible of the excitement she always felt each time she discovered a new place, and she believed that by taking her girls away with her she was showing them that there was much more to life than the small area where they had always lived.

All her girls were hard-working and loyal employees. Florence appreciated their efforts and felt a responsibility to help them realise that they should not be held back by the traditional expectations put upon most of them. She found it upsetting to think how few choices many of these women were given and, as their employer, she intended to show them their true worth.

'These girls need to believe in themselves,' she said to Miss

Tweed as the two sat checking through Florence's endless list while planning the Skegness trip. 'I have the means and also the opportunity to help make that happen for them, and this outing is going to surpass all the other events that I've arranged previously.'

Florence watched Miss Tweed as she continued making her list of things she thought they would need to pack for the day out. She was another hard-working woman, always on time, immaculately turned out, and thoughtful. Florence knew she was lucky to have such an excellent secretary.

She turned her attention to the neat invitation booklet on her desk and studied. It might only be three inches tall, but she thought it looked smart with its slim red cord hanging down between the two pages.

'I don't think we've forgotten any details,' she said, checking each page for the first time since it had been brought to her from the printing department.

Miss Tweed looked at the one she was holding. 'The first page details the saloon carriages and then goes on to add where they're going and what will be happening when they get there. Then about dinner being served at noon in the Pavilion and the menu.' She smiled and looked at Florence. 'I wish I was going. I haven't been to Skegness for years, and this menu looks very enticing.'

Florence also wished her secretary was able to come along, but Miss Tweed's mother had been taken poorly the previous month and was still battling with a dreadful chest infection that didn't seem to want to budge. 'There's still time to change your mind, Agnes,' she said. 'Are you certain you won't?'

Agnes shook her head. 'I'd love to, really I would, but I don't like to be so far away from Mother in case she might need me. At least when I'm here her neighbour can send word to me if her condition deteriorates.'

'I understand,' Florence said. 'However, I'll make up a hamper for you to take home and share with your mother as compensation for not being able to join us.' It made her feel much better to think that her secretary wouldn't entirely miss out on a treat. She decided she would ask Mrs Rudge to cook a ham and some vegetables, as well as put in a plum pie, apple pie, and some jellies. At least that way Agnes would taste some of the delicious menu on offer to the others who were going on the outing. She would also speak to Jesse about the latest medicine to ease a chest infection and add that to Agnes's hamper.

Miss Tweed gasped. 'That is most generous, Mrs Boot, thank you very much. Mother will be touched by your generosity. We will make a special occasion of eating it.'

'It will be my pleasure entirely,' Florence replied, happy to have thought to make the suggestion. 'I just wished you weren't missing the band of Pierrots playing in the Pavilion.'

Miss Tweed pointed to the line in the invitation that mentioned the number of donkeys they had hired specially to give employees free rides. 'I shan't mind not going on the donkeys though; I'm a little nervous of them.'

Satisfied that the invitation card was perfect, Florence slid a copy of the Skegness Party timetable over to Miss Tweed.

'Please read through this again, while I do the same. I need to be certain there are no errors before sending everything out to the women who'll be joining us.' She read each line through to the end. 'You'll see that I added a note for attendees to bring wraps, as I suspect it might be a little cool by seven-thirty when the train leaves Skegness Station to return to Nottingham.'

'That makes good sense.' Miss Tweed smiled at Florence and handed back her copy of the timetable. 'Everything looks perfect as far as I can see.'

'Good.' Florence took a deep breath, relieved to have completed this part of her planning. 'Now, if you could arrange for each of the women to receive these, I'll continue working through today's diary.'

'Would you like me to make you a cup of tea now?' Miss Tweed asked, tidying up the documents they had been checking and placing them on a side table. 'Then I can start sending out the trip invitations.'

'That would be lovely, thank you.'

Florence needed a final check-through of her list of things to do for the outing. She didn't want there to be any dramas, and by making sure that every effort had been taken with the planning and communicating her wishes to each member of staff, she believed it was less likely that any would occur.

Jesse always left the planning and arrangements of the excursions to Florence. She thought back to one of the first outings she had arranged, the day trip she and Jesse had taken the staff on to Castleton in Derbyshire. She could still see the huge group of employees smiling at the camera as they posed on the hillside.

It had been a splendid day and she had recently heard two

of the women reminiscing about the photo she had handed out to each of the members of staff who had come with them. It had made the perfect souvenir and Florence had written, 'With kind regards from Mr and Mrs Jesse Boot'. One of the women had recalled how they had all sung the song 'Mr Warings's Glee Party' at the Great Peak Cavern. Yes, it had been a day to remember and there had been many more since then.

The difficulty was coming up with new ideas and making each special and memorable for the staff. She was delighted that Lily Buttons was joining them for the outing, as she had all the others Florence had invited her to since coming to work at Boots.

At the thought of Lily, Florence mused about how much she was proving to be an asset of the company, just as Florence had expected her to be when she took her on. There was something worrying Lily though, Florence was certain of it. She had seemed a little glum on one occasion when Florence had caught her off-guard and she decided that the only way to find out what was going on with Lily was to ask her. She would go as soon as she finished her tea.

She hoped it wasn't anything serious but sensed there was something amiss. What though? she wondered.

Florence left her office and went downstairs to find Lily. She had to stop several times to speak to a couple of customers who wanted to compliment Florence on the beautiful silverware that they stocked, and then she had a brief conversation with a manageress about a new member of staff who wasn't fitting into her role as well as she had hoped.

Florence spotted Lily. She was talking to a young man, but it occurred to Florence that Lily didn't appear to be as calm as usual. Florence studied her for a moment. Lily's jaw was clenched and her hands were clasped together tightly. Something was wrong.

'Who is the man speaking with Miss Buttons?' she asked the nearest shop assistant, a young girl who had worked with Lily for several years. 'I don't recognise him as a regular customer, do you?'

The girl's cheeks turned a deep shade of pink. 'No, Mrs Boot.'

Florence could tell the girl knew more than she was letting on. 'Have you seen him here before?'

The girl shifted from one foot to the other and chewed her lower lip before replying. 'He was here the other day. Lily, that is, Miss Buttons asked him to leave and not come back, but, well, here he is. I'm not sure who he is, just that she doesn't want him to come here.'

'Thank you.' Florence was grateful for the girl's honesty. She looked over at Lily once again and could see the man was becoming slightly agitated.

Florence didn't want to embarrass Lily but decided that it was time to intervene.

'Good afternoon,' Florence said, smiling brightly first at Lily and then at the man she was speaking to. 'Is there anything I can help you with, Miss Buttons?' Before Lily had a chance to answer, Florence gave the man her full attention, aware that she could come across as rather severe. 'I'm Mrs Boot, and you are?'

'T-T-Thomas Danby.' When Florence didn't say anything else, he added, 'I've come to ask Miss Buttons something.'

'He was just leaving, Mrs Boot,' Lily said quietly, glancing around her.

'But, Lily, I mean Miss Buttons, we haven't finished our conversation yet.'

'We have.'

Florence could feel the tension emanating from Lily, who was well aware that conversing with friends on the shop floor was not acceptable. 'Mr Danby, I believe Miss Buttons has work to be getting on with, so if you would accompany me to the door, I'll show you out?'

'No,' he argued through clenched teeth. 'I have no way of contacting her other than to come here. Please, I need to make Lily understand why I did what I did.' He looked past Florence. 'Please, Lily. Just give me one more minute to try and explain.'

Florence was grateful that he was at least keeping his voice low enough that others couldn't hear what was being said. She forced a smile and rested her hand on Lily's right upper arm. 'I believe that this conversation is finished, as far as Miss Buttons is concerned. Is that correct, Miss Buttons?'

'Yes, it is,' Lily answered without taking her eyes from his face. She leant a little closer to him and, lowering her voice even further, said, 'If you come here again I'll ask the doorman to call the constable. Now please leave and don't come back.'

'Would you come this way please, Mr Danby?' Florence asked, her arm out to her side to encourage him to join her.

After a brief hesitation and one last pleading look at Lily, he did as she asked.

Florence walked through the store to the front entrance with him. 'Mr Danby, it is not acceptable for you to bring your personal matters into this store,' she explained as calmly as she could. 'In fact, by doing so, you are putting Miss Buttons in a very difficult position, so I would ask you, as she has done a few times, not to return.'

Florence looked up at Albert who was frowning at Mr Danby.

'Trouble, Mrs Boot?'

'No, there isn't,' Thomas Danby muttered. 'I was going.'

Albert ignored him and waited for Florence to answer.

'No, thank you, Albert,' she reassured him. 'However, please see that Mr Danby here doesn't return to the shop. Thank you. Goodbye, Mr Danby.'

She returned to Lily's department and on the way it occurred to her that Lily wouldn't be able to speak openly to her on the shop floor. Florence would need to speak to her in private if Lily was to confide in her.

She didn't wish to draw any further attention to Lily so returned to her office. She ran her eyes over the day's jobs outstanding in her diary.

A few minutes later, Miss Tweed entered Florence's office and placed a cup of tea on Florence's leather-topped desk.

'Please could you ask Miss Buttons to be sent to me when she has a free moment?'

'Of course, Mrs Boot.'

Florence had finished her drink and was replying to an

invitation that had come for her and Jesse when a knock on her office door alerted her to Miss Tweed's presence. 'Miss Buttons is here to see you, Mrs Boot.'

Florence screwed the cap back on to her fountain pen. 'Thank you, Miss Tweed. Please show her in.'

Miss Tweed stepped back into the hallway and waved for Lily to enter the office.

'Hello, Lily. Would you like some tea?' Florence asked as she entered the room.

'Yes, please.'

'I'll make some and bring it right in,' Miss Tweed said, picking up Florence's empty cup and taking it with her as she left the room and closed the door quietly behind her.

Florence stood and motioned for Lily to take a seat. Her young friend's face seemed pinched and tense, and she wasn't surprised after what had happened a little earlier. Florence noticed that Lily had lost weight, but made sure to hide the concern on her face.

'I'm sorry to take you from your work, Lily,' she said sitting back down behind her desk, 'but I wanted to speak privately with you about Mr Danby.'

Lily studied her hands. 'I'm so sorry about what happened,' she said, looking close to tears. 'I told him the last time that he mustn't ever come to the shop to speak to me, but, as you saw, he didn't listen.'

'I know this isn't your fault, Lily.' She was relieved Jesse was out checking on other stores otherwise he would have made much more of a fuss, and Florence knew that would have mortified Lily. 'Even before today, I've had the feeling

248

that something was worrying you. I think it has been for a while now.'

Lily didn't answer.

'You might not wish to discuss it with me, and of course that's fine. But I wanted to ask you, in case there was something I might be able to do to help.' She raised her hands.

Florence waited a few seconds while Lily sat thoughtfully. She hoped she hadn't made the wrong assumption, or, worse, offended Lily. Florence was about to apologise for bringing her to the office when Lily shook her head.

'You're not wrong, Florence,' she said quietly. 'I have found myself at somewhat of a –' she hesitated, struggling to find the words '– disadvantage lately.'

Florence couldn't imagine what she meant but sensed it was about Mr Danby. Then a troubling thought seeped into Florence's mind. Could Lily have found herself in the same predicament as Nellie had? If she was pregnant, would Lily tell her? Florence wondered. She hated to think of Lily living hand to mouth like Nellie had after having her son. She would find a way to help her, but whatever she did, Florence knew that having an illegitimate baby would cast a long shadow on Lily's future life. She hoped she was wrong.

'Do you wish to confide in me about it?' she asked, hoping Lily would do so.

Lily nodded and picked at the skin on the side of her left thumb. 'I do, yes.'

Miss Tweed knocked once on the office door and walked

in carrying a tray. 'I've also brought a plate with a few biscuits,' she said, setting up two cups and saucers, the teapot, a jug of milk, and a smaller pot with cubes of sugar.

'Thank you,' Florence said, giving her a grateful smile for being so thoughtful. Miss Tweed always seemed to know when something extra was needed.

Florence held out the plate to Lily, barely aware of the office door closing behind her secretary. 'Take one and eat it while I pour us both a nice cup of tea.'

Florence poured the tea, placed a cup in front of Lily, and took one for herself, before sitting back in her chair.

'What is it?' Florence asked, believing that being blunt might spur Lily to share whatever it was that she was embarrassed to mention. 'Tell me.'

Lily cleared her throat and took a deep breath.

'I know you're a kind and generous person,' Lily said, 'after all you've done for me.'

Florence tried not to let her imagination go into overdrive. 'You're really worrying me now. Please, just tell me, whatever it is.'

'I've had a bit of a difficult time lately,' Lily admitted, the words rushed, as if by saying them more quickly they wouldn't be so upsetting to her. 'And now I find myself . . . without a permanent place to stay.'

Florence remained silent. Her mind had whirred with several worrying possibilities of what might be bothering Lily, but this hadn't been one of them. Florence tried to understand why Lily should find herself in such a situation.

'Whatever happened?' Before Lily had a chance to answer,

it occurred to Florence that this situation might not have occurred that day, or even the day before. 'How long ago?'

'Two weeks.' Her voice cracked with emotion and Florence could see Lily was struggling not to cry.

Florence opened her top right drawer. She hated to see someone who was usually so composed being this upset. She withdrew a fresh handkerchief before hurrying around her desk and putting her arms around Lily's shoulders. 'Oh, my poor dear girl. Here, take this,' she said handing her the hanky. 'Wipe your eyes.'

'I . . . I feel such a failure,' Lily gulped between sobs.

'That's nonsense,' Florence argued, returning to her side of the desk and sitting back in her chair. 'Firstly, I need you to tell me where you're staying at the moment.' She almost held her breath, hoping that Lily had found reasonable rooms since she'd left her previous address.

'I've found a couple of rooms. They're not ideal, but they're warm and near to Pelham Street, so I'm happy enough with them.'

Florence was hurt to think that Lily hadn't come straight to her when her situation had changed but was worried Lily might clam up if she admitted how she felt. 'And why did you have to leave? I thought you were happy in your place.'

Lily cried fresh tears. 'I was, very happy.' She took a shuddering breath before continuing. 'However, a few months ago I, well, I began courting my landlady's younger son.' She glanced up at Florence, who nodded for her to continue. 'She caught us kissing two weeks ago and insisted I leave immediately.'

'I didn't know you had met someone,' Florence said, half to herself. She was surprised Lily hadn't confided in her about the young man she had been seeing.

Lily cleared her throat and stared at her hands. 'Yes. I thought we would probably marry, but when his mother insisted I leave he didn't say one word to stand up for me.' Fresh tears began to fall as Lily continued. 'I can't believe he cared so little for me that he simply let her throw me out. She only gave me two hours to pack and go.'

Florence clenched her jaw, wishing she knew where to find the landlady and give her a piece of her mind. She studied Lily's heartbroken face and knew that she needed to be a support to her, not act as a parent might and confront the other woman. Florence couldn't help feeling furious on her friend's behalf.

'That's monstrous behaviour, from both of them,' she snapped, her anger taking over from her good intentions to remain calm. 'If you wish, I'll go and speak with them. You only have to give me their names.'

'No, please.' Lily's eyes widened. 'I don't ever want to see him, or her, again.'

Florence was shocked by Lily's story. How could anyone evict a young woman? Lily could have found herself in all sorts of terrible situations. Florence was relieved that she had found another place to live, but couldn't help feeling hurt that Lily had chosen not to confide in her about all of this. This hard-working girl had still turned up to work each day immaculate and on time, despite dealing with heartbreak.

'I wish you'd come to me about this, Lily,' Florence said

softly. 'I want you to promise me faithfully that should you find yourself needing a friend for anything at all, you'll come to me immediately.' She waited for Lily to agree.

Lily nodded. 'Thank you, I will.'

'Good.'

Florence arrived home later, still slightly upset that Lily hadn't confided in her. She couldn't help thinking that she should be helping her friend somehow. An idea had been brewing in her mind since she left the store, but all the way home Jesse had been chatting about a meeting he'd endured earlier that day with the owner of a small store that he'd approached and made an offer for. She decided to speak to him about her thoughts once they had changed for dinner and were sitting quietly later.

She watched Jesse eat his meal. He placed his knife and fork on his empty plate and wiped his mouth with his napkin.

'I was speaking to Lily earlier today,' she began. 'She's had a few issues with her lodgings.' Florence refrained from mentioning the gentleman Lily had spoken to her about. 'I was thinking that maybe we could help her in some way.'

Jesse frowned. 'How exactly?'

Encouraged by his question, she said, 'Well, I thought maybe she could move in here for a while, or we could help her find somewhere else to live.'

Jesse took a sip from his water glass. 'She's homeless?'

'No, she's found somewhere to move to, but . . .'

'Then I don't see why we need to become involved. And I definitely don't think she would feel comfortable moving into our house. The very idea is alarming.'

Her temper rose instantly. 'I don't see why.'

Jesse reached out and took Florence's right hand in his. 'I like Lily, you know I do, but how do you think it would appear if we gave her preferential treatment over the other female staff?'

Florence sighed. Jesse did have a point there.

'And,' he continued, 'do you honestly think Lily would accept such an offer?' Before Florence could answer, he added, 'I presume she knows nothing of this idea?'

Florence shook her head. 'No, I thought I'd speak to you about it first.'

Jesse let go of her hand. 'That's a relief. No. I think we should leave matters well alone.' Florence wasn't convinced. 'Do you want to put her in a difficult position?' Jesse asked.

'How so?'

'She works for us and she's your friend. How will it make Lily feel to have to refuse an offer of a home from you?'

Florence nodded. Jesse's argument made sense, whether she liked it or not. Maybe the idea of Lily moving in had been more for her benefit than Lily's, Florence thought. She would have enjoyed having her in the same house and being able to confide in her whenever she wanted. Lily was the one person she truly trusted outside of her family. She had known Florence before she became the grand lady she now was and Florence always felt able to speak to her and ask her advice if she had a problem that she couldn't go to Jesse about. No, she was being selfish.

'You're right,' she conceded. 'I'll not mention anything to her.' Instead, she thought, she'd ask Lily if there was anything she could do to help her with her career.

Chapter 22

23rd August 1902

Florence sat next to Jesse in their saloon carriage on the train to Skegness and watched the scenery pass. She had been up since before dawn, excited about the day ahead. She took care to hide the nerves that she felt each time she took a large number of the staff out for the day. She was responsible for all these women and believed it was up to her to make sure that nothing untoward happened to any of them. There had been very few incidents since she and Jesse had begun arranging these events, but when they were accompanying five hundred women on an outing, who knew what might happen. There was a lot of excitement involved – in fact there had been since she had announced the event weeks earlier.

'Don't fret, Florence,' Jesse said quietly. 'All will be well.'

She loved that he knew her well enough to sense any concerns that she might be harbouring. On the other hand, his intuition about her feelings could also be annoying, especially when she was planning a surprise for him or had something she wasn't quite ready to share with him.

The weather was warm, and Florence was glad she had chosen to wear her new pale blue dress with touches of lace on the sleeves and bodice. She was pleased she had thought to have a hat made with matching material and although it was hotter today than she had hoped, she was relieved she had thought to bring a parasol to keep off the worst of the day's sun.

The train was shortly due to arrive in Skegness and was running only one minute late. Everyone had their own specially printed timetable and a pass. These documents furnished the women with admission to the pier as many times as they wished during the day without any of them being expected to pay. The guard opened the door and Jesse stepped down carefully, his stick in one hand. He held out his free hand to assist Florence. Florence stepped down and watched happily as a swathe of women disembarked from the four carriages kept exclusively for their party. She laughed as, moments later, there was an enthusiastic rush towards the sands.

Florence and Jesse smiled at each other. 'We should also stretch our legs, but I think we should make the most of having a gentle stroll on the pier,' Florence said. 'I'd rather not spend my journey home bothered by sand in my shoes.'

Jesse laughed. 'My sentiments entirely.'

They exchanged conversation with girls from the shop and factory when they passed by and stopped to take two seats just before eleven o'clock to enjoy the concert being held for their party on the pier.

Their noon dinner was delicious with Florence deciding

on the roast beef with vegetables and Jesse choosing the roast lamb.

'This mint sauce is the tastiest I've eaten for a long while,' he said wiping his moustache on the linen napkin.

'You'd better not let Cook know you think it's better than hers,' Florence teased. 'Anyway, I'm glad you enjoyed it,' she said. 'I had been told that the food here in the Pavilion was good and I'm relieved that it is. Will you manage a pudding?'

Jesse nodded. 'I was thinking that the blancmange might make a nice change.'

Florence was surprised; she had expected Jesse to choose the plum pie, which was usually his favourite. 'I'll try the plum pie,' she said, hoping her corset would allow such a big meal.

They decided to walk off their large lunch with a slow stroll to the top of the Pier Saloon to take in the view over Skegness and the North Sea, followed at five-thirty by tea in the Pavilion, consisting of cold meats, salad, and fancy cakes, then another performance by the band of Pierrots there.

By six-thirty Florence and Jesse were happy but both ready to board the train for their journey home. 'We still have an hour to wait until the train departs and takes us back to Nottingham,' Florence said, wishing her feet didn't ache quite so much.

'It's been a triumph of a day though, don't you think?' Jesse asked as they sat quietly in the shade near one of the windows of the Pavilion.

'Yes, I do,' Florence agreed, satisfied that everything had gone as well as she had hoped. She took a sip of her tea from the cup in front of her and spotted Lily walking quickly, her face pale as she glanced through the Pavilion windows as she passed. She seemed to be looking for someone.

Lily stumbled inside the Pavilion and scanned the room.

Florence nudged Jesse. 'Lily looks upset, don't you think?' Florence stood and gave Lily a discreet wave, relieved when Lily saw her. 'Something's wrong,' she whispered to Jesse, keeping a fixed smile on her face so as not to alert any of the others to her concerns.

'Mr Boot, Mrs Boot,' Lily said, using their formal names as she always did when they weren't in private.

'Take a seat, Lily,' Florence said, wanting her to sit so that their conversation could be conducted more privately than if they were standing. When Lily was sitting, Florence leaned slightly closer to her. 'Are you all right, Lily?' She noticed a waitress nearby and waved her over. 'Another pot of tea and a fresh cup and saucer, as quick as you can, please.'

Lily fanned herself with her timetable. 'I'm sorry to disturb you both,' she said, still breathless. 'There's a group of about ten of the women – we work on adjoining departments,' Lily explained. 'We decided to stick together for the day. We thought it would help the quieter, shyer girls in the group to feel like they were joining in and would also have someone to accompany them.'

'That sounds very sensible,' Jesse said, looking a little perplexed. 'Has something happened to one of them then?'

'Yes. It's Daisy Foster, one of the younger girls.'

Florence's heart pounded in panic. The tea arrived and she thanked the waitress and poured Lily a weak cup. 'Carry on.'

'She seems to have gone missing.'

Florence gasped and looked around to see if anyone had noticed. Thankfully everyone seemed too busy chatting and having fun to have done so. 'Are you certain?'

Lily nodded. 'Yes. We all arranged to meet up half an hour ago. After waiting for her for twenty minutes one of the girls sheepishly told us that she and Daisy had met up with two gentlemen.' She reddened slightly. 'It seems that Daisy decided to spend a little time alone with one of them and, well, she hasn't been seen since.' She shrugged. 'I have to admit that I'm worried.'

Florence was too. She looked at Jesse. 'What do you suggest we do?' she asked. 'We can't possibly leave without one of the girls.'

'No, we can't,' Jesse grumbled. 'Think of the damage to the Boots brand if we did such a thing. Our competitors would have a field day saying it was our fault to attempt such a large outing with staff and that we were only showing off.'

'Nonsense,' Florence snapped, irritated with Jesse's focus always being on his competitors and the business. 'I was more concerned about leaving a young woman in a strange place. If she's lost then she will be frightened.'

'Silly girl should have stayed with the others like she was supposed to then, shouldn't she?'

Jesse looked away before she had a chance to answer and tapped the table with the tip of his fingers. 'Let me give this some thought.'

Florence shot a reassuring smile at Lily. 'I'm sure we'll think of something,' she said, wishing she felt as confident as she sounded and hoping Jesse would hurry up and offer some advice.

'We still have time,' Jesse said, obviously annoyed by the turn of events. 'You finish your tea and then return to your group of friends. If you tell us where they are, Florence and I will make our way to them. If Daisy hasn't returned by the time we meet you, then we'll split up and all start looking for her. Quietly, mind – we don't want to alert too many people to what's happened.' He caught Florence's eye and cleared his throat. 'There's a young girl's reputation at stake here.'

'Yes,' agreed Florence, her mood soothed slightly by his change of tone. 'We must do our best to keep this between as few of us as possible. This might be a perfectly innocent case of Daisy losing track of time and we don't want the others to come up with notions of what's happened to her this afternoon. That's how gossip starts and we must avoid that at all costs.'

'Of course,' Lily said, looking horrified at the prospect. She quickly finished her tea and left them to return to the others.

Florence and Jesse stood, and, smiling at the others still enjoying their afternoon, began to stroll slowly out of the Pavilion.

'I do hope Daisy has found her way back to the others by now,' Florence whispered. If she hadn't, she wasn't sure where they would start looking for the girl in the busy town.

Jesse didn't reply as they walked the rest of the way in silence. Five minutes later, they saw Lily. She wasn't with a group of women but speaking with a man. Florence squinted in the sunlight and after a moment realised it was Thomas

Danby, the same man she had insisted be evicted from the Pelham Street store a few weeks before. By the look of things Lily seemed rather agitated.

'Jesse, do you see that?' Florence asked, picking up speed slightly to reach her friend quicker. She decided to let Lily explain to Jesse exactly who Mr Danby was.

'I most certainly do,' Jesse snapped.

They hurried up to the man, who was pleading with Lily about something. Florence was furious that he had managed to find a way to contact her and even more so that he had the temerity to appear upset with Lily. How dare he? she thought, wishing they were in private and she could give him a piece of her mind without others hearing.

He reached out to take Lily's hand but she snatched it away before he could touch her.

Florence felt Jesse tense next to her, and a moment later he raised his walking stick and tapped the man, none too gently, on the back of his shoulder. 'I'll thank you to step away from this young lady. Immediately, sir.'

The man spun round, his mouth open, a look of anguish on his face. He stepped back. 'Sir, um, Mr Boot,' he stammered, then, noticing Florence, added, 'Mrs Boot, um, this isn't as it probably seems, I can assure you.'

'I sincerely hope it isn't.' Florence linked arms with Lily. 'I thought I made my feelings towards you perfectly clear the last time we met.'

'What?' Jesse bellowed. 'You've met this miscreant before today? Where?' He glared at Mr Danby, then at Florence. 'And why have you not thought to tell me about it?

261

'Jesse, please lower your voice,' Florence hissed, aware that Jesse was drawing attention to them.

'Right, yes, of course.' He scowled at Mr Danby once more. 'Do you care to tell me where you've come into contact with this person before, my dear?'

'It was my fault,' Lily said. 'Mr Danby came to the store to speak to me.'

'During working hours?'

Florence closed her eyes pointedly and shook her head. 'Firstly, Lily, none of this has been your fault, as far as I can gather. Mr Danby took it upon himself to come to the store on a couple of occasions, despite –' she turned her attention to the man, who was now staring at his feet in embarrassment '– being asked not to do so. I then had a word with him and made sure that he was escorted out of the building. He promised not to return. Isn't that right, Mr Danby?'

'Yes, madam, it is.' He looked up at Florence and their eyes met. 'I was true to my word and didn't go back to Pelham Street, like you asked.'

Florence couldn't hide her annoyance. She turned her attention back to Lily. 'You're all right?' she murmured, relieved when Lily nodded.

'Maybe we should ask Miss Buttons what's been happening?' Jesse said scowling, his eyes like flints of steel.

'This is Thomas Danby,' Lily explained. 'His mother is my former landlady.'

'That still doesn't explain his determination to speak to you, Lily.' Jesse frowned.

Florence could see he was becoming exasperated by the

incident, so decided to push the conversation along. 'And was it a coincidence that you happened to be in Skegness on the very day that Miss Buttons came here?' she asked, trying to keep the sarcasm from her voice.

'No, it wasn't,' he admitted.

'Then what exactly are you doing here, young man?' Jesse tapped his stick against his knee breeches.

'I recalled Lily mentioning that she was going away on a work outing,' he stammered. 'I know I should have stood up to my mother over what happened, but she can be a very difficult woman. Then, when Lily left my mother's lodgings and I realised I didn't have a forwarding address for her, I tried to look for Lily, but couldn't find her. I went to the Pelham Street store a few times to speak to her. Each time I visited her department, I couldn't see her anywhere and I didn't like to ask anyone in case she wasn't to have friends calling on her at work.'

'I told you never to come to the store,' Lily said angrily, 'but you ignored me.'

He gave her an apologetic look. 'I'm sorry, but I was desperate to explain,' he hesitated. 'There are things I needed to speak to you about.'

Florence suspected that Lily was not in a forgiving mood and didn't blame her one bit. She recalled her and Jesse being pressured to stay away from each other when they first met, and shuddered. They would never have married and enjoyed these past few years together if they had allowed her mother to have her way.

'I thought I'd come here and see if I could talk some sense into Miss Buttons.'

'Sense?' Jesse bristled. 'I think, young man, that if Miss Buttons had wanted to have any contact with you, she would have made certain you had her forwarding address.'

Florence realised she needed to defuse the situation before Jesse lost his temper. She also remembered that they were supposed to be looking for Daisy. If they were to keep looking for her before it was time to return to the station and catch the train home, then she needed to concentrate her efforts a little more. 'Lily, do you have anything you wish to speak to Mr Danby about?'

'No.' Lily shook her head slowly. 'I think we've said all we need to say to each other.'

His mouth fell open and Thomas Danby looked stricken. 'Lily, please. I've tried to apologise about what happened.' He went to take her hand again, but Jesse raised his stick and held it between them.

'Miss Buttons said she has nothing to say to you, young man. Now, I believe you should do the gentlemanly thing and abide by her wishes. Please, leave her to enjoy the rest of her day out.'

Thomas Danby looked distraught. 'Yes, of course. I apologise for my behaviour.' He gave Lily a pleading look. 'If you change your mind about speaking to me, you know where you can find me,' he said, before Jesse stepped forward. He gave them a courteous nod and walked away, his shoulders slumped.

Florence couldn't help feeling a little sorry for the dejected man. He had seemed pleasant enough, despite his persistence, but if he couldn't stand up for Lily when she'd needed him to, then he really wasn't gentleman enough for her. Also, they didn't need men turning up at Boots stores demanding to speak to the shop assistants, so in that respect Florence was relieved that Lily had decided against seeing him.

'You are a brave girl,' she soothed, wondering if Lily regretted her decision to have nothing more to do with him.

'Thank you for coming to help me, both of you,' she said, pulling a handkerchief from her handbag and blowing her nose. 'Oh, and we've found Daisy.'

Florence sighed with relief. 'What happened to her?'

'She forgot the time, that's all. They had walked further than they had intended, apparently. She's back now with the other girls and seems perfectly fine. So, no harm done.'

'That's a relief,' Jesse said, shaking his head as he took his pocket watch from his waistcoat and studied it. 'I believe it's time we made our way to the station.' He grinned at Florence. 'I know that I, for one, will be happy to sit down again for a while.'

'Me, too,' Florence said. She was relieved that everything had turned out well in the end, as she knew Jesse must be. Thankfully, all the women were accounted for, but she would make certain that strict instructions were given before future outings, to ensure that no other girls would go missing like Daisy had done. She shivered despite the heat of the late evening sunshine and couldn't help thinking how very differently their day would be ending if something untoward had in fact happened to Daisy.

'Are you quite well?' Jesse asked, linking his arm through hers. 'You're not coming down with a chill, are you?'

She shook her head. 'No, I was thinking about how things might have turned out if we hadn't found Daisy.'

He patted her arm lightly. 'Don't ruin your day by worrying about such things. Daisy is fine, as is Lily.'

Florence hoped he was right.

'Now, let's get ourselves back to Skegness Station.'

Chapter 23

Two weeks later, Florence arrived home from a musical concert with Jesse. They liked to support local bands and so when they had received an invitation to attend a concert at a nearby parish hall, had decided to go. She didn't like taking time away in the evenings when John was home because she liked to make the most of having him at St Heliers.

She walked into the hall to hear their children's laughter emanating from the living room. It sounded like John was entertaining his sisters with a story. Florence and Jesse glanced at each other, amused.

'Good evening, Mr Boot, Mrs Boot,' Meadows said. 'I'm sorry I wasn't at the door to greet you.'

'No matter, Meadows,' Jesse said as he and Florence unbuttoned their coats and handed them and their hats to him to put away.

'Have the children eaten, do you know?' Florence asked.

The footman shook his head. 'I believe so, but I'm not certain,' he said folding Jesse's coat over his arm. 'Would you like me to go and check with Mrs Rudge?'

'Thank you, yes,' Florence said. As Meadows walked down

the hallway towards the green baize door separating the main house from the kitchen and servants' quarters, Florence touched Jesse's forearm lightly. 'Shall we go and join the children?'

'Yes, but I'll need to go to my office to do a little paperwork before retiring later.'

Florence wasn't surprised. Jesse often worked from seven in the morning until late and continued to look at paperwork once he was home. Wasn't she also guilty of doing the same thing, on occasion? she mused.

As Jesse opened the living room door, Florence saw Dorothy. She was standing in front of her brother and sister. John had returned home from his trip away the previous week and it was obviously Dorothy's turn at charades.

Florence and Jesse stood there for a little while, watching the fun in front of them, until John noticed them and ran up to them. Jesse had been trying especially hard to get along with John this holiday and she appreciated his efforts.

'Mother, Papa, you're home. You have to come and join in,' he insisted taking one of each of Florence's and Jesse's hands in his and stepping backwards, drawing them to the nearest sofa to sit down.

'Dorothy's not doing very well,' John explained. The girls giggled and Dorothy pulled a face at her brother.

'She's rubbish, Mother,' John said, teasing his sister. 'She's almost as bad as you are at charades.'

'I play perfectly well, thank you.' Florence frowned, amused at her daughter's teasing. 'You're worse than me.'

'Yes, John,' Margery agreed, nudging Dorothy gently. 'You're not losing because of anything we've done. Anyway, Dorothy and I can usually understand Mother's clues. You're the one who can't work them out.'

'There, you see?' Florence laughed, smiling at her son to soften any offence he might take from her words. 'I'm not that bad a partner, after all.'

Dorothy went to Jesse and gazed up at him. 'Papa, you join Margery and me, and Mother can help John.'

'I'm not sure,' Jesse said. 'I still have work to finish tonight.'

'Not yet, you don't,' Florence said, irritated with him for even contemplating missing a fun evening with his children. She knew it would do him good to spend some time with them. For once his work could wait. 'You know you love playing this game.'

Jesse grinned and to Florence's relief gave in without further argument. She sat watching as he gave the next clue. She wished Jesse would relax a little more with the children and wondered if his austere way was because his upbringing had been so much harder than her own. She knew he had enjoyed very little freedom as a child, having to leave school early and help his mother run her small shop after his father's premature death.

Shrieks of laughter snapped her out of her reverie. Florence had to pretend she'd been watching and joined in with the applause. It seemed that Jesse's team had done well and now it was her turn.

Meadows returned to the room shortly after. Florence stopped trying to re-enact the book *Dracula* by Bram Stoker and waited for him to speak. She had forgotten that she'd asked him to find out about the children's supper. After all, she'd spent more than enough time with them to ask them herself whether they had eaten yet.

'Madam, Mrs Rudge said she gave the children their supper about an hour ago. She wanted to know if you and Mr Boot would like any refreshments?'

'Jesse?' Florence asked.

Jesse nodded. 'I'd like some tea, I think.'

Florence looked at the children. 'Anyone else want anything to drink before going to bed? Cocoa?'

'No, thank you,' they all replied.

'I'll join my husband with a pot of tea. Thank you, Meadows.'

He gave her a nod and turned to leave.

The rest of the evening was fun. Florence enjoyed having her son back at home with them and taking part in their after-dinner parlour games. The house seemed much more vibrant when John was at home, Florence thought, watching her children playing. The girls loved having their brother back at home with them, and Florence didn't mind that it was much noisier in the house, with his laughter ringing out through the hallways, his footsteps thundering around the house as he ran up the stairs, and the shrieks of laughter from one or both of his sisters when he played a prank on them. She relished every chaotic moment of it.

She wished he didn't have to return to school in a couple of weeks and dreaded having to wave him off, but he had assured her he was settling in as well as the other new boys. He hadn't asked to leave yet, either, which gave her a little confidence that he didn't mind his school.

She sent the two girls to change for bed and walked with John to his bedroom. Florence leant against his desk and folded her arms, watching as he chose a pair of pyjamas to change into.

'You would tell me if you were unhappy at boarding school, wouldn't you John?' She waited for him to answer and wondered how she would persuade Jesse to allow John to return home if he did admit that he hated being away.

He turned away from his chest of drawers, pushing the open drawer closed with his knee and flung his pyjamas onto his bed.

'I'd rather be here, but then no one chooses to go away to school, do they?'

'I suppose not,' Florence said. 'But the masters are all right, are they?'

John shrugged. 'Most of them are very strict, but that's to be expected.' He stared at her thoughtfully for a moment, then walked over to her and gave her a tight hug. 'You've no need to worry about me, Mother. I'm fine.'

Florence's emotions threatened to overwhelm her. He hadn't hugged her like this for a couple of years, and it felt wonderful.

He let go of her and stepped back. 'My form master spoke to those of us who began at the school at the same time and told us that we are almost men and learning to be parted from our families is something that we need to do.'

Florence shook her head. 'You're far from being a man, John. Nor should you be expected to act like one, not for many years yet.'

He laughed. 'I don't mean literally, but I think he meant

for us to know that if we did find it a bit tough to settle in at first, then we needed to see it through and that soon we'd feel much better about being away from home.'

'And did you?'

'Yes. Sort of.' He scanned the room. 'I miss you, Father, and my sisters. I also miss my room.' He pointed at his ancient teddy sitting on a chair. 'Even that old thing that I don't need any more. I also miss Mrs Rudge's food. Everything about being at home really, but it's fine there. At least I'm not like my friend Frank.'

'How do you mean?'

'I can come home on exeat because we only live a couple of hours away. He can't go back and visit his family in Canada for a weekend, or even the shorter holidays.'

'No, I suppose he can't,' Florence replied, thinking how heartbreaking it must have been for his mother to send him all the way from Vancouver to England to study. That was something she never would have agreed to.

'Mother, do you think I might be able to invite Frank to come and stay for the half-term holiday?'

Florence loved the idea. 'Yes, I think that's a wonderful thing to do, John.'

'Should I ask Father, or will you?'

Florence smiled at her thoughtful son and ruffled his hair. 'I'll speak to your father about it, don't you worry.'

That night as she sat in front of her dressing-table mirror brushing her hair, Florence turned to Jesse.

'Jesse, I was speaking to John earlier about his friend Frank.'

'Who?'

'His schoolfriend who's from Vancouver in Canada. The poor boy is so far from home that he's obviously unable to go home to see his family for short periods.'

Jesse closed the notebook he was writing in and stared at her. 'Go on,' he said, his eyes twinkling in amusement.

Florence struggled not to smile back. She wanted Jesse to listen to what she had to say and take it seriously. 'John asked if his friend could come and stay with us for the next half-term holiday. I thought it was very thoughtful of him to think of it. What do you say?'

'I agree. I think we should ask him to stay. He can mess around here with John for a few days, play tennis, that sort of thing. Then we can all go down to Plaisaunce. I'm sure the boys would love to swim in the river like I used to do.' He gazed dreamily at the bedspread covering his legs and Florence's heart contracted at the sadness Jesse must feel at not being able to do all the things that he used to do as a younger, fitter man.

'Wonderful,' she cheered, hoping to distract his mood from becoming maudlin. 'I'll let John know first thing in the morning. He can write to Frank straightaway, so the boy has something to look forward to.'

She could picture John and Frank in their dormitory planning their half-term break together; the thought made her very happy.

'Now,' she said, placing her silver-backed hairbrush down on the walnut dressing table and standing up. 'It's been a long day and I think it's time we both got some much-needed sleep.' She walked over to the bed and, taking Jesse's notebook

273

and pen, took them over to the nearby cupboard and placed them on the top, too far from the bed for him to be able to reach without getting up.

Florence pulled back the bedspread on her side of the bed and got in. She leant over and gave Jesse a kiss, then rested her right palm on his cheek. 'Good night, darling Jesse,' she said before switching off the light and lying down.

Jesse lay on his side, his back to her, and within moments she heard his gentle snoring. She was happy he had agreed so readily to John's friend coming to stay. If John was finding it difficult despite his reassurances that he was coping perfectly well, Florence felt comforted to know that he now had a friend, and she looked forward to meeting the young man.

* * *

The weeks passed far too quickly for Florence's liking and it seemed like no time at all before the new term began at John's boarding school. Florence, Margery, and Dorothy, along with the servants, stood on the front steps of St Heliers trying not to show how glum they all felt as they waved goodbye.

As always, Jesse accompanied John back to school. Florence had offered to travel with them, but John had insisted that he found it easier with his father and didn't want her to become upset when the time came to leave him at the school.

Florence was relieved to stay behind. The last thing she wanted to do was make John's return to his school any harder for him than she imagined it must be. She also liked to think of Jesse and his son spending the time alone together. She suspected Jesse might also be hoping to speak to John about what he expected from him during the rest of the school term.

Florence felt the familiar pressure at the back of her throat and coughed. She had no intention of crying in front of everyone; she would save that for when she had a chance to go up to her bedroom on the pretext of collecting the latest novel she was reading.

Florence hurried up to her room and had barely closed the door when her threatening tears began to slide down her face. She hated having to see her son leave after such a wonderful summer at home with them again. She supposed it was more difficult because John had been with them for so long, and she wished she could keep him at St Heliers with her permanently. He had come this far, though, and didn't need his mother making a fuss. She knew John would hate that and find it embarrassing.

At least the girls were still young enough to live at home, she thought, wiping her eyes on a handkerchief and then blowing her nose. What on earth was she going to be like when they all married and moved away for good? Florence felt the rise of fresh tears and pushed the thought away. Thankfully they were still only twelve and ten years old, so she had a long time to wait before she needed to worry about that happening. Florence cleared her throat and checked her reflection in the mirror to make sure there was no sign that she had been crying. She picked up her copy of *The Hound of the Baskervilles* and went back downstairs to spend some time reading with her daughters.

It was a warm late-September Sunday afternoon and

Florence was looking forward to returning to work the following day. Being in the office always kept her mind busy and stopped her from worrying about her children. She entered her bright, sun-filled conservatory and her mood lifted as she was greeted by the sight of her two beautiful daughters sitting on cushions reading. They were absorbed by their books and seeing them cheered her up slightly. She might not have her boy at home with her, but her girls were still here.

Florence fanned her face with her hand. The room was stifling so she walked over to the double doors leading to the garden and opened them.

'Wouldn't you both rather sit outside in the shade? It's a beautiful day and it'll soon be October and too cold to want to read outside.'

Dorothy placed a card bookmark in between the pages she had been reading before closing the book. 'I don't know why we didn't think of that ourselves,' she said, standing up.

Florence was pleased. She believed everyone should have as much fresh air as possible to keep their constitution healthy. She assumed it might be her upbringing so near to the sea in Jersey that made her love being outside.

'We're lucky enough to live in a beautiful place with little noise and should make the most of this garden during the warmer months.'

The girls stood and followed her outside to take a seat at the oak table on the patio to the side of the house.

Dorothy caught Florence's eye as they both settled in their seats. She giggled. 'What's so funny?' Florence asked, unable to help laughing at her daughter's amusement.

'Mother, you say that we have to make the most of sitting outside, but I've seen you sitting out here on sunny days in the winter and reading.'

Florence shrugged. 'Yes, I've done that many times, but it's not something I imagine the two of you doing without much persuasion.'

Margery gave a mock shiver. 'I'd rather sit inside where it's warm and comfier,' she said. 'Dorothy would too, wouldn't you?'

Dorothy agreed.

Florence shook her head and couldn't help thinking of Lily when she had first met her and how, at just a few years older than Dorothy, Lily was caring for her siblings and going without food to make sure they had enough to eat. She was relieved she had been able to protect her daughters from the difficulties so many other young girls faced on a daily basis. It occurred to her that maybe she was shielding Dorothy and Margery too much and it would soon be time for them to become aware of how so many young women lived.

Chapter 24

December 1902

It was early December and much colder than it had been in recent weeks. They had experienced a few flurries of snow, but thankfully nothing had settled.

Florence sat at her desk reviewing the silk banner in her hand. She was glad she had chosen the third and fourth verse of the poem and used it for her moral verse for this year's Christmas gift to her female staff. Her intention had always been that these banners should be given in appreciation of her girls' hard work and also to support them through any difficult times they might have the following year.

She held it up for Miss Tweed to read. 'What do you think of the verse I chose this year?'

Agnes Tweed smiled. 'Mrs Boot, you must have asked me that question ten times over the past couple of months. I think, as I do each year, that you have made a perfect choice and I'm certain the women will cherish them.'

'Thank you,' Florence said, wishing she was as confident as her secretary that she had chosen wisely.

Florence liked to be fair and so thought that to give the women the same gift – and one to which she had given so much thought – was the perfect way to show how much she valued each of them. For Miss Tweed and Lily, she would privately give something extra. As she did each year, Florence would arrange for a hamper to be delivered to Miss Tweed's home that she could share with her invalid mother. For Lily, though, she still had to find a present that she felt would suit her. Florence wanted it to be something more personal that Lily could make use of. She still had time yet, she told herself.

Florence enjoyed Christmas and each year it seemed more fun than the last. She had loved the magic that the children had felt when they were younger, but even at their ages they very much looked forward to the festivities and sharing gifts out to the servants, as well as celebrating as a family.

Florence was as organised as ever and looked forward to starting a new year. She stroked the leather cover of her Boots scribbling diary, recalling how she had been inspired by the Pears Annuals that she treated herself to each year from her father's stationery shop. She had tried to persuade Jesse seven years earlier that they should produce and sell them. He hadn't taken to the idea, so Florence explained that they could include adverts for their entire business in these books. She had also cheekily suggested that they fix the price at sixpence to encourage customers to make it their tradition to buy one each year.

She smiled to herself, recalling Jesse's horror after speaking to their printing department and discovering that Florence was expecting him to sell something for the same amount that it cost the company to produce it. However, she had insisted that she was right and was thrilled when she'd persuaded him to at least give it a try. Now, their Boots scribbling diaries sold more with each passing year. She loved hers and it still brought joy to her each year when she received her new one.

Her thoughts returned to Christmas preparations. She had already bought most of the presents she was giving to her family and the servants. Being Head Buyer of the Boots stores enabled her to source items that others would not have come across before. She enjoyed surprising her family and friends with these new and exciting gifts each year, and this year would not be any different.

After a lot of thought, Florence had commissioned a painting to be done of her and the three children for Jesse's present this year. It had been difficult at times to make appointments for sittings, especially as there had only been a few weeks when John was home over the summer and the girls weren't busy on outings with their friends.

Florence struggled with the feeling that she wasn't needed as much by the children now that they were growing up. She ached for their family life to be like it had been when the children were small and she and Jesse had spent all their time away from work with them, reading them stories, planning days out, and going on picnics together.

Jesse noticed her deep in thought one evening as she sat in the living room in front of the fire, the book she had been reading now resting in her lap.

'You look as if you have the weight of the world on your shoulders. What's wrong?'

She shrugged his comment away. 'It's nothing,' she fibbed. 'I'm just a little tired, that's all.'

Jesse raised his eyebrows. 'Florence, I know you too well to be fobbed off by that answer. Now, are you going to tell me, or am I going to have to take that book from you and hold it ransom until you do?'

Florence laughed. Jesse knew better than to take one of her books from her. 'I was thinking how little the children seem to need me nowadays.'

'Ah, so that's what's troubling you.' He smiled, looking relieved. 'I'm sure all mothers feel the same.'

'Probably,' she agreed. At least she had her work to focus on each day, she mused. How did other women cope when their babies grew up and didn't rely on them any more? She wondered why she had never wondered how she'd deal with this time in her life. The transition was traumatic.

'Is there anything I can do to help make you feel better?'

Florence loved him for caring so much. 'No. I'm luckier than most women. I have you and the children are still at home for a while yet. I'll just have to keep myself busy with my work. I'm just finding it a little difficult to come to terms with my role as a mother changing. Nothing more. I'll be fine.'

* * *

It was Christmas Eve and the children were in their beds and supposedly asleep, and Jesse had followed a couple of hours before. He was exhausted from working even longer hours recently and Florence was happy that he would now have a couple of enforced days away from the business. She was always at her most content when her brood were around her.

An hour earlier, Florence had finished carefully wrapping her final present. Meadows and Harriet had helped her carry all the gifts from the back of the library out to the hall to place each of them haphazardly under the vast Christmas tree. She thought back to their first Christmases at St Heliers and how their Christmas tree had been put up in the living room, so that the family could spend the festivities cosily together. Now everything seemed bigger and more elaborate.

She looked at the many presents; they weren't all for the children. Florence always bought one for each of her servants, Miss Tweed, and a couple for Lily.

She took two boxes from Meadows's hands and noticed that although he was his usual polite, immaculate self, there was something different about him. He seemed lacklustre and there were dark shadows under his eyes. He didn't seem to exude his usual brightness.

'Like this, Mrs Boot?' Harriet asked, moving the last present into place and distracting Florence from her concerns.

'Yes, that's perfect. The children will be very excited to see this display when they rise in the morning.'

'They will,' Harriet agreed, smiling.

Florence knew her children were much luckier than many other children, but it gave her joy to treat them in this way. Christmas should be magical, she thought, remembering hers as being very much that way despite her parents not having the money to pay for more than one gift each. She recalled only too well the joy she had experienced every

Christmas morning when she pulled on her dressing gown and crept with her younger sister Amy into their parents' small living room.

The air in her parents' flat matched that of the hall and was filled with the delicious pine scent. Florence recalled the thrill of anticipation they all felt and how each of them looked forward to unwrapping their gift on their return from chapel. Florence wanted her own children to enjoy that same excitement. She looked down at the display in front of her. Florence wanted it to look as if Father Christmas had visited and had strewn a pile of brightly coloured items under their vast tree.

Since they had first set up their tree in the hall, it occurred to Florence that it was the one place in the household where everyone would see it many times each day. Why choose to keep something this magical hidden away from the servants who would have no cause to visit the living room? It was now one of their festive traditions and she hoped the servants enjoyed it as much as they did.

Nellie poked her head around the baize door. Florence noticed her and waved her over to where she was standing.

'What do you think, Nellie?'

The young woman's eyes were wide as she stared up at the tall, intricately decorated tree. 'It's perfect.'

'Are you happy with the one in the servants' quarters?' Florence asked, referring to the smaller one in their living room that Meadows had set up earlier in the week.

'It's beautiful, Mrs Boot. When I went to speak to Mr Meadows in the servants' sitting room last week and saw Mrs Rudge and Violet decorating the pretty tree that you and Mr

Boot ordered for us, I couldn't help thinking how very kind you are to us all.'

A lump constricted Flornce's throat. It mattered to her that those in her house had a special time over Christmas. Most of them had now worked for her family for several years and seeing their delight each year brought it home to her how special this time should be.

'We want you all to treasure this time,' Florence said. Then, thinking of Nellie's mother, brother, and son, asked, 'How's your mother? Is she well?'

Nellie gave Florence a tight smile. 'She's much happier since I've been working here, Mrs Boot. She feels like we've got back some of the respectability the family lost since, well, since what happened when I fell for my boy.'

'I'm glad, Nellie.'

'You've done more for me than anyone else ever has, Mrs Boot.'

Florence was relieved that after her initial misjudgement that had caused Nellie and her family so much humiliation, she had been able to make things right. What Nellie didn't realise, though, was how much Florence appreciated having the means to be able to help her, and her other female staff when they needed her to. It was a luxury few could afford.

Chapter 25

Spring 1904

The following months passed quickly and despite Jesse's assurances to the contrary, she couldn't ignore the signs that his health was continually declining. It had been doing so steadily since his physical collapse three years before. She watched him attempting to mount his horse to conduct his usual store visits and, unable to bear the pain of seeing his increasing frustration as his groom failed to get him up onto the saddle, Florence went outside to confront her husband.

'For pity's sake, stop being so feeble,' Jesse shouted at the poor man attempting to assist him.

'I'm sorry, sir. I'll try again.' He glanced at Florence, his face red from effort and humiliation, and she decided that he had endured enough.

'Jesse, please come inside for a moment. I need to speak to you about something.'

'Now is not the time, Florence,' he snapped, taking hold of the front and back of the saddle while he waited for the groom to try once again to give him a leg up onto the horse.

'Now is exactly the time,' she argued, standing with her hands on her hips, aware that he would know by her stance that she meant business and would not accept any further rebuttal.

Jesse stared at her for a moment before letting go of the saddle. 'Wait for me. I shouldn't be too long.'

Florence walked with Jesse into the house and drew him into the living room, closing the door behind them. 'Sit down, Jesse,' she said, taking a seat opposite his usual chair.

Jesse sighed heavily. 'I think I know what you're going to say.'

She hoped so, because it would save a lot of time and worry about how best to say what was on her mind. 'Go on then, what do you think it is?'

Jesse unbuttoned his jacket and sat back in the chair. He was perspiring and she was angry with him for pushing himself unnecessarily.

'You are angry with me for shouting at the groom.'

Once again he was in denial about his physical wellbeing. 'Yes, I am,' Florence said, 'but not only because of you giving that poor man a difficult time.' She leant forward. 'Jesse, you know as well as I do that you shouldn't be riding horses any longer.'

He frowned indignantly. 'I disagree . . .'

She shook her head. 'No, you don't, not if you're being honest. We both know that you don't have the strength in your legs to control a horse. Do you? Honestly.'

Jesse lowered his gaze and seemed to age in front of her eyes. She glanced at his poor hands, becoming more misshapen by the year. He struggled so much with his walking now, too. It broke her heart to see her beloved husband in such a state, but mostly she was frightened for him when he pushed himself too far.

'Jesse, you have to accept that you can't do all the things you used to do.'

'I can't do very much at all,' he said miserably.

Florence moved to sit next to him on the arm of his chair. 'It's unfair and heartbreaking for you, I know that, but I also know that you have no choice but to give in to some of the restrictions you now face with your body. Like riding horses.'

'I need to inspect the stores,' he argued, but she could see it was only a half-hearted attempt to fight back.

'I couldn't bear for you to fall off and hurt yourself, or even worse, be killed. Jesse, we both need to be sensible. There's no reason to stop your visits to the stores, but you need to change your mode of transport. You could go by carriage. It would be more comfortable, and at least you would stay dry when it rains. I always worry about you catching a chill when you're caught out in bad weather.'

'You're always fretting about me.'

'Yes,' she said, smiling at him. 'I know, but that's because I love you and want you around for as long as possible.'

'It's so damned unfair,' Jesse shouted. 'I used to be such a fit young man, always swimming, walking for miles and miles.'

Florence's heart ached for him. 'Yes, I know. It is horribly unfair. But we have to face the fact that there are certain things you need to change and one of those is riding horses. Right away, Jesse. Now, will you tell the groom that you won't be going out on horseback again, or would you like me to do it?'

'No,' he said after a moment's hesitation. 'I'll do it.'

Florence helped Jesse to stand and watched him walk with great difficulty out of the room. Why was life so cruel sometimes? she wondered. It was agonising to watch someone with Jesse's determination and zest for life being constricted by his physical weaknesses. They would need to sell the horses too, she thought sadly. It would be too painful for Jesse to keep them and not be able to ride them. She struggled to hold back her tears.

Florence hoped Jesse would be able to continue as the head of the Boots empire, but worried that if his health continued to deteriorate at its current rate, he would have no choice but to stand down and spend more time at home taking things easy. She knew it was an impossible notion for Jesse not to work; Boots was his life.

She decided to go and sit quietly in the library. Maybe a book would take her mind off her worries about Jesse. Florence walked through to the next room and stood in front of the rows of books that she and Jesse had chosen over the years. They had a massive collection that they were so proud of, but now she stared at them and couldn't think of one that would stop her from fretting about her husband.

Eventually she decided against bothering with a book and instead sat by the window looking out at her rose garden. She and Jesse had chosen the roses with care when they had first moved in to the house. She loved the different colours and scents, especially of the tea roses closest to the window, and on warm summer evenings the delicious scent would waft into the library, making her smile and think back to those first few years living here when the children were toddlers.

'Florence?' she heard Jesse calling from the hallway. She stood up to go to the door to let him know where to find her.

'I believe Mrs Boot might be in the library, sir,' Meadows said, just as Florence went to take hold of the door handle. 'Would you like me to have a look for you?'

Jesse must have said yes, because a moment later Florence heard Meadows's footsteps nearing the library door. Just before he opened it, she let go and stepped back.

'Oh, Mrs Boot, I didn't hit you with the door, did I?' Meadows asked, looking stunned to see her standing immediately inside the room.

Florence shook her head. 'No, I heard you coming and stepped back.' She stepped forward and spotted Jesse. 'I'm through here. Shall I come to you?'

'No,' he snapped angrily. 'I can still walk, you know. Just about.'

They went back into the library and sat on the nearest chairs. She could see a sparkle in Jesse's eyes but couldn't imagine what had caused that to happen.

'You're looking rather pleased with yourself,' she said, hoping that he was happy and that she hadn't read his expression wrongly.

'I am. I went to speak to Sam, the groom.'

'Yes,' she said, unsure why he was telling her something

she already knew. 'And what did he say? He must have realised that if you didn't need the horses you would also not be needing his services in the future.' She was confused. Why would Jesse look happy about letting someone go? That was not like him at all.

'He suggested that if I can't ride horses, maybe I should purchase an automobile to take me wherever I need to go instead.'

Florence stared at him, trying to gauge if he was serious. 'An automobile? Would you want one? Are they safe?' She tried to think of all the benefits of Jesse being able to drive around on four wheels rather than in a carriage.

'Yes, I think it's a tremendous idea. I told him that if he learnt to drive the thing, then he can be my chauffeur. Don't you think that's a good idea? I might even learn to drive myself around. Wouldn't that be fun?'

Florence wasn't so sure. At least, she reasoned, it would mean Jesse giving up riding, so this had to be a preferable option. 'I think it's a marvellous idea. And if Sam learns to drive the automobile then you won't have to let him go. Then everyone will be happy.'

'Especially you,' Jesse said with a grin.

'Yes,' Florence smiled. 'Especially me.'

'We could go on outings together. Drive out to discover new places on the weekends. It would make travelling from here to Plaisaunce much quicker.' He thought for a moment. 'I could visit more stores at a time, too.' Jesse nodded. 'I'm liking this idea of Sam's more by the minute.'

All Florence knew was that Jesse had found an alternative

to riding his beloved horses, as well as a way to keep his independence. Jesse's fears about losing his mobility had once again been soothed. He wasn't going to have to find a way to take a step back from his position at the helm of his business empire, and for that she was enormously grateful.

the roll of his fickle'd horses as well as a way to lose the hard-earned money he'd been about losing his coin. He had once again been sickened. He was going to prison and it was just like a trap. Jack Benny's position at the helm of his business empire, and for that she was enormously grateful.

Chapter 26

Easter 1904

John had invited Frank to stay at St Heliers for the Easter holidays. Florence and Jesse liked him very much and were happy for him to stay whenever he wasn't able to return home to Canada for the holidays. It was hard to believe that John was now fifteen. He only had two more years before leaving school, although Jesse was determined for him to continue his education and go to university.

Florence knew by reading John's school reports that passing many exams was not presently something that his masters expected of him. Jesse, of course, disagreed and believed that if John applied himself more diligently to his studies, then he still had time to achieve something worthwhile.

'How are you getting along with your studies, Frank?' Jesse asked over lunch on Frank's second day staying with them. 'Do you expect to pass all your exams and go on to university?'

Frank finished his mouthful of boiled potatoes and nodded. 'I hope to pass all my exams, sir, apart from German,' he said. 'I'm not very good with languages, but my father said I won't need them when I start working with him full time on the farm.'

Jesse looked confused. Florence wished he would stop questioning Frank and knew it was only so that he could bolster his argument when it was time to speak to John about returning to school after the holidays.

'If you're returning to Canada, then will you attend university there?'

'No, sir. My father doesn't think it's necessary that I do. He said after I finish at this school, I'll learn all I need to know from him to carry on our family business.'

Jesse nodded thoughtfully and glanced at John, who, Florence noticed, appeared to be trying to make himself as inconspicuous as possible. She didn't blame him; conversations about his schooling always seemed to rile both John and her.

Later that afternoon when the boys were out for a walk, Jesse and Florence sat in the conservatory reading.

Jesse was the first to break the silence. 'Do you think I'm wrong expecting John to continue with his education and attend university?'

She placed her forefinger in her book and partially closed it. 'I think it's worth him going if he does well in his final exams, but I don't expect him to do all that well. We both know John is a kind, thoughtful, and caring boy, but he's not the most academically gifted.'

'He would be if he focused a little more on his studies.'

Florence tilted her head to one side. 'Jesse, I long for the day when John has finished his education and can be the man he's meant to be.'

'What's that supposed to mean?'

'That we can discuss this endlessly, but all that happens is you are disappointed and I'm frustrated that you expect things from John that he is unable to give you.'

'I only do it because I worry that if I don't he won't make anything of himself.'

Florence softened her tone. She knew that Jesse cared what happened to their son, but she wished he wouldn't be so hard on him all the time. 'Just remember, Jesse, John is not you. He's had a very different upbringing to you, and to me. We can't expect him to see things as we do, or to worry about the same things. I know you want the best for him but he needs to be allowed to become the man he's meant to be.'

Jesse stared at her. She could see he was nonplussed and knew that she was wasting her time trying to change his mind about John and his expectations of him.

'Can we at least wait and see how well John does before jumping to conclusions?'

Jesse stared at her thoughtfully. 'Yes, I'll do as you ask.'

* * *

The following morning, Florence was relieved to return to work and have something other than John's education to focus on. She had left the boys at the house and Dorothy and Margery were visiting their friends for the day. What she was looking forward to today was giving Lily and two of the other women in her office the news that they had been promoted to oversee larger departments in the stores.

Florence knew that Lily's career was paramount to her. She couldn't help thinking that if Lily hadn't come across Thomas Danby when she had and been put off by his spineless treatment of her, then maybe she might have met and married someone else by now. As soon as Florence had the thought, she felt guilty. It wasn't as if Lily had ever acted, or admitted that she felt, dissatisfied with her life. Lily enjoyed having a career, as did she, Florence mused.

Lily had made friends with a large group of the other women at Boots and never said she felt lonely. Florence was grateful to her friend for always being there whenever she needed someone to confide in. She was happy to be able to reward Lily for all her hard work over the years at Boots and knew that the validation this promotion brought would mean a huge amount to Lily. She also hoped that the extra money in Lily's wage packet might help her to afford a few luxuries now and then.

Lily's promotion also meant an invitation for her to Plaisaunce, along with the other staff who would hear today that they were being rewarded for all their hard work.

Florence checked the twenty letters to the relevant members of staff, then asked Miss Tweed to arrange for each member of staff to come to her office individually so that she could personally thank them and tell them the good news.

When it was Lily's turn, Florence told her about her promotion and the increase in her salary and then handed over the letter and enclosed invitation to Plaisaunce that weekend.

Lily read her letter and beamed at Florence. 'Thank you so very much, Florence. I'm delighted and I know you well enough to understand that this truly is because of my work and nothing to do with us being friends. I really appreciate that, too.'

Florence was relieved she didn't have to reassure her friend. 'You deserve this, Lily. You've worked tirelessly for Boots since your arrival and it's because of your diligence and thoughtfulness that you have reached managerial status in the firm.' Florence smiled at Lily and lowered her voice in case the next member of staff she was to meet was already waiting outside her office. 'I'm proud of all you've achieved. When I think back to that frightened young girl coming to work at Rowe's Stationers that first day –' she sighed and placed her hand on her chest '– well, I find it hard to imagine that she grew up to become not only a dear friend to me but also one of Boots' most valued members of staff.'

Lily opened her mouth but didn't say anything. She shook her head. 'You were always so kind to me, Florence, and gave me a chance when I had no experience, and little confidence. I always wanted to emulate your work ethic and this huge honour shows me how far I've come. You've made me very happy.'

Florence gave her friend a tight hug. 'I hope you'll be free to come down to Plaisaunce for the weekend?'

Lily nodded. 'I wouldn't miss it for the world.'

* * *

Florence loved the riverside summer home in Plaisaunce that she and Jesse had built with its recreation club house and extensive grounds. They had chosen the large plot on Wilford

Lane, in the pretty village of Wilford, and had already spent many weekends there with their family. It was only twenty minutes from their home by carriage, and even less now that Jesse was going to buy a car, but Florence always felt like she was on holiday when she was staying here.

Jesse had wanted somewhere for them to retreat to as a family, mostly in the summer months, but also a place where they could entertain managers and members of staff from the various Boots stores or factories. They often invited them to stay with their wives and enjoy social events and musical evenings, wanting their guests to be able to relax away from work among the furnishings that Florence had enjoyed taking months to track down. It had been important for her to achieve just the result she wanted – something between a home from home and a private members' club. Everything had to be just right for their guests' experience at Plaisaunce because Florence and Jesse were determined that everyone they invited to their summer home would remember their time there with fondness.

Today, twenty managers and their husbands, or wives, including the newly promoted staff, would be visiting. Florence had also invited her servants from St Heliers and from her chair on the veranda she could see some of them enjoying the lawn tennis. Two teams were also competing on the bowling green and Florence grinned as she thought how noisy they were being and doubted members of an actual bowling club would be so exuberant.

She looked over at her guests taking in the fun atmosphere. Some were reading, others were chatting, and by the whispered conversation next to her, it was clear that some were catching up on gossip. She looked around her at the happy, smiling faces and knew that she was incredibly lucky to be in a position to be able to provide such a welcoming place for these wonderful people. She only wished she could help even more people.

Florence especially enjoyed watching Jesse relax. He was now dressed in his smart brown velvet jacket as he sat on the veranda in his bath chair and enjoyed an in-depth conversation with one of his managers.

Florence noticed the two women on the next table had finished their conversation and were watching her.

'I think it's time I do what I expect of everyone else and start having fun. What do you think?' She closed the folder on her lap, shutting away the work that she had been doing.

'Quite right, Mrs Boot,' the older woman, Mabel, said reddening slightly. 'You should be enjoying today as much as the rest of us.'

'Yes,' agreed her companion, whom Florence recognised at Ethel from the Dry Goods Department. 'We wouldn't be here having this lovely day without your invitation and you deserve to enjoy time away from work, like we do.'

'Thank you, ladies,' Florence said, their kind words making her happy. 'You're enjoying yourselves then?'

'We are,' they agreed.

'Ever so much,' Mabel added. 'We all love working for you and Mr Boot. We know we're very lucky to have such thoughtful employers.'

Florence was touched. 'That's very kind of you to say so. I

hope you're going to enjoy listening to the brass band. They're made up wholly of Boots employees. Have you heard them before?'

Mabel and Ethel shook their heads.

'They only formed last year, but they're extremely good. Well, I'll leave you to enjoy your afternoon,' Florence said, not wishing to impose on the women any further.

She had already checked with her staff at Plaisaunce that all the preparations had been finalised for the rest of the Boots employees that were expected to arrive for the event in the next two hours. Her final duty had been to ensure the gentleman delivering and setting up their firework display had also arrived and she had been assured that this was the case

Florence momentarily looked across the immaculate shrub-filled flower borders surrounding the lawn as a cheer interrupted her thoughts. She smiled, relishing seeing so many people enjoying the entertainment that she and Jesse had laid on for them.

She hadn't noticed Lily coming to join her. She stood by Florence's table and cleared her throat. 'Good afternoon.'

Florence studied her friend's expression and couldn't miss the strained look on her face. 'Hello, Lily. Please, sit down. Would you like me to ask for some tea to be brought through to us?'

Lily shook her head. 'No, thank you.'

'You seem worried.' Florence folded her hands in her lap. 'Is something the matter?'

Lily grimaced and stared across the garden to the river

where several male members were splashing each other at the water's edge while their wives sat chatting in the sunshine.

A thought occurred to Florence. 'Shall we take a stroll?' she asked, aware that Ethel and Mabel were close enough to hear their conversation.

'Yes, that would be lovely. Thank you.'

They walked down the nearest pathway, past the people bowling and on towards the lawned area by the river. 'We'll have more privacy down here.'

They walked in silence for a few moments and finally, just when Florence thought Lily had changed her mind about speaking to her, she cleared her throat. 'I bumped into Thomas Danby the other day.'

Whatever Florence had been expecting to hear, this was not it. She stopped walking and turned to Lily. 'Are you all right? Did he say anything to you?'

Lily bent to pick a long blade of grass that the gardeners must have missed. 'It was strange. I did have a pang of regret that I had never married.'

Her admission saddened Florence. 'Oh, Lily. Are you all right?'

Lily dropped the grass and smiled at Florence, who hoped it wasn't too forced. 'I'm fine. I only felt that way for the briefest moment.'

'Truly?' Florence studied her friend, hoping she was being truthful about how the unexpected meeting had made her feel.

Lily laughed. 'Yes, I had the tiniest pang of what might have been. Not if I'd married him, because I know that to have done so would have been a disaster, but it made me think how life might have been if I had married.'

Florence rested her hand on Lily's arm. They walked on together.

'Florence, please don't worry. I'm only telling you because I wanted to share this with someone who knows me well enough and who had met him. Nothing more. I soon recovered from my momentary lapse of sense and have been relieved ever since that I'm a career woman, valued by my employers. I can do whatever I choose to out of work hours. I live where I want, as long as I can afford it, no man tells me what to do, or treats me like their private servant, and my time is my own. I love my life, I really do, and I wouldn't change it for anyone now.'

'You sound like I used to before I met Jesse,' Florence said with a laugh. 'If I'm honest, I wasn't surprised that you didn't crave having your own children.' She wondered if she might have overstepped the boundaries of their friendship when Lily didn't reply. 'I'm sorry, that was rude of me. I should never have—'

'Nonsense, Florence. We have been friends for years and I'm sure you know me better than anyone else. You are right. I've never longed to have children. Being the eldest child and having the constant responsibility of caring for my siblings – and most of the time my mother – since I was eight put paid to any notions of parenthood.'

Florence stared at the river as they walked along the grassy bank. She was relieved she hadn't insulted her friend by her remark and understood completely why Lily would think in such a way.

'No. I'm happy working and making my own decisions,' Lily continued.

Florence nodded, relieved. 'Good for you.' She spotted two of Lily's colleagues waving in their direction from the tennis court. One was holding up a racquet and pointing to it.

This was Lily's time and Florence was delighted that her friend was relishing every moment. 'I think you're wanted,' Florence said, laughing and pointing over to the tennis courts. 'It looks like your friends are hoping you'll play doubles with them.'

Lily grinned. 'Do you mind if I cut our conversation short and go to join them? I'm not very good really, and only ever play when you invite me here, but I do enjoy the exercise.'

'Not at all,' Florence said, waving her away. 'Go, before they find another player to take your place.'

Florence watched Lily run along the grass towards the tennis area, thrilled to see her friend enjoying her day out so much. Yes, Lily Buttons had exceeded all Florence's hopes for her, and it made her want to do much more for the many other women who worked for her.

Later that evening, as Florence and Jesse waved off their guests who were not staying at Plaisaunce for the firework display, Lily greeted them on the pathway with the two women that Florence recognised from the doubles match earlier.

'I hope you've enjoyed yourselves today?' Jesse asked.

'Very much,' Lily said, and the others agreed. 'We're going to fetch jackets and then watch the fireworks.'

'Splendid,' Jesse said. 'We're also looking forward to them, aren't we, dear?'

'We are.' Florence noticed that he was having difficulty walking again today and hoped that the chair she had arranged to be set out for him was waiting. 'You three run along for your jackets and make sure you have some of the hot drinks that will be laid on in front of the pavilion. It's been such a warm day, but this evening is rather chilly for my liking.'

The women ran off and Florence linked arms with Jesse. 'Would you like me to ask for a blanket to be brought out for you to cover your legs for the display? I wouldn't want you to be cold and you'll be sitting still for about fifteen minutes.'

Jesse leant over and kissed her on the cheek. 'You look after everyone so well, my darling. I worry sometimes that you're so focused on me, the children, and all your girls that you occasionally forget yourself.'

Florence hugged his arm to her. 'I don't worry about me. I know you're making sure I'm well cared for, so I don't have worry, do I?'

Jesse nodded. 'I suppose you're right. We make a good pair, don't we?'

'We do,' she agreed, enjoying having some time alone with him during their busy day to reminisce before the evening entertainments began. 'And we always have done.'

Chapter 27

June 1904

Florence could barely take in that the months were flying by so fast. It had been a busy spring and Florence was enjoying the warmer weather. She was also looking forward to the summer holidays and having John back home once again.

She had finally caught up at the office since her arrival back in England from a shopping trip to the continent a few weeks before. It had been tiring, with back-to-back meetings with suppliers and being entertained in the evening over meals by producers of the products she was looking to source for the Boots stores.

Most importantly, her shopping trip had been a huge success. Jesse had been delighted with all the deals she had made and had assured her that her hard work would pay off over the following summer and winter now that they could introduce exciting new stock for their customers. He always enjoyed supplying items that other local stores weren't able to sell.

'Do we really have to go on an outing to the Ivory Palace?' Jesse asked, lying on his bed resting his eyes. 'The Midlands Industrial Exhibition isn't going anywhere for a while yet.'

Florence knew he was right, but John's Canadian friend Frank was staying with them for a few weeks while his mother recovered from surgery that she had unexpectedly needed. Florence had promised the children on several occasions that she would arrange a family outing to the exhibition and her latest trip away had delayed it for a second time already. Now that she and her lady's maid, Harriet, were back, Florence knew that she had made the children wait as long as her conscience could bear.

'No, Jesse,' she disagreed, sitting at her dressing table and noticing how lacklustre her skin appeared. She needed more sleep, that much was obvious. She couldn't afford to look unwell, especially being married to the owner of the most famous chemist shop in England, not if she expected customers to buy the latest cosmetics they sold. 'They've been good enough to wait this long. Poor Frank needs cheering up now that his return to Vancouver has been postponed.'

'I suppose you're right.' He winced as he moved slightly. 'He doesn't seem all that miserable to me though. He and John have been making a dreadful din down at the tennis courts all morning. I'm surprised none of the neighbours have come to the house to complain about their rowdiness.'

Florence made a mental note to ask the boys to contain themselves in future. 'They're young boys, Jesse; they're bound to be lively. Would you rather they were sullen and morose?'

'You know I wouldn't, but if you'll have a quiet word with

them to tone down their enthusiasm, just to an acceptable volume, I'm sure our neighbours will be very grateful.'

Florence walked over to Jesse's side of the bed and bent over to kiss his forehead. 'I'll certainly do that,' she said grinning.

She sat back at her dressing table and took the combs out of her hair. Florence went to say something about the exhibition trip, then caught sight of Jesse through her mirror. He didn't seem very well today and she hoped he wasn't going down with a bug. He'd been taking things a little easier lately, but only because she was keeping such a close eye on him. She tried not to nag him too much about cutting back on his hours at work, but knew he struggled more when the hotter summer months arrived. It was the only thing she didn't like about the better weather.

She wanted to ask if he was all right, but, aware that he hated her fussing, continued with what she was going to say. 'I'm looking forward to the exhibition, aren't you?'

Jesse muttered something and then, looking across the room at her and catching her eye as she watched him through the mirror, gave a reluctant smile. 'Yes, I am, I suppose. I think it's just the effort of getting there. I'll be glad I've been and seen it all once I'm home again.'

'I'm sure you will love it,' Florence assured him. 'The exhibition has been open for over a year now. We surely must be the last people out of all our acquaintances to go to the Ivory Palace and look round all the exhibits.' She unclipped her necklace and lowered it into a drawer in her jewellery box. 'I heard that over three hundred people visited the attraction over the first fortnight.' She turned to face him, pulling off her wedding and engagement rings. 'Even Queen Alexandra and the Prince of Wales went there, last year. It's said that the exhibition is the greatest event that Nottingham has probably ever seen.'

When Jesse didn't respond, Florence opened the lid of her hand cream and dipped two fingers in before wiping it onto the back of her left hand. She turned around to face Jesse as she worked the cream into her hands. 'I know John is looking forward to showing Frank all that the exhibition has to offer before his return to Canada. Frank is always saying how much bigger and better everything is in Vancouver and John wants to show him what Nottingham can do.'

Jesse grinned at her. 'Does he now?'

Florence wasn't sure if he was referring to Frank's boasting, or John's determination to show his friend some of Nottingham's highlights. She did know Jesse well enough to be aware that she had appealed to his competitive side. Now he'd surely give in and agree to accompany her and the children to the exhibition.

Jesse pushed himself up higher on his pillows. 'The Ivory Palace does look impressive, I have to admit that. And if our John wants to show his friend how we do things in Nottingham, then that's what we'll do.'

Florence had to control herself so she didn't laugh. 'Marvellous. I thought we could travel along the river by steamboat as far as the Trent Bridge and alight there. That way John can point out all the places along the riverbank to Frank.' She didn't add that it was also a gentle mode of travel, which would make the afternoon less fraught for Jesse, especially as he didn't seem to be too well.

'Anything you wish,' he said, rubbing his face with his hands. 'I read in the newspaper that there's a Japanese tea house and some sort of water chute that's about one hundred feet in height.'

'And a rollercoaster, oh, and a maze,' Florence added, excited to think they would be seeing it for themselves soon. 'Margery wants to go on the Fairy River and go through caves where there are magical scenes. It does sound incredibly impressive.' She rubbed cold cream into her face. 'I'm more interested in the concert hall and electric theatre, to be honest.'

* * *

The following day was warm and sunny with very little breeze. Florence was relieved that the boat trip to the exhibition would be calm. Growing up, she'd never minded being out in all weathers on boat trips with friends.

Her only sad note to the day was Lily's absence. Florence had invited her to accompany them, but her brother Ben had unexpectedly travelled over to Nottingham on the day Florence arrived home from her travels. He had come to collect his sister and take her back home to Jersey to spend time with their ailing mother. Mrs Buttons had been unwell on and off for several years, but this most recent bout had been quite unexpected and had upset Lily deeply.

Florence had waved Lily and Ben off from Pelham Street earlier that week. She was sorry to see her friend leave under such sad circumstances and hoped Lily would find the support she needed from her younger siblings. As she watched Lily settle into the hansom with her brother, Florence recalled how Lily had wanted to return to Jersey for many months. She knew that Lily hadn't expected her next trip there to be for such a sad occasion though and Florence's heart ached for her friend.

Ben had explained to Florence and Jesse that he hadn't wanted Lily to hear how ill their mother was by letter. Florence reflected that his thoughtfulness might help Lily cope with what she was about to face. Ben added, with barely concealed emotion, that, having suffered a heart attack, their mother wasn't expected to live more than a few weeks. Apparently their doctor had been surprised she'd survived as long as she had, and so when she told him to go and collect Lily because she wanted to see her once more before she died, Ben said that he had felt there was no time to waste.

Florence wasn't surprised when Jesse immediately arranged for Lily and Ben to travel back to Jersey that afternoon.

'This is fun, Mother,' Margery giggled, taking Florence's hand in hers.

She grinned at her excited daughter. 'I told you it would be, didn't I?' she said as they stood next to the mahogany rail on the side of the boat.

They had been right to be excited, Florence mused. She watched the delight on her husband's and the children's faces as they stared up in awe at the looming Indian-inspired building as the pleasure steamer *Empress* neared the grand white building with its minarets. Other visitors near to them gasped and the astonishment in their voices was obvious as they chatted about all that they were expecting to see once inside.

'Mother, look,' Dorothy exclaimed, pointing up at the ornate towers above the Ivory Palace. 'Will we be able to see everything inside, do you think?'

'Hopefully, yes,' Florence said, hoping that Jesse was able to cope with all the walking they would possibly need to do. She looked forward to discovering exactly what goods had been supplied to the exhibition from all over the world. She was intrigued to find out if any of them were items that she and Jesse might stock at their stores. She decided that she would intersperse all the walking with rides so that he could sit and take a breather at intervals.

They entered and made their way past displays of Nottingham lace, pottery, glass, and even jewellery. Florence and Jesse tried out new teas and ordered several boxes to be delivered to their home. She and Jesse were relieved to see that various local artisans had been well represented in this magnificent exhibition. Florence would have liked to take more time to survey the oriental goods as they passed by, but the children were impatient to see the exhibition grounds out the back.

They stood on the veranda looking at the splendid view over the rides and huge array of entertainment. Florence refused to allow the children to go on the water chute ride, but left John to spend some much-needed time alone with his father doing something that amused them both. They might bicker sometimes, but they did have a similar sense of humour and she knew that within a few minutes they would be amusing themselves in the 'Palace of Distorting Mirrors'.

Florence took the time while the men in her life were

occupied to accompany her girls in a canoe on the Fairy River, enjoying the experience of gliding along the water to the prettily decorated grotto with its impressive stalactites.

By the end of their visit each one of them was weary, apart from John and Frank, who grabbed the tennis rackets and ran off to the courts for another few games. The rest of them were happy having spent a fun-filled family afternoon together. Jesse was too tired to travel back on the pleasure steamer, so they took a carriage home.

'Was it as impressive as you expected?' Florence asked Jesse quietly, as the children excitedly exchanged their thoughts on their outing.

'It was, extremely so,' he said. 'It was a remarkable place and so well planned and put together. The chaps who set up the exhibition know what they're doing and deserve to do well out of it. I think we all enjoyed it very much. Well done for arranging everything, dearest. A memorable day for us all, I believe,' Jesse said, giving a pointed look in Frank's direction.

Florence smiled. Typical Jesse to think of how big an impression the event had made on their guest. She looked across the carriage at her son and his friend, chatting excitedly about all the different stalls and sites they had seen that afternoon.

Seeing the boys and her daughters so happy, Florence couldn't help wondering how Lily was getting on at home in Jersey. She had told her friend not to fret about returning to work at the Pelham Street store. Florence reassured Lily that she should take as much time with her family as necessary and also that she should stay with her mother for as long as Mrs Buttons needed her by her bedside.

Lily hadn't enjoyed the best of childhoods, Florence thought, as the horse trotted through the streets on their way home, but Lily loved her mother and that, Florence thought, was important and as it should be.

They arrived home and the children ran up to their rooms, exchanging their thoughts on what had been the most exciting part of their day. Meadows held open the front door for Florence and Jesse. He watched as the children ran along the landing upstairs, and smiled at her and Jesse. 'I see that your afternoon went well.'

'Very well, thank you,' Jesse said. 'If you haven't already visited the exhibition, Meadows, you should make a plan to go. I had expected it to be impressive, but it had much more to offer than I could have ever imagined. I enjoyed it immensely.'

'I think we can safely say that we all had a marvellous time,' Florence said, pulling the hatpin from her hat and pushing it carefully back into the straw crown before handing it to Meadows. She untied the ribbon from the neck of her jacket and handed it to him.

Meadows indicated the silver salver on the hall table, as he took their coats and hats, and with one glance Florence could see she had received a letter from Lily.

'Thank you, Meadows,' she said, picking up the letter and leaving the rest of her mail to look at later.

'Would you both like tea, madam?' he asked as Jesse walked towards the conservatory leaning, Florence noticed sadly, heavily on his walking stick.

'Yes, please. The children will probably want something

cool to drink too, but I'm sure they'll be down in their own time. Just ask Mrs Rudge to pour four glasses of her delicious lemonade she made this morning, and then please ask Annie to check on them shortly, will you?'

'Of course, madam.'

Florence followed Jesse into the sun-filled conservatory, opened two large windows, and sat down to read her letter. She hurriedly skimmed the words on the two pages to discover how things stood in the Buttons household. She smiled when she reached the end of the letter.

'Lily is all right?' Jesse asked, taking a seat by the open French doors in one of the shadier areas of the bright room.

Florence nodded. 'Her mother deteriorates by the day, according to her letter. It seems that she's still fighting though. She must be far tougher than they expected. Lily says she's fine. I think she's kept busy looking after her mother and is enjoying spending time with all her siblings. It's the first time they've all been together for a couple of years,' Florence explained, wondering why families waited until there was a reason, usually a sad one, to bring them all together. She thought of her own siblings and made a mental note to return to Jersey and visit them as soon as she had a quieter week in her diary.

Chapter 28

July 1904

'You'll never guess what's happened,' John shouted, running into the dining room, closely followed by Frank and interrupting Florence and Jesse's breakfast.

'Don't barge in here like a lunatic,' Jesse shouted waving his butter knife in the air. 'What's wrong with you, lad?'

Florence cringed and motioned for John to take a seat at the table. John did as he was expected and glared at his father, his expression sulky. No doubt he was embarrassed at being told off in front of his guest.

'Tell us what's happened then,' Florence said quietly.

John immediately brightened up. 'The Midland Industrial Exhibition, you know, the one we went to at the Ivory Palace?'

'Yes, of course I remember it.' Florence laughed, intrigued.

'It burnt down,' Frank shouted. 'Last night.'

John glared at his friend. 'Yes, he's right. There were hundreds of people watching from the steamer boats on the river and others on the Trent bridge.'

Florence gasped and her hand flew up to her mouth. 'Jesse,

no. There must have been hundreds of people inside there at that time.' The thought of people trapped inside a burning building horrified her. She looked back at John and then Frank. 'Do you know if everyone was saved?'

John shot Frank a glance, as if daring him to reply. 'Meadows said that everyone managed to escape. He was saying that they don't think that anyone was killed. Which is incredible news.'

'Yes,' Florence agreed, closing her eyes in relief and saying a silent prayer that her son was right.

'And how does Meadows know all this?' Jesse growled.

'One of the tradesmen who brought a delivery earlier this morning had a brother who was there,' John said, his blue eyes wide. 'He told Meadows all about it.'

'And he told you?' Jesse asked, giving John a disapproving glare.

John shook his head. 'No, I overheard him telling Mrs Rudge when I was going into the kitchen to ask for some glue for a picture that I wanted to paste into a book.'

Florence almost sighed with relief when Annie entered the room with a plate of scrambled eggs and bacon for the boys' breakfasts.

She watched her son eating and giving a satisfied sideways glance at his father. No doubt, Florence thought, because he had found out some intriguing news before his father had. Why were the men in her life so competitive? she wondered.

* * *

The following day, Jesse and John accompanied Frank down to Southampton for his voyage back to Canada. Florence was thrilled that she had been able to keep Frank busy and his mind as much off his mother's operation as possible. She hoped that he would have a safe journey home. They had invited John to go to Canada for a few weeks' holiday, but once again, Jesse had decided that he should spend his holiday with the family. Florence hadn't argued with Jesse about his decision as she was relieved to have some time with just her family around her.

She received a letter from Lily the same day as Frank's departure. Lily wrote to say that her mother had finally succumbed to her weakened heart and died two days after she had sent her previous letter to Florence. Florence noted that Mrs Buttons's funeral was to be held the following day and immediately wrote to her own brother, Willie, asking him to arrange for flowers to be sent from her and Jesse and to please keep in contact with the Buttons family and kindly represent her and Jesse at the funeral.

Florence was relieved to be able to welcome Lily back to Pelham Street at the end of the month.

'I have to admit I'm delighted to be back,' Lily said when Florence asked her to come to her office for a catch-up. 'My mother made us all promise that we wouldn't spend time grieving for her but go out and live our lives as best we could.' She picked a piece of lint off her sleeve. 'Our time in Jersey was spent sitting with my mother, all of us crammed into her small room at my aunt's house.'

Florence listened, silently glad that Lily was opening up about the difficult time she had been dealing with.

'We were there day after day. We'd almost run out of things to talk about. None of us spoke as my mother slept, which she mostly did for the last week of her life.' Lily wiped away a tear with the back of her free hand. 'It was awful. She had so many places she wanted to visit and things she still wished to do. Although she didn't have the means to do most of them. It's like being able to breathe properly again, now that I'm back here in Nottingham and able to work again.'

Florence's throat tightened with emotion. To be told that her job meant so much to her made Florence immensely grateful to have the means to help her find the freedom she had always longed for.

Chapter 29

July 1904

The terrible event of the beginning of the month had shocked Florence more than she had expected. The news of the Ivory Palace fire had dominated the local and national newspapers and Florence and Jesse were relieved and stunned to discover that despite the number of people attending the exhibition that night, everyone had managed to escape.

'You're not still dwelling on the fire, are you?' Jesse asked over breakfast one morning. 'You've read the reports in the papers yourself that there were no fatalities.'

'I know.' She buttered a piece of toast and ate it. 'But it's made me think.'

'You're always thinking,' he teased.

'Yes, but this time I'm thinking about family and how I should return home to Jersey at the end of this month.'

Jesse pushed his fork into a piece of bacon and looked up. 'To celebrate your birthday, you mean?'

He knew her so well, and she loved him all the more for

it. 'Yes, exactly.' I probably should have invited my mother and father here for my fortieth last year, she thought guiltily.

'You've been over to see them several times, so please don't worry about last year's birthday.' He ate a mouthful of food. 'I do think it's a good idea to go and see your family later this month though. Would you like me to ask Miss Tweed to make the arrangements?'

Florence didn't mention that she had already asked their secretary to look into boat times. 'No, it's fine. I'll do it when I get to work. I'll arrange passage for us and all the children. Mother and Father will want to see them, and I think it's important that the children also spend time with their grand-parents.' She didn't add that the shock of what could have happened to three people close to her had made her consider her own mortality and that of her parents.

She couldn't help thinking about the human frailties that caused so many of them, her included, to be spurred into action and take time to see their families only after something amiss happened to give them a fright.

Florence finished her breakfast and went up to her room to fetch her lighter coat. It was a warm day again today and she had been too hot travelling home the previous day.

She stared out of the window at the bustling pavements. She really did love this vibrant city that she had made her home. There was always so much going on and although she was looking forward to returning to Jersey for a holiday and to breathe in the salty sea air, she now found that Nottingham was somewhere that truly felt like a home away from home.

* * *

Florence's mother pushed the knife through the delicate sponge birthday cake and lifted a tempting slice on to one of her best side plates.

'Take this to your mother, Dorothy.' She placed a cake fork on the plate and handed it to her granddaughter.

Florence took the plate from her daughter and gave her a kiss on her forehead. She pushed the fork into the sponge and took a mouthful. It was as light and delicious as she had known it would be. Her mother had always been a skilled baker and even though Jesse had offered to pay for the top baker at a nearby bakery on the island to make a cake for her birthday, her mother had insisted that she be the one to do it. Florence was secretly pleased. She often reminisced about coming home to her parents' flat for a get-together after her father had closed the shop, as it always brought back memories. However, eating her mother's cake was certainly the most nostalgic part of her birthday.

Jesse cleared his throat, interrupting Florence's thoughts. 'It's such a beautiful day, finally.'

It was. Florence was relieved, especially as the summer had, up until now, been mostly dull and warm rather than hot and sunny as she preferred. She smiled at Amy, who at forty years old was happily unmarried and still living at home with their parents above the shop.

'Florence,' Jesse said, interrupting her thoughts, 'I was saying about the lovely weather today.'

'Sorry,' Florence said, aware that she hadn't been paying attention. 'I'm listening. Please carry on with what you were saying.'

'I was saying that this beautiful weather has got me thinking that we should make the most of it before we return home to Nottingham.'

Florence knew without Jesse saying anything further that he had arranged a surprise for them all. She caught her father's eye and knew by the smile on his face that he was thinking the same thing and was also anticipating an exciting announcement from Jesse.

'I've hired a cottage by the sea for us all to spend the next three days.' Jesse turned to his father-in-law and then Amy. 'I know you'll both need to return to open the shop tomorrow morning, but I thought you could still come back to join the rest of us as soon as you've closed up.'

Florence's father beamed with delight and even her mother looked happy at the prospect.

Her mother sliced through the cake and placed a portion on a plate for Jesse. 'When do we need to leave?'

Jesse grinned. Florence recognised that smile, too. He was about to shock her mother. She held her breath, waiting for his reply.

'We have enough time to eat this birthday cake and then pack a few things for three days at the beach cottage.'

'How long exactly?' Her mother asked, one hand on her hip and the other holding the knife absentmindedly.

'The charabanc will be waiting outside for us in –' he took his half-hunter watch out of his waistcoat pocket and squinted, before replacing it and replying '– forty-five minutes.'

'Forty-five!' Florence's mother shot her a horrified glance, as if she was in a position to cancel Jesse's treat for everyone on her birthday. 'I don't have enough time to prepare for us, not if we're staying away tonight.'

Florence's father stood and walked over to her mother. He took the knife out of her hand and passed it to Dorothy. 'You finish slicing up the cake for everyone. Margery can hand out the pieces. You, my dear, take some for yourself first and sit down for a moment to enjoy it. We have plenty of time. What do you say, Florence?'

'We do, Mother,' she agreed, relieved her father had stepped in to stem her mother's panic. 'Knowing my husband, I'm sure everything will be waiting for us at the cottage and all we need to take are our clothes.' Her mother opened her mouth to argue. 'And if you forget anything, Father, or Amy, will be able to fetch it for you when they come back here to work tomorrow.'

Her mother took the plate with her cake and fork and went to sit near the living-room window. She ate a mouthful thoughtfully. 'It will be fun,' she admitted after a few minutes' contemplation. 'And I would hate to be the one to ruin your birthday treat, Florence.'

Florence continued eating her cake, happy to have this treat to look forward to. She caught Jesse's eye and gave him an amused smile. He really was clever, coming up with a surprise and announcing it when her mother wouldn't be able to refuse. Florence knew her mother would enjoy a few days by the sea. She spent far too much time at home, and rarely ventured out from the confines of the town area.

'I'll help you pack, Mother.' Florence finished her cake, collected the empty plates, and took them to the small kitchen to wash them.

Amy joined her with a few more. 'Adelaide is popping home to pack and I'll help you with Mother and Father's things.'

'What do you think of Jesse's surprise?' Florence placed the first clean plate on the wooden drainer.

'I think it's a splendid idea. Very thoughtful of him to include the rest of us, too.'

Florence thought so too but wasn't at all surprised. Jesse knew how much she valued spending time with her family, as he had always done with his own.

It dawned on Florence that she hadn't packed a bag for her, Jesse, or either of the children, but knew well enough that if he had thought to arrange the cottage then she had no doubt that he would also have remembered all the small details, like having one of the hotel maids pack bags for them to take.

She was right. The charabanc arrived at six-thirty and everyone, including her mother, was waiting to be taken to the cottage. As they all settled onto their seats, Florence turned to Jesse and whispered. 'You never said where we were actually going.'

'I didn't, did I?' He tapped the side of his nose. 'You'll know soon enough.'

He took her hand in his. Florence closed her eyes briefly, thinking yet again how lucky she was to have met this wonderful man nineteen years before. Nineteen years. Was it really that long ago that she had met him, and right upstairs in her parents' shop? On the one hand, Florence could not recall a time when she didn't know Jesse, but on the other, the years had flown by.

The driver clicked the horses into action and soon they

were trotting along the street making their way east. Florence loved the east coast of the island, with its wide expanse of beaches of fine white-gold sand. Then again, she thought, they weren't that different to the west of the island, although there were more coves and cliff faces.

She and her family waved to several people they knew and a few who stood at the side of the road watching the family's charabanc as it passed. The sun was beating down on them and becoming a little hot, so Florence and her sisters took out their parasols and held them over their and their mother's heads. Dorothy and Margery were wearing their straw hats and giggling about something, and John was fixated by the sight of the sea as the vehicle moved slowly along the coastal road.

It took a while but eventually the driver brought the horses to a halt at the end of a small lane along the road at Grouville.

'I won't be able to turn around if I go down there,' he explained. 'I'm afraid you'll need to carry your bags from here, if that's all right with you, Mr Boot.'

'We can manage,' Jesse said, stepping down from the charabanc and holding his hand out to help everyone that needed it.

Florence's father passed down each of the bags and everyone took their own, apart from Florence's mother, who didn't need to as her husband had kept hers to carry.

'This is fun, Mother,' John said, taking Florence's bag from her. 'Papa told me this morning that he had planned something fun for us, but I never expected us to be doing something like this.'

'He told me, too,' Dorothy said quickly.

'And me.' Margery took Florence's hand and walked alongside her and Jesse. He led them down to the property and announced they would be spending the next two nights.

Florence stood facing the sea and took in a deep breath, relishing the saltiness of the air. Even though her family shop was only a few minutes' walk away from the waterfront, the sea air was even better when you were standing over the beach.

'What do you think of your temporary home?'

She turned and, standing with her back to the sea, stared at the beach villa in front of her. It wasn't very big, but Florence made a quick calculation. They needed a room for her and Jesse, one for her parents, one for Adelaide and her husband, and two more for Amy and the children. If necessary, the girls could share with her and Jesse and she could make up a bed for John in the living room.

'There are six bedrooms,' Jesse said without needing to be prompted. 'Two are quite small, but I'm sure that won't worry anyone for the length of time we're here. I have another surprise for you inside.'

Florence couldn't imagine what it might be. Jesse opened the French doors and waited for her to walk in, a big smile on his face. Florence gasped. Standing at the door of the large sunny living room were Harriet and Mrs Rudge.

'How wonderful,' Florence said, walking over to greet her lady's maid and cook. 'I hope neither of you minded coming here?'

They shook their heads.

Mrs Rudge pointed to the beach behind Florence. 'How could we mind coming somewhere this beautiful?'

'Well, I'm thrilled to see you both here. I know we'll all be extremely well looked after, but I'm going to make certain that you both have time to go and explore some of the island. I want you two to experience the joys of Jersey for yourselves.'

Harriet smiled even wider than she had before. 'We've been here since your arrival two days ago. Mr Boot put us up here so that we could make everything ready but also gave us a lot of time to ourselves and we've had a fun time walking on the beach and paddling.' She turned to Mrs Rudge. 'It was your first time in the sea, wasn't it?'

'That it was. It was colder than I expected, that I will say.'

Florence and Jesse laughed.

'This is a big beach, isn't it?' Mrs Rudge added.

Florence loved Grouville Bay's wide horseshoe shape, with Mont Orgueil castle up to her left. Then again, she loved many of the beaches on the island. 'It's a beautiful beach and we must make the most of staying next to it.'

'We've prepared some squash for everyone to have a drink at the table out front,' Mrs Rudge added. 'There's some shade there from the pine tree and if you like I can serve your supper outside, too.'

Florence decided that would be a perfect way to end her birthday. 'Thank you, that sounds ideal.'

While Mrs Rudge served drinks to Florence's family, she, Harriet, and the children went with her father to arrange who would sleep where in the villa, and place their bags in their respective rooms. Half an hour later, Florence sat next to Jesse, listening to Amy regaling them with anecdotes about people she had met in the shop recently.

Florence kept an eye on the children. They could all swim but had been warned before changing into their sun clothes to stay away from the sea. 'This water is tidal,' she explained, although they heard the same information each time they visited the island and spent time on one of the beautiful beaches. 'There are rip tides and you must have a deep respect for the sea. None of us must take our safety for granted, do you understand?'

They each nodded. Moments later, John and his sisters were down on the sand playing with a ball that they had found in one of the villa cupboards. Margery had insisted on taking a bucket and spade down with her, too, but that had been discarded in favour of taking part in John and Dorothy's game.

Florence watched her son, happy that at fifteen he still enjoyed having fun with his sisters. Dorothy, at fourteen, was growing up quickly. Florence wanted them to enjoy their childhoods for as long as they possibly could. Her heart raced as twelve-year-old Margery fell over the ball, doing a somersault into the sand. There was a moment's stillness from the children as her youngest daughter seemed to decide whether or not she had hurt herself and then guffaws of laughter when she shook her head and sand showered down past her shoulders.

Florence thought how special the day had been and knew that it was one she would never forget. She realised her father was speaking and turned her focus away from the children to hear what he was saying.

That evening, Florence went to bed feeling truly blessed to have enjoyed her birthday with all her siblings, apart from Willie, who had been unable to join them. She would make the most of seeing him before she went, and invite him out to lunch, she decided.

The following morning, the party went for a stroll along the beach towards Gorey before a late breakfast. The sun was shining once again, and the temperature hadn't yet risen to become uncomfortable. They walked as far as the common, where families were already gathering to meet up with friends and pass the time of day. Children played and Florence's son and daughters found others their age to talk to for a while.

Jesse called them back when it was time to return to the villa. 'There's a small farm on our way back to the villa and I thought we could try and buy some fresh milk and a dozen eggs. I'm sure Mrs Rudge will be pleased to have them for tomorrow's breakfast.'

Florence agreed, happy to do whatever Jesse chose. She didn't mind where they went, or what they ate, as long as the weather held, and everyone enjoyed themselves.

They reached the villa just as Mrs Rudge stepped outside with a tray of cutlery and napkins to set up the large table on the veranda.

'We've bought these,' Jesse said, holding out the milk churn, a basket of eggs, and some butter. 'I promised to return the container and the basket later today.'

Florence showed her the two cabbage loaves she was

holding. 'These are freshly baked. In fact, they're still warm.' She breathed in the delicious scent of the crispy loaf and longed to have a slice slathered in the creamy butter Jesse had bought.

Mrs Rudge's mouth opened to speak, but seeing the rounded loaves Florence was carrying, she frowned. 'Those are cabbage leaves on the top of them loaves?'

'And on the bottom, too,' Florence smiled. 'Don't look so shocked. I promise you this is the tastiest bread you'll ever eat, apart from your own,' she added hurriedly, so as not to offend her cook. 'I'll carry them through for you and we'll have a quick slice to show you.'

'Ooh, I'm not so sure I'll like it, madam.'

'I'll try some, if you don't,' Harriet said as they walked through the living room on their way to the kitchen.

Florence placed them down on the pine dresser. 'You'll both try some. Just a little,' she added, giving Mrs Rudge a pointed look, 'in case you don't actually like the taste, but I'm sure you will.'

She watched as Mrs Rudge took the breadknife and cut them each a piece, slathering them with the rich yellow Jersey butter.

Florence took hers and as the other two women studied theirs, then she took a bite and relished every morsel. Mrs Rudge and Harriet followed her lead and both took a tentative bite of the slice in their hands.

Harriet groaned in pleasure. 'This is incredible,' she said, immediately taking another bite.

Cook was last to finish hers.

'Well, Mrs Rudge, what do you think?' Florence waited for her cook's verdict. She knew that Mrs Rudge always liked to feel superior when it came to her knowledge of food, but wanted her to agree that this particular loaf was, indeed, delicious.

Mrs Rudge's lips slowly drew back into a wide smile. 'I have to agree with Harriet, madam. I thought I knew about bread, but this is something that's new to me. I think I might even try to replicate it for the other servants when we return to St Heliers House.'

Their weekend by the sea passed far too quickly for Florence's liking and on Sunday night she stood hand-in-hand with Jesse staring at the incoming tide.

'Thank you for arranging this for my birthday. It really was a perfect treat.' She gave him a quick kiss, aware that her enjoyment of his surprise had made him happy.

'I'm pleased that everyone had such a good time.' He checked his watch. 'It's time that we left now though. The charabanc will be waiting to take us back to town.' He waved at the three children making the most of their last few minutes on the sand. 'Hurry now, children. Come and fetch your bags.'

The children grimaced and then did as they were told.

'I wish we didn't have to take the boat back to the mainland in the morning,' Florence groaned.

Jesse put his arm around her waist and pulled her gently towards him. 'We can come back any time.'

She knew he was right but doubted they'd be able to replicate the joy that each of them had experienced over the past few days. It had been truly perfect.

PART THREE

Chapter 30

May 1907

Florence gazed happily out of the library window and watched Jesse being driven out of the driveway. The vehicle had given Jesse a new lease of life. He loved the speed and got along well with Sam. The last three years had been busy, but satisfying ones, despite Jesse's deteriorating health.

John had left school the previous year, unfortunately without passing any exams. Jesse had been furious and, yet again, they had quarrelled. Florence wished Jesse would stop expecting John to be a replica of himself. She couldn't understand why he wasn't as proud of John as she was. Their son was a kind and decent man, and she never minded that he hadn't excelled in his education despite Jesse's annoyance. Florence believed that everyone's strengths, and weaknesses, were different to everyone else's; it was what made them all unique. John would find his way in the world, of that she was certain. She believed in John; she just wished Jesse would begin to, too.

Now, with the latest upset when John had dropped out of

his place at Jesus College in Cambridge a few months before, Jesse's irritation with their son had escalated, culminating in a row the previous evening after dinner. Florence exhaled sharply at the memory of what had happened.

'You will do as I say,' Jesse had shouted, glaring furiously at John, who paced back and forth in the living room. 'I'll give you until Monday and then you'll begin working for the company. Boots is your heritage, for pity's sake. Most young men your age would be only too pleased to be given a position at the firm. You, of course, aren't interested. You're ungrateful, that's what you are, John. And I won't stand for it a moment longer.'

Florence had been pretending to read her novel when their quarrel had begun. Her breathing sped up as she tried to refrain from becoming upset. 'John is not ungrateful, Jesse,' she said as calmly as she could manage, hoping that her intervention might reduce the tension between them.

'I don't know if I am interested yet,' John snapped before her words were barely out of her mouth. 'What if I want to build a career for myself in an entirely different field?'

Florence immediately looked at Jesse to see his reaction.

His mouth fell open for a couple of seconds before he closed it. 'What career? You've never shown any interest in anything else. I might be able to understand your reluctance to work for me if you did have a passion for something else, but you don't, do you?'

John glared at his father. He looked as if he wanted to tell him something, but changed his mind before he actually said anything. Florence wished he would share what was on his mind. Maybe then she could help father and son find a way to bridge their differences.

'John, darling,' she said, going over to him.

'No, Mother,' he said angrily. Then softening his tone, he added. 'I'm sorry. I know you want me to work at Boots with you both, but I don't know if I'm ready for it. Or if I ever will be,' he added before leaving the room and closing the door quietly behind him.

Florence went to follow him, then thought better of it. John was upset, that much was obvious. He was struggling and it broke her heart to see him this way. She decided to let John calm down. She would speak to him tomorrow when Jesse was at work.

* * *

'You can't expect John to want the same things that you do,' she had said over breakfast that morning when Jesse had brought up the subject yet again.

'He's not going to spend his time sitting around the house and vegetating,' Jesse grumbled, before eating his last mouthful of egg. 'He can come and work for Boots. It's the family firm and it's about time he started paying some attention to it.'

Florence had known Jesse wouldn't back down. When an idea formed in his head he was rarely able to let it go until he discovered that it wasn't going to work. Unfortunately, in this instance, his determination was causing friction within their family. The girls were beginning to make excuses not to share breakfasts with them and Florence suspected it was because of Jesse's annoyance with John.

Even John hadn't come down to breakfast this morning, which was out of character, and this upset her deeply. She didn't want her son to feel like he had to stay away from Jesse to keep the peace. What would he do next, she wondered: plan to move out of St Heliers? She hoped not. It had been bad enough when he was away at boarding school, and she wasn't ready for him to move out of the house for a long time yet.

'I think John should be allowed to find something he wants to do,' she argued. 'You're both so different, and he's still only young. Give him time to find something that suits him.'

Jesse drank the last of his tea. 'He is eighteen, Florence. It is high time he stopped messing about and did what's expected of him.'

Florence could see the hurt in Jesse's face and it occurred to her that he wasn't trying to be difficult, but that it was upsetting him to think that John didn't have the same passion for the business as they both did. Florence didn't blame either of them for struggling to cope with each other, although she knew that if she was the one at the helm of the business, she and John would have little problem working together.

Jesse wiped his mouth with his napkin. 'I'm getting older, Florence. I need to train him up so that he can at least take on some of the work for me. At this rate, I don't imagine he'll ever have enough knowhow to take my place in the company.'

She wasn't sure either, but didn't say so. 'Right now, you have a great team of managers working with you, and you also have me, don't forget.'

Jesse's expression softened and he sighed. 'I am eternally grateful for all that you do for the business, and for our family, Florence. You are the glue that binds everything together for me, do you know that?'

She was aware that this was how he saw her, as he'd told her many times over the years, but hearing Jesse telling her these things never failed to make her heart swell. 'And I've loved every moment.' She took his hand and kissed the back of it.

She turned away from the window and left the library. Apart from the quarrel with John and Jesse's increasing frailty, the rest of their lives were wonderful. Florence was grateful for everything that they had together. Their daughters were happy, if growing up a little too fast for her liking. It only seemed like a year or so when her children were small. Now Dorothy was seventeen, beautiful and confident, as was Margery at fifteen. Even the business was going well. It had taken them many years to get to this point and in a few months she and Jesse would be celebrating twenty-one years being married.

She needed to take her mind off Jesse and John clashing with each other. It was a beautiful spring day after several days of intermittent rain, so Florence decided to pick some roses to display in one of her crystal vases. Jesse rarely noticed flower arrangements, but the floral scents in her living rooms always made Florence's day a little brighter. She fetched her favourite wicker garden trug and secateurs and went outside. The sun warmed her face as she walked over to her rose garden. It was looking especially colourful this year and the scents transported her thoughts away from her worries.

Her favourite rose was one that Jesse had surprised her with several years before. She had loved her Belle of Tehran rosebush so much that she had treated herself to several more and now had a rose bed purely for that one rose. It was situated outside the library where she could look at it from her favourite chair. Often she felt compelled to step outside and breathe in the heavenly scent emanating from the pink-tinged buds that opened into full white cushiony blooms.

The day was peaceful and the only sound, other than that of a neigh from a horse, was the birds singing in the trees. Florence lifted the final bloom to cut and was relishing the beautiful scent of the velvety petals when she heard Margery calling for her.

'Mother!' Margery shouted from somewhere inside the house.

Florence called back to let her daughter know where she was. She thought that Margery sounded tense, but, aware that it could be anything from a falling-out with a friend to discovering something she needed in a magazine, Florence wasn't overly concerned.

'There you are,' Margery said, a little breathless and red-faced. 'I couldn't find you.'

Florence was used to Margery's tendency towards the over-dramatic on occasion. She smiled at her younger daughter and held out the rose she had just pruned for Margery to smell.

'Breathe in this delicious scent,' she said. 'It will make whatever's worrying you less important. This rose is nature at its finest.'

Margery glanced at Florence as if she wasn't convinced, but after a second's hesitation did as she asked.

Satisfied that her daughter had taken a moment to calm herself, Florence placed the flower onto the others she had cut. 'Now,' she said, her instincts telling her that Margery was still agitated, 'why are you frowning? Shall we sit down out here and you can tell me what's happened?' Florence placed her trug on the table and went to pull out one of the heavy wooden chairs to sit.

When Margery didn't move to pull out a chair for herself, Florence turned to her. 'What is it?' She took hold of Margery's arms lightly. 'Has something happened to you?' she asked, trying not to panic.

Margery shook her head slowly, her eyes never leaving Florence's. 'I almost don't know how to tell you this.'

Panic welled up in Florence's chest. 'What? Tell me, right now.'

Margery frowned, then held out a folded piece of paper that Florence hadn't noticed she was carrying until now. 'I found this.'

'Where?' Florence asked, reaching out to take the note from Margery.

Margery hesitated before letting it go. 'In John's room. When I went to see where he'd got to. He had agreed to go into town to meet some friends with Dorothy and me later on and I wanted to know exactly what time I should be ready.' She let go of the letter. 'He's gone, Mother. John's packed his things, and left.'

Florence didn't understand what she meant at first. She

stared at her youngest daughter trying to take in what she had just told her, then looked down at the piece of paper in her trembling hands and unfolded it. She read it silently to herself.

Dearest Mother,

I'm sorry to do this to you, and know that you will be shocked and probably angry when you read this letter and discover that I've gone away. I know also that you will be disappointed with me for not staying and sorting everything out with Father. I was going to, but I can't see the point when there is little chance of him changing his mind, and I'm not ready to change mine either.

Florence gasped. Maybe John and Jesse were more alike than either had ever imagined. She read on, horrified.

I booked a passage to Canada. By the time you read this I should hopefully have departed from Liverpool. I am truly sorry to do this to you Mother, but I don't feel that I have any choice. Please don't worry about me. As you know, Frank Hamilton always offered for me to stay with his family in Vancouver and so that is what I'm going to do. I don't know when I will return, but maybe I'll be able to make a life for myself there. He's told me so much about his home and I feel certain that I will love it. I do hope so.

Please tell Father that I love him, but I can't see how I would fit in with the company, or working for him at Boots.

He's never thought I could do the work to his satisfaction and, rather than disappoint him, again, I believe it's better if I leave now before we fall out any further.

My love to Dorothy and Margery. Please apologise to them for me. I had agreed to go out with them, but didn't want to confide my plans to my sisters and put them in the difficult position of knowing my intentions and having to keep them from you.

My love to you, too, dearest Mother. I know that out of everyone you are the one I shall miss the most. Please try not to worry about me. I am fine and believe that this time away in Canada will be the making of me.

I will write again as soon as I'm settled.

Your son, John

Florence's knees gave way and she sat heavily on the oak garden chair behind her. She blinked away tears that made his words swim in front of her eyes, and cleared her throat. Then she read her son's words several more times, trying desperately to absorb that he had indeed gone. She battled to compose herself. She didn't want to upset Margery any more than she had already been. She took a deep breath and brushed the tears away with the back of her right hand, only for her cheeks to be wet with fresh tears immediately after.

'He's gone? You're certain?'

'I am,' Margery cried. 'I checked his wardrobe. Most of his clothes are missing.' She hugged Florence from behind. 'Do you think he'll be all right where he's going?'

Florence realised she needed to pull herself together. This

was no time for weakness. She needed to be strong for the rest of her family. John's departure was going to devastate Dorothy, too, and Florence could only imagine what it was going to do to Jesse. She just hoped that the shock of discovering what John had done would not bring on another breakdown. Jesse was too frail to cope with another emergency like that.

Florence stood up and pulled Margery into her arms. 'Your brother will be fine,' she reassured her. 'I'm certain of it. I don't believe John should have gone, but he's no fool and can look out for himself. Besides, we all know Frank well, and if his family are nearly as kind and thoughtful as their son, then John will be well cared for.'

As she said the words, the realisation of what had happened began to sink in further. Margery must have taken some comfort because Florence could feel the tension in her daughter's body relax slightly.

'I'm glad,' Margery said and sniffed. 'I wish he hadn't gone though. I'm going to miss him and I know that Dorothy is going to as well.'

'We all will,' Florence said, her chest aching at the thought of her precious son going to the other side of the world. 'You must remember how Frank always used to tell us how Canada is such a magnificent place? He showed us photos once of some incredible views near where he lived. At least we know that John will have a wonderful time.'

As Florence spoke she knew she was trying to reassure herself as much as Margery. It did help though to think that her son was going to stay with someone they all knew and were fond of. Frank's family had written to her and Jesse to thank them for inviting their son to stay at St Heliers during holidays when he was unable to travel back to Canada. They had offered for John to stay with them several times, hoping to repay Florence and Jesse's kindness to Frank. It helped her to focus on this, but only a little. She was going to miss him dreadfully.

Florence let her arms drop from around Margery's slim back. 'I need to go and check John's room for myself,' she said, wanting to be sure that there hadn't been any mistak. Maybe her son had changed his mind at the last minute and had forgotten to dispose of his letter.

Florence hurried to join Margery in John's room. By the time she reached her daughter she was standing next to John's open and empty wardrobe.

'You see?' Margery said, indicating the bare hangers and near-empty cupboard drawers nearby.

'There can be no doubt about it then,' Florence said miserably, half to herself. 'I was hoping . . .'

'I know, I was hoping I'd imagined this when I checked in here the first time.'

Florence stared at the light-filled room, still containing most of John's personal treasures, but somehow already lacking his warmth and personality.

'We could try to pretend he's away at boarding school, then maybe we won't feel so miserable,' Margery suggested, her eyebrows raised in a hopeful gesture.

'We could,' Florence agreed, putting her arm around Margery's slim shoulders. She doubted there was anything she could do to persuade herself that John was only away for a short time, but if it helped Margery to feel better, then she wasn't going to dissuade her.

Florence stared around the room, at a loss for what to do next. Then, taking a deep breath, she decided that she was going to do her utmost to bring her son back to where he belonged. There had to be a way to persuade John to return home and she was determined to find it. Then she would somehow make John and his father learn to muddle along together. Other fathers and sons managed it, and there was no reason why the men in her house couldn't do the same thing.

'Margery, close the wardrobe,' she instructed, pushing the drawers closed. 'We have to let the servants know what's happened, but not until much later when I've had a chance to speak to your father about this. He can't be the last to find out; he would hate that. Close John's door behind you, too. We don't want to draw attention to anything in here and alert the household before I'm ready for them all to know.'

'Yes, Mother. May I tell Dorothy when she comes back from playing tennis with her friend?'

'Yes, but make sure you're not overheard by anyone and tell her to keep it to herself for now.'

Florence needed to manage the situation. The last thing she wanted was for Jesse to decide that John had turned his back on them and wasn't welcome home again. She was good at finding solutions to issues at work; now she needed to put all her expertise into practice at home. The first thing she was going to do though was sit quietly in her bedroom and write to her son trying to persuade him to return home. At least then she would be able to tell Jesse that she had already begun to deal with the issue before he had even been made aware of it.

She went to leave the room but her daughter's sad expression stopped her. She took Margery's face in her hands and kissed her forehead. 'Thank you for bringing John's note directly to me and for being quiet about it. You did very well.' She forced a smile that she hoped would help reassure Margery. 'Don't worry too much; John will be home again soon. I know he will,' she insisted, hoping she was right.

Florence went to her room and closed the door. She sat down at her Davenport and, opening the desk, took a piece of her personal headed paper and stared thoughtfully out through the window. What to write? she wondered. She needed to find a way to make John feel compelled to return home. She understood his need to leave, but running away to Canada was not the way to solve this issue.

John was a young man, who didn't quite know what he wanted out of life yet, but like the rest of them he needed to face his responsibilities. He couldn't do that on the other side of the Atlantic. Florence's upset turned to frustration. She unscrewed the top of her gold fountain pen, and began to write.

Dearest John,

I hope that this letter finds you well after your voyage to Canada. I have to admit that I am almost at a loss as to what I should say to you. Almost. I am, however,

349

preparing to break the news to your father about your unexpected departure and I think we both know that it won't be a calm conversation. It certainly isn't one that I'm looking forward to.

Whilst I understand your need to leave, I just wish you hadn't thought to travel so far away, because I could then come and visit you and speak face-to-face about this situation. I know that you wish to find your own way in this life, and that is commendable, but there is so much on offer for you here. I truly believe that you should not dismiss the notion of working for Boots when you've never taken the time to see whether you would like working at the company. Who knows, you might find that you love working for the family business?

I am writing to you therefore, to implore you to rethink your decision and return home at the earliest opportunity. I have never asked anything of you, but on this occasion I am. Please change your mind and come home. Do this one thing for me. We both know your father can be a hard taskmaster, but that's only because he wants the best for everyone connected to Boots, and it's not as if he doesn't lead by example, is it?

I know I am asking a lot from you, John. I want you to be happy, and I'm sure you will be when you find the right path to follow. However, you cannot discard an opportunity if you don't take the trouble to try it first.

I anxiously await your reply. Please know that you are very much missed at home, yes, even though at the time of writing this letter you have only just left. Your sisters

send their love and I send mine. I know, too, that your
father, once he has had a chance to calm down after he
learns what has happened, will send his too.

Please thank the Hamilton family from me for making
you welcome at their home.

With love,

Your loving Mother

Florence finished the letter. She took a calming breath and stared out of the window as the ink on the paper dried. After a few minutes, she reread her words and, unsure what else to say, but wishing the letter to catch the day's post, she folded it, took an envelope from one of the cubby holes in her small desk, pushed the letter inside, sealed it, and then looked through her address book for Frank's address. She was relieved to have written it down, thanks to having the family on her Christmas card list. She had no idea what she would have done if she didn't know their address.

Florence stood and held the envelope as she raised the mahogany lid of her desk until it was closed. How could John go without saying goodbye to any of them? She didn't blame him for not wishing to speak to his father before going, because Jesse would have forbidden him to leave and John would have ended up quarrelling with him. John could have spoken to her though, or one of his sisters. Dorothy and Margery would have cried to watch him go, but would have hugged him, and wished him well.

Florence put the letter down onto her dressing table and peered into her mirror. She looked ghastly. Her eyes were red and her face ashen. She sat and dabbed a little powder onto her cheeks. She really needed to gather herself before Jesse's return that evening. Florence hurried downstairs and handed Meadows the envelope.

'Please arrange for someone to take this to the nearest post office, as soon as possible,' she said. 'It must be posted today.'

Meadows turned over the envelope and read the front. 'To Canada? Master John has gone to Canada?'

'Yes,' Florence said tensing. Now that Meadows had been alerted, she knew that the rest of the servants would become aware within minutes. She didn't want them gossiping about why he had left so suddenly. Although she knew that they would probably work it out for themselves by Jesse's reaction later that day when she broke the news to him. 'He's gone to stay with Frank Hamilton's family in Vancouver. Frank always wanted to show John the sights of the mountains and the ocean nearby. John couldn't go before now because of his schooling, but now that he's finished his education, he's free to take time to travel there for a while.'

Meadows listened intently as Florence spoke. She could see he thought John a very lucky man to be able to travel to the other side of the world so easily.

'Master John must be very excited,' Meadows said. 'Canada is so far away. Mr Hamilton spoke to me and the other servants a few times about his father's apple farm. It did sound very different to anything here.'

Florence could see the envy in the young man's face. His wish to do the same as John was almost tangible. 'Would you like to travel across the ocean one day, Meadows?'

His eyes narrowed dreamily. 'Yes, Mrs Boot. I've always wanted to go somewhere on a ship. Somewhere that's different from anything I've ever known.' His face reddened and he stepped from one foot to the other. 'I'm sorry, I do enjoy my work here. I don't want you to think—'

Florence shook her head. 'I asked you the question and all you've done is answer me. I think it's wonderful that you have ambitions to travel, and I'm sure that you'll make many amazing discoveries when you do go.' She gave him a reassuring smile. 'You're only young, Meadows, and there's a whole world waiting out there for you to discover it.' She laughed. 'But not too soon, I hope. For now, I'm very happy that you stay here with us at St Heliers.'

Meadows relaxed and smiled. 'I can't see me leaving for a few years yet, Mrs Boot.'

'Good, that's a relief.'

He seemed to recall that he was holding the letter and held it up, giving it a tap. 'I'd better go and see that this catches today's post.'

Chapter 31

Florence was in the conservatory with Dorothy and Margery arranging the roses she had taken from the garden earlier into two vases. She listened as her daughters asked questions about John leaving, wondering what she thought might happen next. She couldn't worry them by saying that she didn't know, or, heaven forbid, mention her greatest fear, that he would never return to Nottingham. Instead, she told them she believed he might take a few weeks out to enjoy the beautiful area in Vancouver where Frank's family lived and have a holiday before coming home. She hoped she was right.

Florence tensed when she heard Jesse's car pulling up outside the front of the house. She looked up to see both girls staring at her, their eyes wide.

'I think I'll go to my room and read,' Dorothy said quickly, giving her sister a knowing look.

Margery nodded. 'I'll come with you.' She gave Florence a questioning look. 'Is that all right with you, Mother, or would you like us to stay with you while you break the news to Father?'

Florence was touched by her daughter's feeling of responsibility towards her. 'No, darlings. Thank you but I think it's better if I speak to your father alone. I expect him to be upset, so don't be surprised if you hear him bellowing. You know how he tends to make a fuss when he's angry.'

She couldn't actually think of another time when something like this had happened, but she did know her husband well enough to prepare for a noisy reaction. 'You two go upstairs. I'm sure Father will calm down once he gets used to the idea that John has gone and there's not much we can do now except wait to see what your brother does next.'

She put an arm around each girl's shoulders and kissed the tops of their heads. Hearing Jesse's voice as he spoke to Meadows near the front door, she pushed them gently away. 'Off you both go now.'

She watched them run out of the conservatory into the garden, no doubt to then enter the house by the front door once their father had come through to the conservatory.

'Florence?' Jesse bellowed.

'I'm in the conservatory,' she shouted back, saddened at the cheerful note to his voice. He must have had a good day. It upset Florence to think that she was about to ruin his happiness with the news she was about to break to him. She reached for the bell. They would need tea and maybe some of Mrs Rudge's Victoria sponge cake. Anything would be welcome that might reduce the sting of what she was about to say to him.

She waited for Jesse to remove his coat and hat, and no doubt pass them with his briefcase to Meadows. She could picture him doing it and also knew exactly how long it would take. Then the door to the conservatory opened and he appeared, beaming at her as he walked towards her.

'My darling wife, how has your day been?'

She forced a smile. He really was in a good mood, she thought sadly. 'I'm fine, thank you. I can see by the look on your face that you've had a positive day.' She motioned to the table and chairs. 'I've rung the bell for Violet. I thought we could have tea and cake in here; it's not too hot and should actually be rather pleasant.'

'Good idea.' Jesse sat and rested his sticks against the side of his chair. 'I was speaking to . . .' He stopped mid-sentence and frowned thoughtfully. 'Something's the matter. Sit, tell me what it is.'

Before Florence had the chance to do as he asked, Violet entered the room.

'You rang, madam?'

'Yes. Please bring tea and some of Mrs Rudge's Victoria sponge if she's baked any today. We'll have it in here.'

Florence waited for Violet to leave and sat opposite Jesse. She smoothed down her skirt, trying to find the best way to tell him that John had gone.

'What is it, my love?' Jesse reached out his gnarled left hand to take hers. When she didn't speak immediately, his face blanched. 'Tell me. You're not ill, are you? Or one of the children? Please don't tell me that there's something wrong with one of you.'

Florence hated to frighten him and could see that the longer it took her to speak, the more concerned Jesse was becoming. Aware that she had no choice but to hurry up and say what was worrying her so much, Florence took a deep breath and taking her hand from Jesse's, she pulled John's letter from her skirt pocket. She unfolded it and placed it on the table, pushing it towards him.

'I'm so sorry Jesse. You'll need to read this.'

His eyebrows lowered and he stared at her for a second before looking down at the piece of paper in front of him. 'It's John's writing,' he murmured.

'Yes, it is.'

Her hand went to her chest as Jesse read, his expression changing from shock to anger and then pain as he reread John's letter. He was so still that Florence wondered if he was taking in the spiky words in front of him.

Jesse pushed the letter back towards her before looking at her. 'You've checked his room? This isn't some childish prank of his, is it?' he asked, hope obvious in his voice.

Florence wished she could say that it was a foolish joke but shook her head. 'He has gone, Jesse. I believe he left during the night sometime, so even if we chased him to Liverpool we wouldn't find him in time.'

She needed to put a positive slant on the situation. 'It will probably do John good to spend some time in a new environment, don't you think?' she asked, warming to the notion. 'Staying with Frank's family on their apple farm, where according to him the day's work is long and arduous. I think it'll do John good.' It really might, she thought. John had never had to do any menial tasks, apart from any that he might have been given at boarding school. Maybe helping out on a farm might be the experience he needed to realise that the only way to succeed in business is to put in a consistent effort.

'He could do with a bit of hard labour, I think.'

Jesse's words angered her. They were the reason they now found themselves in this miserable situation. 'He's gone because he feels you're too hard on him. That you're never satisfied with anything he tries to do.'

'Do you think I am?' Jesse snapped.

Florence ignored the question and continued with what she was trying to say. 'Maybe, though, if John sees Frank working with his own father and experiences how much focus other families need to put into their business, he might come to see that we are no different to them. That people with a business to run have to be dedicated and make difficult decisions.'

'We are different, though,' Jesse argued. 'This isn't one small store we're trying to keep running, it's many stores and thousands of staff. Surely John can understand some of what it takes to keep up the motivation to stay on top of everything that entails. After all, he's grown up in the same house as you and I. We both work hard all year round and never expect others to do anything we haven't done ourselves.'

Florence couldn't argue with what he was saying. It was true. John should have some idea of the dedication it took for a business such as theirs to succeed.

There was a gentle knock at the door before Violet entered the conservatory and carried over a tray of tea things and plates of cake.

Jesse muttered something to himself. Florence could feel his frustration that he was having to wait to continue with what he was saying. Violet lifted each item from the tray and began setting it neatly onto the table. She moved to straighten a cake fork but Jesse snatched it from her and said, 'Yes, thank you, Violet. That will be all for now.'

Violet gave a little curtsey and hurried out of the room.

Florence hated it when Jesse was impatient with the servants. 'That was rather unnecessary, Jesse,' she said. 'Violet was only doing her job.'

He closed his eyes and sighed heavily. 'Yes, I know. I'm sorry, but she takes too long prettying things up on the table.'

Florence didn't argue. She didn't want to make Jesse wait any longer to continue with his diatribe. 'You were saying, about John.'

Jesse slammed the fork down onto the table and glowered at her. 'What was he thinking? Who does he think he is, upping sticks and marching off like a sulky, spoilt schoolboy? Just because I told him a few home truths.'

Florence had to concentrate on keeping her temper. To lose hers now would only end up with them arguing and neither would manage to get their point across.

'I'm as upset as you, Jesse. Please don't think that I'm not, but we have to calm down and work out what we're going to do next.'

'We're going to demand he returns home immediately. That's what we're going to do.'

'Yes, I agree, which is why I've already written to him and had the letter posted today. The sooner it reaches Vancouver and John reads it, the sooner he can plan his return home.'

'Plan? There's no planning about it, Florence. He will book

a passage back to Liverpool and come home on the first available ship. I don't care whether he wants to, or not. How dare he upset you like this?'

Florence took Jesse's nearer hand in hers. Jesse knew her well enough to see beyond her calm reaction and be aware that inside she was heartbroken that John had gone without any word. 'He's a young man, Jesse. John is trying to spread his wings a little. He's spent his life doing what others have told him to do and now he needs time to make a few decisions for himself. I am upset, of course I am, and I'm angry with him. I do, though, understand his need to do this.'

'I'm glad you do, because I'm struggling to accept that he's done such an impulsive, selfish thing without a second's thought for us, or his sisters.'

Florence couldn't let him say such a thing without trying to placate him. 'We don't know that he hasn't been planning this for months. I doubt it was too impulsive. After all he's been hearing Frank telling us all sorts of wonderful stories about his home for several years. And as far as being selfish, I think he's simply a young man who doesn't know how else to go about leaving.'

'What do you mean? He didn't have any problem packing his bags and booking his fare, as far as I can see. He must have been saving all his allowance for months to afford this.'

Florence wasn't surprised by Jesse's reaction, or that he was hurt by what John had done, but she also tried to picture how it would have panned out for John if he had done as Jesse said and spoken to either one of them before leaving. She knew full well that neither of them would have let him go and both of them would have done their best to persuade him to stay and think things over.

'Jesse, both of us, you especially, are very strong-minded people. We both, yes, mostly you, know what we want and sometimes find it difficult to hear other people's points of view. If you really think about it, you'll know that poor John wouldn't have stood a chance if he had spoken to you about his idea to go and stay in Canada. You have to admit that, don't you?'

Jesse thought for a moment. 'Yes, I suppose you're right,' he admitted eventually.

Florence poured their tea and handed Jesse's to him. 'This is probably lukewarm by now, so we'd better drink it while it's still reasonably nice.'

They sat in silent contemplation as they ate their sponge and drank their tea. Florence was relieved to have shared the news with Jesse and that his initial reaction was now over with. She knew though that once he had spent time mulling over what had happened, he might still become much angrier with John. She hoped he wouldn't. Florence didn't want Jesse any more upset than he was already. He needed to focus on his health rather than being angry about things, although this was exactly the sort of thing he would be upset about. Not that she blamed him.

Florence would never admit how upset she was with John and, she realised, also rather angry at him. If only he had tried to work with his father before going to Canada, then she could argue in his defence over his departure. He hadn't though, and that was the thing that troubled her the most. Apart from how he'd fare in Canada.

Jesse finished his sponge and wiped his mouth with his napkin. 'What will we do if John refuses to come home?' he asked quietly.

Florence didn't want to think about that happening. It would break her heart. She decided that if John did make that choice, she would book a passage and travel to see him. John was less likely to be able to refuse her something when he was face to face with her. 'I honestly don't know. What I do know, though, is that you and I are going to find a way to get through this, together. It's what we've always done.'

Chapter 32

Three weeks' later, Dorothy ran into the dining room. The earlier rain had dried up and there were hints of blue sky appearing. It promised to be a beautiful sunny day. Florence was finishing her breakfast. 'Look, Mother,' she whispered, as if nervous someone might hear what she was about to say.

Jesse had left moments before and Florence was aiming to follow him to the store as soon as she had finished a few things she wanted to speak to the servants about. She looked over her cup as she took a sip of her tea, alarmed to see her oldest daughter's anxious expression. 'What's the matter?'

Dorothy closed the door and walked over to Florence holding an envelope. 'There's other post in the hall, but this one has John's handwriting on it and I thought you'd want to read it as soon as possible.'

Florence had been trying to keep from worrying as she waited each day to see if a letter had arrived from John. It was a huge relief to finally receive his reply to her. Florence placed her cup down on the saucer and took the envelope from Dorothy.

She picked up a clean butter knife from Jesse's place setting and slid it into the envelope, slicing it open at the top. 'I'm almost afraid to see what he's said,' she admitted quietly. She took a deep breath and withdrew the single page before taking a deep breath and reading.

Dearest Mother,

Thank you for your letter; it was wonderful to receive it. I'm grateful to you for not being as angry as I had expected you to be. I have to admit that I am missing you, Father, and my sisters. Please send them all my love.

It can't have been easy to break my news to Father and I hope he wasn't too disappointed in me. I expect that he was rather angry and I don't blame him for one minute.

I will make this letter brief because I want to reply to your request for me to return home as soon as possible. I know you will be waiting each day to hear from me.

You make a lot of sense when you say that I should have at least spent some time working with Father at Boots, and I know it was utterly selfish of me to leave like I did. But I knew that if I didn't go when I did, I might never have had the courage to do so. I wanted to go to Vancouver ever since meeting Frank and hearing how beautiful this place is, and it is, Mother. Vancouver is the most enchanting place I've ever been. I would love you to come and see everything that it has to offer. The clean air and beautiful scenery would probably benefit Father's health, too.

However, that said, I must tell you that I don't feel ready to return home to Nottingham yet.

Florence's hand flew to the pearls around her neck. No. John was not going to refuse to come home. She wouldn't allow it. She read on.

I am sorry that I feel this way and know that you will be upset by this reply, but I've come this far and I would like to continue with my stay here, for the time being at least. There is so much that I wish to explore here in Canada, and I worry that if I come home I might never again have the chance to visit here.

Frank's family are as kind and welcoming as you would hope. They have made my stay exciting and a lot of fun, although I believe they were rather more surprised at my arrival than I had expected.

I will sign off now, Mother, and write again in a day, or two. Once again, I apologise for not giving you the answer that you will have hoped for.

With love,

Your son,
John

Florence swallowed the nausea rising in her throat. The thought of not seeing her beloved son again was not something she was going to accept. She took a sip from her glass of water and tried to calm down. He hadn't said he wouldn't ever return, she reminded herself, only that he did not intend returning yet.

She realised Dorothy was speaking to her. 'Mother, may I read John's letter?'

'Pardon? Oh, yes, of course you may.' Florence handed the

letter to Dorothy, her hand shaking so much that she almost dropped it.

She waited for Dorothy to read John's words, not wishing to give in to her tears in front of her daughter.

Dorothy finished reading and stared up at her. 'John will come home, won't he?'

'Of course he will,' Florence reassured her despite her own fears that he might change his mind and decide to stay in Vancouver. 'Why don't you run along and quietly tell Margery what he's written to say? I know she's been waiting to hear from him, too.'

Dorothy put the letter onto the polished table. She went behind Florence and putting her arms around her mother's shoulders rested her head against Florence's back. 'I'm glad he likes it there though. I would hate to think of John as being unhappy.'

What a kind girl, Florence thought. 'Yes, that's very true, Dorothy. You're right. We should be relieved that John is safe and happy.'

She waited for Dorothy to leave before rereading John's letter. She needed to be positive. All was not lost and he would be returning. One day. Florence gave in to her tears. Moments later, she pulled her handkerchief from her skirt pocket and wiped her eyes and blew her nose. This wouldn't do. She needed to be strong. Then she would take a hansom to Pelham Street and let Jesse know what John had said.

* * *

Jesse reacted as she had known he would. She let him have his say and vent to her for several minutes about how he had always worked hard and only took time out of the business once he had made a success of himself.

'The youth today have no idea how it was for the rest of us.'

'Jesse,' she said calmly when he took a breath from his ranting. 'We've discussed this before. John needs to work this out of his system and then hopefully he'll come home to Nottingham and begin working at the company. Nothing is final yet.'

'He will work here if I say he can. The longer he's away the less likely I am to agree to give him a job. I can't wait for ever for my son to decide what he wants to do with his future.'

Florence groaned. 'He's young. Give him time to discover what he wants out of life.'

Jesse glared at her. 'What? When did anyone wait for me to do such a thing? I was young when my father died and I had to help my mother keep her business, his legacy, going.'

'I know, but times are different. John has been luckier than you, but that doesn't mean he isn't allowed to make decisions for himself.'

'I beg to differ.' Jesse pushed a file away from him, knocking other paperwork to the floor.

Florence looked at him for a few seconds, to let him know she was not amused by his behaviour, before bending to retrieve the papers. She tidied them and placed them back on his desk.

'Losing your temper won't change the situation. It won't do your health any good either. Now, I suggest you calm down. We have more than enough to focus on with the business. We can't force John to do anything from here anyway,' she said not adding that if John didn't return then she had every intention of going to Vancouver. It was something she would begin planning over the next few days.

* * *

The following afternoon, Florence and Jesse arrived home in the motorcar, just as a hansom cab was pulling out of the driveway.

'Who that can be?' Jesse frowned as their car slowly drew in once the carriage had cleared the entrance for them to pass.

'I've no idea.' Florence was exhausted and past caring. It had been an upsetting couple of days. She couldn't admit to anyone how hurt she had been by John's refusal to do as she had asked. Florence had thought herself closer to her son than she obviously was and the realisation stung. 'Maybe we've had a delivery of some kind.'

Jesse's car drew up outside the front door and Sam stepped out and opened the doors for them. Harriet pushed Jesse's bath chair outside for him to use.

'Why is Harriet coming out to fetch me?' Jesse grumbled. 'That's Meadows's job, not hers.'

'He must be busy elsewhere.' Florence stepped out of the car and walked around it to greet Harriet and help her move Jesse from the back seat of the vehicle and onto his bath chair. She glanced at her lady's maid and couldn't miss that she was looking a little flushed. Something had obviously happened here, but Florence didn't want to set Jesse off on another rant by hearing any bad news.

Florence helped Harriet push Jesse's chair inside. 'I'll take over from here,' she said catching Violet's eye as the maid almost ran from the baize door carrying a tray of tea things. 'Are those for the girls?'

Violet glanced at Harriet and then blushing, nodded.

What was going on? Florence wondered. 'Where can we find them?'

'The living room, madam,' Violet said, just as Meadows hurried down the stairs.

Jesse grumbled to himself. 'Where on earth have you been hiding, Meadows? I expect to see you outside to greet me, not my wife's lady's maid.'

'Sorry, sir.' Meadows exchanged glances with Harriet and Violet. 'I was caught up with something for a moment.'

Violet continued carrying her tray to the living room. Florence watched her and was beginning to feel uneasy. What were the servants keeping from her and Jesse? Jesse passed his hat to Meadows and Florence unbuttoned her coat and unpinned her hat and handed them to him to put away.

'Come, Jesse,' Florence said. If the servants didn't feel able to share what was happening with her and Jesse, then she was sure her daughters would have no such qualms. 'Let's go and say hello to the girls.' She smiled at Harriet. 'Please arrange for more tea to be brought in for Mr Boot and me.'

Harriet nodded. 'Right away, madam,' she said, a secretive smile appearing on her lips before she left to do Florence's bidding.

She pushed Jesse through to the living room. Dorothy and Margery's shrieks of laughter cheered Florence and soothed her taut nerves. Her daughters always made her arrival back at the house feel much lighter. If only John were here, too, she thought miserably, her heart aching as she recalled the words in his letter to her.

Violet opened the living room door for them and waited for Florence and Jesse to enter, before closing the door behind them. Florence noticed the back of the head of a gentleman sitting on the sofa. It couldn't be. Could it? The man rose and slowly turned to face her and Jesse.

'John?' she asked, her mind taking a moment to catch up with what her eyes were seeing. Florence opened her mouth to say something further, but the words wouldn't form. It was John. She raised her hand to her mouth as his lips slowly drew back into a smile. Her boy was back.

'Hello, Mother.' He looked at Jesse, his expression more serious. 'Father.'

Florence stared at him for a few more seconds before taking a deep breath. He had come back home to them, after all.

'Oh, John,' she said going to him, her arms opened. 'You're here. I can't believe it.'

John stepped into her hug and held her tightly. 'It's good to see you.'

After a few moments, Florence lowered her arms and turned to Jesse. She took John's arm and led him around the sofa to stand in front of Jesse's bath chair. 'Look, Jesse. Didn't I tell you John would be back? Isn't it wonderful?'

She hoped that Jesse would say the right thing now and not antagonise John into storming out. She wished Jesse would stop staring at John. She wasn't sure if he was trying to think of the right thing to say, or if he was trying to show his disapproval by not immediately welcoming their son back home.

'Jesse?' Florence said, willing him to say something. Anything at all that would encourage John, since he had travelled half way around the world because she had asked him to.

Then she remembered that Jesse didn't know exactly what she had said in her letter to John, so maybe he assumed John had come home because things had not turned out as well as he had imagined in Vancouver.

Jesse reached out his hand, and smiled. 'It's good to see you, son.'

John's shoulders relaxed and he took his father's hand. 'Thank you, Father. I'm truly sorry for leaving the way I did. I felt guilty as soon as I was on the boat and had time to think clearly about what I'd done. I hope you'll both forgive me. And, if you're happy for me to, I'd like to come and work for Boots in whatever capacity you choose, Father.'

Florence mouthed a thank-you to John over Jesse's head. She could imagine how much John had given up to do this for her and loved him all the more for it.

'Let's not talk about any of it now,' Jesse said, letting go of John's hand. He looked up at Florence, before turning his attention once again to John. 'I'm happy for your mother that you've come back to us, and naturally for me, too.' Jesse motioned towards Dorothy and Margery, who were still standing where they had been when Florence and Jesse had arrived. 'I know your sisters have missed your presence in this house very much. They'll be delighted to have you back, as I'm sure will Mrs Rudge. You eat more than the rest of us and I think she was starting to worry that she wouldn't have enough cooking to keep her busy without you here.'

Florence laughed at Jesse's teasing. She relaxed, realising that every muscle in her body had tensed while she waited for the two men in her life to react to each other. Now they had done so, and all seemed well. It was more than she had hoped for and her life could carry on once again.

It only occurred to her, now that John was back, how disheartened she had been while he was away in Canada. She supposed it was because, like Jesse, she had always hoped John would go on to work with his father for the company. She had imagined he might choose to try other jobs first, but she had never expected him to leave like he had done.

Now he was back though, and he and Jesse seemed to have made some sort of pact to at least attempt to work together. She was grateful to both of them for doing so. She suspected they were probably putting their own feelings aside to please her, and if that's what it took to bring her husband and son back together, then she was all for it.

John pushed Jesse's chair closer to the fireplace, so that the rest of the family could sit down in time for Violet to enter the room with another tray of drinks for them.

Florence sat next to John on the sofa and poured everyone a cup of tea. This had turned out to be a much better day than she had dared imagine. What next, though? she wondered.

Chapter 33

Late July 1907

Jesse and Florence sat together eating with their children in the dining room. John had been as good as his word and begun working at Boots. Florence took him aside every so often to check how he felt things were going. She was nervous in case he found working closely with his father stifling. The last thing she needed was for him to pack up and leave again and was determined to make sure that didn't happen.

Florence was proud of her son for the way he was conducting himself at work, especially on the days when Jesse was particularly grumpy due to the pains in his body. She suspected John's new-found maturity must be as a result of his experience seeing first-hand how it was for a father and son to work alongside each other during his visit to the Hamiltons' apple farm in Vancouver. She was grateful to him for trying to please his father and for fitting in with his working life as well as he had done. She hoped that by letting John know how proud of him she was it might encourage him to keep going if he were ever tempted to give up.

Today was another warm day, and Jesse had spent most of it closeted in his home study as he insisted it was the coolest room in the house. He disliked the heat more and more each year and especially when he was feeling unwell, or the pain in his joints was troubling him more than usual.

Now though, as they ate their meal, Jesse seemed thoughtful.

'A couple of days ago, Dorothy came to me with an article in a newspaper,' Jesse announced, making all of them look across the table at him.

Florence caught Dorothy's eye and looked at her questioningly. She wondered what the article could have been about, but knew she didn't need to ask as Jesse was obviously about to tell them. 'Go on,' she said.'

'Do you want to tell them what it was, Dorothy?' he asked.

She shook her head. 'No, Father, you'll explain it better than I can. You tell them.'

Jesse gazed at their eldest daughter proudly. Florence hoped that he would look at John in the same way one day, but maybe the issue between Jesse and his son was that they were both men, with a natural instinct to want to take charge.

'As you know, Florence, I've been hoping for our personal funds to increase so that we can take on board larger philanthropic projects and do something to help the welfare of the working class somehow.' Florence nodded. It was the subject that had been closest to both their hearts for many years now and they were frustrated that most of their money was tied up in the business.

'I had been thinking about what to do with the extra funds that I should have at my disposal next year. My lawyers are confident that we will be able to free money for new projects,' Jesse continued. 'Then, when I read the article that Dorothy handed to me about Miss Florence Nightingale becoming the first woman to receive the Order of Merit, I thought it the perfect opportunity for me to do something constructive.'

'That's good news,' Florence said, intrigued. She was always pleased when a woman received acknowledgement for hard work and in Florence Nightingale's case, she thought her very deserving of the recognition. 'Yes, I do. I believe people should be acknowledged for their hard work.'

Florence continued eating her roast chicken. So often it was men who received awards for their work. Women, as she knew only too well, had to work harder than men to be noticed and if they weren't fighting for the right to carry out their work, they were having to fit it in with social expectations and, more often than not, a family's needs. She wondered if women would ever be considered equal to men. She doubted it. She realised Jesse was speaking and turned her attention to him.

'Reading this feature gave me an idea,' Jesse explained, and waited expectantly for her reply.

Jesse's ideas always meant a lot of hard work, for him especially but also for her, and Florence was immediately intrigued to discover his latest plans. 'Go on. Tell us about your idea.'

'Thinking about her fame stemming from everything she achieved during the Crimean War, I began to wonder about the veterans who fought in the Indian Mutiny and more recently in the Boer War. There must be many injured men who can't provide for their families as they could once do.'

Jesse sighed. 'I want to build almshouses.'

'Sorry?'

'Homes for army veterans who've given the best part of their lives and themselves to protecting the Empire, and also their wives, who probably now have to care for their husbands.' He placed his knife and fork down on his plate, his food only half finished, and looked at Florence for her reaction.

As Jesse had been speaking, she pictured some of the veterans that she saw in the streets of Nottingham. He was right; this was a marvellous idea. She couldn't help wishing Jesse would learn to take things easier and accommodate his own disabilities, but how could she expect him not to carry out this project now that he had thought of it? It would be wicked to try to change his mind and deny these deserving families much needed homes.

'I think it's a marvellous idea.'

'I thought I'd name the new homes in your honour, Dorothy.'

'Mine?' Dorothy looked confused at the notion.

'Yes, you were the one to show me the feature that gave me the idea. So they'll be known as The Dorothy Boot Homes.'

Dorothy and Margery gasped.

'Oh, you lucky beast,' Margery said with a scowl.

'Now, now, Margery,' Florence said quickly, desperate to defuse any jealousy between her daughters. She could see Margery was put out by Jesse's intention. 'I'm sure your father will think of something for you at some point.'

Dorothy threw her napkin onto the table, pushed back her chair, and ran to her father, wrapping her arms around his neck. 'Thank you very much, Father. That's jolly exciting.'

Florence mouthed for Margery to stop sulking.

Dorothy returned to her seat at the table, her pretty face beaming with joy at her father's announcement.

Jesse turned his attention to Florence. 'So, my dear, what do you think?'

Florence thought it was an excellent idea. She swallowed the lump in her throat, delighted that Dorothy was to have a project named in her honour.

'How kind you are to think of this, Jesse.' She smiled proudly at him. 'I think you should definitely go ahead.'

'Where will you build these homes, Father?' Margery asked, cheering up at the excitement around the table.

'I bet I know,' John said.

'Go on then, where?' Jesse rubbed his right knee a couple of times. Florence could see he was in pain and decided that as soon as supper was over she would check he had taken his latest dose of painkillers.

John finished a last mouthful and placed his knife and fork neatly on his plate. 'I thought that land you have in Wilford would be perfect for the project. Don't you think?'

Florence was impressed. She agreed with John's suggestion and tried to picture new buildings on the land near to their home Plaisaunce. 'I think that sounds like the perfect location.'

Jesse raised his eyebrows, obviously impressed with John's idea. 'That's exactly where I was thinking about. Well done.'

He seemed surprised and Florence was relieved to see them both agreeing so easily on something. Maybe the way forward with them both working at Boots wasn't going to be as difficult as she had expected. It gave her hope that every-thing would work out well.

'You've given this a lot of thought already, haven't you?' Florence said, smiling at Jesse. 'How many properties do you think you'll build?'

'I was thinking about ten, or twelve, but I'd need to see some architectural drawings first to be certain how many can comfortably fit on the land.'

It was just like Jesse to be thoughtful. She loved the enthu-siasm in his voice whenever he began planning a new project; it seemed to instil a new lease of energy into his weary body. The one thing about Jesse that she loved above all else was that he always found his best inspiration when trying to help others.

Intrigued by the thought of the houses, Florence was looking forward to hearing more about Jesse's plans. 'When you say comfort, what exactly did you have in mind?' she asked, aware that although this was a recent idea, Jesse would have wasted little time in making plans either on paper or in his head. He always knew exactly what he wanted and rarely took long to make a decision. It was why, she imagined, he had achieved so much in his life.

'Things like heating, and I thought each must have a bath. I know how much a bath soothes my poor body and these veterans will all have some sort of injury to have to cope with.' Florence opened her mouth to speak, but before she managed to, Jesse continued. 'And free medical help, whenever required.'

'And a garden,' shouted Dorothy.

'What about a clubroom?' John suggested.

'Yes, those things, too.' Jesse beamed at them all in turn.

Florence took his hand in hers. 'You are the kindest man I've ever known, Jesse Boot, and this is a brilliant idea. I look forward to seeing the plans when you've had them drawn up.' She studied him silently for a moment.

'What?' he laughed.

'You've already written to an architect about this, haven't you? Go on, admit it.'

Jesse threw his head back and guffawed loudly. 'You know me far too well, my dear. I have to admit that I did dictate a brief letter to Miss Tweed before leaving for home this evening.'

Florence was not at all surprised.

Chapter 34

June 1908

Florence sat in her office watching Agnes Tweed leave the room, a pile of papers balanced on one hand. It had been a busy year since John's return from Canada. Florence pictured her nineteen-year-old son standing in his Territorial Army uniform and how proud he had been to be gazetted as a Lieutenant. She was thankful that this interest kept him busy during non-working hours. The thought of him looking for something more fulfilling and setting off once again to the other side of the world worried her. But he seemed happy now and that was all that mattered. John had been working for Jesse for almost eleven months now and rarely complained about his job to her.

John worked hard and did his best to take some of the pressure off Jesse, but Florence knew that her husband hadn't made life easy for John where work was concerned. When she confronted him about it, Jesse had been insulted and insisted that he didn't want any of his managers thinking that he was guilty of nepotism. She understood what he was aiming to do and hoped that by her mentioning her concerns to him about his attitude to John, maybe Jesse would ease up on their son a little.

Dorothy was now eighteen and had delighted Jesse by going to visit him at his office and requesting a position in the business. Florence had hoped that Jesse might offer her something in one of the stores, but he had asked Florence to find Dorothy a position at the Island Street factory. Florence had been relieved when her daughter had shown herself to be a diligent and popular member of the Dry Packed Goods department. She had visited the department on several occasions and always found her daughter working hard and seemingly enjoying her time at the factory.

Now all she needed to do was to persuade Margery that she might want to become involved in some way with Boots.

Florence rested her chin on her clasped hands. Her relief at her children's participation in the business had been counteracted by her mother's devastation, and her own, at her father's death earlier that year. While they both knew he had been rather unwell neither they nor the other siblings had expected his illness to take his life. Her father's passing made Florence concerned for Jesse. He was now fifty-eight and his mobility was decreasing by the month. It hadn't stopped him wanting to grow the business though and take over the Gas Works in Nottingham and work hard to finalise the Dorothy Boot Homes project.

She hadn't noticed Miss Tweed coming back in to her office and realised she was speaking to her. 'I'm sorry, I didn't hear what you said.'

'I can come back later, if you're busy,' Miss Tweed offered.

'No, please carry on. I'm afraid I'm still a little weary from the upset of my father's recent passing and all the travelling back and forth to Jersey that I've had to make. I do appreciate your help with these arrangements.' It had been hard work for both of them. 'Did I mention that my mother's coming to stay for a few weeks? My sister Amy is travelling over with her for a holiday.'

'That will be something to look forward to, I'm sure,' Miss Tweed said, her usual cheerfulness returning to her face.

Florence had been thinking that now her mother and sister didn't need to work in the shop they could do with some time to enjoy St Heliers and the beautiful restful gardens. Her mother always enjoyed having a household of people to look after her and ensure that her every whim was catered to. Florence was also planning to take them to Plaisaunce for a few weekends while they were staying.

'The children must be excited to have their grandmother and aunt to come and stay?'

'They are,' Florence admitted. She was grateful to have such a close family and after the less than perfect start to her mother's relationship with Jesse, Florence enjoyed seeing them spending time together in the garden chatting and getting along famously.

Florence was happy to focus on work. Every time she thought about her mother, her mind would then whirl back to some memory of her working with Florence's father in his shop. She missed him. Most of the time Florence was relieved to be able to pretend that he was simply back in Jersey.

However, when her mother was staying with her and Jesse, Florence was unable to keep thoughts of her father at bay. It was especially difficult when at least several times each day her mother mentioned him, which, Florence knew, was only to be expected.

Florence couldn't help thinking back to when she was a young mother fighting against social expectations of how the wife of an up-and-coming entrepreneur should remain at home and care for her new baby. She had expected some people to look down on her for making the decision to continue working, and especially because she insisted on taking John to work with her. However, she naively hadn't expected the worst offenders to be women. Maybe they were voicing the concerns of their husbands, but she doubted it.

If Florence hadn't realised what a devoted husband he would be when she married him, she certainly had done when he backed her decision to continue working and not retire from the business. They might have had many disagreements during their marriage, but he had allowed her to do as she wanted when it came to work. Probably, she thought, because work was so important to him. Still though, most men only thought about life from their own perspective.

Florence was surprised that so little had changed where women's welfare was concerned, including the traditional expectations of them as married women and mothers. She thought back to how stretched she had felt at times, trying to care for her children while running a household and keeping on top of everything at work.

Would she have made different choices back then if she

had known how much of a struggle it would initially be to juggle motherhood with working long hours next to Jesse? Probably. Should she have spent more time with her children when they were growing up? Maybe, Florence mused. But she also knew that, unlike so many other women she had met over the years, she had always felt fulfilled as a mother, as a wife, but mostly as a woman. No. She didn't have any regrets. None as far as her life was concerned anyway. She did wish that she could have helped more women, but she was still only forty-five and had plenty of time to find ways to help make other women's lives better.

Florence arrived home later that day and quickly changed out of her work clothes and into a lighter dress to go and find her mother and sister. She spotted them sitting under a large sunshade at the side of the house. Her mother had her eyes closed and Amy was reading a book, as she always did when she had any time by herself.

Florence strolled over to them and took a seat next to Amy. 'Enjoying yourself?' she asked quietly, not wishing to disturb her mother.

Amy placed her cloth bookmark in between the pages, closed her book, and placed it on the table next to her. 'Mr Meadows brought this jug of orange juice out to us only a few minutes ago, so it's still cool. Shall I pour you a glass?'

Florence could see that her mother's glass hadn't yet been used and presumed that she must have been dozing for a while. 'Yes, please. I am rather thirsty; it's been a long tiring day at work today. It's a little hotter out here than I had realised. How is she doing?' she asked indicating her mother with a nod.

'I think Mother's feeling a little better today,' Amy whispered. 'It was definitely a good idea of yours for her to come here to stay here with you. She needed to get away from everything that reminded her of Father, even if she didn't think so.'

Florence was relieved. Her mother hadn't wanted to leave Jersey initially and insisted all her friends and everything that was familiar to her were there. Jesse had suggested that she simply come to Nottingham for a holiday and take it from there. There had been no mention of her wishing to return home to the island since her arrival, and that pleased Florence very much.

She and her mother had always been close and it was only when Jesse and Florence had become close that the distance between them had come about. Now, though, they were good friends. After all, thought Florence, how could her mother still be unsure of Jesse's ability to give her daughter a good life? Hadn't he proved himself time and time again since they married twenty-two years before? Florence believed it was her turn to care for her mother at this later stage in her life, and she had more than enough space to do that at St Heliers. She also had enough servants to enable her mother to do as she liked without feeling as if she was troubling Florence or Jesse in any way.

'Where are the children today?' Amy asked.

'John is still at work and will be going straight to meet his Territorial pals afterwards,' Florence said before taking a sip of her sweet drink. 'Dorothy will be working until later, too, and Margery is out with friends for the day. The girls will be back later for supper though.'

'You must be so proud of them, Florence. I know that if I had been lucky enough to have children I would want them to be just like yours.'

A lump formed in Florence's throat and she swallowed it away. She would have loved to see her younger sister with a family, too. 'You've been happy though, haven't you?' she asked, having always believed Amy when she had insisted that she enjoyed being an independent woman.

Amy gave her a reassuring smile. 'You know I have. I also think that if you hadn't met Jesse then you would never have married either. You still would have been happy though because you'd have done the things you chose to do. You're just luckier than most woman, Florence, in that your husband not only allows you to do all that fulfils you, but he encourages all your endeavours.'

'Well, most of them,' Florence said with a laugh. 'Don't think there aren't times when we have to battle out our opposing ideas.' Her sister was right though; she would always have worked whether she was married or not. It was good to know that if she had her time again, she would almost certainly make the same decisions.

They heard movement and noticed their mother rubbing her eyes and looking a little bemused as she sat up straighter in her chair.

'Mother, you're awake,' Amy said, no doubt to alert Florence that their conversation could now be overheard.

'You're back, Florence,' her mother said, checking her hair was tidy.

'Yes, how are you feeling this afternoon?'

'Relaxed enough to fall asleep in this pretty garden of yours. I'm feeling a little more like my old self today.' She glanced at the two half-filled glasses.

Florence remembered that she had used her mother's drinking glass. 'Sorry, Mother,' I'll go and fetch you a fresh glass so that you can join us and have a cool drink.'

Florence stood and walked back into the house, happy to have seen for herself a marked improvement in her mother. Her parents had been married for so long that it was going to be difficult for her mother to fill the chasm left in her days without her husband. The children had initially found it different having their grandmother staying with them as opposed to Lily, who was much livelier and less strict, but they were all settling in well together as the days passed. All Florence knew was that she was doing what her father would have wanted her to do and taking care of her mother in the best way she knew how.

Chapter 35

29th July 1908

Florence couldn't believe she was about to celebrate yet another birthday. She had noticed the appearance of more grey in her hair these past few years, so much so that it was almost impossible to hide it any longer, but she still felt young at heart, despite what the mirror told her.

As usual, she had arranged an outing for her girls to celebrate the occasion and six days before had taken nine hundred and fifty-three of them to the Franco-British Exhibition. It had been exhausting, but as her outings usually were, great fun as well as educational for everyone involved.

She and Miss Tweed had finalised all the arrangements in good time and although Miss Tweed would have liked to join Florence on the outing, this time it wasn't her sick mother holding her back. Her mother had passed away the year before and unexpectedly left her a small legacy. She had approached Jesse and Florence months before, asking for advice about buying a small cottage that was up for sale, and was now in the process of moving into it. Florence was delighted for her and happy that her loyal secretary was moving on with her life after so many years looking after others.

The women surprised Florence with a presentation to thank her for all she had done for them. Florence gasped when she was shown the large heavy book that seemed to resemble an ornate photograph album.

'Ladies, I don't know what to say,' Florence said when she finally managed to overcome her shock and speak. She brushed her fingers across the top of the leather cover and opened it to reveal many thick pages.

'This is a thank-you from all of the women you took to the exhibition with you and to show you our continued appreciation for all that you do for us.'

Florence opened the book and looked at the many names each written in a member of staff's own hand. It was something she knew she would always treasure. 'I'm going to take this home with me and show it to my family,' Florence said. 'Because I simply don't have the words to describe its beauty, or, for that matter, how much your thoughtfulness means to me.'

Florence asked for one of the porters to carry her gift to the car. She was sorry when Sam told her that Jesse was held up in a meeting. She would have preferred to stay and wait for him, but knew he would rather she went straight home, and that once Sam had dropped her off he would immediately return to collect him. She led the way as Meadows carried the gift into the house for her when she arrived home.

'Please bring it into the library for me, Meadows,' she said. 'I want my mother and sister to see this magnificent gift. It's from the women at Boots who came with me to the Franco-

British Exhibition.' She waited for Meadows to place the book carefully on one of the tables in the library and opened the cover. 'See for yourself. Isn't it marvellous?'

Meadows stared at the colourful inscription on the first page. 'It is splendid, madam.'

She pictured each of the women concentrating to write their names as neatly as possible. No one would have wished to be the one to smudge their signature on one of the neat pages, each with the heading of where their store or factory was located and then above each list of names, the department name where the women worked. It would be a treasure for her to keep always and it meant a huge amount to her.

Jesse arrived home half an hour after her. Meadows pushed his chair into the library so that Jesse could see the book. At least that was what she had expected, but when Jesse came into the room, she could see he was holding an envelope tightly in his hand and had an expression on his face that she didn't recognise.

Florence thanked Meadows and stepped towards Jesse. 'Is everything all right?'

'It's more than all right,' he said, holding out the envelope for her to take.

She glanced at him before taking the single sheet letter and reading it. Then she read it twice more. 'You're to be knighted?'

Jesse beamed at her. 'It's not something we can share publicly yet and won't be until next year, but yes. I'm to be Sir Jesse Boot. You've always been a lady, as far as I'm concerned, but after I'm knighted, you'll be one officially and it's no more than you deserve. What do you say to that, Lady Boot?'

Florence had no idea what to think. Jesse knighted? Her a lady? She laughed. 'From shop girl in Jersey to being a Lady. It's extraordinary.' Then, bending down, she kissed Jesse. 'I'm thrilled for you, Jesse,' she said, her heart pounding at the enormous honour being bestowed on her husband. 'You thoroughly deserve this recognition.'

'As do you, my dearest one. I couldn't have achieved all that I've done without you working beside me.' He cleared his throat. 'I'm more delighted that you'll be Lady Boot. It has a pleasant ring to it, don't you think?'

Florence heard footsteps outside the library and recognised them as her mother's, then heard Amy's voice. 'Do you think we can tell my mother and Amy our secret?' she whispered. 'No one else, I promise.'

'Yes, but they must swear not to share the news with anyone else. I don't want this getting out into the public. Imagine if it did and the honour was cancelled before we ever received it. That would be ghastly.'

She knew Jesse was teasing, but shuddered at the prospect of him not receiving his knighthood because of something she or her mother and sister did.

'We've been told by Meadows that you have something special you wish to show us,' Amy said, holding the door open for her mother. 'We're intrigued.'

'Actually,' Florence said, keeping her voice quiet and motioning for Amy to close the library door. 'There's something else we want to share with you both first. Then we can show you the surprise Meadows mentioned.'

Florence showed them the letter Jesse had received. She

quietly explained about his impending knighthood being in the strictest confidence. Both nodded silently, her mother's eyes wide. Florence thought she seemed awestruck by the unexpected news.

'Now, I'll show you my surprise. It was presented to me from the women who came with me to the exhibition.' Florence indicated the large book and left them to it, going to sit on the nearest chair by Jesse. She waited while they studied it intently.

'It's magnificent,' Amy gasped, stroking the beautiful cover. She opened it and gazed at the British and French flags depicted at the top of the first page with, 'To Mrs Jesse Boot', printed in large type and then, written in a neat hand, the words that the women had decided upon to thank Florence for the 'pleasure and enjoyment you have so kindly and thoughtfully provided for us on many of your birthdays'.

'Mother, look,' Amy said, turning each page slowly. 'Every store is listed and then below that each department. All the women have written their names in their own hand under their department.'

Her mother didn't make a sound while she studied the gift. Then she shrieked, making them all jump in surprise. 'Look, there's Dorothy's name.' She gazed up at Florence, tears glistening in her eyes. 'This is such a well thought out gift, Florence, and so heartfelt. You are truly loved and respected by these women.'

'I am a little overwhelmed by it, if I'm honest. It took me a while to be able to show how much I appreciated their thoughtfulness when it was presented to me.' Florence dabbed at the corners of her eyes when her emotions overwhelmed her.

Amy left their mother to gaze at the pages and stepped back. 'It makes me think that maybe we should have done a little more for your birthday ourselves.'

Florence shook her head. She knew her mother was not up to people coming around to the house for a party, and more than anything she wanted her to enjoy this special day.

'Not at all. I told you that having my family together was all that I wished for this year. I haven't changed my mind. I've told Meadows that as it's going to be another sultry evening we should eat outside in the garden. We should make the most of this glorious weather, don't you think?'

'Yes,' her mother agreed. 'It'll be turning soon enough and we'll only regret it if we don't make the most of what chances we have to eat outside.'

Jesse had wanted to arrange tickets to the theatre for all of them, but Florence persuaded him that her mother wasn't ready for outings and that she wanted them to share a quiet evening together. She was also worried that if they did make a big deal of her birthday, it might remind her mother how Florence's father had always been the one to make a fuss of her, taking them to the beach to celebrate, or for a ride in a charabanc. He always liked to celebrate their birthdays with something special and she didn't want to do anything that might make her mother miss him even more than she probably did already. Jesse had agreed. They finally decided that they would ask Mrs Rudge to make her special chocolate sponge cake to mark the occasion and they could all enjoy it in their garden.

Florence heard Dorothy's voice and then Margery's out in the hallway. Then came John's deeper voice as the three of them spoke with Violet. Moments later they all burst noisily into the library, giving her mother a shock.

'Do you always enter rooms in such a chaotic way?' she snapped, frowning at them.

'No, Grandma.'

'Good. Now come and give your grandmother a kiss while she tries to calm her nerves.' She indicated the book in front of her. 'Look at the beautiful gift your mother has been presented with from the women at work.'

They did as she asked, but only after each had stopped to give Florence a brief hug and a kiss and wish her happy birthday. Florence watched her children as they stood around her mother and all studied the huge book.

Dorothy looked across at Florence, grinning. 'It was difficult keeping the surprise from you, Mother. Did you notice that I was allowed to sign my name too?'

Florence nodded. 'Your grandmother noticed it first. I'm glad you signed it. You do work there.' She didn't add that having Dorothy's signature in the magnificent book made it all the more special to her.

'I was very excited to be able to sign my name in something so lovely. I was terrified I'd make a mistake, or smudge the ink, but I didn't. I bet you were thrilled to receive it?'

'I was,' Florence answered honestly. 'It's something I'll treasure always, and having your name in it makes it even more precious.'

'What do you think of it, Grandmother?' John asked. 'It

looks heavy, doesn't it? The pages are very thick. Look at the gold on the edges of each page.'

'It's a magnificent book,' Florence's mother said thoughtfully. 'And shows her how much she's loved and respected by those who work for her, if she didn't already know it.'

She walked over to Florence and took her hands in her own wrinkled ones. 'Do you know, Florence, I've been wrong about many things. You know mostly what they are. I've been feeling more and more lately, as I live here with you and see for myself how well you run this home and all that you fit in to your days, how very much you've achieved in your life.'

'Thank you,' Florence said, touched to hear her mother saying such a complimentary thing. She was surprised to hear her talking so openly about her feelings. It wasn't something she had ever done, not like this, anyway, and certainly not to her. 'It's kind of you to say so.'

Her mother gave her hands a gentle squeeze as if to accentuate her point. 'You don't understand. It's important to me that you know how proud I am of you.' Her expression softened. She turned and gazed at each of the children in turn. 'Not just of you, but of your children too, and Jesse. I've criticised your choices over the years, but you have both done so much. Not only by building your business so successfully, but in the way that you've helped so many other people.'

'Thank you, Mother,' Florence said, her voice cracking with emotion. She had never heard her mother speak like this. Never imagined that she knew why she worked so hard or believed that what she did was acceptable.

'I haven't finished.' Her mother took a deep breath. 'In your case, you've helped many women. I hear about these things from your sister, and I've read about how you've given many women opportunities that they otherwise would not have had or helped them in other ways. I'm inordinately proud of you, Florence. Despite my earlier reservations about you continuing to work after the children were born, you've proved me wrong. With all that you've achieved in your life, as far as I'm concerned, the greatest achievement of all has been producing these three darling children of yours. Well, they're all nearly adults now.'

Florence couldn't imagine her mother would ever understand how much it meant to her to receive this commendation from her. She wiped away a stray tear.

'You're not crying, I hope?' her mother asked, embarrassed.

'Not at all,' Florence fibbed. 'I'm touched by what you've just said, that's all. It means a lot to me. Truly it does.' She hesitated before putting her arms around her mother and hugging her, hiding her smile when her mother stiffened at this unusual expression of affection between them.

This was her mother's way of saying that all her misgivings about Jesse being older, and her concerns about Florence's life if she married him, had been completely unfounded.

Florence had never expected her mother to admit such a thing. She had never needed her to, but hearing her mother opening up and sharing her pride in her meant the world to Florence. She knew it was a brand new start for both of them. It was the best birthday present anyone could have given her.

The End

Author's Note

Dear Reader,

Thank you very much for choosing to read *Mrs Boots of Pelham Street*.

Like me, Florence Boot (Née Rowe) was born in Jersey. When she married Jesse, she moved with him to his home city of Nottingham where they brought up their son and two daughters. Florence and Jesse moved to the South of France later in their lives, finally returning to Jersey where Florence died on the island at her beautiful home Villa Millbrook on 17th June 1952, aged 89. It was a special place to both of them.

Florence and Jesse were great philanthropists both in Nottingham and Jersey. They donated much to the island including St Matthew's Church (known as The Glass Church) with its incredible array of crystal created by Réne Lalique; Coronation Park, next to the church where I was taken to paddle in the shallow pool as a child by my mother; FB Sports Fields, where most school children have their sports days, and much more, including cottages and maisonettes for those they wanted to help.

It was a delight to spend many months researching Florence and Jesse's life for these books. I had thought I'd known quite a bit about Florence Boot's life before setting out to research for these two books, but I knew the tiniest amount. There is so much more that I could have included in this book and although I've kept as true to Florence's story as possible, I've had to leave an enormous amount of information out. Ultimately, this is the story of an amazing family, their devotion to each other and dedication to building an empire and helping as many others as possible, while facing their own private conflicts.

I've been lucky enough to get to know Florence through my research, but especially from personal accounts shown to me at the Boots Archive in Nottingham and also from stories told to me by her great-granddaughter, Allison Barrington, I've learnt that Florence never wavered in her dedication to help others. She was an extraordinary lady who was very much ahead of her time in her beliefs that women should have the freedom to work and live their lives as they chose and not as tradition expected, and I am honoured to have been asked to write these books inspired by her.

I hope you enjoy reading them as much as I've loved writing them.

Thank you,

Deborah

Acknowledgements

To the entire team at HarperCollins/One More Chapter who help make the experience of writing a book a very special one. I'd especially like to thank Charlotte Ledger, Editorial Director and huge supporter of her authors, I still can't believe I'm lucky enough to be one of them. It was Charlotte's idea that I write the *Mrs Boots* series inspired by Florence Boot and her incredible life, and I'm forever grateful that she did.

Being able to work with a brilliant editor can make all the difference to a book. I was lucky enough to write *Mrs Boots* and *Mrs Boot of Pelham Street* with the help of the brilliant, hard-working Emily Ruston. These books would not be the books they are now without her support and wonderful suggestions.

I'd also like to thank my copyeditor, Lydia Mason; proof-reader, Tony Russell; and Bethan Morgan, Assistant Editor, for all their hard work.

Thanks also to my agent Kate Nash for sending me copies of the various censuses mentioning Boots family members.

I'm delighted to have met Allison Barrington, Florence and

Jesse Boot's great-granddaughter and Dorothy Boot's grand-daughter while researching these books. Allison, together with her daughter, Heidi Lewis, and granddaughter, Lara Lewis, have been very kind meeting me, sharing their personal photos of Florence and Jesse, and private family anecdotes. Even if I am unable to use all of them in the books, they have helped me visualise Florence and Jesse's life together so much better.

Thanks to Claire Fenby, Digital Marketing and Publicity Assistant at One More Chapter, for accompanying me to the Boots Archive last April and helping make the day so enjoyable and memorable.

At the Boots Nottingham Archive, I had an unforgettable day being surrounded by many fascinating documents. I read letters written by Florence to her *Dear Girls*, saw silk scrolls that she had made to gift to her female employees, and so much more. For this I must thank Sophie Clapp and Judith Wright, Boots Archivists, for their wonderful welcome and hard work arranging everything that day.

I'd also like to thank Michele Leerson at Jersey Archive for connecting me to Allison Barrington and her family and for helping me with research about Florence's life. Also, Toni Wolstenholme, Linda Romeril, and Stuart Nicolle from the Jersey Archive for their assistance with my research.

I wouldn't have the amount of free time I enjoy now to focus on my writing without my biggest supporter, my wonderful husband, Robert.

I'd also like to thank my son James, who, as well as the rest of my extended family, allows me to regale new stories about Florence's fascinating life as I find them.

Also, to my fellow Blonde Plotters, Kelly Clayton and Gwyn Garfield-Bennett, two great friends who are always there to encourage me.

Finally, to you, dear reader. Thank you for choosing to read *Mrs Boots of Pelham Street*. I hope you enjoy getting to know more about Florence and Jesse's lives as much as I did.